LEGENDS OF HERTON

A Novel By

Peter Clarke

First published 2007

Copyright © Peter Clarke 2006
All Rights Reserved

ISBN 980-0-9559915-0-9

Cover Design: Lulu.com

Peter Clarke has asserted his right under the Copyright, Designs and Patents Act 1988 to be identified as the author of this work.

No part of this publication may be reproduced, stored in a retrieval system, or transmitted, in any form or by any means, electronic, mechanical, photocopying, recording or otherwise, without the prior permission of the copyright owner.

This book is sold subject to the condition that it may not be resold, hired out, or otherwise circulated without the copyright owner's prior consent in any form or binding or cover other than that in which it is published and without a similar condition including this condition being imposed on the subsequent purchaser.

By the same author:

A Corner Known As Parliament Square

CONTENTS

CHAPTER ONE
Murder Most Fowl
Herraton Bonville
The Deep Lane
Éclair
Stoke Kevelle

CHAPTER TWO
Sunset
The Sketching Pad
George Jago
The Outhouse Revisited

CHAPTER THREE
Ralphe Mareschal
Gift Horse
Marshburgh
Ill Met By Moonlight

CHAPTER FOUR
An Old-Fashioned House
Free Passage
The Proximity Of Men
Riding The Crops

CHAPTER FIVE
Johanna
How Perfect She Is
The Siege At Gernsea
Revenge

CHAPTER SIX
Atmospheric Pressure
Mr Digweed's Retirement
Wild Garlic
In The Lock-Up

CHAPTER SEVEN
Bandit Country
Oblivion
The First Homecoming
The Second Homecoming

CHAPTER EIGHT
Obscene Publications
Jago Canadensis
Rude Awakening
The Final Set

CHAPTER NINE
Pete Florence
A Small Collection Of Relics
The Antiquarian Imperative
Starshine

CHAPTER TEN
The Mobile Home
Hardly A Love Nest
Cold Madonna
Marshall's Wood

CHAPTER ONE

Murder Most Fowl

I'm walking down to Herraton again this morning - can't seem to keep away - and I'm sorry to say my mind's wandering a bit. Oh Lord it's my foot, the old wound, it hurts so much I know it's nearly Spring. I am an old soldier, disposessed, the first man I killed was an English sargeant, I was very young. My name is Guillame Mareschal, you will get used to me.

I'm near Herraton now, I can hear the crooning of broody hens and I can tell you, there's an awful lot mankind could learn, just observe your poultry and see how they live in peace. That's right. Look to your chickens.

When I was a boy, my mother gave me tasks, and each morning yoked with buckets I would struggle down to the sow and the younger pigs. I enjoyed the task not so much for the swine (though I had no dislike of them) but as soon as their feed was tipped I'd be quickly away to the hens. I had names for them all ... the Upright Chicken, the Boring Chicken, the Hungry Chicken, the Naughty Chicken ... in the scramble for each scat handful of grain, many beaks would dart and stab but with never a cross word. I let myself be drawn into the world of those fussy, pretty fowls; their lives became mine and I followed each quizzical scratching and crank of the head with fascination, I gave them words to speak. I imagine now (as we all do) that because I was young, I must have been happy.

There was a particular morning, when I looked down toward the sea, and a shroud of mist lay in the cleft of the valley between the slopes of ash and oak.. The trees were turning, so it would have been late autumn, possibly the ninth or tenth year of Stephen. The Dancing Chicken and the Moody Chicken were circling an invisible iota of grain, eyeing each other sideways. Amidst the bargaining I thought the Moody Chicken might be testing the pecking order, for I knew her as a bit of a mutineer ... then a tiny sound (which I said later – not quite truthfully – I heard too) set off one of the half-collies that roamed about, whinnying and barking high with his ear cocked: then all of them were baying and yelping, geese honked and laughed, all the hens scattered, human heads turned.

And there *was* something nudging its way out of the gauzy fog and poking blackly through, like a stain on white cloth (a mysterious wound, bad humours, black blood). I was aware of shouting, men running hither and thither. The sun was just becoming strong, I had to peak a hand over my eyes. Dark serrations emerged from the surface of the mist like the ridged back of a big fish. Helmets, heads, then shoulders, broke the strange still waters: horses with coloured trappers, staves held upright, three mailed knights and some two dozen infantrymen. Low sunlight glanced off their armour and liveries, bright pennants hung down straight: they seemed merry as strolling players, grave and beautiful as icons of The Christ. They approached in tidy order without words or shouts or gestures; I remember the heavy treads of marching, the pleasant jingle of fine trappings, the grinding together of other less pleasant loose metal. I realized, even at my young age, that the chances were they were not benevolent. I'm afraid only the vaguest of gestures of defence could be gone through since my stepfather, as was his habit, had taken the handful of cavalry and foot we had left here, they were campaigning yet again in Somerset. Men did what they could, went through the motions of manning the walls, but in essence we were defenceless. The closer the strangers came, the more people looked uneasily at each other. Soon one man threw his weapon aside, then another, then all. The gates were opened, and we waited.

The column crossed the moat and passed through the gates without altering its pace, the whole company halted in order on the green in the centre of the bailey. They stood quite still amidst a heavy silence, and their eyes roved. The leading knight spoke with a bass and rather sweet voice, announcing himself as Oliver Verraby. Here was a well-groomed, slender man with a pitted face, long dark hair, and silken beard. His surcoat showed a barn owl and was stained green and brown, and flecked with blood. The withers of his heavy horse were caked with soil; it shook its head, snorted and shifted its feet whilst its rider surveyed us and all we had with his charmless eye. No one could meet this eye, most lowered their heads as though waiting for the judgement of the axe. He said he meant no harm to us. No one believed him.

So he was quickly down to business. The King, he said, counted for nothing. The King, he said, no longer held this place. He demanded ... well, what didn't he demand? ... more or less everything, whatever coins we had, whatever food we had, shelter for his men. Even as he was speaking, they were sticking one of the pigs and I saw another grab the Hungry Chicken and wring its neck. How easily then our animals, our sustenance, and most likely our lives, could be taken. Verraby did not dismount, nor did the men of his retinue, but he sat quite still amid the crying panic of the remaining pigs and watched his men account for the Naughty, Boring, Dancing and Moody Chickens and one of them, a thin scabby rodent-featured man, was pointing at me (*pointing!*) ordering me to collect eggs (he called me 'laddie'). I did not move, why should I?

My mother had emerged from the hall and stood at the top of the stepway. She made a shooing motion with her hand as if to say: 'go on it's alright, do as he says'. This Oliver Verraby – I watched him closely all the time, I learned his type on this day and never forgot it – who had already assessed the entire value of Herraton with a cursory glance and decided there was little worth staying for after routine looting, turned and saw my mother. I thought she looked angry. Her face was thin and highly coloured, her head was uncovered and she wore the plain white gown she slept in, her hair hung in two long braids. Verraby immediately and without a word swung his horse's head and walked the animal across the bailey toward the motte. A minion appeared from nowhere and after the knight had dismounted he led the horse off. Verraby had a very deliberate and unhurried way of walking, I watched him (everyone watched him) ascend the steps. He kept his back very straight as if to move it naturally would be unwise, and held one of his arms rather stiffly. As he approached, *maman* turned her back and walked away into the hall. I did not see her again for three days.

So the retinue and infantry of Oliver de Verraby, forced to stay as long as their master chose, made themselves thoroughly at home and took all we had as they required it. After they had eaten their first, very generous, meal at our expense, including the eggs that I had collected and my chickens they had killed, they demanded that everyone – men women and children – be gathered together in the bailey. We assembled uneasily expecting execution, but it was only to be humiliation, which we could take in our stride.

When the whole of our small settlement was gathered (daughters and younger wives had gone off at the first alarm – there was a hideaway in the woodland, long–prepared, well concealed) we were encircled by a far from sober company of the commonest possible soldiery. The other two gentleman knights who rode with Verraby had made themselves at home in the hall, which was now out of bounds, even to me. A stocky, neckless, sergeant wearing grubby hose which once were red, a short hauberk of mail, and sporting a huge axe in a sling on his belt seemed to be in charge. There are any number of boneheads in this country who, given the chance, like nothing more than to abandon the few rudiments of civilisation they have acquired and revel in the luxury of anarchy: it is the nearest they will ever get to being in a position of power. Position without responsibility suits them well, a means of following any inclination, any whim, through to its conclusion. The sergeant (whose name I later discovered was Martin) stood with folded arms, looking us up and down, one eye closed, head cocked, mouth twisted in a parody of speculation, a face that said: what shall we do with this lot, we can do what we like, so what shall it be? And he started to pace slowly about in front of his smirking men, arms still folded. He spoke in a flat English accent I found hard to follow but it seemed we did not impress him at all. This Martin looked the few older women who were left up and down with some distaste. 'Hags, bags and boilers' he said, much to the merriment of his men who never missed a chance to applaud manifestations of their sergeant's wit.

However, these men stayed with us but two or three days and, when they had eaten and drank more or less everything that could be eaten and drunk, and liberated anything they could carry, and rounded up a selection of our best livestock, then they readied themselves for departure. They had made up straw tapers, ready to finish the job with fire. But as before there was a concentrated barking of dogs and our distinguished visitors, being more prepared for travel than for fighting, were surprised completely by the sudden appearance of our lord and master Guy de Bonville crashing out of the woodland. He had most of our normal garrison with him jaded from hard fighting and not pleased. At all.

I, like everyone else, ran. I saw Verraby making his slow, cautious, way down the steps from the hall and my mother behind him. As he took an arrow, he slumped and she stepped quickly over him and made for the old charnel house in the side of the motte which was not locked because two or three of the common infantry had been sleeping in it. I followed her in and we lay side by side, too terrified to speak, and outside we could hear men running heavily past, strange thuds and screams, the bellowing of cattle, the barking of dogs. My mother looked ill, she was still wearing her white gown but it was crumpled and stained, her hair was loose and greasy, her face was bruised. I was going to ask her what had happened but a man suddenly came backwards through the door, shattering the plankage, falling across us like an ox. Between us we rolled the sergeant's heavy body away, until he was half-lying, half-sitting against the wall. He had mislaid a good part of his confidence and some of his head. Anyone else I might have felt sorry for.

His helmet was breached down the middle, and the top of his skull was split; his skin was drawn, his face was covered in blood and he was breathing heavily. Though still alive, he couldn't move and though his eyes were open he was drowning. He could still feel more pain, I was sure. But he couldn't do anything about it. *Compos mentis* but helpless. Perfect.

This revenge was to be very sweet indeed. I had a small dagger that I always carried about for this and that purpose, most boys did. I told *maman* (very gravely) to look away and whether or not she did I don't remember. I let the good Martin have a long look at the blade, turning it before his eyes this way and that.

And he was afraid. I said not a word but closed my right eye and looked into the sergeant's left until I felt we knew each other. He could hear the fighting outside still going on, his eye said so – he knew all his company were being slaughtered. I rested the blade under his eye and pushed it slowly in. He made not a move but I could read his left eye. Blood was coursing down over my hand, between my fingers and the blade handle. And my gaze never left his until I saw the loss of focus, which led to the passing of the soul and the extinction of all thought.

'That man Martin you finished off ...' my lord Guy de Bonville said to me many years later '... a good job done, I knew him once you know, he used to be my man ... absconded, disappeared ... he hated your father and meant him harm. It was he who guided Verraby and his bunch to Herraton .... so there, you did your father a favour after all ...' As I said, the English sergeant was the first, but he would not by any means be the last man I killed; a few years later I embarked on my career – still rather young but quickly successful. I saw the tail end of those days of what came to be called the Anarchy when murder was routine. Rightly, you should be on one side or the other but if you were mobile or solitary, you could be on neither side and would have to kill those on both. *Maman* was not pleased with me then (nor is she now I think). And strangely, I was sustained through all the violence by memories of those few innocent fussy little fowls – some things have that effect. The sergeant was ugly in body and soul and too ignorant to understand blamelessness. I avenged the Upright, Boring, Moody, Dancing, Hungry and Naughty Chickens, and have been avenging them ever since. Go on, say it ... you don't believe me!

De Bonville and our men killed or put beyond usefulness nearly all of Verraby's crew. Only two escaped. That knight himself, Roger Verraby, had expired on the steps where he fell and the other two knights were taken alive. My Lord de Bonville had the walking wounded clear up and dig graves then, with surprising kindness (but that was the man) he sent them on their way. But for the knights there was good money to be had, and they were tied to trees in the wood until Bonville was ready to move. They were ignored by everyone and, to their credit, did not start begging for water until three days and nights had passed.

I was able to return to my house, where my mother had been put to bed curtained off in her privy chamber. I think she slept for a full two days. At night I left the spot near the hearth where I usually slept to Bonville's knights and found myself a corner. Sometimes, my lord de Bonville entered my mother's chamber; he never slept in there, but I heard the murmur of their voices. On the second night his voice rose to a shout: '*quoi?*' he kept saying that word '*quoi? ... quoi?*' then my mother was sobbing and gasping and Bonville burst out of the room, wrapped himself in his deerskin, and slammed himself into a chair. I don't think he slept much because every time I woke up I could see firelight in his open eyes.

I was proud of my trophy, the axe of the sergeant Martin, that I was allowed to keep. I leant it against the wall near me where I could see it. In the morning it was gone. At first light my lord de Bonville had emerged from the hall with the axe, his own sergeant and a milking stool, and strode off toward the wood. The knights were still bound to their respective trees ... *young ash I believe, slender and smooth, they will have been able to bend them a little, entertain ideas of snapping the trunks and getting away* ... Bonville's man stood behind each knight, grabbing fistfuls of hair, showing each neck to his master in turn. And de Bonville took the heads off both of them ... *he will have fussed with the stool in between, adjusting its set, even though its tripod form guaranteed stability, he will have muttered and coughed as he fiddled about, whilst the next victim looked on, showing an improbable grin through lips pulled taut, spots of his comrade's blood on his forehead* ... Guy de Bonville, balanced on the silly little stool, swung the axe for the second time, coppiced the tree and the man at once. The head fell with a soft thud like a windfall apple, the trunk of the young tree, branches and all on the ground, cut clean and all bloody ... *'Better this time' I can hear him say to his man 'cleaner I thought'* ... and they each carry a severed head back to Herraton and left the bodies for the fox, or anything else that might have been abroad and hungry. That's the gist of what happened, told me by the elder shepherd Oswald, whose accent is as thick as the fleeces of his sheep.

Herraton Bonville

I have survived now to the age of five and forty. I am honoured to be well acquainted with my lord de Bonville, who in due course became my stepfather. My real father, Ralphe Mareschal, fought with him in Somerset, before I was born, raiding against the various armies of Stephen. I did so myself, as the battle went on over a generation. The careless child to his cheery uncle I was and shall remain: my lord de Bonville was spectacular of beard and jaunty of walk, arms swaying, palms backward and his body hardly moving as though someone had wedged an ash cane across his shoulders. He was a first class horseman, and natural commander. He is one of the few *chevaliers* I ever came across who was on crusade. And he told me tales to impress the young son of his new wife, full of colour and thrill; tales of how the Saracens were terrified by the sheer weight of our armoured charges. We rolled them over, he said, swept them aside like corn, collapsed them in hundreds ...

I think I'm a selfish man, that much is clear from what I say. You must have noticed. I will tell you what I think of myself whether you're interested or not. So I am calm, not especially friendly, and I don't like adversity. Of course, I can cope with it ... adversity I mean ... but I don't thrive on it. Really the best way I can put it is that if the rest of my family were water in a cup, I would be the drop of oil that finds itself in the cup and, though it might float about hither and thither, it will never mix and mingle, dissolve, or lose itself in the mass. And that is it. Simply. And for these reasons I've kept away from Herraton for years, but these days, I seem to be haunting the place.

I must assume that the Lord is watching over me as he does over us all and that He knows my mood, so why is it He has made these past few mornings so lovely, so fresh? Showers puttered thin on my thatch all through last night and the morning is clean, clear and perfect – big blue sky and washed green hills. Primroses and little celandines, their leaves like hearts and tongues, speak yellow to me, the new leafage is well broken above the old beaten path through my own acres of timber. But here I am, a retired fighting man who should know better, not enjoying it, merely trudging dogless (poor old Chretien died a fortnight ago) up to old Herraton – or Herraton Bonville as it will come to be known. Day by day ghosts of memories are passing by never to be seen again. Rebuilding has started, even before the demolition is done. I struggle to be myself. Things slip away and unravel. And in these past weeks I have felt what I can only assume is loneliness. I'd like to call it sentiment but I know it's worse than that. Time is suspended. I feel obliged to keep looking in to see if there's anything I can do, pacing back and forth during the protracted death of an old friend and kinsman ... and think how much better would it be if the poor old boy would just drift away into the dark night where you need no longer worry for him?

Ah yes (to speak of the old) I have just caught the sound of Oswald out there on the breeze: my old friend, his angry voice. Good now ... there's a very funny man! I can't see him but I can tell he's up there on the Bonville pasture trying to gather his flock, struggling with the new collie I have seen run low and keen round the sheep, hanging its pink tongue, a glossy and fit young dog. And poor old Oswald, a measured and taciturn man at best but now he whistles like a mad blackbird and screams and swears. Like all the English, his repertoire of curse-words is staggering; such a range of profanity must take a lifetime to learn! I can't pretend to understand the half of it. That native tongue is blunt indeed and never heard in polite circles; but how can all that thwarted rage, bitter and sarcastic profanity, be expended on an innocent dog? Sheer entertainment. I laugh aloud.

Oswald's people held Herraton before we came. Of course he knows of the change that comes over a place when it is possessed by another power. Do we displace each other habitually, we men? I can accept that Herraton will not be disappearing from the earth, merely being rearranged. But ... was it ever really mine? We Mareschals were here only by the *noblesse* of my lord de Bonville and he only by dispensation of the King.

The old place looks well enough in the morning sun. The *motte* shrinks a little more each day. I can see figures posing on its lopped-off top, there's one with his hands on his hips, elbows crooked, tatty scarlet hose fired by the sun, stupid head thrown back, mouth wide open. I know this man, long hair flows away from his bald crown, he'll be singing away at the top of his voice, one of those empty songs, filth dressed up as sentiment (they *all* sing *all* the time, goddam them!) One of them is half-heartedly swinging a two-bill, but most are standing, listening to the minstrel. Then suddenly there is action: a scattering, a hurried assumption of stance and tools, pretence of work. My half-brother must be about.

The trees that my father's grandfather, also Guillame Mareschal, cut down and rooted out, again are being allowed to grow from seed scattered in their heyday, and the fine new house my half-brother is building where our humble old hall stood on the old motte will be ringed in years to come by ash and oak. The land can be screened off in these days free of war, only seen when it suits from an angle of your own choosing. Richard will leave the south prospect open, where the Nole River and the road cut down through blooms of trees to the sea. His door will look that way simply because it is pleasant, because it is *bon*.

Richard's bonehead rabble has hacked the rampart away with hoes, in the last fortnight, since the ground's dried out. They've scat clods of turf and stones around the bailey with shovels. And another gang are slicing the head off the motte and pitching down the spoil, gradually filling the inner moat. So it will all be different now. The last of the bleached timbers that made the old stockade were used for firewood years ago. The old stables, too, are pulled down. The cavalry garrison, disciplined men which I sometimes led myself out into the country, have gone and along with them the best of the horses. A new chapel is, of course, under way and worship is done for now only in the village where the *abbé* has gone. There is (I understand) a very able carpenter, a cut above the locals, who is in charge of building the new hall. His plans are grand (so I think), even a new bridge over the moat. And what amongst all these works that upsets me most? Not Richard's improvements, but what he's taking away.

I am now slithering with arms spread among the alleys of the old bailey yard between the decaying hovels and empty storehouses. I know the people here by name, and I know they're harassed, some of them desperately poor, but still a few familiar old faces look up and touch their foreheads, spare a moment to nod: even though I myself live in a hovel no better appointed than theirs on the other side of the wood. I still have *status*, some acreage, men still work my land. These are the few who have escaped being roped in to the workforce and they raise an eyebrow toward the old fortification, shrug a shoulder at the hopeless vanity of it. There are various tradesmen from outside, along with people from all over the demesne working as pairs of hands: and all are united in singing, whistling, cursing and bantering: wrecking the place. And they won't be troubling my half-brother's pocket in any way (*I would have paid them – even the young boys who struggle with baskets of earth and stones –* which is most likely why my home is a hovel).

In my time as a *chevalier* of sorts there were dozens of castles appearing all over the country. There are rich men who can afford armies of labour to raise ramparts of masonry and high towers they call keeps. The building takes years, any one of these fortresses would replace a dozen humble outposts like Herraton. Even the exalted Richard de Bonville will never be able to build such a structure. Turning the rustic old Mareschal royal fortification into something less modest must satisfy him. Old Guillame Mareschal, my namesake, made us our old fortress a hundred years ago – in a fortnight they say! ... *and I cannot call him our great–grandfather for he is not Richard's relation in any way – our mother is the same but our fathers are quite different, as chalk is to cheese.*

We survivors are lucky that for us the horizon will never again pulse with shields and spears – who will attack us now? Oswald the shepherd (who might have cause since all this land once belonged to his father's father)? Sturdy villeins armed with forks? And the greatest danger I know came from our own countrymen, falling out with each other – it's what they say isn't it, that thieves soon fall out? The Time of Anarchy has gone into the past, Stephen of Blois has been dead now for twenty–five years ... defence is no longer a priority, so says my esteemed half–brother.

Talking of Richard's oafish workforce, the fools burned the old hall to the ground in a day ... the fucking idiots! ... speed and economy was the reason given. Lady de Bonville's poor old dog slept soundly inside, and by the time the absence of this venerable and happy animal was noted, the fire was too hot for anyone to go in. My mother cried bitterly at first but, strangely, instead of bearing a grudge, she soon became philosophical and in the end resigned – not like her at all – as if she was afraid to state her case. The dog was old, she was soon saying, his time was nearly up and it was better that he died in the house he had always lived in, he will have breathed smoke and passed away without suffering ... *she said this!*

But, of course, she will live in the bold new edifice with Richard – and I can't blame her – I could hardly expect her to stay in my ramshackle place. She lodges for a time with the seneschal in his passably comfortable house until the new hall is built. I tell myself I come up to Herraton just to see her (*does everyone lie to feel better?*) but of course it is the building work that draws me up here like a toper to his skin. Of course Richard is friendly enough in his sporting way. I must tolerate him. I was happy enough to tolerate his father .... obviously I am supplanted by a richer man. It is the Life, as we say. My life? Me? My own company suits me best. I never married. I don't need a wife and I don't like children. My father? I don't recall him. My mother? She is a silly woman but dear to me, it's for her sake I tolerate Richard, and 'show an interest'. My Lord de Bonville who of course is a man of property much wealthier than my own father, Ralphe, has given Richard large amounts of coin. But that's not to say that Jeanne married Guy de Bonville for his money. She married him for safety. You could say she is blameless, only doing what is best, and Richard is creating a better chattel to pass on. But, I say to *maman*, I have no children, nothing of mine will be passed on. 'Your good will?' she hopefully suggests.

'You know I bear Richard no ill-will' I say truthfully 'he's just not my type, I don't especially like him, but I can put up with him.'

'Good' says my mother. 'That's all I ask. Your hair is greying, it was never so curly'

'It has always been curly, *maman*, perhaps it is just longer now'

'So, Guillame …' says Richard later, brisk and bright as ever, 'what do you think?' *What do I think?* I think I'm standing here now on the motte, a man long in the tooth, surveying the property he has forsaken, ignored and dreamed away.

'Seems to be coming along …' Sadly, it's all I can think of to say. I sound weary, tongue in cheek, but I know he won't notice. Bluff and stout like his father, he plants himself athwart the soil with his elbows bent and his hands resting on his belt. A man without doubts. I myself am rather wiry and tall. In no wise do we resemble each other; it's hard to believe we share the same mother.

'Cheer up for God's sake!' he says 'help me out here … I mean, this is so interesting. Do come take a look!' He guides me toward a trench in which the wild-haired songbird of earlier is standing and pounding clay with a block of wood on a stick. '… The old place just rested on the ground but here we're having foundations (no less) and the walls will have these heavy posts (he points to a stack of trunks which carpenters are adzing) set in a stone plinth'.

Though I seem to listen my eyes are roving. There's another, younger, man further along the trench apparently digging a narrow hole some four feet deep. With each thrust he follows the momentum of the spade into the hole, digs and leans awkwardly backward, remaining plumb more by luck than judgement.

'That man is drunk' I point out, interrupting Richard's architectural lessons 'and the sun has only been up three hours'

'Maybe' says Richard 'but he is paid by the hole. If he doesn't sober up I'll kick him down the motte'

I have to laugh. But the details that are disappearing! That round stone driven in to the foundation was one I found when I was a child and kept near me for years until one day I just threw it in the inner moat without a thought, that charred piece of timber with the long split was part of the fowl house. Yes, it was a lintel. I know it.

'There'll be plenty of room…' my brother (half-brother) is saying '… you could live here with us'

'I'm happy where I am, Richard, as you know'

'Of course' he says, rather seriously. He seems genuinely upset at my lack of desire to be domiciled in this palace. 'But think on it, Guillame, things you've never had before … a tiled roof, an aisle, a great oak door that has a lock!'

'I will stay where I am, but thankyou for offering'. I know I sound prim. We are standing in the way of two boys but we don't move and they must struggle around us with the basket of clay they've dragged all the way up the motte up from the old ditch. Baldy with the tamper scowls as they heave it into the trench. The boys run off toward the edge of the motte for their next load.

'Well done lads' says Richard. 'How long before you start the wall, Kenred?'

'The day after tomorrow messire' answers Baldy. His voice is girlish, lisping, and offensive.

'Excellent!' Richard claps and jigs a little on one foot, swings an arm as though swatting a fly 'I have a first rate carpenter advising the local man on the roof trusses, he's going to do it in some new complicated way, all to with balance and stress and counter-stress to make it strong enough to take the weight of the roof tiles...'

Oh God he warbles on and I glaze over. His lips move, his tongue forms words ... all of it the most utter shit! And the tamper thuds away in the background. The breeze is growing chilly ... the trouble with me, my mother is always saying, is that I worry at a subject like a dog worries an old shoe. That there is *no* answer is not acceptable. Twelve years younger, and my stupid half-brother can still manage to make *me* feel stupid! You see, so narrow is his field of view that he always has a very simple answer to everything. I don't have his command of easy chitchat and so often there's something I'd like to say waiting on the tip of my tongue, but opportunities just go by untaken. And the more time trickles away, the more ridiculous it will sound. And that face of his – still the same one as he had before he could walk and talk – oh it's weathered, it's aged, but it still has the same stupid expression.

' ... just imagine' he is saying 'interior arches of timber a foot square'

Finally, transfixed by the tamping minstrel (*Thud. Thud. Thud*), I manage to speak. 'You know' I say 'that tale of my father brought in dead, slung across his horse like a sack, the usual version. Mother's version actually ...?'

'Tale? How should I know, Guillame? Before I was born, before you were born ... Is *maman* not telling the truth? You still think my Lord Bonville killed Ralphe?'

I do not reply. I have made a mistake. A blunder of speech. I am talking to someone who knows nothing, whose head is empty.

'Guillame, Guillame ...' Richard puts his hand on my shoulder, rather kindly. I feel grateful. Richard is good after all, is he not? 'Are you going back over to your place?'

'Soon'

'Well come down and have a mug of cider and a bite'

'I won't thankyou' I say 'I've already seen *maman*. I must get back'. But we stand a moment, seeing different things in a very familiar view. Richard sees potential, I see fixity. How I hate change. A silence has grown between us; we watch the young delver, a thin weasely man with a sallow face, a dark beard, and ratty hair. As he approaches the bottom of the hole he stops every so often, gets to his knees and gropes in up to the armpit, throwing out fistfuls of black earth. The thrusts of his spade are ever deeper, his body bends like a hook, and he pushes himself back off the handle, sways like a tree in a gale. When he eventually falls on his back he just grunts and lays there, making no effort to get up. Baldy gives a cynical laugh but carries on thudding his block of wood on the clay. Whilst Richard stands here he will not stop. Bless him, he strides over and yanks the fuddled delver upright (by the hair!), throws him over his shoulder like a flour sack, walks a few paces and pitches him over the edge of the motte! 'Well, I shan't be paying him' he says 'not a man who's left his hole unfinished, and has a broken back!'

A man with a broken back, no use to his family, maybe dead. Tragic. Brutal. But we laugh together as we walk across the scattered débris of the old bailey, watching our footing. Richard sees the two boys who were carrying the basket: 'you two lads finish off that hole and you'll get all the money for it'. They run for the spade and fight for it.

Me? I have no vanity, if you want to know. No trappings, and I'm proud of that (which must be a joke). My retinue? Just the two men who are with me to this day. I like to grind my own sword, and finesse the edge with the fine oilstone so that you could shave with it. I like to think I am as careful with my killing. And it will be sad if what I've come to think is true: that my stepfather was responsible for Ralphe's death. I'm tempted to believe it, and vengeance must be exacted.

And to speak of the art of death, as I got older my Lord de Bonville told me more about the Saracens. They were men, he said, like you and I and they did not stand still but instead learned. So they took to showering the proud knights with quick storms of dense archery, then disappearing. So, like a bear with a sore head, our great war machine lumbered on, thrashing blindly, drawing further away from supply bases, inevitably becoming exhausted by heat and hunger.

The Lesson? Might is only right when it's winning. I too learned from that – speed of movement, lightness of action, quick and decisive changes of direction, small but deadly weapons: all these can triumph over the apparently invincible giant. And so does the terrible Exterminating Angel, armed to the back teeth, metal-clad and fearsome, run out of steam and fall in a heap …

The Deep Lane

Ees father and mother was lovely dugs y'knaw … but thissun! There iddn no means uv workin a flock without a prapper dug. I'm tellin it. No way at all. I've shouted meself hoarse up yer, used up a month's cuss words in one go. I need to get some prapper work out of the dug and I'll be beggered if that's ever goin to come about … summin just iddn there … should've had a bitch, er'll stick close sure nuff … Now, I knows all these things I'm saying to meself, knows em fer sure – I've bin a shepherd man and boy – but I've bin a fool to meself landing up with thik cakey fuckin dug. I don't take me own advice … I'm like the old Maister Marshall. Oh you know … ee (the dug I mean, not the maister) jest looked up at me with they brown eyes and thumped ee's tail a couple of times on the ground and I was caught waddn I? I fell for un. But ee's more keener to show off how quick he is than to do a prapper job. Ee'll even be abroad een the middle of the bliddy night roundin up the flock fer the ell of it and they things is just a pain in the arse.

Tis just as well I've got ee's sister, she's the one who's got em moving … the whole flock's out yer on the Bonnyville Acres at the minnit and I've got to get um over by Cliston afore th'afternoon. They'm coming over now in a long wave, trotting nice and prim. 'That's it Jessie, good Jessie …'

There ee goes limpin down drew the woods, the Maister-that-was, down to ee's mother at the old fort shouldn't doubt (I see ee's without a dug at present) twas really our old place. My grandfer wouldn't let they frog-eaters just walk in and take what they wanted, although maybe ee should've cos in the end they hanged un. Then th'old Maister Marshall, hard old basterd by all acounts, was put in there by the Bonnyvilles.

What goes about comes around or summin like that. Me and the young maister's in the same boat alright. We'm both sittin in little more than sheds, I've got no land to speak of and nor has young Marshall specially seein ee's a frog-eater. And ee don't like it at all, young Marshall, don't like ee's brother in charge at all.

'Gitonuparound! ... Jed, Jed! ... Bugger me! Git on!' If I was another sort of chap I'd take a log to the bugger's ade. But I knaws I iddn gwain do that. He's gwain to be biding home after today and I've got my eye on another bitch over to Thorneys, to work with Jessie. For sure.

My vather told me how they iron-nose basterds come along on a sudden and ripped the place apart, torched it, ridin out of the woods swinging swords. Anybody they could collar was put to work casting up that gert hump they call a motte and the pointy stakes, the banks, the water. Twas all done in a fortnight, parrently. They was organised, see, and serious armed, up to the teeth. I have to admit it, they'm great riders, never seen no one who could manage an orse so well as they. We was only farmers, see, and my granfer lost the lot to um, even ee's life. And me, I learned shepherding because it's the only way to be a little free of em. Shepherds is left alone, see ... that's no bad thing I s'pose. Money talks enough and I don't want to speak to um. The shape's better company. But to give im ees due, I s'pose young Marshal's alright, ee'll talk to ee like you'm summin.

Well .... tis a wonder, but I've got em in hand and us is all walking up the brimbly old lane – there's Herraton Marshall on the one side and Cliston on t'other. This yer lane was yer lung afore the frog-gobblers came, and tis only wide enuff fer two shape so they fit neat between the banks and we'm traipsing alung up it een close order. Tiddn a bad day fer it, sunny and blue ... I s'pose you could say they'm sauntering, the flock, sauntering tidy. Both the dugs is alright, trotting along back of the last ewe, panting and grinning (but I won't change me mind about Jed, ee's gwain soon as I can find un somewhere). And that's when I seed un comin up behind at tother end of the flock ... draggin ee's leg a bit like ee do, the young Billy Marshall.

'Bonjour Oswald!' ee's calling, all beard and teeth.

'Mornin messire!'

'I heard you up on Bonville Acres earlier .... in cracking form' He's trying to work ee's way up drew the shape. The dug's lickin ees hand. 'Do you still have trouble with your dog?' ee says, a bit smirky like ee knows fuckin well I am.

'Don't mention thick fuckin dug! More trouble than ee's wuth'

'He looks keen enough', says young messire. 'He is clear of eye n'est ce pas? His coat shines, his tread is jaunty and sure'.

'Oh aye, ee's keen ... (nessypa I'm thinking) ... too fuckin keen. Ee'll have to go. My wife's brother over to Thorneys has a bitch goin beggin ... fuckin dug's got too many notions'

'When you say "go" you mean you'll break his neck?'

'Best way' I said this even though I knawed I couldn't kill the dug and I was getting a strong scent of an ome for un right yer and now.

'I'll take him off you' young Marshall is saying 'I'll give you something for him. I don't like to see a healthy animal killed'

'You take un messire, I don't want nothing for un, only don't bother to try working the bollocky-headed bugger'

'I've a place for him' ee's saying 'My old collie recently died, there's a place for this "bollocky-headed bugger" on an old arming–coat beside my bed. Will you bring him to me when you have your bitch? Oswald …?'

'Messire?'

'Our grandfathers knew each other, and you knew my father'

'True enough' What's coming now, I'm thinking. Ee's a bit of a deep one is the young Marshall.

'This land was all your own once. Aren't you bitter?'

'When I think about it messire, I kin get bitter, so I don't think about it. There's bugger all I kin do about it now, that's fer sure'

'Now I'm less active about the place' says the young maister like ee weren't listenin (you kin say whay you like to un y'knaw) 'I seem to be thinking about my father more *tu compris*? his life, his death, I try to know his thoughts. I don't suppose you care … (I iddn sayin nothing to that).

I cant follow ee's thoughts at all … 'I'm too old to care messire and it seems you are too. We're all people ain't we? What do it matter oo you talk with'

That told un. I ate talkin. I waddn gwain tell un about ee's father anyway. Nobody should, not now, tis too late. No … if ee's mother abbn told un, then nobody should! When come to, us went our seperate ways at the the top of the lane where the gate opens on the hillside and the walls bend off and the trees stop. One way goes down to Cliston and t'other way cuts up the slope, cross the pasture and back into Maister's woods. Ee crouched down, young Marshall (and I seed a bald spot on top of ee's ade I'd never noticed afore) and give the dug a stroke afore he went off. Me? I penned the flock fer the time bein and walked off with the dugs down to the corner of the pasture, where the track to Thorneys goes off. The bitch is weaned now and l'll fetch her out and start her trainin, the sooner the better. I seed the yung dug looking after Maister Marshal as he was limping off up the slope. I seed it raise its snout and seperate ee's smell from the general. And when ee turned back to me and looked up, for the first time I gives him a pat and a kind word. I iddn so bad as I likes to think I could be.

Éclair

Allez! He has bounded into my life, Oswald's awkward collie! Though he came with the name Jed, I must call him Éclair because he's like a flash. And I knew when I first came across him in the brambly lane that he was a good friend. So energetic and playful, always ready for action, he leaps like a motley fish and nips my elbow as we walk out in the mornings. He jaunts on ahead all the way up to Herraton, grinning with his tail swinging, tongue lolling, clouds of breath. Can one fall in love with an animal? Ah, Herraton … the further work progressed the more restless I was becoming, but at last nostalgia is waning. I have realised that my memories of the old Herraton are all of my jovial *pére*-by-proxy lord de Bonville, but now I have taken to thinking more about my blood father. It's my age, isn't it? My 'time of life'?

And there were many years, when I was working on my land or off campaigning, when I never gave Ralphe Mareschal a single thought – who was he but a man who sowed his posthumous seed, a man whose face I never saw, whose touch I never felt? I feel I must undertake one last journey so that I can pass whatever time is left to me in peace and quiet, I'm going to go to see Guy de Bonville before the old sod tethers his mount and walks away into the west, and I will ask him what happened to my father.

And what a coarse ungodly place the world is: all about power, just a rabble of selfish men striving to sense out the right side and stay with it, sustained by never having enough. For one to have more someone else must have less: since what there is to go round is finite … and that's all the more reason to own it. But I have the luxury of not being distracted by this crude dog-eat-doggery: there's no mark I need to make, I earned my money as a warrior. I can if I wish take only a passing interest in the farm. Being the eldest, the few dozen acres I hold happen to be the best cropping land and they bring in enough to keep my small household running well. Some would say I'm lucky. My life is my own. All I have is a couple of horses, a couple of pack animals, two men of my own plus the work of sundry villeins, the woodland, a small flock, milk cows and heifers …

But *maman* will say I have too much time to think. It's true, I wake in the night and think away. I am quite good at pitying myself … a bit of a lost soul, a wanderer, a man with a halting gait and a frown out of step with a whole world full of the optimistic, the cheerful and the firm of tread. Or that's how I feel anyway. Some nights I hear every fox-scream, every cat that creeps across the thatch, the wind tussling in the dark beeches and I think all night … I have no *penchant* to make an issue out of Richard de Bonville's acquisition of Herraton. I can't stop him. I bear him no ill will, as I have truthfully told Lady de Bonville. When I am dead my land will be his and so the name of Mareschal will be gone and he will celebrate new acreage with another wing on his grand hall. So that's it. Quite. So why don't I shut up and go to sleep?

Most mornings I'm off up to Herraton and Richard brings me up to date on the work, the skeleton of the hall looms before us, a frame of cross-bearers morticed to the heavy posts on their narrow plinth of stone. I appreciate vaguely the wondrous feats of the imported carpenter, the profound depths of trenches, lengths and levels. At last I ask him, rudely interrupting him mid-sentence, in a strange high voice, where my stepfather is at the moment. He looks askance, raises an eyebrow, I look straight into his eye, he says then that Guy de Bonville is at one of his holdings in Wiltshire, Stoke Kevelle. A long journey indeed. 'I know it' I say.

'You are going to see your stepfather?' My mother says when I call on her. 'But why? He will be here himself in three months'

'I need to, mother, I need to travel while I still have an inclination. And there's something I need to ask him …'

'It can wait surely?'

'No. I want to go to him. I just need to clear something up and I think only he knows the answer, or you, but you won't tell me'

'Guillame, when you were a child you played alone because you had to, for a while until I married your stepfather you were alone, I thought that as the family grew you would be less solitary. Let me tell you, you never came to me even if you were hurt, you never gave me the chance to give comfort you'

I try to take my mother's hand, tell her about the chickens, and that I never needed comfort, but she pulls it away. She has never spoken so before, piercing the skin of neutrality our relationship has always had. There are even tears. 'Now you're doing the same to me' I say, uttering words that I know are false.

'All your life you've kept out of others way, never married, never needed anything. Everyone needs something! Your father came back here from Somerset with a terrible wound in his side, in agony, and he died two days later, stinking and screaming if you want to know …. you were all that I had then. So picture that'

She gives way and lets me hold her head in my hands, I feel what must be human warmth, and I have her blood in me after all; and strange tremors enter me through the grey cotton of her hair. 'I'm so sorry maman it's been so long since I've touched you'

'You have *never* touched me!'

And I have a picture of all the wasted time, all the years in which I'd never given her affection in that way human beings or even the lowest of animals, even dogs, and cattle in the field comfort each other by simple contact. She is now well over sixty, her body is bent, she walks with a stick: and all those years have gone. There is nothing I can do. But then I am full of hope, what about those simple things she has always done, domestic things she dealt with ever since I can remember. Keeping up appearances, running the household. She still has the battered old box of coins and the reckoning beads here with her, even the keys. Those magic shapes that fascinated me so much when I was very small. I remember reaching up to her belt and making them ring together, I was holding her hand that was hot and big, and we walked round through the buildings that were busy and noisy. And she looked down at me with a smile. I *did* know the kindness of her. What's she talking about?

'Those keys unlock nothing now, mother' I see them hanging on a nail behind the door over her shoulder.

'Yes' she sighs, raising her head, holding my face in her palms. 'I suppose they might as well be thrown away since the few doors they unlocked are now burned to a cinder. Oh, but this one' she has got up and taken the keys down, she separates a small one from the bunch, 'this one might still have a use ... the charnel house, of course'

That musty secret place set into the motte, on the far side where the graves were dug. The door was now so aged and weak that a lock was unnecessary, a sneeze could collapse it. About thirty-five years ago the door had been damaged, I have told how it was damaged, and afterwards it was renewed. As far as I knew it had been locked ever since. 'I don't think even that key has a use, neither you nor I will ever want to go in there'

'Oh mother ...' I say as if it's an afterthought, over my shoulder as I am leaving 'could you look after Éclair whilst I'm away?'

'Éclair?'

'I have him here' I pull the door open and pat my thigh. 'Actually' I say 'his name's really Jed, but try to call him Éclair and he might get used to it. He eats at six after noon'.

'Oh Guillame!' she laughs delightedly as Éclair puts his paws up on her lap, wags his tail furiously, grins and licks her face. 'Oh he's a grinner! Like old Belle!' One thing my mother cannot resist is a good dog.

Stoke Kevelle

I'm not looking forward to it and I'm feeling tired. Once, the thought of a journey of any length would excite me; sometimes I could hardly sleep the night before, and at the setting out I'd be that jaded and chilled, sad and petulant, and only gradually would horse-warmth seep into me and the ease of riding thaw me out. Then I would enjoy and never tire of travelling the whole day. But now a simple adventure of only two horses and a donkey, just nine days of riding ... I've hardly got the stomach for it. The thought of it alone is tiring. Age. It must be age. Since

I am now officially over the hill I can sense, when I'm out and about, only the loyalty of those of my own generation and older – the young will see me as a nice old chap, never thinking that I was as strong and fearless in my day.

My weapons, mail and surcoat, long shield, helmet, aketon, and sundry paraphernalia of war are still with me, carefully wrapped and kept dry in the roof space of my house. I have a mount called Ponchard, an aging warhorse like myself, that was once strong, a little long in the tooth now, but still game. I'm not going off to war, only to visit my dying stepfather but am *I* still game? Can I handle myself out there? I mean, there's lack of inclination for a start, and lack of practice (I've been a bit of a farmer lately, a bit of a poultry breeder). Of course, everyone will think this journey pointless, dangerous, and ramshackle but it's simply got to be done. And how do I know that there's urgency about my visit? I have not seen my Lord de Bonville since last autumn. How do I know he's dying? I don't. I just *feel* that if I don't see him now I never will again. I couldn't say that to my mother but it's true. Even though he's an old man, I must ask him to his face if he killed Ralphe Mareschal and naturally he will tell me: he has nothing to lose. I will take Jakon, my 'squire' (whether or not he likes it!) and leave young Martin who can be trusted to keep the stock in good health. So, everything is organised.

I know the roads well. There are two routes. One is a good wide way that the Latins built, that runs from near the moor all the way to Sarum (but we won't be going that far, Stoke Kevelle lies well this side of that town). This road is rough now, churned rubble, but with remnants of such a surface that must once have been smooth (and so straight!). Speaking of past glories, of building castles, I saw one that no man could build today: the great shoulders of a stone giant turned to me as I sailed on *La Manche* many years ago. It sat on its own across the chill grey sea beyond the pooled mud and the salt marshes, a huge shell of masonry, and you could see through its wide gateway the empty enclosure within: and there was a cart, an ox, figures were loading stone. But however many farmers, however many masons robbed it of its stone I'm sure they could not make it any smaller.

I remember then, young as I was, wondering how the men who built these roads, these castles, could possibly have declined and vanished. How could they be mortal? Where have they gone? But I know now that even the strongest of armies is not invincible. Great empires come and go, the sun gives way to chilly cloud, like men and like the green stem that gives way through a season to the sapless haulm that withers by winter into the wet ground.

Enough … enough! Now, the road we will use, and keep ourselves out of harm's way, is the wide lane the animal drivers use, or rather used to use: the flocks and herds nowadays are few and far between and sorry-looking – and it is us, the lords who are my countrymen, who must stand the blame. Even my Lord de Bonville has done it, as an official of the English Crown, taken the best animals out of Wessex flocks bred with care over a long time and left the people with no good stock. The cattle you see on the drover's way are indeed slight of bone and gaunt, the drovers themselves have a hungry look about them, a lot of them going underdressed, some of them are drunk. They go through the merest motions of deference as they pass, an almost imperceptible raising of a hand, a salute disguised as a headscratch. Deference? I must overlook its lack. These are quiet lanes, fine for the horse and mule, easy for us, avoiding towns and trouble.

When we set out it is June and the weather is hot and dry. We tread carefully on the high ground where a breeze always tempers the heat and ryegrass flowers free over vast ungrazed acreages. Nights are warm as spring days; we make good time in comfort. Some of the country is still ruined from the troubles and terror, the godless evil, that my father and myself and my lord de Bonvillle were all involved in. Approach the land on the edges of Somerset and there is dereliction, a rioting of ragged wort, thistle and willow saplings. Where deer and roaming sheep are protected from the hungry people, the fallow is different but no less depressing. There are villages here left to die, never reoccupied after thirty years. These troubles lasted all through my childhood, boyhood, youth, manhood – I have known little else. Even a remote and insignificant place like Herraton, its few rebels gone off to fight leaving only poor men, women and children, was attacked as I have recalled. We were easy meat for such roaming bands as de Verraby and Martin the fugitive and it was such as they that I went to fight.

Now we must travel quietly, avoiding even the drover's lodges. We sleep outdoors, away from people; it is better that way, better not to accept anyone's hospitality unless you know them. I am lulled by the slow rhythm of old Ponchard and the twitter of Jakon's conversation, though even he can be silent for longish periods (which is why he has survived with me for fifteen years and not made a widow of his wife). I have been to Stoke Kevelle only once before, and I remember it as a prosperous place (even now, people seem wealthier up the country than they could ever be in my neck of the woods). I think this must be my stepfather's original home, it's where he was born. For two days we have ridden with the wide plain of Somerset on our right and now the hills are long and rolling, open and airy, full of great standing stones and raised mounds. You come into the home grazing of Stoke Kevelle through a long shallow valley where the flanks show patches of bare chalk and the road is strewn with flinty pebbles and the sheared Bonville flocks are etched on the Bonville pastures, smooth white on green as the sun breaks through the morning haze.

Of course there is no ruination here. It is because my lord de Bonville has seen himself alright. Such is the life. He protects his own acres, he has his loyalties. If he is attacked the whole system of vengeance and justice will pursue the attacker and eliminate him without mercy. And through that same system he has seen myself alright, indirectly, through my mother (at first the girl Jeanne Warenne, then Jeanne Mareschal the young widow, finally Lady de Bonville). When I cannot fall asleep I see the many fine stems of family that come from deep roots, like the binding weed I have pulled off a favourite bush and cast away, for a time it is forgotten but look again and it is back, its white bugles and its mass of leafage regrown. But I am so lazy boned! I live a life of comfort through my relationship with Guy de Bonville and I don't look too much further. That is that. *Ça va!* Fancy *maman* telling me straight I don't love her, fancy that …

So I approach Stoke Kevelle in the balm of this morning light, through the vacuous bleating of his massed animals, fancying that my lordly stepfather owes me a history, he owes me the truth. These hills are like the moors in Devon but stretched and dried, Stoke Kevelle lies tucked into a neat fold of one of these wide downs and a stream flows noisily down the slope behind. I can hear it, and see its *mousse* of foam, and it flows away from a culvert out of the moat, down steep between trees, over boulders. As we get closer I can see that Guy de Bonville, like Richard his son, has been rebuilding. Last time I saw this hall it was timber like ours but now it is all heavy masonry, the earth banks now revetted with blocky stones, the gate most impressively pillared, and the moat deep and dark.

The bridge is down (it's a real one, what Oswald would call a prapper job one, with ratchets, pulleys, thick ropes) and we can see through. It looks like the bailey is empty, we are not challenged. But the noise of our crossing brings out three men, one with a sheathed sword, two with crossbows. I tell them my name and that I wish to see my stepfather and they tell me that he is very ill, they add that a man has been sent to Herraton to fetch my mother to him. 'We must have passed each other on different roads' I say.

My stepfather's chamber is approached through a maze of passsages with solid stone walls tidily rendered and washed. Like son, like father: I can hear them eagerly consult. He and Richard comparing notes on the various techniques of building, extolling the skills of great craftsmen they have known, talking sagely of wall thickness, of the pitch and lean of stonework, and neither of them having a clue. I follow in the foxy wake of the old retainer 'Monsieur la Grillade'. Grillade looks and smells the same now as ever. He has always been old; a cumbersome warty man, huge ears tufted with spills of dark hair, a mesh of fine blue veins on his red face, swags of loose flesh beneath the eyes, ponderous head pitched forward by its own weight, like an ill–formed child. He slides a dragging foot and walks with a heavy tread. We have that in common, the lameness, we make a pair. Lost in these unknown passages I must gaze at the stooped, vulnerable back of Grillade. An inexplicable, almost tearful sympathy comes over me (yes, to me! Sympathy! By God I must be old!). Grillade has a bald patch at the back of his head, at which I stare in sentimental wonder as though it was a holy image. How does such a man bear up to life, his whole being subjugated to the welfare of another, his only purpose to be reliable. And my God whatever the season, he has worn the same heavy garments, the same deep red coarse woollen cloak with many mended holes and rents – it must be the same one as he wore three decades ago when he first appeared at Herraton, no wonder he smells like a stable. A dear old chap, Grillade, a pity that I cannot understand three parts of what he says.

'My lord buzzard awake' he says 'and how fare you, young Master Marshall?'

'Very well' I say by way of conversation 'the work done here is quite excellent!' I draw level with the old man and cast my hand expansively around the walls.

He meets my eye briefly and seems to laugh, a scornful bark without mirth. 'The pointy crumphole all the ready' he seems to say.

'It must have cost my lord a lot of money' I venture (our limps really are very similar, as though we are mocking each other). I have fallen back behind him again and I feel like the naughty boy who apes the grown-up for laughs.

'Three under cod pieces and sum shillins' old le Grillade says over his shoulder. I smirk at the ground, avoid the joints of the flagstones. How nimble, how young the old chap makes me feel!

Guy de Bonville lies in a chamber full of dust in a vast bed like a raft, and he is clearly drifting up a creek from which there is no return. An elderly crone sits patiently beside him on a hard stool. She nods to la Grillade and smiles patiently. To me she inclines her head. 'Angelica …' I say her name uneasily. It looks as though my journey is wasted. The firmament parts reluctantly with each draught of air, as though my lord de Bonville, or his skull that lies on the pillow rasping like a saw, is so near to closing his account that the Creator has decided that providing him with sustenance is wasteful. Here lies the last remnant of that undefeatable *seigneur* himself built like a castle wall, now reduced to a derelict old outhouse whose tired door creaks on its hinges in the breeze.

Old Grillade leans over the bed and bends his huge head toward the piebald ear of the pillowed skull ... 'Gee-am Marshall shear alway frameratun'

'Hwhere ... is Jeanne?' (So he can speak)

'Onway ...' says Grillade

The old lady Angelica is on her feet quickly and smoothes the thick white hair of the skull. Yes, he could inspire devotion. Bonville was a good man. I look up in amazement at the thick cobwebs in each corner of the arched frames, martins are already nesting in the purlins, as if the castle has been built to be a ruin. A dusty place indeed to take one's last breath. At least it is summer, god knows ...

'Guillame, Guillame' (the skull has turned toward me) 'young man'

Grillade steps away and I bend toward the sunken face, hardly blanching at the musty, dungy smell. Bonville takes two or three of his sawtooth gulps. He seems to know why I have come. 'Your father, Guillame ... was not your father ... no one knows who he ... your mother was Johanna ... bastardy I'm afraid ... Ah!' My stepfather clenches his teeth and opens his mouth for more of his ration of air. He cannot get enough. And to think I had been minded to kill him. He will die without my help and some of the truth with him.

'Did you say Ralphe Mareschal is not my father?' I have to ask though I'm aware of the impossible complexity of the question. The skull of my lord de Bonville takes another agonising draught; he winces his brown teeth and screws his eyes shut. Was that an affirmative, was it pain, was it frustration that I hadn't understood? It was then that I walked away. He would not speak to me again. I knew that whatever of the rest of his family could be mustered would soon be here, I moved away from the bed and left my stepfather to the ministrations of the faithful Angelica and Grillade. I needed solitude. As I left Grillade said: 'Abbayonway ... seenyourgonesoon'. I smiled politely, like a mourner who has turned up at the wrong burial.

In the end, I sent Jakon back to Herraton on his own. I told him to go on the Roman road and tell my mother and Richard, as he would surely meet them, to hurry. I wanted to meet no one. I wanted to be back on the drover's way and return to Herraton as slowly as I could. My mother? Richard, my half-brother? Who were these people? Have I spent my whole life in the company of strangers?

CHAPTER TWO

Sunset

In a town the new house of Mr William Digweed Esq. would be fairly unremarkable – imposing and solid, the mark of a well-to-do man, nothing very special. But in the sticks, it is simply glorious. Even Mr Albert Thomas, General Carrier, of Rafton, is astonished. A very steady man, Mr Thomas has guided his light waggon (very steadily) round the curve of the rolled gravel drive and into the rear courtyard and stables. He gazes in wonder at the arched walkways, tubs of Wallflowers and Sweet Williams, slate flags and lamp standards. Turning to his pale grey mare, old Annie, he says 'well now, iddn this an expensive do? I'm almost afeared to ring the bell!' Indeed, after working the bell-pull, he uses his sleeve to wipe his fingermarks from the brass knob.

He waits on the threshold for a response and becomes aware of the sun on the back of his neck. It has come to rest, very red and fiery, in the trees on the crest of the mound at the end of the garden, and thrown a tracery of shadows onto the walls. The day has been one of fitful brightness, an afternoon of broken cloud and showers, not many folk about, but as he was on the road to Rafton, he did see Miss Jane Digweed on the dyke leading her horse and walking slow, a sight that always warmed his heart (*lovely girl, a real father's daughter – if I had the choice, if I could have one girl on top of the pack of boys the missus've come out with, 'twould be Miss Digweed*). He could imagine a painting Miss Digweed might have done: a big blood orange veined with dark branches, its redness melting into the ground, colouring each pane of the new white casements, and shadows of leaves dappling the walls (*God knows the walls is bland enough, tidy like, but not pretty*). He could see her in his mind's eye, out by the Coley, sitting in the marshes with a sketch book on her lap, working the pencil hard (*Tis a shame she's not here, someone should catch this moment, but she's on her back, out by the Coley*).

Dreaming away, Mr Thomas is on the brink of risking the arrogance of a second pull on the bell, when at last the door is opened by Mr Trelease himself. 'Lovely end to the day' says Mr Thomas to the factotum, before walking back to his waggon for the flat, oblong package marked **Handle with Care**.

'Surely it is Mr Thomas' Mr Arthur Trelease is a tall fair man with a North American accent 'and I reckon this'll be the long–awaited photographic likeness of Mr Digweed. One moment, please …'

Mr Thomas leads his horse and cart over to a drinking trough and paces around the courtyard, one arm palm-outward across his back, whilst the mare drinks. As the factotum returns with Mr Thomas' payment, he finds the carrier minutely examining the trappings and blinkers of his old beast.

'Trouble, Mr Thomas?' asks the factotum.

'No trouble at all Mr Trelease, thankyou fer askin'' He clears his throat, slips the coin into his waistcoat and tips his hat.

When the photograph of Mr Digweed, having been unwrapped personally by the factotum and its gilt frame quickly dusted, reaches the inner sanctum of Herton House, reactions are certainly not mixed. On the contrary, the reaction amongst all those present is uncannily the same, but there are variations in the manner of its concealment.

The photographer has certainly captured Mr Digweed's essential qualities. His hands, keen to return to their tireless industry as soon as possible, rest only for a moment on the curved handle of his stick; his tall hat is inverted on the desk beside him ready to be redonned and used as an offensive weapon in whatever pressing business will be afoot as soon as the photographer is finished. He sits on a plain well crafted wooden chair with a leather seat. Behind him the walls are panelled and lined with books. So there he is. A man under threat but statuesque in his defiance; as though an unbearable sum of money has been suddenly suggested to him, or his elevated position has been ignored by a creature lower than himself. His mouth is closed tight and drawn down, his eyes give no quarter, his posture, though seated, is uncompromisingly stubborn, almost dangerous. Quite honestly, if appearances were all, Mr Digweed would not be out of place in a madhouse.

Of course he is a man not to be trifled with whose time must not be wasted. Though he is now known for a gentleman he has worked his own land with his own hands for most of his life and he owes much of his current wealth to his expertise as a breeder of cattle, there is no one who knows the Devon better than he. Others now work his land on his behalf, others tend his herds, and he has absorbed many of the acres of his less financially resilient neighbours. His new house, perhaps his greatest achievement, stands well away from the farm buildings. Double–fronted, porticoed, with a crenellated annex in honour of the castle that once stood on the same spot, its chimney stacks are multiple and smooth, seated astride each gable end, its casements are tall and wide, its front door oaken, black and immovable. Any of those former small (and not so small) holders who are now forced either to work for Digweed or move to town cannot fail to read the unwritten message of Herton House. *What you see here is Land become Wealth beyond Subsistence. That is the privilege of the Few. One of the Few lives here. Knock not upon this Door unless you have an Income.* Or words to that effect.

Expressed opinion of the new photographic portrait amongst those members of the Digweed family present at Herton House is cautious. Mrs Digweed is fussily wiping the glass, using her own breath on smears or fingerprints, real and imaginary, peering closely and buffing away with a soft duster. Elizabeth and Rebecca, the two of her daughters who are in the room (Jane, the third, as we know is out riding) manage to make no sound but are forced to avert their heads. Her two sons, Charles and John, must risk leaving the room rather hurriedly in order to be out of earshot before their restrained mirth becomes vocal.

Albert Thomas the carrier, having made his last delivery and gained the road homeward, is forced to pause above Herton House to allow the passage of cattle and has a moment to observe the very last beams of the sun canting low across Digweed's fields. The air is cold, clear and silent but for a burst of high laughter and the two young Digweed lads rush through the nodding grasses and disappear behind the mound, finally giving way to unrestrained whoops of mirth. Mr Thomas assumes the photograph can't be quite how Mr Digweed might have imagined. He has a bit of a smirk himself, as if for his own lost boyhood. He adjusts the brim of his hat and softly clucks his tongue, jerking the reins of his old mare; the shadows of standing cattle grow long and the light is cooling to blue. The mare walks on, in no special hurry...

'You must be happy with it' says Mrs Digweed, very carefully, for even she could succumb.

'Marvellous!' says Mr Digweed. 'That's me meself, no doubt. Where've them boys gone?'

'I think they've gone to fetch a hammer, dear' Mrs Digweed improvises wildly.

'Us don't need an ammer, the nail's already in the wall, I got Joe to put one in t'other day'

'Of course.   Perhaps it was a screwdriver ... well, they'll be back in a minute I expect'

Mrs Digweed, desperate for distraction, continues to clean the glass. 'Hanging's too good for it' she thinks, but with masterful control brought about by years of practice, no words pass her lips and her expression does not change. Though she loves her husband, is dutiful toward him and finds him, contrary to popular opinion, a generous man, he has never been possessed of a sense of humour. In fact, the photograph has captured her husband's essence to perfection. She knows exactly why her sons have left the room and why her daughters are standing together, backs to the room, staring out toward the mound.

When the boys return, John, the eldest, has recovered his composure enough to hang the portrait on the prepared nail and screw the small silver label (***William Digweed Esq., Herton House, 1863***) to the wall beneath it. Though Mrs Digweed herself must not yield, she notices the embers of a recent conflagration of serious laughter on her son's face: a fading flush, exhausted eyes, traces of a smirk. Mr Digweed sits quite benign and smiling, absolutely his usual self, as the table is laid by both maids and those present sit down to take tea (this is what is done nowadays in the Digweed household, tea is 'taken').

Now, some of Mr Digweed's older employees can recall being seated as a body either side of the long table in the kitchen of Herton farmhouse, where as soon as the maister's mumbled few words of grace were over straightway came a gaggle of conversation and laughter. Bill (as he was known then) Digweed's vast brood and everyone else's vast brood all together. And these same older hands could easily call to mind, during numerous discussions amongst themselves as they rested from their work, the old yard – which was now the paved 'expensive do' that Mr Thomas had noticed at the rear of the new house – as mere brown earth scratched bare by the poultry which Mrs Digweed herself and her eldest Jane used to tend. And the missus would be in the dairy too, churning butter and making cheese. A sophisticated man would dismiss these fond recollections as sentimentality, that there can be no kind of perfect world in the present because the notion of paradise is a desire or a memory, the finest landscapes are those that are lost etcetera, etcetera. But he would be wrong. '*They'm too well–off now to be sharin ort with the likes of us*' these recollectors will say, without bitterness.

And so it is. Since Farmer Digweed became William Digweed Esquire, and since his transformation to gentleman farmer, he will not allow his wife to do anything that does not pertain either to administration of the household or suitable hobbies and the men, with their honest but coarse ways, are no longer admitted into the house. Mrs Digweed would perform her chores still with a good heart and roll up her sleeves in the dairy or tend the fowls but it is too late; the order of things has changed irrevocably, as if there has been a realignment of the universe itself, and the Digweed household has become an example of decorum (would seem to be Decorum itself). One example will serve to show how fully aware Mr Digweed has become of the requirements put upon him by his status. If he wishes to break wind when others are present (as he does with increasing frequency as his years advance) and circumstances cannot guarantee inaudibility, he will leave the room and seek privacy. He prefers to be out of doors. Only when Mr Digweed is safely in his garden can the noxious ethers of his digestive system be expelled to the four winds, along with any accompanying sound, with complete abandon and discretion. The first few times he absented himself, he said he was going to 'listen out for the cattle' and now it has become accepted that Mr Digweed leaves the room for this reason. And his guests can see how exactly how the farmer has become so successful, for surely no other herds could be so carefully fussed over by their breeder.

What a contrast to those Arcadian times mentioned above (but are they so distant? They are within the memory of Jane) when such bouts of flatulence, from either of the customary orifices, occurred audibly at the table they were discreetly ignored or, if they were in any way prolonged or notable or have an unmistakable musical *timbre*, greeted with unashamed laughter. But now, in the conservatory where the family customarily 'takes tea', a particular kind of bland gossip where rogue comments have no place is conducted almost entirely between Mr and Mrs Digweed. The food is both trivial and excessive. The boys are quiet, the girls are quiet. The only sounds are those of mastication (unavoidable), the humph of a minor throat clearance or the discreet impacts of the family cutlery. Mr Digweed sips his tea from the petite, almost transparent, cup he holds in his left hand. His right rests on his thigh where he is working the heavy, silky tablecloth between his thumb and forefinger. He is slightly distracted, for he finds it difficult to stop his eye straying to the newly-mounted photographic portrait. Oh yes. He is a happy man. In this agreeable situation the audible release of wind, in any form, would indeed be an unforgivable transgression.

The Sketching Pad

As Mr Digweed employs men, so he employs his money. From Herton, down through the wooded slopes and water meadows he has a distant view of sandy burrows, along the curve of the River Coley to the sea. Until a decade ago, this silty river with its racing tides was much wider and a sizeable area of marshland between it and the Warrens was regularly flooded. Local landlords formed a consortium, Dutchmen came and built a massive sea bank against the river and the whole thousand or so acres was drained and reclaimed; many of the old tidal creeks were deepened and straightened to gather the waters of tributary streams and drain the marshes, sending them out through the sea dyke via a sluice. Mr Digweed, as a major tenant, was more than able to cope with the rents of the large acreage on which he grazed and fattened his Devons. And even if he had not already been wealthy, he would have raised the capital somehow, for he could see that a land already rich had been made much richer and such pastures, though distant, could not fail to nurture sleek and productive herds.

The Coley Levels, as some call it now, is a place of quiet where numerous ducks and swans cruise the slow reedy waters of the drains, and other wading birds pass through, and the lanes are straight and hedged with golden sedges. The sea dyke, curved and battened to a flat top, is three and a half miles long and the river, its shallows clefted with salty creeks blurred green by tiny plants that thrive on being drowned, comes right up to it. Jane Digweed, in no particular hurry, leads her mare Dido and breathes the heady stench of the grey sucking mud that blows brackish off the Coley as if it were a tonic. To landward, groups of her father's russet bullocks stand in the fields with bent heads, peacefully swatting their tails; and sometimes they will all run suddenly, pursued by the warble fly from one hedge to another. She stops to adjust the dark mass of her hair, raising her arms behind her head, pinning it back with a slide. Jane is heavy and dark, fleshy, robust and rather serious. Her skin has a fashionable milky density, but there's a flush to it that cannot help but suggest the outdoors that her younger sisters (pale creatures of the house and garden) would never want to emulate. But then Jane is a law unto herself.

Since she was old enough to ride a need to escape from her sisters has drawn her out here and now she has other reasons, other interests. Her favourite spot is where the stream of the pill joins the banks and channels of the Coley where a few long–abandoned hulks of small boats lie moored to rotting posts driven into the shingled mud around a derelict fisherman's hut. A desolate spot you could say, quiet but for the calling of oystercatchers and curlews, the occasional human voice on the breeze from the river, or the bland haronies of flocks on the levels.

Jane has a way about her that does not encourage the imposition of control. Her father permits the eighteen year old Jane to ride alone, or rather she rides alone, the question of permission has never really arisen. She believes that no one knows she comes all the way out here, only two are allowed to know: she has been kept company on occasions over the past year and a half (but never at the same time) by Geoffrey Trelease, the son of her father's factotum and George Jago, the son of someone unknown to her called Jago. The former friendship is well–established and years old, expected to lead to marriage and approved of by her father. Of the latter friendship Mr Digweed has no knowledge and, if he did, there are no circumstances under which it would meet with his approval.

She trusts Dido to wander and graze nearby and flops down at the foot of the dyke onto the blanket she carries behind her saddle. The sloping side of the embankment makes a perfect rest for her back, and she sprawls like a rag doll left on a pillow, with her legs apart and stretched flat on the ground, fingers linked on the nape of her neck, eyes closed, face to the sun, exploring the air like a dog (*Oh Jane, do try and sit more like a lady!* But Mrs Digweed could never hide a smirk). Then she shades her eyes and gazes out along the deep navigation channel which never empties, a river within a river, roving toward the open sea through the stranded pools and sandy banks where here and there grounded barges are being filled by distant men with shovels. Though it would be more comfortable, she avoids raising her knees because of the Finger Thing, and she's succumbed once already today even though she's let her nails grow long. She is sure the Finger Thing is wrong. The Bible must say it, surely.

Sighing, she nuzzles her ear into the fine grass. The Coley smells best at low water and it sounds best, not only the gatherings of wading birds and gulls but the faint effervescence of the brackish mud itself, alive with thousands of tiny creatures going about their business between tides.

Of late, she has felt not the slightest desire to open the little volume that lives in whatever outer garment she is wearing so that her mother when rifling her pockets will be reassured that her eldest daughter goes out riding to sundry places so that she can better appreciate our literary heritage. She has read the anthology quite thoroughly anyway, made sure it is suitably worn and dog–eared, she knows the poems by heart so there is no chance of being caught out. She is now more interested in sketching. Miss Sheldrake taught her the rudiments of drawing when a child but she had little interest and hardly picked up a pencil for years until during the last twelve months she has developed something of a passion for Art. Why bother, her father would say, to go to all the trouble of drawing when there's these photographs and you can't get no realer than they? Oh, but you can, she knows you can. Her current sketching pad is buried in a corner of the old hut, wrapped in oilcloth and tied with raffia. It is her most prized and secret possession.

And now her eyes have come to rest on one of a group of figures around a distant barge and quite suddenly she is on her feet. A year ago she purloined a small trowel from the gardener's store, she fetches it from her saddlebag, draws the nail from the latch on the door of the hut (which reminds her a bit of the battered old door of the faithful old outhouse in the side of the mound at home) and retrieves her pad and pencils from their hiding place. Sketching excites her for several reasons; propositions come to her out of thin air. Music is all very well but a passing and not especially private thing, it suits her sisters well enough but she finds practice very boring. With drawing, with art, when it's over and you haven't thrown the thing away there are shapes preserved on paper which mean something and can be kept forever. From the first bold strokes of foundation to fine details of grasses, plants, and hair, all of her is in her drawing; she mythologizes what she knows in order to know it better. She views each sketch as though it was the work of someone else, and she cannot say whether or not they are 'good' but she knows they are interesting, so interesting that she goes to great pains, as we have seen, to ensure that her mother, or any member of her family, or any other living soul, ever sees any of them (for there are other books, three or four, hidden in the old outhouse in the side of the mound).

She would be alone until later. Geoffrey was away in Marshbury all day and Jago would only appear after high tide, sailing on upriver to the quay. In a while he would walk back down to her. There was a gamy, wet dog smell ingrained in the fibres of the rough but indestructible clothes he wore day in and day out, like the labourers at Herton. George Jago (she preferred to call him Jago to herself, to his face she never used a name at all) could be somewhat more fragrant if he was wearing his best but she preferred him fresh off the boat, salty and hungry. He was a strong, hairy, and frankly ugly man whereas Geoffrey (smooth, fair Geoffrey) was more handsome and *his* clothes didn't smell of anything. Geoffrey was her most cherished human being, but such knee-rising, thigh-spreading thoughts had come to her as she had lain against the bank that her book and pencil must be in her hands before the Devil found other work for them.

If she hadn't found a way to weave herself into the fabric of the landscape, Jane would have tired of drawing before now. With a few sweeps of her pencil, the riverscape appears, a scene she could probably sketch with her eyes closed so often has she done it. 'The Coley Strands' by Jane Digweed, it could be left at that, but she has a life and the river has a life, the two must dovetail. Not for her the pretty doodle, the nodding flower, the sylvan glade. Jago was to be made of three triangles. She laid his right leg out straight and the knee of the left she raised crooked, with its ankle at rest in front of the knee of the right. His torso inclined away at a shallow angle (about thirty degrees she thought) supported by the flat of his palm, and the strut of his canted arm. The other forearm rested casually on the raised left knee with the fingers trailing as though idling in water. The natural fulcrum of his pelvis and buttock made the two halves of his body agree. So the three triangles were Jago. One (right–angled) his inclined torso, the river horizon and his slightly bent arm; two (isosceles) the straight leg and the raised knee; three (scalene) the oblique thigh of the folded leg, the relaxed straight arm and the pelted flank of his chest. The geometry was apparently random and quite perfect, she was well pleased. The figure took up the top two-thirds of the sketch, his right leg and pelvis resting on calm waters, his supporting arm planted firmly on the riverbank. With its half-formed beard and strong throat the head, plumed with a cliché of dreamy curls, looked skyward with its eyes wide open.

Through the first triangle distant sand barges lay scattered on the banks; a sky of broken cloud passed through the second, and the third showed a view across water to a stretch of level sands where the bones of an old hulk lay like the remains of a beached whale. In the close foreground, she used the hull of a boat to run its prow out past the headland of his flank and obscure with its sail what he called his tackle. She contented herself with rendering the thing in its limp state, for the boat was only a lugger with a single sail – a larger craft would have ruined the ratio of the figure to the river, and an equation was an equation.

Though some were of Geoffrey, most of her recent efforts depicted Jago. She knew she *ought* to draw Geoffrey but he was simply not drawable in the same way and, of course, she had never *seen* Geoffrey, let alone drawn him, naked. Her favourite of favourites, coincidentally the most trivial and disgusting to date, was four pages back from today

… All horses love to run, and last week she had walked Dido right across the sandy burrows, right over to the wide beach where she gave the animal free rein and let her canter steady along the shore. She ran about four miles, to the remotest point of the sands, and was glad to rest. Jane herself sat, leaning back where the dunes had been cut straight by winter seas and rapidly sketched in breakers, flat horizon, and cormorants ranked on the surfline. Working from memory, a stark naked Jago appeared and stood in profile, arms stretched out ahead of him, fingers spread, and palms inwards. With teeth bared and hair improbable, the maid of his dreams had been seen, he was ready to embrace, hold and impale her.

He was indeed huge, so that his upper body reared out of the sea, its wet pelt plastered down. Waves were breaking around his lower buttocks and all the way along his cock the line of cormorants hung out their wings to dry. The one on the extreme left was taking off, as though launched away by the bulbous tip as it quested proud of the rolling surf. For the first time, she felt like putting a name to a drawing. In the bottom right hand corner she wrote *Jane Digweed 1863*, and in the top right hand corner she wrote *Life on the Ocean Wave*. And she laughed so loud and sudden that Dido seemed to share the joke, whinnying, cantering in circles, and shaking her head at the breeze.

George Jago

The bargee pauses, leaning on the long handle of his shovel, squinting into the light.

'That old man Digweed's a bigheaded old bugger y'know, thinks he owns everything' he says finally.

'Ee do more or less don't he?' says Bill Painter.

'Do what?'

'Own everything. Ee owns a good bit round yer …'

'Alright. Alright. Spose ee do … sort of own it, rents it don't ee. But that don't make him a bedder man than you or me'

'Makes him a bedder man than you, boy, you kin be sure'

'Well ee ain't no bedder than any of us … I'll tell you one thing then Mister Painter sir, when I was walking down past Herton t'other evening … you know ee's new house don't stand all that far back from the lane … well, ee couldn't see me but I seed ee, or more like I heard un. Ee was there paking about een the garden, only just over the hedge from me, and as God's my witness ee were lettin rip like the best of um, like a mains'l tearin drew een a gale. So ee can flex ee's guts and let fly a crackin fart good as any of um.'

Bill Painter can't help but laugh. 'Alright … alright then young George. So in they ways ee's the same as thee and me. But if you take my advice, I wouldn't be caught with a want of respect for un. Ee's on the bench y'know. You can think what you like of un, thinking idn no crime, but just don't go sayin yer pinions where anybody can hear em. Believe me you will be shat upon from a very great height. What makes you mention Bill Digweed anyway?'

'Nothin particular …'

It was at this moment that the daughter of the subject under discussion, her cheek in soft grass and her eye roving over the Coley banks and pools, separated Painter and Jago from the rest. Everyone has his or her own way of leaning on a shovel. Jago's *stance* was unmistakable – spread legs, broad shoulders, and the shaft of the tool between his knees. Jane's fingers, flexing and creeping over her clothes, must get round a pencil and set to work straight away.

'Talk of the Devil …' says Bill Painter 'that's ee's daughter over be th'old huts …'

'What? The Devil's …?'

'No! Digweed's, you fool. Ha! Good solid young maid her is too. I shouldn't doubt she'll make somebody very happy.'

Jago made no reply. He was glad of the chance to stare at the grazing piebald and the sprawled figure of Miss Jane Digweed.

'Her've always spent a lot of time with that Trelease lad. I wouldn't be surprised if the banns was read out forelung'.

'More than likely …' Jago is staring over toward the huts and he doesn't turn his head. *Well no* (he's thinking) *old man Digweed don't own everything, he don't own his daughter for a start.*

Wisely, the bargee never mentioned Jane Digweed to anyone. He well knew their connection could not last – hay must be made as the sun shone, gift horses should not be looked in the mouth, and all that. Miss Digweed didn't care who or what he was and he was happy to act the part expected of him, produce for her the coarse and slangy talk he heard all the time (but rarely used himself). His body, and the part of it that most fascinated her, cost him nothing, nor did he begrudge her the use of it, and that use of it was pleasant to them both. When she married Geoffrey Trelease he would, in the unlikely event of his opinion being sought, wish her well. No one could call George Jago unkind.

'… seems like a nice young chap (Bill Painter was saying) mind you ee'll have less money than she'

'Reckon so' says Jago with a sniff, spitting on each palm, gripping the shaft of his shovel. 'Best get on!' he said rather loudly, plunging the shovel sandward with a grunt. He worked with a relentless energy in all weathers. He was well–known for it.

… I'd never have thought it, but then I didn't know the maid. Jane Digweed, old Bill Digweed's eldest, plummy lips and brown eyes, one of us. Was her kind or unkind? I dunno. Both, maybe. Last summer was when I first come across her, I was walking along the dyke and her was sitting with that blessed book

on her lap scribblin, I was hopin her wouldn't, but her looked around. I touched me hat, wished her good afternoon – I didn't think nothin but to just pass by, and mind me own – but her kept on looking up at me, into the sun, either dazzled or smilin, I dunno which. I s'posed her was gonna to say summin so I had to stand to and wait. Her's a big maid, not that good a looker but warm and friendly enough, it felt like her was lookin me over, you know, like I was an effer at the market. But I didn't mind too much the waitin. When come to, her laid the pad down off her lap, t'were just a picture of the river and the sky (I couldn't help thinkin as I'm stood there like a lemon tis alright for them as got the ease in their life to sit by the river drawin). But there was summin made me want to ang about apart from manners. I waddn that happy to be talking to gentry. But I was trapped waddn I? Couldn't be rude could I?

    Then her was patting the turf beside her, askin me to sit. I reckoned her wasn't more than seventeen, I'm five yer older, I hadn't felt butterflies in me tummy since I was a youngster. But I sat, beside her. Her kept on staring then, even when I was sot there in me patchy old clothes and clod–hoppers – but there's nort funny about her, her's just a plain maid really, like I said. There's more than a few round Rafton handsomer, they just iddn so well–dressed. The clothes her was sittin about on the grass in is better than some of our maids have fer best.

    'You want to talk to me, Miss Digweed?' I said.

    'I will talk to you, if you like' her voice was sweet and low, with just a smidgin of the local 'but most of all, I want to sketch your head'.

    'Oh ...' I must have laughed then, because I remember her smiling back at me 'Right ... righty–o ... how d'you want me to look?'

    Her said, a bit schoolteachhery, 'Look up the river, and narrow your eyes as though you've seen something really interesting away in the distance. It won't take long. I hope you don't mind, it's just that you have a very nice head'.

    I must have laughed again. 'Good of you to say so, a nice head, that's a new one I'm sure!' As her was drawin, I was looking over her head, out across the Coley. Her skin was white with a blush of blood in it, her had nice teeth, her was smilin as she flipped her pencil about. Her hair was very dark and thick. The way her looked at me when I was stood before I sat, her was poking me flesh with her eyes, seein if I was really as fine an animal as I looked – and I could have told her I was a very fine one. I'm thinkin a tumble of different thoughts, you know what I mean, and tis just as well I'm sittin down cause I've got the orn summin chronic, could've rowed a boat with it, wouldn't go away.

    'Just keep sitting forward as you are now' her said 'keep upright (no trouble!) and just look up the estuary – empty your mind'. Her was flirtin! I were bliddy sure of it. Flirtin! With me, George Jago!

    'Tis already half–empty' I said 'so it won't take a minute to finish the job'.

    Didn't take her long to finish the picture and her thanked me very polite afterward and showed me it. It waddn bad, though I don't remember bein such a looker as all that. And I don't remember the stubbly chin neither, I'm particlar about shavin. 'We might come across each other out here again' her says, as we both stand up. I was still a bit flummoxed, I just touched me forehead and walked away reasonable as I could in the circumstances – the minnit we stood up, of course, the old thing was there stiff's a poker. Did her know? Could er tell?

    And that idn all. The next time I'm out there and I'm on foot, her's ridin with that young Mister Trelease so I walks on like I don't know her. A few days go by and I'm walking down that way again with me tool bag to the river strand to caulk a leak in Ted Passmore's dory. I'm passin by the old tackle shed and I seed her mare tethered but no sign of her, so I creeps over and has a peek round the doorway and her's een there, just standin up and flexin her back, looked like her'd bin bent over doing summin or other. I was bound to give her a shock, and when her turned round her looked sort of drained and tired, and I says I'm sorry I didn't mean to creep about, I was just on me way down to fix a boat.

I adn't bin close by her when her was standing up before, and her was tall for a maid. Her says very nicely with a little smile 'It's alright. I didn't know you worked on the boats'

'I do a bit now and then, little spare time jobs, on the small craft'

'Is it one of these here?'

'Oh no' I says 'one of they out on the shore. These yer's well past it, tis a sort of graveyard this, none of these'll ever see water again ...'

Her made me feel so easy I took a bit of chance – so what if her was Digweed's daughter. The words just come out. I says: 'you don't wanna draw me again then?'

Calm as you like, her says 'well, yes, I would'.

Then her thinks a minnit, turns her back and walks over to the doorway. Her hands is restin on her waist and her head's down and I was studyin her back and her shoulders, the dress her wore was dark green and her back was straight and broad. Then her turns round sharp and says would I take all my clothes off. I would've run a mile, I iddn really that bold, but there was summin so calm about her and her give me such a smile, without no craft or mockery. All I could find to say was 'All of um? Now? Right yer?' Her nods her head slow and meets me eye, neither of us looks away. So I makes a start by hoppin on one leg and pullin off me boots. 'I don't have t'be clean do I? Cos I iddn ... tis only Thursday.' Her said it didn't matter. When I'm down to jest me trousers I hold on a minnit, in case, but there's a little pink tip of tongue between her lips and her've got dug's eyes like when ee's waitin fer the rabbit. So there I am bullock-naked! Her looks me up and down, and walks round me, runs her hand over the hair on me back like her old man sizes up a bull I reckon. Of course, long afore now our friend's been stiff's a mast but I don't feel no shame at all.

'It's bigger than I was expecting' her says 'are you big? I mean bigger than others?'

'I dunno, Miss Digweed, I dunno. I don't think about others that way'

'Of course, I'm sorry. If you could just stand with your legs a bit spread, and...' her reaches round me, takes me wrists and guides me hands onto me backside. Her stands away a bit with her back bent to save touchin the end of un with her dress 'now bend back slightly, that's it...good, very good'.

Her stands a minnit with her head to one side, one eye open. 'Good' her says. Then her picks up her book, and her's away and at it, quick and sure, pencil flyin about all over. Just as well her was quick, I waddn too comfortable, stood there stark naked, hands on me arse, like I got backache. 'What d'you think?' her says, and shows me a picture of me own cock, sticking out of a hairy thicket like a thigh–stump. 'It's just a doodle really' her says 'I'll improve on it later'.

I can't think of nothing to say. But her's right – it's a doodle sure enough! I would've laughed but it didn't seem right. The poor thing's so hard ee's almost sore and I'm not gonna be able to keep me hands off un much longer. 'Can I get dressed again now?'

'In a minute' her says (that's right In a minute!) Her's still lookin at un, like un's gwain speak. I reckon her's tryin to decide whether or not to touch un. Then, out of the blue, her gives it a flick with her fingernail. 'Fuckinjesus!' I'm doubled over.

'Oh, I'm so sorry!' her shouts out and lays a hand on me shoulder (and her meant it God Bless her). 'I didn't know it would hurt you so much. I just wanted to see how hard it was, that's all. I could have used a more subtle method'. Honest to Gud, the things her would come out with! I've stood up straight again at least, but me eyes is still watering. 'There's ways kinder on a man than that one ...' I managed to say 'I hope twas as hard as madam expected.'

Her laughed shortly at that. Then her says a bit sharp 'thankyou for being so kind, I'll have to go now'. Her walks away quick then, out the door. And then I hear the ring of the mare's bit and bridle, and the swish of her skirt as she mounts. I'm still standing like a fool, still naked, when her's there again in the doorway and pointin to the book, saying would I mind wrappin it back in th'oilcloth and stickin it in th'ole and kickin earth over it. Then her's gone again. Me, I'm so flummoxed I couldn't care less about the bliddy book, I stand there and cuff un off meself, there was the sound of oofbeats as I grunted the stuff out over the wall. I buries the book after I've chucked me clothes on (can't blame her fer keepin that out of the way, I'm sure) and gets on quick. I'd forgotten all about Ted's bliddy boat. Tis wimmen see, they makes ee late fer everything.

Well, I knew I shouldn't but I took to gwain alung the dyke when I didn't ave no need to. Soon enough there was a next time. And now twas her who took all her clothes off, insistin that I stay dressed. For all the country colour in her face, the rest of her was smooth and pale, and her bubbies was big with a dark centre and the thatch between her legs was as thick and black as that on her head, her legs was strong and firm, her feet small and nicely arched. Her was a fleshy maid, but cause her was so tall twas well spread out. 'What d'you think?' her said 'we're even now, I've seen you and you've seen me'. I would never have thought this could happen. 'What I think is that in a minnit I'm gonna wake up ...' Her asks me, since I'm 'decent' to go outside and get the blanket off Dido and while I was out there I was lookin about – what if some bugger happened along? But I spose twadden so likely, out yer.

When I gets back in th'old tackle shed her unrolls the blanket and lies right down on it. So I'm kneelin between her legs and unbuttoning, it takes a bit of time afore ee's free and when her sees un her smiles, more of a smirk... I'll tell you one thing for nothing, I thought, if her's never done it afore her's bin plannin it sure enough! I says to her I'd be happier if she'd put it in cause I still couldn't believe twas real and I thought it would make it more alright. So I lower meself down and keep me arms straight and her takes un in one hand and grips me shoulder with the other so that her can watch un down her nose, I can see a tip of tongue between her teeth, as if her's threading a needle. Once the tip of un's in the folds of her cunt, she lays down flat but keeps hold of un and moves the bulb of un up and down in the soft parts just inside her.

'I think' I says 'you've bin lookin forward to this'. Her lets un go then and leaves me to push un in and catches her breath like her's cut her finger sudden; her lays her arms flat beside her and widens her legs. At first ee's tight in there but

I'm behavin meself and slowly her reams out inside and leaves me to it. And all the time her eyes is wide open, maids keep um closed as a rule, they'm lookin straight at me and her's breathing heavy through her nose, grippin her lip with her teeth. I'm determined to string it out long as I can, so I spend a while lying quietly on her with me cock docked in tight, rolling a hard nipple between two fingers. But her've got other ideas and starts kneadin me chest and pushin me up, pinchin me own nipple with her fingernails. No man can stand that. I can't stop un now! Tis a matter of pushin the thing all the way in and half the way out, I catch her eye and tis hungry and drownin, lovely brown eyes her's got. Then at last they close and I can see bared teeth and a pinky blush is spreadin over her face. Her throws her head aside and grins at the wall, soft palms is pushin me away and the stuff's spreadin out hot inside her and I'm growlin like a soldier's dug.

After, I wanted to get away quick. Well, I did...and I didn't. I was worried. I mean this waddn any old maid, twas old man Digweed's daughter. No offence I said as I bunged on me clothes but I've gotta run. Her's still lying there with her legs spread wide, I can see a wad of seed gathered in the pink inside, and there's bloodstains on the blanket. While I was lacing up me boots, her brought her legs together and lay watchin me with her hands clasped on her belly. 'What's your name?' her said 'I've never asked have I?' Her sat up and crossed her ankles. I tried not to look. I told her.

'We'll meet again I should think' her says. 'You've been very considerate. It was everything I'd expected, but I think next time we should kiss.'

Next time we should kiss! The things er'd come out with! Not this time, next time. And when I got outside I ran all the way along the sea dyke till I could run no more, and slept fer a good two hours curled up like a tired-out dug in the bottom of an old boat.

The Outhouse Revisited

'I thought I was going to bust! ... I've not laughed so much in ages!' Young Johnny Digweed sat with his brother on top of the mound in gathering darkness, on the rustic bench which the lad had recently made from hazel sticks he coppiced himself in Marshall's Wood. 'That picture last night ... oh my god I'm getting the stitch again ... it was Pappy to a tee!'

'You know' said Charlie, apparently not listening to his brother 'considering that you made this it's remarkably unrickety, surprisingly stable. Ah, here comes big sister'

Much of Long Lane can be seen from the mound, where it runs through the water meadows and starts to rise toward Herton. Jane can just be made out in the dusky light, ambling her mount up this last inclining mile.

'Do you know where big sister goes, slowly on that dozy mare of hers, Charlie?' asks John.

'Somewhere out on the marshes, I've heard'

'Oh I know she goes *there* with Geoffrey. So she goes alone too, all the way out there? It's miles away, how *does* she get away with it. Girls don't do that.'

'Well this girl does. Jane is a law unto herself. She fears no one, you know that – not even father has the whip hand there'

'But she's so *lumpy* and quiet and *dreamy*'

'She just doesn't care.' Charlie breaks a twig he's been fiddling with in half and throws the pieces across the mound. '*I'm* scared of her. I don't mind admitting it. I think only Geoffrey really knows her'.

'Charlie …?' John changes the subject suddenly, as he likes to 'What is this mound? It's not natural, y'know. Somebody made it. Do you know who it was?'

'John, you've asked me that same question so many times before – and still I don't know the answer. How should I know who built it?'

'Well you're the clever one, the one who's off to be a lawyer'

'All I know is that it's an old fort, you can see for miles can't you? So if anyone was going to attack … say Jane and her mare was a foreign army tramping up the road, its the only road, and they'd have to come along it. So you, being the medieval garrison, would see them and get ready to fight'

'The Medieval garrison! That's very jolly! Man the battlements, raise the drawbridge, and fill the buckets of boiling oil! Aren't we lucky that we've no enemies, unless there's an uprising amongst all pappy's sheep and they all come charging in to get us. Serve us right for eating them! And talk of the Devil …'

'Are there sheep in the garden or do you refer to the *paterfamilias*?'

'To Pappy of course, he's taking his ……'

'Pre-prandial perambulation? suggests Charles.

'Oh get away with your silly big words!'

Compared to the paved rear courtyard and its cloistered walkways, the main area of gardens at Herton House has, at Mr Digweed's insistence, been left wild apart from the digging out of brambles and ragwort. It consists of the mound with its covering of trees, and a number of mown paths tending toward it from different directions through a pale sea of cropping grass and drifts of dandelions. A few hollies, elders, privets and buddleias, all self–sown, have grown large enough to be tolerated and give some cover from the winds. The house may be grand and new but its garden is much older, being an appropriated section of the rambling plots and orchards surrounding Herton Home Farm. Barely visible at present, a new hedge of box plants twelve inches high, heeled cuttings from a mother plant which has flourished on the edge of the farmyard for decades, serves as a boundary. Mr Digweed, though he takes an interest in the kitchen garden of the old house, cannot be doing with tilling plants for their own sake. He has no time for transactions which *only* consist of spending! If a plant cannot be eaten or sold to others who wish to eat it what possible use can it be?

All that being said, in most weathers Mr Digweed will pace about the garden for a while before the evening meal. Quite possibly he reflects on his lot (or he might reflect on nothing at all). Sometimes his head is bowed toward the turf and he walks with his hands clasped behind his back; other times his small sharp eyes are alert and scanning, his nose scanning the air for any subtle change that would give away how the weather will stand in the morning, when arable acres are to be drilled. Or he may be contemplating further refinement of his breeding skills – although this is most unlikely. As everyone knows, no one senses the good provenance of an animal, the reproductive charge with which an apparently ordinary ewe or young heifer is loaded, better than William Digweed Esquire.

At times he could well be thinking (with a degree of self–congratulation) about the impressive brood of young that himself and his wife have managed to produce despite their not being wed until they were both in their thirties. Where the act of human coition is concerned, Mr Digweed's habit (in his heyday) was to set about it at a point between his entering the bed, usually at ten o'clock, and his rapid descent down the shaft into the pit of sleep, usually at about a quarter past ten. Brevity, therefore, was inevitable. But he responded to the requirements of procreation with energy and determination, never failed to complete the act and was not afraid in those days (and nor was his wife) of making a certain amount of noise. If any of the children remarked in the morning on having heard strange sounds of suffering in the night, Mrs Digweed would tell them that their father was 'having a bad dream' or that it 'must have been the dogs'. The very young Jane, until she was much older and knew better, would sometimes quietly watch her father and think him awfully strong to be able to go about his daily business unaffected by the painful encounters with she knew not what, the struggles with grunting things along the roads of terror his mind travelled at night. And the dogs, with their strange nocturnal pantings and howlings, it was no wonder they spent so much of the day snoozing in the yard.

As Mr Digweed fades into late middle age, he has developed a round-shouldered stoop, he cuts a rather lonely figure in truth with his tall hat and dark suit of clothes, strolling through his half-wild garden toward the mound. But he has little reason to be discontented. From nothing but the raw materials with which he was born he has fashioned his life: though he is a man of few words his brain is sharp, his grasp of the value of commodities and manpower, his command of respect, is faultless. He is always about his bits of business.

He has a family where the sexes are evenly distributed and for which he can comfortably provide. He fulfils God's and Nature's purpose for man, of course he does. There is no need (or time) for modesty; he will not look away as he meets the world's eye. Those men who devote less than their whole time to business and family will never gain his trust.

Yet, there are moments of regret. If he drives to town with his wife, or walks the crops with Arthur Trelease, all around he sees men working out in the fields on his behalf and with a straight face he stares ahead as though keeping his dignity. Or sometimes he is about in the early morning and he comes across one of his sons, sees him in the lantern–light supervising the milking in one of the shippens. Again Mr Digweed will slow in his tracks, cast down his head, almost through shame. Of course, he too worked with his hands and looked up to others. He once shared in the lives of other men. It is not that he would wish to return to the fields, but he has reached an age where decisions come only through measuring the ups and downs of known factors against each other within a closed scale – gainful experience is all behind him and he can learn no more. A more or less satisfied mindset which is more or less impervious to doubt is the most one could hope for; an agreeable generality of situation and not too much disturbance. There is no such thing as perfection. So ownership has become Mr Digweed's purpose in life – there is much that he owns and many people owe him their living. He has constructed his own isolation.

Only one factor cannot be measured against any other, and that is his eldest daughter. He asks himself the same question which intrigues his sons – where does she go and why? Often she is out for long periods. Hard-headed enough when it comes to business, Mr Digweed is not an unkind man; though he could, he will not go as far as to have her followed. His wife assures him that Jane is a great reader of poetry, she has found the battered and well thumbed copy of McGovern's *Verses of Field and Forest* in Jane's pocket and, as everyone knows, such poetry is best appreciated out of doors. Superficially, Mr Digweed defers to this view but does not have much of a belief in the power of the written word, and he has seen something in his daughter's bearing he cannot put a name to that scares the life out of him, and he knows it has no connection with verse.

His son Charles has ambitions to study the law, and John will stay and learn the full gamut of Digweed responsibilities so when Mr Digweed is gone, there will still be a Mr Digweed. The twins will marry and leave to be with their husbands. But surely Jane is unknowable. *Jane ... Jane ...Jane!* At times Mr Digweed hears the voice of a Stranger. Not whispering demons, he is not insane, but ungovernable thoughts which are audible (*She is female, Digweed, your daughter! Tall and dark and soft. Eighteen? She shouldn't be out for hours alone. What things will happen to her, what things have happened to her?*)

With his sons he talks easily, rough wisdom gets him through, but where Jane is concerned, he hears what he wants to say quite clearly inside himself, but when the lines are ready on the tip of his tongue, she will meet his eye without fear and the words have flown. He becomes a small silly smile and small talk. (*She does just what she likes, knows the names of birds, how they sing, where they come from and where they nest. Her eyes are deep; she is in rude health, rude health. Can't you see, Digweed? Can't you smell? Give in to your nose and take a deep draught of the salty tang on the careless bitch!*)

But Mr Digweed, though frightened by the Stranger he doesn't really hear, knows for sure that his daughter will marry Geoffrey Trelease, who will be his father's successor, and she will never leave Herton. For that certainty, he will put up with any number of bogey men saying awful things into his ear, out of the corners of their filthy mouths. Even possession by Old Harry himself, and bugger the Parson!

Rounding the base of the mound, he strolls back toward the house. Dangerous talk preoccupies him. He has lately heard about the design and construction, to be carried out by his younger son, of a 'summer house' on top of it. But he stops in his tracks, having noticed the body of a young field mouse that one of the cats has killed for sport. As he picks up a length of dead wood and makes a scrape in the soil nearby Mr Digweed's thoughts are jumbled. He hates cats, he worries as his children slip through his fingers, and he can appreciate that a summer house, though he has never come across the notion before, sounds an agreeable sort of thing (*your daughter'd like a summer house for her "poetry reading"*). He cradles the field mouse in his palm and places it gently in the earth. As he is firming the little grave with the toe of his boot he notices that the grass outside the old outhouse, wet and thick after winter, is flattened where the door has recently been opened. He has strictly forbidden that anyone should go into this curious little shed let into the side of the mound, he considers it dangerous. 'Who's bin buggerin about in yer' he mutters. (*Picture it, Digweed! Your daughter's white thighs astride a roughneck labourer, and she impaled to the hilt, screaming with pleasure!*)

He knows there can be nothing in there, but he must open the door and look. Mineral damp has leached from the old mound into its timber linings making them fungal grey and friable; Mr Digweed shrugs and sneezes, a chilly, earthy finger runs down his spine. He thinks of slugs that came under the front door of the old house at night, bloody slugs, he'd forget about them until he'd find something soft and cold under his bare foot (there isn't anything that's soft *and* cold!) fear and disgust made him run up stairs and rub his foot on the boards and leap into bed curled up in a ball. The outhouse never was much of a place, no one ever used it, Jane and Geoffrey only played in there until he stopped them. As he is about to return to honest daylight, and shut the door behind him, he sees a greenish ear–shaped thing sticking out of the beaten earth in a corner of the floor. And the earth around it has been disturbed. Who on earth would bury some dead creature in here? (*Devils! Cats! It's a cat's ear, you old fool!*) Angry suddenly, he clears some of the earth around the ear–shape with his toe, puts a handkerchief on his hand and pulls on it. There's no fetid head of any wretched feline, but an oilcloth package which sheds damp ashy soil and begs to be unwrapped. 'Books' he mutters 'what's um burying books out yer for?'

Taking them out into the light, he sees what books they are, and he comes to realise why they are buried out here. Of the three sketchbooks, the first is full of unremarkable landscapes of the woodland round the old farm, grazing sheep, an old cart which has been rotting in the yard for years. Mr Digweed smiles to himself and the Stranger He Doesn't Hear is quiet. Some of the sketches are signed *J Digweed 1860, Jane Digweed 1861*. Pretty enough pictures, these. She had shown them to him; his dainty flocks, the ash and oak, the twisting earth tracks of Marshall's Wood. But why on earth is she keeping them out here?

Near the end of the second book the year becomes 1862 and the works take on the character already described, leading on to the outrages of the third, only placed there the previous evening. Mr Digweed turns the pages not so much with disapproval as desperate relish. Despite the cool evening he is aware of a gathering heat at the brim of his hat. Though agitated beyond anything he has felt before (and he a man of some means approaching fifty), he remains perfectly still: only his fingers tremble and his eyes search. (*You see, Digweed, what your daughter…*) but, yes, he does see, and the Stranger is shocked to silence. Mr Digweed approaches exhilaration; the veinwork, the keel, and the polished tip, the sea breaking, the ludicrous cormorants. Closing the book with a bang, he staggers back; a stifled cry from the pit of his stomach breaks out of him as a single bark. Sitting heavily on the wet grass he firms his hat like a noonday drunkard and wonders amid the darkness of his silent laughter, and the tight ache of his diaphragm who was the sitter for these pretty pictures?

'Pappy, are you alright?' The voice of his eldest son interrupts Mr Digweed as he is replacing the books in their wrapping and carefully re-burying them in the corner where he found them, replacing them in the right order, leaving the same cat's ear of cloth protruding from the soil in the same way. 'Yes …yes' he says removing himself from the outhouse back first and shutting the door. 'I must get a lock on this door – had one years ago you know – I think somebody's been buggerin about in there. What have you lads bin up to?'

'Just sitting, talking, up on the mound' says Charles.

'Are we to have the summer house pappy?' asks John.

'I'm thinkin on it … now tis near supper and I've got to have a word with Jane'

The two boys exchange a glance. Jane, with her measured rolling walk, is just crossing the courtyard from the stables. 'I'll see you boys in a moment' he says and walks away toward his daughter.

Baffled and smirking, his sons look after him as though observing an unknown species for the first time. 'Is he alright?' asks Johnny 'he's a bit odd isn't he? He was sitting on the grass, the back of his coat's all wet …'

'I don't know if he's alright. His eyes were all red, as if he'd been crying'

'Or laughing ... he might have been laughing!'

'Pappy? .... laughing?'

'Evening father' Jane's manner is brisk, quite unlike the dawdling rhythm of her walk. She carries a bonnet, she wears a choker with a cameo, some kind of sculpted face but so tiny. 'And how are you?'

Pleasant ride?' Mr Digweed's voice sounds flat. And he knows it (*Her skin! Such skin! Smooth white, an artful sheen of blood. Cow's eyes*).

'Oh yes, lovely. Did you see the sunset?'

'No. I was busy. There've been people in that old outhouse ... can't think who'd want to go in there' (*Watch her! Watch her! Is she wilting, is she cowed, does she know? There's the scent on her again, she's walking loose...round face, wide forehead with just a little crease...I can't believe she's your daughter, what she wants is nobody's business!*) 'I'm going to put a lock on it, soon as I can' (*So she'd better find another place to hide er pictures and when she does we'll be lookin fer it!*)

'But, father, there's nowhere else to shelter from the rain' 'Young John's going to make us a summer house up on the mound' (*That darkness on her lips... struggles, bruises, teeth, tongues!*)

'Oh, lovely. Now I must go in, I need to change' She does not slacken her pace. 'I must call on Geoffrey, I think he returns tonight. You should repair the old outhouse and not lock it up. It was Geoffrey's and my den. And it could be used to store things'

(*Den? Earth, she means. Earth. The vixen!*) 'What things?' (*Answer that one, mistress!*)

'Oh ... just *things!*'

Mr Digweed stares after his daughter, her riding boots a crisp signature on his flagstones, all laxity gone. She vanishes into the rear door, into the fastness of Herton House. Mr Digweed distracts himself by peering upward at the chimneystacks. Earlier he was almost sure he saw a weed, in the pointing, but the light is now too low to make it out. But he knows the spot; he will wait until the morning. Grass, it was. Grass! In his chimneystacks! How in the Lord's name did it get there? Someone must suffer for it.

CHAPTER THREE

Ralphe Mareschal

There was a child, he just knew it. It was nothing Jeanne said, oh no, she *said* not a thing. He stood, patient and uneasy, steadying the nose of his heavy horse. The animal was restless too, and keen to be on the road. It was a bright and brittle morning, the first that year to show a light dusting of frost on the back edges of the fields, and a settling of fog in the valley. The long summer of steady dry weather was at an end. Jeanne was still sleepy after a late night. She didn't want him to go. Unusually, he was up much earlier than she was, she had kept on lying, sleeping back upward, head turned away.

Now, out in the yard, she gave him a look, nothing he wasn't used to, a long look as though to fix him in her mind. 'I'll be back by All Soul's' he said. And the horse gave a snort, something like her derision might have been had she uttered it. He laid his hand on its nose. No, there would not be 'words' with his wife; no blame could come his way. And she came to him when he held out his hand and drew him to her. After all, there was just him. Herraton *was* Ralphe. 'I know you'll be back', she managed to say at last 'you must come back' and she tilted her head away to look at him, let her wrists rest on his shoulders and the horse nudged his forearm and tossed its head. They both laughed, for just a moment, as though there was a chance he might stay, just for the enjoyment of a little awkwardness. But she knew as well as he that he had to go. Obligation. On the nearest they had to a battle horse, towing a laden donkey, no squire: completely alone. A journey in a bad time through land as well known as it seemed foreign, as far as Cleeve where de Bonville was waiting with the garrison (which he had once again appropriated) and others. Jeanne had only one look for her husband. No words. With this look she told him she was carrying and that he had to come back. The last thing he did was to place his hand on her belly. And she held his gaze, held the same look. When he got into the saddle and settled himself, the dogs sat patiently; they expected to stay and guard, gathering from the air that this was to be no mere traipse about the flocks. Ralphe Mareschal gave the reins the slightest flick and bade the old courser walk on. The first few leaves were floating from the hazels and thorns in shafts of light and woodsmoke. The air had caught the nip of autumn; a heavy dew soaked the fields. A baby could be born in May, he thought, an excellent time to be born.

On the way, he forfeits the easier routes because he delays and dawdles like a girl and is forced to short cut over long miles of high moor that not a soul would cross without good reason. Following only sheep tracks his progress is poor, picking a way round treacherous sucking bogs, plodding through tough heather, yellowing wiregrass and soft rush. But the weather keeps his spirits up, threads of high cloud and a light breeze, still warm as summer during the day: and he's feeling relaxed. And clean. The previous night he was camped by a small deep pond. After waking he had such a shocking picture in his head for some time, he was working up to something he had never done in all his eighteen years. Finally, he threw his fur blanket to one side and rolled into the pool, without a splash, like a log. When he stood shivering soft silt spread warmly between his toes, stickle fish nipped at his ankles. He clambered out, rolling over and over on the turf, like a dog on a beach, shouting and laughing like a fool.

In early afternoon, as the sun had climbed and was falling again, he stops and smiles as the donkey brays in raucous disbelief at the nap of a turf so razed by sheep that she can only nose it. He rests his back against a rock, knees drawn up, staring over acres of budding pink heather at nothing and his eyelids droop and he sleeps, only to wake shivering on his bed of pink ling and see the hazy ghosts of the blue hills near Herraton ... *oh, that look Jeanne gave me: it's a game we play, a game of wordless talking. The last night we spent together, three nights ago...two? Oh God I was tired, tense with thoughts of travel, I couldn't sleep or relax but she wanted it over and again. I was as hard as a pole but there was no heart in it, I provided and she made use. And the game prevailed ... conversations with tongues. I did, before we slept (and she lay on her stomach) take a light–fingered journey over the knobbles of her back and nibble her ear. And she was so exhausted she slept in, was still bleary as I left bright and early. As she finally stirred in the bed I was there waiting: and she turned and flopped on her back, crooked her arm over the top of her head, pouted and squirmed like a child but gave me blessing through her eyes ...*

Of course he misses Jeanne but he is not so unhappy. The only advantage of his route is that it is very much quicker, even though he's wasted time, so he can waste even more time. A whole day, actually. So he closes his eyes again and his second traveller's catnap is of Jeanne, left in charge and having to talk more than just a few words. She would have to abandon the game. And soon the hills around Herraton will be lost to sight altogether. And she, his waxing wife, also lost to him. He feeds like a nomad or a prisoner, waking in the friendless cold, drawing a hard lump of bread from his coat and chewing on it slowly.

Ralphe set camp within two miles (he thought) of Cleeve, at the end of the next day. He had been forewarned. Both he and the animals would need a full night's rest to be fit of limb and fresh of mind for the last couple of miles of descent. And now he saw why. He found himself working his way down one side of a steep combe on a beaten track of milled grey silt and bare rock. The slope above was covered in bracken and close turf, and he looked down over a scree of flaked shillet, scraps of furze and heath, twisted thorns and stunted oaks that fell away to a winding shallow stream. The way seemed no wider than a man's flung arm, crossed by deep cuts where winter rain made its way down to the floor of the valley from the high moor. Occasionally, strange outcrops of rock and turf overhung the path and all the ground was ripped away, exposing a thin crust of dark loam on greyish brown soil where, having only air to feed on, roots struggled in the breeze like the legs of beetles on their backs. Rounding one of these catheads of rock, he met the green stare of a lone sheep with a shaggy fleece and a lean face sitting at rest beside a large boulder. A bold sheep for it met his eye steadily as he passed. A dead sheep. Without a mark on it.

He stopped briefly to get his bearings, looked down into the valley, and followed the stream toward a small cluster of walled fields where a corner of moorland was tilled and grazed. He could just discern a man and a single ox working a plough on a strip of meadow before dense woodland and the pall of thin smoke that he assumed must hide the buildings of Cleeve. And, turning in the saddle, he looked along the stream as it grew into a wide shallow river, foamed white over reefs of rock until, flatter and much better behaved, it crossed a cove of pebbles, gravel and boulders and into the sea.

Obligation has brought him here and he knows that obligation is inescapable, that he is merely one of many dogs obeying the twitch on one of de Bonville's many long leads. But he sits still on his horse, unwilling to move, determined to linger ... he remembers that there was something of the unknown in his wife's look the other morning, had he missed a clue. Of course she knew my lord de Bonville as well as he, the Warennes and the Mareschals had both fought and won those old battles for the King. It was she who had warned him of the dangerous approaches to Cleeve. She knew it, yes; of course she knew it. And there was nothing strange about that – but what was that pessimistic desperation about her, on the night before he left? A hand he didn't know kneaded the flesh on his back, drowning fingers gripping anything that might save them. Instead of Jeanne, his wife, there was a tongue, a sucking hollow, and a mouth eating him.

Though he woke and broke camp in bright sunlight, as he moved on the weather darkened and a clammy wind with the hollow sound of winter blew in buffeting drizzle that soaked him in no time. Up here, any death natural or otherwise could long go unnoticed. He could become the keeper of the wretched staring sheep. His ageing horse might go wrong–foot and send him into the valley the quick way. But he must think of Guy de Bonville, of course he must trust him. And why shouldn't he? The man was his lord and master after all. Harassed and uneasy, a foreign traveller in a desert place, all his concentration was needed simply to stay on the path. He had never seen Cleeve: he knew it by reputation only. A hidden place where no one goes, Guy de Bonville's most remote holding. And was it not a curious choice of muster point? Is some secret expedition being assembled, something *extra murales*, unofficial and not quite wholesome?

But when the track levelled out to surer ground the weather seemed to clear again and he joined a wider way of beaten earth crossed here and there by groping roots, staying close to the shallow curves of the river and the tiny walled hideages of grazing and meadows on the other bank. He could sit upright in the saddle and approach the settlement with some ease and dignity. When precarious on the bleak hill, he found he could master his own fear by struggling to keep the animals calm: but all the way down an ooze of sweat had accumulated under the padded stuff of his arming coat and now lay cool and sticky on his back. He was forced to stop a moment, take the mail shirt and the aketon off (he had only put them on to make an impression), hang them over a branch to air, splash water on his face and body, let the animals drink and generally compose himself. Brushing away sheep pellets with his foot he sat on the turf beside the river, resting back on his elbows, studying the progress of that solitary villein, the one he had seen from afar. A stooping unwary man with a hung head, hatless and chinless, steadying the coulter behind a peaky piebald ox, eyes fixed on the tawny furrows littered with stones unfolding from his ploughshare. But he had seen Ralphe, and he turned his drooping face and therein lay only empty curiosity, as though he could muster no more wisdom than his beast. Ralphe was thinking with a grin that he had certainly never seen a man who looked quite so stupid. But as the old labourer dutifully raised his hand to his forehead, a strange false smile appeared, the dullard's eyes came to life as though he were peeling away a mask. He was just like a player miming a jest, a fool whose simpering submission itself was the point of the joke. With a half–shrug his finger glanced off his forehead and he beamed, showed his palm, disappeared behind a stand of alders much as an actor leaves the scene, his lines delivered.

Gift Horse

He entered the manor through a rocky cut of oaks and sweet chestnut, and a din of white water. Long before he saw them, he heard the chatter of three bondmen bandy about the pitched chasm. They were larking about and crossing the river on stepping stones, shouting and whistling, using their forks and shovels as balance poles. Though he still considered English a bland, coarse tongue he now thought he could hear a charm in it; dainty sounds that he took to be birdsong translated into the chit–chat and laughter of a pair of girls scattering seed for the fowls. They watched him walk his beasts over toward the tethering posts, smiling.

Sleek and weighty Warhorses worth fortunes are being led to water by liveried grooms, fresh hay was being forked from a cart into clean stalls by a large-boned youth. A blacksmith and his boys hammered out red–hot iron, setting up a clanging like a peal of dead bells. Men are loading pack animals; a glossy black courser is having its red cropper folded away, ready for travel. So he must be later than he thought. Amid the noise and action of the place, he guiltily recalls his fitful napping on the moor, his sketchy dreams, and his morning roll in the cold pool, his leisurely observance of the strange ploughman. He feels many things in an instant: that his body is of no particular shape, that his clothes are unconvincing, that home is a fantasy which he cannot take seriously and that, most of all, that he prefers his own company.

Instead, he has drifted into the orbit of a stocky untidy man with curly hair exploding from a battered leather hat that is working his way round a tethered bay, cradling each foot between his legs and checking the shoes.

Ralphe, desperate for human company, moves his mouth and hears the sound of his voice: 'an out of the way spot, is it not …?' He is uncomfortable with his agricultural English for days had gone by since he had spoken to anyone in decent French (but himself and his animals) let alone cod Saxon.

This man, this 'squire', lets the foreleg of the bay rest back on the ground and raises his head. There is a curious silence, as though a storm is about to break. Drifting smoke and a queasiness of rendered fat air hang on the air; somewhere pigs are squealing, and Ralphe stares after an old grey dog that wanders between them, nose to the ground. The squire, steward, or whatever he is, runs his glance up and down the offering that is young Ralphe, surveys his ageing mount, his quiet pack mule, and his minimal armour, stares straight at him, standing back on his heels in a parody of admiration. He seems to say, without a sound: *who the fuck are you?* Then aloud, quite aloud, he says (in French): 'Just yourself is it, sir?' Ralphe, hearing his own tongue spoken to him thinks sarcasm does not become it.

He is aware that the two girls have stopped casting seed for their fowls and stand agog (one has her hand on the shoulder of the other) and the whole world is halted, waiting. Something is expected of him. The same breeze that moves the leaves is pressing on him from all sides, heat prickles on his face and he stares in disbelief at the ridiculous hair, the snail–like back of the groom who has bent again to his work, appearing to examine the other foreleg of the quiet bay.

So Ralphe humps him up faceways by the collar, knocks away the hat and grabs a handful of hair. He catches the steward's eye and is pleased to see only fear. Pulling the groom's head chin up, he lifts him bodily by the groin and wrings out his scrotum like a wet rag. As the groom sinks to his knees, the parting in his hair looks a good handspan broad, the skull pale and scabby. Then he's on all fours, gasping and whining like a dog, and right on the ground, hugging himself into the shape of those low men, those criminals who are swine-tied and thrown in the quag. Once again, that same old grey dog who passed between them before ambles through, investigating the promising novelty of the coiled groom's arse. But the animal establishes in seconds that this is *posterior non grata* and passes on.

'Deference' says Ralphe for the benefit of the poultry girls 'where would we be without it?' But they are running away to their mothers, bursting with news. 'Now then ...' Ralphe inclines himself toward the curled form of the squire, works his foot under the groom's cheek, and turns the face towards him. 'As I think you know, I seek my master de Bonville, by whom I was invited to be here. I'm wondering if you are his man – if you are, he is surely hard done by, we are all on a run of sore luck. Now get on your feet and run along and find him'

But there is no need. Across the way by a rough-built lodge, a pair of collies are getting to their feet, stretching, grinning and bending. A man is striding from the house accompanied by the old grey lurcher dog. A blocky barrel-shaped man, dark beard and white teeth, heavy shoulders and an easy gait, stretching out his hand.

'Young Ralphe Mareschal! ... as I live and breathe!'

'My Lord, you do. And I am glad to see it. Your hair is still black and your back is still straight. You may live forever ...'

'I will not! I can't imagine immortality! All these people I know all dead, all others living their spans and dying but myself living on and on and on ... oh no! And Ralphe, you're looking so well ... it's disgusting! In any case, you look better than the mortal remains of poor Martin' The groom has managed to return to his knees, his head is turned away. He is sniffing and wiping his eyes, groping for his hat where it sits crown down in the mud.

'Ah ... my apologies for the abuse of your man' says Ralphe 'I'm afraid he has acquired ballsache, it came upon him sudden'

'No matter. Unfortunately he will never acquire wisdom. But I dare say abuse will not go amiss with him. True he is my man, and faithful as a dog, but it does a dog no harm to get a kicking now and then'.

'Can I give an honest opinion without giving offence my Lord?'

'Quite probably you can'.

'I find I cannot share your view of dogs. Your man Martin is less use than a dog, neither as clever nor as loveable'.

De Bonville laughs loudly. Martin is walking off stiffly, like a man who has just struggled out of a pond. He slaps his wretched hat on his thigh and curses low.

'Come along in and have something to eat' says the jovial warlord. 'Over the moor? You came *that* way? Worried about being late? Well, you *are* late, but not *too* late.'

The old grey lurcher, who seems to have *droit de seigneur*, enters the lodge first followed by his master. Ralphe, in from the fresh air, the business of the outside, passes under the lintel into a rough and ready domestic scene. The lodge is little more than a cabin of brashed trunks lashed together under a nest of thatch: it contains a long table strewn with scraps of bread and the stripped bones of poultry, plank benches and three men with cups before them and empty bowls. 'This is young Ralphe Mareschal ' says Guy de Bonville 'just arrived from the wilds of Herraton, a sweet enough spot but very near the ends of the earth'

'From the wilds to the wilds, eh?' says one of the liegemen, a heavy, middle–aged man with thick greying stubble who rumbles rather than speaks, and shifts in his seat. 'I can see we'll have to tread careful with you … watch out that we don't get a bollocking!'

'Ah yes … very entertaining!' This speaker is a youngish dark–haired man with a thin choleric face: he rests his back against the wall, stretching his legs along the bench. He runs a finger around the rim of his cup: 'he had it coming, you're lucky to have the privileges of a newcomer. My lord won't let *us* touch him…'

Guy de Bonville gives a sudden burst of laughter. 'Now these gentlemen, Ralphe – of whom you need not be afraid – are Jean Villon (the older, rumbling man), Guillame Canteloupe (the younger, lounging man) or *de* Canteloupe as he styles himself and this (a soft–featured, chubby–faced, bulge–eyed man not much older than himself) … is Jean de Ravelin, mad as a brush.'

Ralphe sits and a spare cup is slid before him. 'Have you been this way before?' asks Jean Villon.

'Never. No' says Ralphe 'and I don't know the road to Bristol at all.' He pours himself cider from the jug.

'Well, I wouldn't call it a road exactly' says de Bonville, watching Ralphe and smirking as he sees his reaction to the cider.

'Good God! It's like vinegar!'

'Indeed it is. Rough stuff, eh? I know your own cider at Herraton is much sweeter and darker. At your age, Ralphe, you won't ever have come across my Lord Robert of Gloucester?'

'True' says Ralphe with a sour face 'I do not number him amongst my acquaintances'

Jean de Ravelin gives a sudden bark of laughter.

'I can tell you'll be trouble' says de Bonville. 'Anyway, my Lord of Gloucester's as crazy as a forked snake and though you wouldn't believe it sitting here, it's madness out there, sheer *madness*. I'm sure you know that no one's in charge, and every man's out for himself. We're going out to see what's afoot, there could anything out there for the taking'

'Where is the Queen?' asks Ralphe, uneasy at this talk of piracy. 'It is for her cause we fight'

Guy de Bonville raises an eyebrow. De Ravelin gives another sudden bark of laughter, Villon shifts in his seat and clears his throat, and Canteloupe takes a drink. 'She lodges as far as I know with my Lord Robert in Bristol' says Bonville. 'More Cider?'

'Thankyou no' says Ralphe.

'You get used to it, you know' muttered the sallow Canteloupe, staring down at the table in front of him. 'It's never done me any harm …' He looks up then, one eye closed, the other sharp, as though inviting dispute.

'*Allez, allez!*' Guy de Bonville is on his feet, suddenly brisk, 'we must crack on – as the English say. Get the show on the road! Ralphe Mareschal come with me, there's a rabble of infantry out in the woods' says de Bonville suddenly as they move out together into a grey, even light 'some of them you'll recognise, my apologies for having to borrow them … and some excellent and very expensive archers whose only fault is that they're Welsh'

Ralphe smiled politely. 'I saw no foot soldiers on my way in' he said 'just some half-witted old villein ploughing in his sleep and a few men off on their way to the fields'.

'It's the odd way you came in, straying off the beaten track' said de Bonville, taking a moment to study the newly-made wheel of a cart, the metal rim still cooling, and the wheelwright waiting, cradling his mallet in his palm. 'You wouldn't have seen the men, they're over that way, either side of the track we'll be following out.' De Bonville gestured toward the denser woods and walked on briskly. 'To be honest', he said, 'I won't be sorry to see the back of this place, been here a week now and though I own it, I can't say I've much of a soft spot for it … inherited, see, poor stuff, no money in it and now that you've finally graced us with your presence' and here de Bonville, bestowing from the height of his rank a friendliness which was necessarily barbed with sarcasm, slowed his pace and showed his teeth. 'You my boy are the last piece, we can move now … get the oxen ready, the wheel's fixed!'

He shouts across the way to where the penned draught cattle stare and an aged man with a thick plumage of white hair leans on a thorn stick 'Everybody's bored stiff!' Ralphe had not seen this side of his lord before: never seen him so candid, so domesticated, so distracted by small details, not at all the legend. 'Can't keep Canteloupe off the drink, just about manage to keep people like Martin off the women. And everybody's a bit odd here … that labourer you saw, mad as the best of them, they call him Chunky for some reason, brain-dead but with a curious kind of wit. Sheer and simple mockery, taking the piss, but he gets away with it because everyone thinks he's an idiot … such is life eh?'

As he followed Guy de Bonville to wherever they were going, Ralphe realised that there was nothing odd about his lord's behaviour: after all, this was the man himself and not his own imagined version. Of course, this was the first time he had been in the company of Guy de Bonville (not as an equal, that would be going too far) as a fledged human being and he was being *treated as such*. And of course he now saw why his warlord had general respect, even in this most poverty-stricken and remote of his holdings. Ralphe admits aloud to playing the part of poor relation as he sees all around him and amongst the rough and ready huts, the well-husbanded animals, the carts, waggons and engines, the armour and mail of the other men being assembled, packed for travel. Here was a man who could make things happen. 'You are all greater men than I' he says 'all I can offer is my good self'.

'I'm sure that will do well enough' says de Bonville 'and you won't be poor much longer'

When they were back near the huts where Ralphe's animals were tethered, the bay, which Martin had been seeing to still, stood quietly. 'You take her', said de Bonville, 'she's a good strong lady. You take her with us or leave her and pick her up when you return. She's yours' And why does one man give another man a horse? Ralphe pondered this question without curiosity, suspicion or ingratitude.

'I know it' said de Bonville later, on the subject of Herraton. 'I've stayed there one night when I was very young, three or four, a pretty place. Not like this'

'It is … It is not. You were with your father, my lord?'

'My father, yes. I recall it as a place of some potential and you'll make a lot of it. Are the fortifications up to the task?'

Potential? Fortifications? Though he found conversation difficult, he was desperate to say the right thing. He wasn't quite like Jeanne whose need for words was minimal but had no trouble saying the right thing, he was sure he could survive without her, he regretted her distance now, and the notion of his child. As for fortifications: the motte was steep, the house was high, and the elm of the outer rampart was brittle, grey, splodged with orange and shelved with fungus.

'The fortifications fortify' he said eventually 'the King's men will not come to us anyway – we're too far away'.

De Bonville wasn't smiling. 'Probably not' he said with a twist to his mouth 'but there is more going on out there than the quarrels of the so-called King and his cousin – let them tear the land apart, they have their own crow to pluck! Let the feathers fly above our heads, Ralphe, abroad in the countryside there's all sorts of smaller men after all sorts of smaller results. It's an ill wind ... you know what I mean'.

'Of those three men in there with whom we are to make "common cause" with Matilda, I would only trust de Tracy ... oh, you may look at me like that! Yes, he is an idle toper but when it comes to it I would trust him with my life. Villon has experience but no money, he will fight for the highest bidder, who at the moment is myself; de Ravelin is deranged and kills for the sake of it, he slaps a man with his palm or if that palm contains a sword he shears off his head, all is the same to him. Your wife, Jeanne Warrene ... (how abruptly he changes the subject! From casual murder to my wife in a blink) now don't look so worried! I was only going to say that I'd met her, many years ago, at her father's house, she must have been barely walking. Do you have children, Ralphe?'

'Jeanne is carrying now'

Then de Ravelin, mounted, charges noisily through the yard, his short sword on the end of his straight arm: cats scatter and dogs press themselves to the ground. He reins to a halt and sits with the weapon at rest on his breastplate. 'Ready to be gone I am, my Lord' he declares.

'Very well! Six days to Bristol, with luck, monsieur de Ravelin!' So saying, Guy de Bonville washes his hands in air, claps them together and the man Martin, still walking rather carefully, emerges immediately followed by the measured tread and composed gaze of his master's smooth-pelted charger. 'Where the blank is the abbé?' calls de Bonville to no one in particular 'we need The Lord with us, get him out here to say his piece. Time, *my* time, is being *wasted*!'

Marshburgh

The next day, way behind the main party, hardly two miles out of Cleeve, the supply column of laden donkeys and ox carts languishes, having struggled to a halt on the greasy tracks of the plain, unable to make high ground. The hills are faint shadows ahead, the sky hangs like a slab of slate, rain falls steadily. The main party itself has no such problems, ascending a long slope between stands of beech. Ralphe, riding not the gift horse but his own old beast, watches water running off the leather of de Bonville's hat brim and down the back of his greased travelling cloak. His mind is elsewhere, in the woods near Herraton, talking to the little girl his wife once was ... *Jeanne, that's your name isn't it, there's something I want to ask you: can you tell me why it is dark at night? ... Why shouldn't it be?* (she says with a frown, thinking who is this now, why does my father do this?) ... *Well* (he says), *there's all those stars out there shining away and yet we can't see a metre in front of us ... Easy* (says Jeanne with a smile) *they're too far away ... How far away? ... So far away that their light is too weak ... Are they moving away from us? ... Don't be silly ...* He was ten and she was nine, their fathers were talking, standing away from them in the woods and they were waiting for the discussion to end, tending the horses. *You have a look tonight* (he says) *and see if you think they're moving outwards.*

That was his first encounter with Jeanne Warenne, as their fathers discussed boundaries and timber. She looked him straight in the eye, without ill-will. Without even touching, she was introducing him to new sensations: a prickly heat spread over him as though thousands of thin points were bursting through his skin. It was like fear. But it wasn't fear. Each time she looked away he watched her, all of her, hungrily. Here was the beginning of a mystery which would be his to investigate and solve at his leisure (for timber and curtilage were not the only subjects their fathers were discussing that day).

He decided there and then, enclosed in her atmosphere, that she must be a being above all other. He sensed oblivion. Her eyes were amiable and greenish – her hair was the colour of ripe straw, her skin was very pale, and of course she was girl. Though he well knew what girls looked like underneath their clothes, he was curious to know the very deep inside. Always curious. Even later, resting his ear on her navel and probing the silken reams and nodes of her vagina with his fingers, wedging them as far as he could inside her, and he would have to know what it was, or where the stuff went. 'Oh Ralphe!' tremors of laughter on his cheek 'I don't know! I've told you! Somewhere up inside, just some thingummy up there, I think it bends round ... oh you fool!'

The next time their fathers were out together, and the boy and girl were left alone again, she said that she did not believe the stars were moving away, that God wouldn't make them do such a thing. She said they were just very weak and we had the moon in any case ... and looking him straight in the eye she declared that the black sky was a dark cloth with pinholes in it held up in front of a great light and that the biggest hole was the moon. And Ralphe stared himself, held her eye and wondered whether her knees were smooth or bony like his own, and how there came to be a little bit of hair missing from one of her eyebrows, and a tiny scar just below ...

And now there is only the shrug of his master's glossy back, the solid noise of rain in the leafage, water murmuring along the tracksides, the standing timber thick around them. De Bonville was certainly right not to call this mule track a road. And nor was Ralphe impressed by the 'infantry'. They were, as the warlord had said, waiting in the woods by Cleeve: and they were a motley crew indeed. Brave men, possibly, with slings on their belts and their hedging hooks attached in various homely ways to stout ash poles. One or two have their own swords, one has a crossbow. Just as well the experienced and properly-armed foot soldiers from Herraton lead them, and keep them quiet and in step. There are five mounted knights (including Ralphe himself), other mounted men and squires, the dozen or so expensive and taciturn Welsh longbow men and de Bonville's own close guard, cowled in fine mail, smart in short surcoats quartered in red and yellow.

Rain falls in equal measure on these sundry men and beasts. No one is happy; everyone is wet and cold. The tracks are rough and narrow, crossed by springs and streams, riven by deep ruts, loose underfoot with that same grey shillet Ralphe knew from the moorland. And on the first night they are forced to camp out of doors in a mossy cove of abandoned stoneworkings beside the path. Ralphe is staring at the last embers of a disappointing fire raised with difficulty out of deadwood and green sticks; he has stripped out of his clothes and lies wrapped in his father's bequeathed sheepskin. His father was a hard bulky man with a smooth hairless head and thick shoulders. But his father-in-law – wiry, short-arsed, with faded yellow hair – could hardly be more different. So what hybrid form can his son be expected to take? In the clearing nearby the men have a good blaze going and they are restless and loud, undaunted by a soaking, gusts of profane laughter rise along with columns of sparks which die in the dark.

...*They're looking over at us again* (he says) ... *Sit down, Ralphe* (Jeanne lays her palm on the riven bark of the fallen sweet chestnut where the horses are tethered) *that means they're talking about us ... Saying what?... Oh, they'll be saying when we'll be married and all that stuff. Now don't laugh ...My father's fatter than yours isn't he?* (he says) ... *A bit* (she says) *now listen, Ralphe Mareschal* (she put her lips right up to the shell of his ear) *when we're married you'll have to 'hump' me, don't laugh I said* (she is laughing herself) *it's what they call it, I've heard the men say it. You've gone red. That's right isn't it, 'humping'? ... Yes that's right* (he says) *I've heard it too, and I've heard them doing it. Sounds like it's plenty of work, sounds as if it hurts. Well, when there's infants we'll name the first boy Guillame, after my fattish father, he's not so bad as they say ... D'you mean that?* (she asks) ... *I mean it* (he says and he sees her private little smile) *Guillame Mareschal he'll be called and he'll have to do just what you tell him to do so help him God!* ... They laugh so much that their fathers turn and stroll away ...

The party emerges from the woods in the cloudy morning onto a stretch of high quiet country of rough pasture, thorn thickets and buzzards. Some people are working on the hedgeless land, keeping their heads down and their eyes averted as they tend their small flocks. In the scattered steads and hamlets they come across, they glimpse only brief human movements – an arm withdrawn quickly through a window, a bare heel disappearing round a corner, a head tugged down behind a hurdle. De Bonville had made it clear before setting out from Cleeve to those who did not already know that (and he cleared his throat) there was a new danger and cynicism presently in the world, that they must carry on in the direction of Bristol, feel their way round the situation and not upset anybody. There were to be no attacks on local populations, and not even (he said) the scraggiest of old hens is to have its neck wrung without proper requisition and payment. There's no way of knowing who else might be about, in what strength and with what intention, assume hostility until you know otherwise etcetera, etcetera.

So, longing for warmth and food after a wet night and an overcast morning, in the late afternoon they are resting, watering the animals where a spring pours from the steep flank of a long bluff of bracken and gorse. Round the shoulder of the hill, the bends of a broad river blend into the distant sea. Ralphe, de Bonville and Jean de Ravelin ride back and find a beaten track to the plateau. 'There it is, Ralphe' says de Bonville 'Marshburgh, or Marshberry as some call it' The town gathers round a high motte at the point where the narrowing river necks in just too much for ships to turn. There are craft of all sizes anchored offshore, docked at the quays or manœuvring in the haven. Only one of the outer walls lies along the strand and a bridge has been built at its end. Outside the three landward walls there is the usual sprawl of shanties.

'What do you think, Bonville?' asks Jean de Ravelin cheerfully 'Does it look hospitable?'

'Can't tell from here, have to be trial and error, haven't been to the place for years ... but we could do with somewhere to bed down. We'll ride in over the bridge and see what happens. Roger de la Moule holds the castle now, I believe'

'Do we know what manner of cove he is?' De Ravelin is craning his body forward, both hands on his pommel, narrowing his eyes. 'He won't be of the King's party that's for sure isn't it?'

'As God is my witness I don't know. I've not heard' says de Bonville 'Ralphe ... have you ever heard of him?'

Ralphe shrugs. 'Me? I've not heard of anyone? But is the king not a generous man? I've heard he is. Does it matter who is of whose party?' He can see de Ravelin out of the corner of his eye, looking at him askance in mock horror.

'Yes, you could say that' says de Bonville dryly. 'Generous to a fault. But there are uncharitable souls who say he lacks all his marbles, that he is a few jewels short of a crown'

Ralphe and de Ravelin laugh aloud. 'Well, young Mareschal!' says de Ravelin settling back in the saddle 'you certainly bring out the best of my lord's wit and it's worth having you along just for that' *And what else? Am I no use for anything else?* and aloud he says: 'so this is why people everywhere do as they like?' But he speaks to the void for the others have already turned their mounts and are on their way back down.

To seasoned men the town is a commodity, a chance or not. But Ralphe has not seen a town of this size before and left alone he lingers, as if he needs to learn its form and setting. He can see there are two towns with what looks like a marsh separating them. The walls of the main town draw a rough triangle – there is a gatehouse at the narrow end and at each angle of the rounded end – and a causey crosses the marsh to the smaller town, a finger of houses along each side of a single sloping street running oblique to the main town like a heart pierced by an arrow.

And Marshberry looks prosperous enough, sheltered from the north, east and south by high verdant slopes full of sheep. Here is the point at which the produce of these animals is transferred to the river that bears it away to the rest of the realm. The ramparts are substantial, revetted with heavy, young timber. The castle, lying in the riverside quarter of the top of the heart, has stone buildings in the bailey and a keep of some size sitting on a motte so high and wide it makes Herraton's look like a molehill. The smaller, finger–like, town has its own quay at the foot of the single street and a narrow gut winds round the marshland near the causey and flows into the main haven. He is aware that de Bonville and de Ravelin are waiting for him, they sit on the track, well down the hill, mounted side by side. Ravelin is beckoning with wide sweeps of his arm.

When they get there just before dusk, the town is neither hostile nor welcoming. The knights sit mounted and the men stand restless whilst the lengthy negotiations which precede the handover of toll monies by de Bonville's factotum and treasurer proceed. Some of the men sneak forward to the gates to steal a glance inside, and the watchmen above on the parapet speak not a word but shoo them away like straying poultry with handclaps. At one point the gate is opened but only to let a troop of knights and liveried foot, presumably de la Moule's men, straight through in tidy order, looking neither left nor right.

Most of the Bonville party have spent at least a fortnight in the dull solitude of Cleeve preparing for this journey. Once in the town they ride in silence all the way to the castle bailey amid shouting, singing and banging, the grinding of wheels, the cries of animals and hawkers on the quaysides where bales of greasy wool are stacked amid strewn webs of rope and the queasy stench of fish. Roger de la Moule himself is standing near the gate. He is a short man with a bland monkish face, and he looks harassed.

'*The King!*' he exclaims, apparently surprised and amused by such a conceit. His scalp is smooth and polished, bordered with a purfling of crisp white hair that he adjusts and smoothes continuously. 'What King is that? ... Oh! *That* king!' He looks straight at you after each morsel of conversation with his small alert raisin-like eyes as if to emphasise that there are facts that must be faced.

'No, no ... we're not worried about the King here or the other woman ... no, no ... let them bang their heads together! Now are you gentlemen wishing to lodge the night? Right. There'll be somewhere, I'm sure, we're rather crowded at the moment, we've some lodgings here, by the hall, and there must be somewhere for your men. I'm sure. Don't you know there's a war on?' He gives a short cynical bark of laughter like a whiplash.

Ill Met By Moonlight

'All men' de Bonville is saying as he and Ralphe sit together that evening in the lodgings, drinking '... or most men, get drunk don't they? Nothing at all wrong with it, Ralphe, nothing. When I've had a few I start repeating words! Some are drunk half the time, some all the time, some some of the time, some only on high days and holidays. But there aren't many who *never ever* indulge. Now your friend Martin, so delightfully insolent to everyone, is by no means an habitual drinker, by no means: but when in his cups he is strangely quiet, tight–lipped and staggering' De Bonville throws back his head and laughs 'like a priestly puppet with elastic strings, only by some mysterious recurring miracle does he reach his lodgings safe and sound. And Canteloupe ... je m'excuse *de* Canteloupe ... is an entirely different kind of cove. He's a young man, twenty-three, twenty-four, ten years younger than I, not a lot older than you, Ralphe. But by God is he a sponge! A firkin on legs, a cistern with a leak! So pickled is he that his vast intake of any and every fermented substance has no visible effect, as though the inside of his body's coated with a patina of alcohol and he only drinks to keep his hands busy. Only in the very early morning does he approach anything that could be called sobriety and, even then, there is still enough drink in his system to keep him in equilibrium, remind him that he needs more. Villon – since I seem to be including everyone – he drinks only a little ale with his food, and tonight he has already gone to bed. De Ravelin is a perfect human being, a complete abstainer, he too is already sleeping '

'So not all men drink then, my Lord' says Ralphe sleepily 'and yourself?' he asks. He is looking slightly upward at de Bonville, cradling his chin in both palms, elbows on the board. He is very tired, he makes his enquiry only from *politesse*.

'Me? I drink *some*what, but only to oil the brain. I like to keep my eyes open, wits about me, take in the information. I know, Ralphe, precisely how much drink it takes to lubricate Master Brain without addling him. *Never* am I befuddled, uh, never. But I do tend to repeat myself ...or have I already said that?'

Ralphe has no views on the consumption of alcohol. Accustomed at home to an average intake of cider, his body rarely demands an excess. But tonight, in strange surroundings, he has consumed rather more than usual. 'Do you know' he says suddenly 'I've never been to a place this big, I'm a real bumpkin, an embarrassment. But you know Herraton ? Is it not a sweet place? I don't think ...

when this jaunt is over I won't leave it again … I'm not one for the roaming about. I'll be there now when you want me, whatever jaunt it is we're off on, I'm not afraid of anything. But this is a terrible thing to say I couldn't make a life out of it, I'm happy jogging along'.

'Yes Ralphe, since you owe me for ever that is rather a terrible thing to say. I'll put it down to youth and greenness. I know lads younger than you who haven't seen home for years. I asked you to come with me on this because your father, a brave man, a man of whom I was very fond, wanted you to know something of what your fellow human souls are up to....'

'What!? You've spoken with *him* about me? When? He's been dead three years'

'The last time he travelled with me, when you were quite small. I haven't seen much of him since, I let him off these jaunts in the end because he hated them so'

Ralphe is in his own world, so sleepy. 'My grandfather' he says 'who neither of us knew, built Herraton when he was young and strong, sixty–seven years ago in a fortnight! He roped in all the locals: bondmen, slaves, women and children. And so we came to control the countryside, the Mareschals, as a privilege of fighting alongside The Conqueror and winning'

'What's your *point*, Ralphe, you're not making sense'

'What threat is it we're under? The fortifications, my Lord, are falling to pieces. There's no threat'

'But Ralphe, when we get out there' he made a sweeping gesture with his arm 'you'll see what the threat is and you'll go back to this "sweet spot" you call home and you'll have those defences back up, a fortnight won't be quick enough! Men, women, children and all!'

Sadly, Ralphe was not listening. 'I'm very sorry, my Lord, but I'll have to go and walk about, my head weighs heavy, bugger the curfew.'

'Be careful, Ralphe. There's all sorts about out there. I'm fond of you as you know, I don't want to lose you. Think of Jeanne'

'I do, I do …'

Ralphe steps out of the lodging into a narrow straw–blown street and a biting breeze, vaguely aware that he's been insubordinate and been threatened. He could be mistaken, but the word 'threat' kept coming into the conversation. Once outside, he has no idea where he's going. The night is serenely clear, the sky crammed with stars, the streets drenched with the moon's cold glow and utterly silent. Yet never quite: by the strand there is activity, men work even at this ungodly hour, lifting bales of wool into a moored vessel with block and tackle. Ralphe watches these men with homes to go to from the shadows and envies them their easy bantering laughter. Wandering back through the warren of streets, he finds himself out on what he takes to be the eastern rampart, near his lodging. He hears the rustle and sigh of settled horses from nearby stables, God only knows what hour it is.

Every so often, he evades Roger de la Moule's men who patrol in pairs, smartly liveried, wearing short swords. A small brown dog follows him for a while and then vanishes. The only human sounds come from the scatter of shanties outside the rampart, some of them no more than hovels of hazel spars and grass: there is some kind of communal clearing where pinched faces, apparently disembodied, swaddled against the wind, are gathered round a twisting fire and a bulbous pot. He thinks he feels the heat of the fire from his distance. The small brown dog reappears in the firelight and leaps for a tossed morsel of food. There is a burst of laughter as he turns away to enter the streets again and find his way back to the lodging.

Taking advantage of a corner in the lee of a barn he stands with his feet apart voiding filtered cider against the wall in a gentle cloud of steam and becomes aware of a figure in the doorway of a house across the way. He turns when he finishes and can see a woman leaning in the recess, a slight girl with a drawn white face and thick dark hair swathed in a blanket of heavy woollen stuff. Her face is almost the same colour as the moonlit timber of the wall and seems to float free above the deep shadow of the blanket.

As he approaches, she looks him straight in the eye with a tremor of the lips that could be a smile and parts the blanket revealing flesh of the same lunar pallor as her face. At this dead hour of the night who will ever know? He feels blood coursing in his body and the cold recede. Only Jeanne, his distant wife, would care: he hears the jangle of keys on her hip as she walks among the outhouses and he hesitates … *But no one will know, you oaf!* … but isn't there a dislocation which this woman cannot set right? He needs her to *accommodate* him for a short while, that's all. As he crosses the street toward her, she nudges herself off the door jamb, wrapping her body in the blanket again, turning her back and disappearing into the house.

The one room she lives in is pungent with poverty and as cold as the grave. Light and shadow are sharpened by moonlight. There is no fire and he can hear her shiver, God knows how long she's been waiting out there. She says to him that she waits for de la Moule's men some nights. There are others sleeping in the room under rough coverings, a sudden deep cough makes him jump. She laughs softly and says it's her father and she carries on chatting whilst she lets the blanket drop and smoothes her hair. The bed she indicates is the only one in the room and, as far as he can tell, has only one other occupant. A profusion of dark hair lies in a trail behind the sleeping head. A sister. And he knows suddenly that this woman has motives like his own: she fucks not for a living but because it is a distraction, because she likes it, because she wants a child – any reason but financial gain. She is not a whore, if only she was. Without the simplicity of a transaction, there's too much to it. And Jeanne demands that he walk away quickly, out of the door and into the night.

Guy de Bonville's account of the reaction of his man Martin to drink was, of course, inaccurate. The groom has spent a good part of the afternoon and all of the evening festering in the same tavern, a simmering broth of spite flavoured with bitter herbs (a far cry indeed from the 'priestly puppet with elastic strings'). And even after a prodigious and sustained intake of strong drink, he cannot easily forget his public humiliation at the hands of Mareschal. Martin has come full circle, passing through the rubber-legged, harmless stage (so fondly described by de Bonville) without even leaving his seat. By way of the parti-coloured yawn at the bottom of the whirling pit, he has drunk himself into a version of sobriety. A stained and malodorous parody of strong and silent *gravitas*, he sits bolt upright and deadpan, having arrived at that state of cold excitement, of vicious melancholia, which calls for either an infamous action or complete collapse.

The bitter cold hits him like a fist as he emerges from the foetid stew of the tavern, forcing him to reel against the wall. But he soon recovers, takes a deep fearless breath and strides away with exaggerated aplomb. Like Ralphe he has no idea of where he is or where he is going and like Ralphe he comes to the same leeward spot and pisses, copious and muttering, against the wall of the barn. He too becomes aware of the female figure who, baffled by the abrupt disappearance of her previous customer, stands in the doorway, swathed anew in her rough blanket. Martin takes his time to conclude his liquid dialogue with the wall and put himself away, and when he turns his stare is deliberate, and paralytic. She does not move, merely smirks. Then Martin quite suddenly sniffs and walks away.

But, having gone only a few yards, a circumstance arises he had never for a moment thought likely: an insistent, almost uncomfortable, erection. His hand confirms it, a stave that could sink a ship. So he hurries back to the doorway, taking the poor girl unawares. Almost before she has pushed herself upright from the doorpost, Martin is down on his haunches, grabbing and lifting the blanket. The girl, bewildered by his muttering haste, appalled by his sour smell, holds the material against her breast as she is forced back against the wall. 'Let's go in at least, it's freezin out here' she says. But the groom ignores her, briefly finding her with his fingers he pushes what he can into her. She is forced to release the bundled blanket as she grapples with the problem of balance. 'Hold on then' she says 'keep it there and don't move'. In one swift movement, she raises her knees and plants her feet on the opposite wall, at the same time locking her arms around his neck by gripping each elbow with a crab of fingers, in this way she houses his whole length and keeps it there.

Ten seconds of stabbing is all it takes for this repellent, humourless man to bang her like a nail into the wall. He fires his charge with a strange high yell like a kicked dog and pulls away breathing heavily. The girl's blanket drops back into place, and she remains flat against the door jamb, her feet apart. 'Most men come in you know' she says 'what if someone'd bin passing, seeing me fucked up against me own front door'. Martin says nothing but stands swaying slightly, with his cock still out and hard, fumbling in his clothing for a coin and sliding it between her lips. She, left with no choice, takes it between her teeth. 'Ha! There, take it and eat it!' he cries as he turns his back and walks away.

He strides quickly, a stiff-legged lope, almost a run, along narrow ways between high buildings in the blue and white light, the deep shadows. His cock he does not, cannot, put away for it still rears in a cold hard fury. He can hear the pounding of his heart, he wants to be alone with his exhilaration. But this is not to be. Ahead is a chapel, half–finished, and someone is sitting in its shadows. The last thing the groom had expected to see was another human being, he had thought he was alone in the world: he must stow away his penis which has wilted as quick as if the Devil had breathed on it.

Ralphe had not gone far since he left the girl, there was confusion in his mind. He came to a place where there was a half-finished chapel, new-built walls clothed in scaffold poles and planking: the shell is almost complete, a few courses short of the roof plate. Heavy, shaped roof timbers are leaning ready at the foot of the scaffold. There are sorted piles of undressed stone, offcut poles thrown in a corner, a heavy waggon with its shafts on blocks, half full of white lime: scattered all over the yard like nuggets of black wax are all the odd-shaped faceless stones of no use to the masons. He sits, suddenly weary, on a rough bench set up in the lee of the waggon …

… isn't it good nobody knows we're out here, isn't it so good to lie flat

on your back and watch the moon but my legs are cold (he slides his arm under her neck) *... we're not meant to be here, no ... I'll have to be sure this blanket's aired, it's my mother's good one she never uses it, she won't miss it ... the moon goes across every night but it's always the same, it never gets any further away ... will you love me Ralphe? Always?... The moon's a lady they say ... you don't say much do you? ... Nothing like as much as you* (he says finally) *I'm happy listening to you* (he is tracing her ear with the end of his finger) *there's dark marks on the moon, d'you think there's anybody on it? ... They were talking about us again today I heard maman talking to your father, it's like we're cattle ... We'll be as happy as cattle* (he says) *... What colour is moonlight?* (she says, squeezing his bare leg) *... I can just about see your hand* (he says) *can you tweak the hairs on my leg, just a bit ... for the sake of the pain, ah yes! That's it! ... moonlight, to answer your question, is the opposite colour to shadows ...*

Then he is aware of a figure emerging at a peculiar stiff jog from the heavy shadow of a tall house and it halts suddenly in the middle of the street resolving itself unmistakably – the explosion of hair, the hat – into the man Martin. He seems to be (the moonlight is merciless) God forbid, getting his cock out.

'It's alright sir' says Martin 'I'm putting it away, not getting it out. I'm not one of those. Matter of fact scored a quick knee-trembler just now, thing is it's such a boner I couldn't get it back in'

'Ah really? And who was the lucky lady? The girl with nothing but a blanket on?' Ralphe stands up, keeping his fingers on the handle of his short knife, as Martin walks on past him, still fumbling with his clothing.

'Ah' says Martin with a sniff of recognition 'it's you sir. Well, I can report (he really is quite a mimic, he has Ralphe's posh gallic accent to a tee) that your effort to rip off my balls has had no effect whatever upon my potency. Everything still works'

'I'm very glad to hear it' said Ralphe, weary and irritated. He would have preferred not to be noticed, not to be forced into the company once again of this unlikely menial with his reckless mimicry, insulting posture, and gross familiarity. 'Now, Martin' he said 'if I were you I'd be off back to my billet now. You do that and I won't say anything to my lord de Bonville, get back and sleep it off. No one will know'

'Kind of you to think of my well-being, sir, but *actually* I'm not that drunk, I was earlier, very drunk, but I'm better now. I can talk and think and fight and walk'

'Then walk away Martin, walk away, there's a good chap'. He was not making a good job of this, he knew this would have to be resolved by weapons. Then it occurred to him that this man might not be a servant at all, had never been, he was something else, entirely bogus, or an agent representing *something* else, he was just *too* vile to be true. Underneath that obnoxious exterior, he was sure there was calculation. 'Walk away?' Martin declaimed 'oh yes, your lordyship, after all it's my place to bugger off ain't it? Disappear when my services ain't required. I could crack your head open sir – right now – and nobody would know it were me.' Even his speech must be affectation. Ralphe became alert and limbered up without moving, he stood on the balls of his feet, flexed his toes and fingers. He was sure he was about to die ...

Guillame Canteloupe has paid for a room in the tavern that played host in its lower public areas recently to Martin. He sits alone in that upper room now.

Goodwife Pilgrim, the *maîtresse*, has been diligent in her offers of female company ('a very cultured young man' she says to her regular ladies 'groomed nice, dark and handsome, has a charming way with his eyes, you know, dark and deep'. The ladies laugh and smile and take each other's measure askance). But nothing offered to him during the evening could light Tracey's fire and prise him away from his flagon and the truth is now it is too late, far too late: so damp has the kindling become that the possibility of ignition has all but evaporated. 'Not your fault, my dear Goody Pilgrim' he says 'what I shall do is walk for a while' he drains his cup with a steady hand. 'I have a notion the cold will do me good, I'm feeling jaded. Who knows? When I return I may feel more open to the charms of your *repertoire*'. But he knows, and Goodwife Pilgrim knows, that sadly all the charm in the world would not now, at this stage, be capable of inducing in him anything approaching a state of priapism.

    Nor did the cold do him as much good as he had hoped. It made him rather cynical. He sighed as the smell of two stains already on the wall of a barn forced him to stop and urinate. He stands splashing his feet, muttering complaints of the demands of the body, and out of the corner of his eye he sees the Blanket Girl in the doorway. When the flow has ceased he turns toward her without putting away his penis. 'And what *bel dam* is this' he asks with a lopsided grin 'blushing – or should I say shivering – in her bower? I'm so sorry but I'm afraid I can be of little use, look at it, see how the poor thing droops.' Lifting what looks like an anaemic slug, he eyes it with sad distaste and lets it fall back to rest.

    The girl had been thinking to herself that this one, with his dark beard and pale face, at least looked quite handsome: especially following on from the nervy one who ran off and that nasty blockhead she wished had done the same. Unfortunately, her encounter with this trinity of fickle clients, one after the other, leaves her with only a tired scepticism. 'All you lot do' she says 'is either piss up that barn, waste my time or *take* the piss!' She turns her back, disappears inside, and slams the door.

    '*Consummatum est*' sighs Canteloupe, walking on.

    Turning away from the street, he passes down a narrow drang between two houses and onto a track running beside the revetted wall. The moon is sailing smoothly through patches of diaphanous cloud, some characteristic of its light brings a stealthy velvet lightness to his step. Something in the air makes him slow his pace to a stalker's creep. And there is a chapel half–built, clad in a skeleton of poles glazed with white light and the shadows of two figures dancing distend across the dark ruts of the yard amongst scattered piles of chunky stones. The breeze has slackened, sound carries well, and quite plainly he hears the voice of de Bonville's man, accented strangely: 'I could crack your head open sir, right now and nobody would know it were me'

    Canteloupe halts and follows the shadows: one leads to a tallish man standing still with his hand on his hip and the other to the stocky Martin, circling and making slicing motions with his arms. Recognising young Mareschal, he is intrigued: what on earth are these two doing out here together in the dead hour of night? The man Martin picks up a sawn pole about five feet long, tests its weight like a *connoisseur*, swings it back and forth in the air. Mareschal stands perfectly still in his cynical posture. Canteloupe finds it all very amusing. The groom is either drunk or playing the fool: his footing is slippery and he seems barely able to control the pole. He lurches suddenly toward Ralphe with the pole at arms, his legs and back bent, a creeping parody of wary skill. 'Come on then' he's saying 'come at me yer bastard!' These were the words of a man who has burned his boats, who is within sight of the gallows.

Ralphe then moves with impressive speed, a pole appears in his hands instantly and he counters the wild swings of Martin easily with measured parries to the left and right. Canteloupe is enjoying the contest: the *thock, thock* of the clashing poles, the hopeless dullard versus the apprentice warrior, he skips and dodges in the shadows like a puppet, but the same thought comes to him as came to Ralphe. Is this man real? Could anyone be so useless?

And Ralphe, at ease with the stave, firm and quick with each parrying blow, enjoys this unexpected bit of practice. But soon his weariness catches up with him and in a last, rather elegant, move he skips to the side and fells the groom with a blow to the back of the knees. Canteloupe then makes his appearance, rolls the servant, leans a knee on him and pins his arms to his lower back.

Ralphe is taken aback, he laughs. 'I'm glad to see you but where did you come from?'

'I appear when least expected, out of darkness!' Canteloupe, too, is laughing. 'Now, there must be a length of small rope about, we'll get this rogue lashed up and take him back. Alright now ' Canteloupe bends his head close to Martin's ear 'you, sir, are in several feet of shit as I'm sure you know – attacking a colleague of your master, out after curfew, drunk in charge of a two–yard pole, verbal abuse … oh dear, dear. The ordure you languish in will pull you down like quicksand. I witnessed the whole shameful episode.' He winks at Ralphe, who goes to fetch rope. 'For now, my friend, you will come with us'.

And he did go with them, up to a point. It was decided they should give him over to de la Moule's men at the North Gate but, as they escorted him along the path that rings the inner wall, he simply melted away. And later, when Ralphe thought about the circumstances of what could be called Martin's 'moonlight flit', he struggled to understand the means, or even the cause. Canteloupe was ahead of the groom and Ralphe behind him. At the first moment of darkness (when a drift of cloud covered the moon) Ralphe heard a movement, very quick, which Canteloupe said afterwards was the prisoner skipping and shooting out his foot. There was the sound of a fall, a groan and a curse. In seconds the cloud had passed, Canteloupe was getting back on his feet and Martin was gone. He must have vaulted the wall (unlikely) or passed through it (impossible) for they are left watching his black shadow lope unhandily out over the marsh, its wrists still tied. The moon hangs, alone and perfect, above the dark mass of the other town across the marsh, called Tawton, and the tide is well in. 'That man is no more a groom than I'm the Pope of Rome' says Ralphe.

'Armless but not harmless, eh?' says Canteloupe, brushing earth from his hose, stone cold sober now. 'He's a snake that one. We'll not go after him – let the sucking mud have him. The causey's underwater.'

And the dark shape of Martin leaps like a wingless duck among the tussocks of thin sedge. When he finally stops, he seems to stand for a moment (is he looking back?) then he jumps and disappears feet first, smooth as an otter, into the steely water. The two men watch in silence as his hat drifts slowly into the shadows. Before they walk away, Ralphe crosses himself. Canteloupe mutters. *Dona eius requiem.*

CHAPTER FOUR

An Old-Fashioned House

After the construction of the new house at Herton, or 'Digweed's Castle' as it is known locally, there was a general redrawing of boundaries. The working parts, that is the orchards, paddock and yards, remained in the curtilage of the old farmhouse but a sizeable wedge of land has been taken into the 'wild garden' of Herton House, with its mown paths radiating from the old motte like the rays of the sun. Mr Digweed had been told by the architect that it was now fashionable to have a 'garden mound' and he, keen as always to conform to enhancing trends, is delighted not only to possess what is *á la mode* but also to have spent no money in its acquisition. If progress suits him, Mr Digweed will adapt to it. Even at his stage of advancing middle age, he cannot simply be dismissed by the rising generation as a relic and therefore hostile to the contemporary. He is nobody's fool. He knows how the world sits. For example, his view of the old farmhouse – though he is not blind to some aspects of its quaintness, or its sentimental associations – is that it is a place where *time has stood still.* Look at its dun thatch and rambling, piecemeal construction, low ceilings, worm-eaten lintels and beams, only a small part of it has two floors. Let's be honest, the old place has *had its day.*

At least he thought it had. Occupied in its dotage by only Arthur Trelease and his son the old longhouse, built in a time when people and animals lived under one roof, was to have been left in peace, like an old horse whose working days are over, to quietly decline. But since the previous September, of 1864, the new Mrs Geoffrey Trelease has joined the factotum and his son so that the old farmstead has gained a new lease of life. And Jane, able to live again in the home where she spent most of her childhood, does not have her father's problem. An immobility of time suits her.

There is a bench seat in an alcove let into the foot of the mound and having stepped over the insignificant obstruction of Mr Digweed's new box hedge, she has gone to sit there, on a cold afternoon in February. A hazel branch hangs very close to her and she pulls it down level with her eyes, stares at the catkins, runs a fingernail along one that is still firm. She finds that she hates change ... *what if one year these catkins never came, or were purple, orange or blue?* She knows her parents, or at least her father, would rather she and Geoffrey had lived in Herton House, but no ... *just look at it sitting there with its nice casements and smooth walls, those awful false battlements, I've heard from Jago that people call it Digweed's Castle* ... she refused to live there, and let it be known to Geoffrey. And her father-in-law (though a faithful retainer to William Digweed & Son), lacking utterly Mr Digweed's desire for social position, having his own means into the bargain, knows his daughter-in-law well enough not to intervene in discussions with foregone conclusions.

Also, her father-in-law encourages Jane, in a way that her own father does not, in her plan to open a school and herself be the teacher of those children of the few labouring families and cottagers who would consent to have them educated. Unless it has the effect of socially enhancing his own children or, in the case of his son-in-law, improving the managerial classes, Mr Digweed does not approve of education. Where the labouring classes are concerned, well there is no self-evident point in teaching letters and figures to those whose lives will only consist of drudgery and obedience. But she *will* do it, she will, and that's not all! Since she's moved back into the old house, she has made a new enclosure and taken on the poultry *and* the running of the dairy, just like the missus used to do. *And* she plays hostess twice per annum to the men and their families, treats them to a meal, and has them all round the table in the farmhouse, like it used to be. Mr Digweed has heard the laughter, he can imagine the ribaldry (*She makes a mockery! And I suppose you know who she's laughing at?*)

So, why is it that Mr Digweed is not utterly scandalised? As ever, he has not succeeded in communicating even the most superficial of his feelings to his daughter. And why? His views are what anyone would call forthright, free of the clutter of nonsense and ambiguity, there are ways things are done and that's that. Is he not a decent straightforward man? So why is it he can muster only tongue-tied resignation? *Afraid, Digweed, frit of your own daughter!* Never has he so much as *hinted* at his knowledge of the outrageous sketch books. He arrives at the barrier of her candid gaze *Them sharp, foxy eyes!* which has no art in it, and he can go no further. Even if he manages to open his mouth only platitude emerges. S*truck dumb again Digweed, you clod-hoppin' old basterd!* But there were other drawings in his daughter's portfolio, much nicer ones of Geoffrey, head and shoulders or full figure clothed: she makes him look like a god. There is one Mr Digweed likes especially where his son-in-law sits a-seat a grey charger like a knight of old – Sir Geoffrey de Trelease winning the hand of the Lady Jayne! *The hand of the Lady Jayne! We know where that've bin!*

Not so much when he sleeps but when he is awake Mr Digweed has a recurring dream. He bursts into her room, splintering the door if he must, slams the pages of vile sin on the table, and she will lay down her head and plead for his understanding. Then, together, in her own small grate, they will burn those wicked pornographs, watch them blacken, curl and disintegrate. There will be reconciliation. 'This need go no further than us two, Jane.' 'Oh yes, Father, that is best – never again shall I use my hands to produce such images, I swear.' Still shamefaced but deeply loving, she entrusts herself into his care, and he reaches out …

At that point the picture dissolves: it will fade completely before the final tender reconciliation, the lingering touch, and the long embrace. He well knows she will not be sheepish, or even remotely perturbed by his dramatic appearance. She will be sitting on her window-seat, head down into a book and those eyes, bemused and compassionate, will look into his and the cresting roll of his temper's wave will brush harmlessly over the sand. He will leave the room, apologetic, closing the door quietly.

And if he were an honest man, who listened to his stranger's voice, Mr Digweed would have to let himself know that he had returned to the outhouse more than once in the last year and studied the pictures again for much longer than the excuse he gave himself (identification of the sitter) would have required. *That length and girth she's had inside her – where did her learn not to be afraid of it? And you can't fathom that leaping seabird can you? Is it freedom. Or worse?*

And the young lady herself? Mrs Jane Trelease the woman is rather busier than was the girl Jane Digweed. No longer is there a current sketching book secreted in the old fisherman's hut: all are now stored in the old outhouse. She has come to think the unthinkable. She can see herself standing quietly in the orchard before long, the next time a bonfire is lit, and feeding the drawings that, unknown to her, have so perturbed her father one by one to the flames. She still rides out alone, of course, to the marshes and the dykes, to the resilient probing of Jago; but the whole business of drawing, of art, seems to need evaluation. It may have served a purpose that has been superseded. She has become immersed in domestic practicalities, creative in itself, and these days the married woman, though not especially keen on writing, prefers to keep a diary.

She found that the responsibility of caring for her husband and household permeated her with a warm well-being she could not understand but only enjoy. Work and housekeeping were necessary exercise. That was more or less all. Oh no, not quite – her father was made *very* happy. 'Don't misunderstand me' said Arthur Trelease the wedding guest aside to his new daughter-in-law among the throng at the foot of the sweeping staircase of Herton House. 'But I've rarely seen Mr Digweed so easy-going and gay'.

'Oh' said Jane with a laugh 'he is quite capable of affability. It would take a brave or misguided person to be the spectre at *this* feast. No one is allowed to spoil a wedding' And all the time she was nodding, smiling and waving to guests who stood in groups with their punch, or wandered by to wish her well.

'I didn't mean that, you *did* misunderstand me' said Mr Trelease, piqued 'God forbid, Jane. I wouldn't suppose for a moment anyone would set out to spoil such a day, least of all the father of the bride. I just meant'

Jane had placed her hand on her father-in-law's arm. 'I am entitled to some humorous licence on my wedding day, Mr Trelease.' He smiled himself then, but uncertainly, in deference to his daughter-in-law's wide grin. A gong was sounded.

'Where is Geoffrey?' cried Jane to the whole room 'Husband! Where art thou?' And the whole company raised their glasses with a cheer as Geoffrey approached his wife and took her arm.

And later Mr Trelease, slightly merry, declaims his long–prepared and rehearsed text over the extended tables, along ranks of bucolic faces and the débris of feasting. He concludes with expressions of unfeigned satisfaction: ' ... myself and many others of you will have seen these two people growing up, and I've always hoped and prayed, been so sure that I would gain Jane Digweed as a daughter. I am a happy man today and I hope that the young people will be as happy in years to come and now I really must sit down in deference to Mr Digweed's excellent wine and of course, Mr Digweed himself.'

Mr Digweed, in common with most of us, acts all the parts in his own small drama himself and only occasionally must learn new ones. He rose, joviality personified, as the good–natured laughter and applause Mr Trelease's speech had engendered began to subside. To an accompaniment of breaking waves of that same good-natured laughter and a tinkling murmur of fine glassware, he provided a shamelessly favourable and endearing estimate of his daughter's virtues. And finally he said: 'there's many a time I've bin glad that this steady and serious young lady's been at me side to make sure folks don't take me for a prapper oaf and I hope her husband'll permit her to remain there for years to come' *But that's just it, Digweed! You are what you are – an oaf. And she knows it! She's free of you now, aren't you glad? And there's satisfaction clinging salty in her hair and in every pore of that creamy skin, there's a good reason to be satisfied* 'So without more ado, raise your glasses please to my daughter and son-in-law Mister and Missus Geoffrey Trelease! Good luck and God Bless ...!'

Actually, Digweed rather envies his daughter her ability to so easily draw lines, to quarter herself like a cheese. Her natural decorum, for example, her mastery of both small talk and informed discussion. 'Mr Digweed' is a figurative skin containing many people, all of them of the genus *Digweed,* but he hopes there might be one or two varieties of the species *William* waiting to be discovered. He could learn from his daughter, how does she keep her social qualities so separate from those dark and shocking female enthusiasms that he prefers not to notice. *You've caught the smell on her, brackish garments of rivermen discarded and strewn about. A mettle smell. You know she still sees him but you can't speak of it. The county people and the pastor – they'll know and you'll suffer!*

Returning indoors at a much later stage of the evening, flushed and philosophical after a cataclysmic, dahlia-withering, release of gaseous energy, Mr Digweed engages the ear of his wife's elder brother. Their conversation is meandering and banal. 'Mind you' Mr Digweed eventually expounds 'tis summat the youngsters do, tis *they* that shows you'm comin up in the world. Charles'll be a prapper elevated man, a barrister I dare say, and John'll take over the estate, be a prapper gentleman farmer, *and* I still got two more aces up me sleeve. The twins'll marry well you can be sure uv it. So I can't see no arm in giving up notions of Jane bringing the Digweeds more respect and leavin er alone to marry where er likes.'

'I've just remembered' his brother-in-law edges away 'I said I would dance with Mrs Digweed before the end of the evening. You'll have to excuse me.' And Mr Digweed is left alone, unencumbered by a partner, watching the couples form up. His daughter, too, is sitting out this dance. She is seated with Geoffrey and they are deep in conversation. *No need for you worry now Digweed.* He catches his daughter's eye briefly, the merest gleam, a glance which struck him askance like a glow-worm in a dark hedge or the distant wink of a lantern on a moonless night. *Your daughter's married now, Geoffrey's problem.*

In the months before the wedding, through perseverance and discreet enquiry, he had managed to put a name to the face of the model for the more scandalous of the drawings. One George Jago, of Rafton, a bargee! And as preparations for the wedding were underway, having considered the serious effect any gossip might have on his own family, Mr Digweed sketched out a draft of a letter. He will send it to an old business associate of his, an Ulsterman who emigrated with his wife to a particularly desolate part of the Americas some years ago. This letter, which a firm of clerks in a distant town writes in fair copy and posts as per Mr Digweed's instructions, begs Mr & Mrs Thomas Hiscock to make a place on their holding available to one George Jago. This young man comes with the writer's own guarantee of his solid qualities, keen ambition, industrious application, etcetera. Mr Digweed adds that he would be most grateful if at no point in their correspondence with Jago they mention the name of Digweed. It only need be said that testimonials and references, provided by a local notable, have been most favourable and that, quite by coincidence, they seek just such a person to help realise their ambitions in taming the land and making it pay. In fact, they would be flattered if Mr Jago would be kind enough to consider and accept their offer. And, amongst other financial inducements, Mr Digweed adds, as a clincher, that they may offer Jago not only payment of his passage (third class), but also one year's wages in advance payable on his arrival, fit for work, in the vast spaces of Rupert's Land.

Free Passage

        Jago! If er called me anythin twas always just Jago! Not that I'm one to mind, you couldn't really hold nothing against er, er was a lovely maid. There's this one day in the autumn or late summer of last year, and I'll never forget it. I like to remember every detail of every thing – gives me summat to think on and keeps me in heart out yer in the middle of nowhere (and tis the very middle o't!). There's three things. One was the master bangin session in the old hut, two was when er called me 'George', three was the letter out of nowhere. But I'll get to that in order.

        The first time us didn't even take our clothes off: er went down like a dug and twas all done quicker than a rabbit. Er didn't say nothing, just flopped down on her arse and slumped against the wall and combed er fingers through er air. I was there on me knees, most devout, with un halfway down to normal – aff-cocked I s'pose you could say for a laugh.

        There was a second and a third time. The second time was slow, like a real job of work: there was moments when twas like cruising drew the sky or floatin naked on a cool pond on a hot day. Weightless. I could see er was miles away somewhere else, some empty place I reckon, like a desert (like bliddy Rupert's Land!) and there's two deep lines in er forred above the nose like twas hurting a bit but twas an operation ad to be done fer the good, and er would bear it (is there such a thing in this world as summat that rises and falls at once? A rising fall?) There was times when us was very nearly there, right on the edge of finishin, then without sayin ort we'd both agree to ease up at the last minnit, postpone it. But in the end twas me couldn't elp settin up a pace, took to slidin in and out like a piston – I could hear an echo in the walls of meself gruntin, and er flung er head aside sudden and laid a cheek to the ground and pink spread all over er face. Er cried out through a clenched grin to be honest it sounded like a cat spittin and that were that, it came sudden like a single thread of hot quicksilver shot deep away into whatever's in there that catches it. Gone. And then us was both lyin on our backs, not sayin much (er never did). And one of er legs was lying between mine, sweat was coolin on me and er was starin at the roof twistin er mouth and blowin up over her face.

        Well the third time – I'll get to the letter in a minnit, but I only really thought about this a moment ago and tis details I don't want to forget cos I don't suppose I'll ever see er again. I spose I want to drive it into me mind, the love parts, like I'm driving these yer posts in, tis summat to fix me mind on (I wish I'd never come out yer, the master and missus is alright but tis so bliddy lonely). Well now then, the third time ... as I said we was both lyin on our backs and I was restin me hand on er thigh near the top, and there's that gentle heat that comes off er cunt and that smell of friction that's a bit like burnin and if I moved me little finger ever so slight I could brush the fine ends of er damp thatch with un. By and by er fingers crept down drew the line of hair on me belly – er was sort of walking two of um along, you know, this little piggy and stuff. Then er closes a fist over un and lifts er ade up to take a look. Course un's there, like a bliddy rounders bat, and I'm already rollin over and meetin er mouth with mine and er's lifting and spreading er legs. Er keeps old of un and ee slides on warm grease right the way in. Er digs an eel into each half of me arse and just slowly grinds away and I reckon, by the patient way er was sort of polishin the tip of un with some little nubby thing she ad in there, er must ave thought twas gwain be another long slow one – but I'm buggered if I could stand more than alf a minnit of it! It all come out in two or three great lumps – buggered if I know where twas all comin from! And that were that.

And after, us was both weary. Er looked sort of helpless with it, er eyes was worried-looking and drained, rovin up and down me face, shocked and fucked out (if there is such a thing as fucked out). It was like all er willpower was used up. The thing was, never appened afore, us both fell asleep! And woke up later when the sun was low, all disorganised and flappin about, chuckin our clothes on. As I put me jacket on I felt the letter in a pocket and I said to er: 'I've ad this delivered, would you read it to me?' or some such thing. When er'd read it through to me, er said twas from Thomas Hiscock Hesquire, of Kirkboys, Rupert's Land.

'Where in buggeration's that? I've never eard of it' I said. Nobody ever sent me a letter afore. I were flabbergasted. The more I heard of it the less I believed.

'It's in Canada, George' er said. That was the first time er ever called me George. And er looked sort of knowing and sad, like er knew what sort of an effort the letter really was. Like it waddn so simple as it sounded.

'Oo's this local bigwig oo's been singin my praises then? They've heard of George Jago in Canada? I can't believe it'.

'Will you go?' er said. Suspicious! That's ow er looked! Like there was somethin afoot.

'I should go, missy. Sure enough. Sounds like I should be rolling in it, a year's wages! In advance! I could buy land and be like your pappy. I might end up with more land than ee!'

'George, you will never be anything remotely like Mr Digweed. But I would go if I were you' Er ad er face turned away and er was fiddlin with er scarf-knot as if er couldn't quite get it right.

Out on the river the day after the receipt of the letter, Jago and his skipper are resting 'A lot of chaps have gone to work out in America or Australia or New Zealand, even chaps I know', says Bill Painter swigging cold tea from a bottle. 'What've happened see is that yers ago, I remember it meself, the farmer and his men used to be out together working. But what's comin about these days is they farmers who've got pots of money is swallowin up the small men who used to have a few acres and get by, smallholders and they, so a lot of they's ended up either working for a wage some farmer pays em, or else having to go and live in town and get work there or else hemigratin to some foreign place where they can be their own boss again. So what you got now is the bottom of the heap's got wider and the top've got narrower and the middle's gone altogether. So one chap's getting richer and richer and undreds is getting poorer and poorer and the countryside's gettin emptier'

Jago is confused: when he asked his skipper's advice he had expected yes or no. He's not thought about variable pyramids. 'Well, Billy, should I go then?'

'Who's given ee these wonderful references, d'ye know?' asks Bill Painter

'I've no bliddy idea'

'Well, must be somebody. Have you upset anybody? For what tis worth, I should think somebody's tryin to get rid of ee'

'Oo'd want to get rid of *me*?' George Jago gives a little bark of laughter.

'Only you'd know that'.

They have hired in a larger boat today, the *Albert Rose*, to fill a big order that's come their way. The loading of it is long, hard and tedious. Jago settles to his shovelling, thinking to make order of events. Alright, a letter comes out of the blue from some land he's never heard of thousands of miles away, someone's got to be taking him for a mug. Who, he can't say. But it's an offer that he can't just turn his back on. Think about it: free passage, a year's wages in advance, nothing to say he's got to stay there for ever. But his mind, deadened by repetition, drifts away on a sea of forgettable dreams as the *Albert Rose* sits ever heavier on the bank. And because of this a good day's work is done, the boat is full to the hatches and water washes over the deck as Jago stands at the tiller guiding her through the bends of the pill with the last rays of the evening sun easing his knotted back.

It waddn just me servin er in the'end (Mister Trelease seemed a nice enough sort of chap, what I knew of un, bit like a rasher of bacon) But when you think on it, er bein married never made no difference, er just didn't care! Frightened me a bit I don't mind sayin. What I mean is I put any amount of stuff into er, buckets I dare say, and er was never caught! I don't reckon er can ave babbies and if that's true er won't be happy, never, and er's such a dear maid, there's none like er, I'm always sayin of it.

In th'end it had to be Farmer Digweed writ that letter. At first I didn't think it made sense, with all ees money ee could have my ballocks on a plate any day if he thought I were poking his daughter. But that's it! The key to it! Ee must have known what was what, but ees daughter didn't know ee knew what was what until er saw the letter! I mean, think what 'twould ave done fer un if people knowed ees daughter (ees married daughter an all!) was getting it regular from George Jago, bargeman ... not a lot I shouldn't think!

So, aside from the fact that I did, I didn't need to go away if I didn't want to, cos there's nothing old Digweed could have done if I hadn't. I don't reckon ee's a good man, tiddn from ee Missus Trelease gets er nature. There's a lot of kindness in er and that's important to us folk down yer. When er was doin uv it there was a warmth about er, tis difficult to describe. I've ad a few quick clinches afore with maids bedder looking and never give um no more thought, been off on me way. But with Jane (there! I know er've got a name so I'll call it er), you knew er liked it fer its own sake (and fer yours) so you try to make it last a while. Er waddn after nothing else and there waddn no more to it – er made me feel like I was doin good to another youman being. I'm rambling off away now like a silly bugger but sometimes I can't get the bliddy woman out of me mind. I said afore er kept er eyes open all drew (or nearly all drew, sometimes er shut um when er was almost gettin there). Bugger me, I bin tilted up on me arms, drivin away there, I look down and there's er eyes looking straight at me, or drew me. Turns me to jelly or most of me anyow. Hayho! what a shock that afternoon! My godfathers! Falling to sleep like that! Anybody could've come along! Mind you, if they did I couldn't have done nothing, not when er ad the soft end of un snared on that fluttery thing. And first off I thought twas me who'd be doin the teachin! When come to I found out more things about the inside of a maid than I thought there was to know.

But now I'm out yer in Rupert's Land – Rupert's bliddy welcome to it – and I shan't never see er again. There iddn no maids out yer. Only th'indian wimmen and Missus Hiscock. Missus Trelease waddn too happy about that letter, er face was sort of bleak and I never quite knew why, I think I'm further forward now.

Bill Painter has emerged from the cabin and readies the ropes as they approach the quay. 'What's Canada like when it's at ome then Billy?' says George Jago.

'I dunno. I should think tis cold ... sounds cold'

'Well, I don't wanna go there!' Jago steers for the quayside and lets Bill Painter off the bow where he takes the line up the rusty ladder.

'You could go and come back' shouts Bill Painter 'there's no bugger can make ee stay out there'

'I've thought of that, and I idn gwain all that way just so's I can come back again'

'Sounds like a good chance though George, I can't pay ee no more than I do now and never will be able to' he catches and makes fast the stern line. 'You'm the hardest workin crew I've ever had and I'll be sorry to see ee go. But there's a lot to be said of this opportunity I'm sure. Think of the money, you might be able to buy some land out there'

'Well' says Jago on his way up the quayside 'I think tis too good to be true, there's a stink comin off it, I don't trust it and I iddn bliddy gwain!'

Six months later, in March 1865, Jago arrived in the port of Bristol flushed, queasy and invigorated from the long airy miles of third class railway travel in clear, cold weather. No footslogging for him. And he wears brand new clothes, carries all his goods and chattels in a box so light he can rest it easily on his shoulder. But, in that city of much noise and chatter and human commerce, as he waits in a queue with many others boarding ship for Nova Scotia, this unencumbered former bargee with his whole life before him stands alone with a bland face, and a roving eye searching the docksides and warehouse walls between thickets of gull–spun masts and webs of tackle, flocks of nodding talking heads and none of them hers.

The Proximity Of Men

23rd July 1864: Given the way I act, can I be said to be in love with Geoffrey? Would the answer make any difference to anything? Now those are Questions! If this is to be a serious diary, I thought I would be brave and honest, and ask serious questions. How is it that I've never considered them before? The fact is, come what may Geoffrey is going to be my husband and I chose him. Marriage, the word, has nothing to do with any other man, and so it will always be (I'm working on the question, taking it seriously, I am trying to define love; that I've heard so much about). After a fashion, we've been betrothed since we were very young (like the marriages of Kings and Queens in the Middle Ages) and Geoffrey, when he was very young, was very pretty and with the years, he's grown beautiful. His skin, once so pale and transparent, is now become tawny from the sun; his hair was once the fairest of blond, almost white, now its the colour of honey with a few darker streaks. His body is tall, smooth and perfect. He has an open-eyed confidence, people like and trust him, as he talks to you his eyes rarely leave your face (they're green as lichen his eyes, did I say?) he laughs honestly without malice and shows sympathy when required. So tell me that a man <u>cannot</u> be beautiful. There are those who will; <u>and</u> they are always men, in dark cloth and tall hats:- the pastor, and Mr Digweed & Co. will admit to the beauty of the male sex as long as it is in a spiritual way. A horse, a baby or a morning can be beautiful, but certainly no woman of proper inclinations would think to so describe a grown man. But I <u>know</u> that a man can be, for I am soon to be married to man that <u>is</u>. Indeed, Geoffrey and I are mutually obverse; it is he who is the fairer sex where I am plain. Geoffrey is ~~perfect~~ (no he's not. Miss Sheldrake taught me a little writing as well as a little drawing and she said not to use the same word again too soon, she also told me about paragraphs but I can't remember what she told me) flawless [Interrupted by mother and a lost kitten] I was about to say I'm sure our children will be divine and they will play together up on the mound, as we all have (even Becca and Liza until they were called in to be ladies). ~~Geoffrey and I~~ Our young selves skylarked around up there among the hazel wands, ferns and brambles and I'd finger-brush his yellow hair as we watched the heavy horses plod across and back before the plough, or the stripped swathe the dusky wheat (was it really so perfect? I can use it again now). How many brackets can I use? I would be kneeling behind him, combing, and Geoffrey would sit cross-legged and utterly still, except that sometimes he'd move his head into my fingers if he thought I was losing interest, like dogs do if you stop rubbing their ears. And we named all the pigs and some of the hens, after those people from church:- Nebuchadnezzar, Og, Jehoshaphat, Abishag, Job, Ahab, Ezekiel. And we made the cubby hole our den and kept secret things in there:- a long rusty blade thing I found in the Seven Acres and a sheep's skull and a little piece of knitted metal; and other things that I can't mention because they're secret. Harmless things, but they're mine and Geoffrey's and they're still there, well buried, deeper than my sketching books. So I must love him. He has all of me. Most of me. All of me but an infinitesimal part. Unfortunately, there are some things that Geoffrey lacks (I always knew it) and these are things I must have, essential things. But no one else has my whole heart. My time is his time. I am a different woman in different places, sometimes I'm still a girl (I don't know if I shall take to this writing habit or not, it confuses me). I'm going out now for the afternoon, this chair I have is too hard, it makes me shift and squirm, I cannot sit still for long enough to be a diarist!

14th October 1864: Still grappling with the same questions as before. In my mind I have three categories of men:- the Carnal, the Trusty and the Divine. Very often, just the proximity of certain men (the Carnal, of course) can make me quite pleasantly uncomfortable; as though there's an itch that I would love to scratch but it's inside and cannot quite be reached. Someone needs to find it, and relieve it slowly, and this can be any man (oh dear, not quite) I mean no particular man on the outside, it is an inner thing (am I <u>really</u> scandalous?). It cannot be "love". A few days before my wedding, I spent a quiet three parts of an hour in the cubby hole glancing through my old sketching books. The ones of Geoffrey were always of his lovely head or him on his horse, or leaning on a gate, or sitting on a stile, or resting beneath a tree. Effortless, euryhthmic (it is a word, I am proud of it, it denotes harmony) quite the opposite of Jago, who is a frankly ugly man; the stink of the river clings to his very skin, along with that frowstiness of animals and damp that all the working men have on their clothes. His face is always rough with stubble, his teeth are stained; and he speaks in that thick local tongue (that has been bred from my family but I understand still). Though he is neither clever nor handsome like Geoffrey, he has skills the existence of which Geoffrey is completely ignorant (is that correct, grammatically?). And this (I must think) is why Geoffrey (Divine) has all my love but yet not every small part of me. Of course, I could never "love" someone like Jago (will I get to the heart of it soon?) but Geoffrey (I should call him my husband now) can be fumbling; he can be slow in inconvenient ways; there can be awkward silences. With Jago, whom I hardly know, there are silences but in no wise are they awkward:- a sight (even a thought) of him and I am ready, we both know why we are in each other's company and he will slide it in without further ado. Something inside me is ready by instinct; and though I have been closer to

Geoffrey than to my own brothers for many years, on our wedding night he was so clumsy I could have laughed. It was actually painful, and, ironically, I had been prepared to feign virginity but was saved from the necessity of acting. He poked the thing in vaguely the right place, I was completely dry, I have no idea whether he spent or not, there were no stains in the morning. What does this tell us about the true nature of love? I lay beside him with my palm spread on his belly and he covered my hand with his, I could not speak:- as far as I (the young uninitiated wife) was concerned that was to be it, my duty, that was the "act of love", that was a "fuck" (I'm deeply sorry, Miss Sheldrake, but I shall write it! I've only ever heard that word once before, concerning goats, and have never repeated it aloud. It describes what Geoffrey does to me perfectly). I cannot blame him, my husband. I, supposedly a mere novice, would only describe what I feel about him as the tenderest of love, but there was never carnality between us before; and I cannot teach him because I am not supposed to "know", and if I could I think he would be a difficult pupil because it's not really his subject. I am ever hoping for improvement. I've read this through, and it is a terrible muddle.

20th October 1864: Why do parents assume that their children walk around with their eyes and ears closed? I can just recall how two months ago, poor mother took me aside and told me that there would be "certain requirements" my husband would need from me; these intrusions, which were almost certainly of a physical nature (I gathered), were something that could be tolerated without too much trouble (I heard her tolerating them when I was a child without any trouble at all), and one should not worry because it wasn't important. How perfectly right she was! Within the institution of marriage almost everything <u>else</u> is important! Domestic duties, stocking the garden, ordering comestibles and when the time comes, tending the children etcetera, etcetera.

There was such heavy rain in the afternoon today that fifty sheep had to be rescued from the Meadows before they were carried to the sea by the swollen Nole!

28th November 1864:   During recent nights, as Geoffrey is having his "requirements", I have taken to making little sounds, gasps and sighs; I think they slow him down, and make him subtle. I can risk guiding him a little now; he'll think I'm starting to learn, and getting to enjoy it, appreciating his efforts. I am not such a bad woman as I think I am, and as others would think I was if they knew; Pastor Davidson (Not Divine) would not understand but I think God might, given time:- did I not give up the Finger Thing for Him?

29th November 1864: The entries are getting thinner, I don't know how long I can keep up this writing. I have tried to canvass some interest in the school down in Rafton and it really is something of a struggle. They all seem to share father's views on the education of the lower classes (even the poorer people themselves share it) and Herton has never been much more than a hamlet:- there's only nine children under fourteen here at the moment. I must be resigned to starting off with a small roll and hoping word will spread; perhaps the children think it will be like Sunday School. I am always up early, attending to the poultry (another battle of glances with father), and getting the day in the dairy started off; but thereafter I would be free to teach, for the rest of the morning. Father said to me yesterday, accompanied by a peculiar look: "drawing (but he said it as drorin) would be a good thing to learn" but I did not flinch.

I <u>thought</u> someone must have been "at" my sketchbooks:- the order they were in appeared wrong, and there were large footprints in the cubby hole. Father cannot touch me now, for am I not safely and happily married to a known quantity? He also still has Becca and Lizzy:- the dullards they are likely to find hereabouts will not satisfy their fine natures, they'll be the ones who marry well, quite likely to men they don't love, and I bear them no grudge. My hope is that they do not come to me for advice about what men will require them to do, of course I shall only refer them to Mother, who knows all about that sort of thing. There is something in this train of thought that reminds me of that peculiar look father gave me on the evening of the wedding (throughout which I have to say he had been the most perfect of hosts); I think he was a bit the worse for drink. I'm sure he was looking at the back of Geoffrey's head, quite leering with satisfaction, as well he might:- I think he thought I could not see him, and I leaned forward as if to say something in Geoffrey's ear and caught his eye. There was the briefest exchange of sharp glances, where I paid him back in kind and he turned away as though struck.

1st December 1864: I was wondering in chapel, as the children were saying their pieces, how it would be when I have my own; and another thought on my new state of matrimony came to me:- it is a sure proof against scandal! Over the last eighteen months I have surely taken in large amounts, pints I'm sure, of Jago's seed, and certainly I worried, though less than I should have (*because I'm a scandalous woman!*); and now my lawful wedded husband is adding to it, therefore I need worry no more.

2nd December 1864: It <u>must</u> have been father behind that letter of Jago's. He has known about my sketches since well before the wedding, I'm sure, but, since he's never mentioned them, it is most unlikely now that he ever will (though he's given me some looks, he is <u>all looks</u> Mr Digweed as though something's on the tip of his tongue, for years now). He is hardly likely to say to me:- "Oh Jane, what a pity you've taken your drawing books away, I was so looking forward to the next one". He could easily have identified Jago by describing him to almost anyone in Rafton, and I know mother has a relative in some wild part of Canada who married a man named Hiscocks. Of course there is no need to worry about Mr Digweed saying anything; he will not risk falling off the social ladder half way up because of his daughter's (*What? What would they call it? Found out, that's the main thing, found out! So it must be...*) indiscretions. Jago will go, and I made it clear to him that he should. Well, I'm going to get rid of the books, for my sketching days are over.

5th January 1865: Though today was rather breezy and variable, I decided not to delay the immolation any longer. After I had finished in the dairy, I went over to the orchard and passed some time with Tom Redfern (Trusty) who has spent the last day and a morning pruning the apples and pears. I saw the fine pile of branches he had gathered, and I asked him to go over to Marshall's Wood after he had got the fire going and cut a few hazel rods, the reason they were required was not his business; and, like the proper man he is, he did not ask. I said I would tend the blaze while he was away. The fire was hot and red, flames were leaping this way and that, the wind was swirling round in all directions through the fruit trees; because I was worried about fragments drifting across into the grounds of Herton House and being perused by the curious, I leafed the books into the heart of the fire page by single page, I could not help having a last look at them. I burned almost all of them, only keeping some of the ones of Geoffrey, and in the end I could not bear to destroy the one I called "Life on the Ocean Wave". There he is, Jago the "gert lummock" standing athwart the sea, waves breaking over his   manhood and the cormorants in a row like soldiers:- was that a mere eighteen months ago?   (*I'll* *have to think what I can do with it. For now I'll tuck inside this book. I certainly can't frame it and hang it on the wall!*)

23rd March 1865: Mr Digweed will be pleased, this is the day Jago sails from Bristol. I have wished him luck, shaken his hand, and almost kissed him goodbye. I think of the sheer oblivion I have experienced in his company, and there was a little sadness at our final meeting, as though something had passed for ever. There was little pleasure in it, and I felt distant; nor was Jago quite himself, above me with his head hanging loose, I held each of his shoulders as he stabbed away, and he spent quickly, frowning and chewing his lip. He was reaching for his clothes straightaway, saying something about catching the tide:- it was then that I quickly grasped his hand and wished him well. In the moment it took me to close my eyes, and incline my cheek for a farewell kiss, the oaf had disappeared, and there he was running off along the dyke like a thief. I wonder if he is so with other women of his acquaintance, in and out quick and on his way (*unkind, Jane, unkind!*). No, I should not say that, poor Jago knew as well as I that it was the last time, and his heart was in it no more than mine.

15th April 1865: On the way back from the dykes this afternoon, I must wait in the wide part of the lane near Marshall's Wood, for the carrier's cart to pass; Mr Thomas and one of his sons (Trusty and Carnal respectively) were on the driving board. I greeted them equally, I think. The elder Mr Thomas wished me good afternoon and the younger was smirking as he touched his hat:- and well he might. Then, as I was almost home I met Geoffrey, riding out to Crocken Farm with papers; and he tells me his father is, more or less, stepping aside and that he will, more or less, be Estate Manager now. Geoffrey, Manager; and my brother John soon to become absolute ruler of all Mr Digweed's acres and men. Is he really to stand aside? It would seem so. Things move on so quickly. I have still not fallen pregnant, or "been caught" as they say, during the day I forget, at night I remember:- I know it is my fault, and I can't say it.

14th May 1865: I have scribbled away in this book for nearly a year now, and looking back over it, it seems too full of my own thoughts. I had wished for it to be more of a humdrum record of my domestic life, and my efforts to start the school:- those are the things that take up my life (truly they are!) but I cannot be troubled to record them. When it comes to it, it is Geoffrey and father, and all these mysteries about love and the Other Thing. I think I would take to writing more if I could invent it, make it all up, like authors do; if I could do that I am sure I would get to the heart of things. Geoffrey and I have our own desks in separate rooms; I have the domestic accounts to do and Geoffrey has the farm accounts; so father won't be able to read this unless he forces the lid, and Geoffrey wouldn't dare. Mother is in the porch and is calling up the stairs (*I can't hear her, whatever is she saying? Just a moment, I'll come down!*)

Riding the Crops

It's surely true these days Bill Digweed lives the life of a squire, for sure he's a wealthy man, but he'll always be a farmer, cattle-breeder, crop-grower. I admire the man. Still got some spunk in him too – fit as a butcher's dog. How old is he? Fifty-six? Sure, I know he can look fierce: that photograph, been up on the wall two years now – my Lord above! I had a quiet laugh at it myself, along with everyone else. He can be bone-headed now and then, but for all that he's a decent enough fellow: if he weren't such a bonehead and such a damned fine farmer, he wouldn't be where he is. Now, he ain't touched a tool for years and he well knows he turns more profit by the work of others, and the laying of his own hands to the pumps won't make a jot of difference, but what's writ on the old boy's face is he wants to be out there with the men like he used to – it's a kind of itch with him – but he also knows he's well too long in the tooth and too high up the ladder now. So he satisfies himself with interfering and criticising.

Even though the two of us, men of an age, are about to move to one side for the next generation, we still can't get out of old habits: and there is nothing in the world Digweed loves more than riding the crops. For all I know this might be the last time. We'll be pausing at every gateway, mulling over every acre of every field, and old Digweed'll be jawing away to everyone who's about. What I gotta do is keep him moving, so the men don't lose the rhythm of their work. And I don't always succeed.

There's been some fine weather lately but this morning's a bit overcast and gloomy and there's no breeze. We're riding side by side through the Long Lane where the grass banks are heaved into all sorts of shapes by the roots of the old ash and oak and studded with primroses, the celandines have just about finished now and the spears of bluebells are poking through – can you ever tire of it? I say to Digweed that it sure is a lovely morning even though it's clouded over and he grunts something or other and then he says (as if it's been on his mind) out of the clear blue that he hopes I'm getting on alright with my daughter-in-law and I say surely, of course I am. Geoffrey and Jane have been in the house now quite a few months, and I tell him that I've no trouble getting accustomed to a little more domestic bustle, a bit more life after I've been a widower these last few years. I say how Jane's such a busy young woman – I'm thinking of the school, the dairy, and the eggs. That's when he leans over to me and says, as if I didn't know: 'she's one who'll have her own way y'know' he gives a short laugh 'I can't stop her y'know! I could keep the missus from getting her hands dirty, but I'm beggared if I can stop Jane'. After that he doesn't say a lot and we ride in silence. I guess I know why he's so amused at what some folks'd call his daughter's defiance: the more Jane does what she wants, the more the twins (his insurance policy) seem to conform. Seems like a law of nature. Now, the misses Elizabeth and Rebecca are pretty and pale indeed, not in any wise inclined to manual work, or being out of doors. Their complexions are unblemished and they speak French. What the old man don't say is that those girls are commodities of real class, high value, so he can give his uppity eldest all the slack she wants.

Here I am saying Rebecca and Eliza are pretty – and surely they are very *petite* – at first sight you might dismiss their elder sister as a homely young lady without sophisticated charms inclined to rude health and heaviness. But you only have to spend a short time in her company to appreciate her beauty. She's full-built and handsome with them brown eyes that don't pass judgement (God damn it! Do I love her myself?), I'm not putting this so well, it sounds corny I know, but there's something floats away from her, creeps around you like a mist and draws you in before you know it. It's not so much physical beauty as a pleasant, confident and straight–talking way she has. She ain't emotional. I would trust her with my (and my son's) life. Old Digweed don't really know what he's got there. I'm glad to have her in my house: she's helpful and calm, and she makes you feel good – that's it, she makes you *feel good!* But the old man's right when he says no one tells her what to do. And she earns that privilege, every bit of it.

I'm looking forward to my grandchildren – breed out some of our rawbone fairness. I don't know what manner of offspring they'll produce but they should understand children well enough. Geoffrey and Jane spent hours together, I know they made up long funny names from the Old Testament for the hogs and hens, sitting up on that motte all day like brother and sister. There was one time when she was a bit older, thirteen or fourteen, Jane was in our part of the old farmhouse waiting for Geoffrey to come home and she was passing the time of day with me, standing over by the kitchen window, chattering on about something or other and the tone of her voice suddenly changed and I could see she'd raised her hand. When I went to the window and joined her I could see my son coming across the yard from the stables. She turned to me and said: 'isn't he beautiful?' like she was seeing it for the first time. Now, young ladies don't usually describe young men so – maybe they do in conversation with each other, who knows? – and I couldn't see what she meant, Geoffey sure was a beautiful boy, but now he was getting on toward manhood. But she meant it sure enough, and I respected it.

And she's that busy she puts us all to shame: there's her projects round the farm and all, and her clerking work for her father where he tells her the gist and she puts it down in the proper way. Old Digweed reckons she's a bit of a mutineer on account of the way she carries on with the old ways which sounds back to front when you think on it and he don't like the idea of educating the poor, oh no, I can hear him now: 'A carter's lad is a carter's lad, what earthly use is letters to un? I s'pose he can read what's on the side of the cart and what's that? William Digweed & Sons! That's what *that* is!'

But, you know, Digweed's close to her and very fond, no matter what he says. Now and then, sometimes when you see them together, it's like he's watching her out of the corner of his eye kinda sly like he's looking for traces and signs of some thing or other. It's like he suspects her of some crime and he's waiting for her to make a mistake. Well, if anyone ever barked up a wrong tree it's him.

Anyways Mr William Digweed and me going about the ritual of riding the crops. That's where I was. I've rambled away here about my daughter-in-law and gotten lost up some creek or other. After we're stopped and the mounts tethered, we sit ourselves down on a length of windfall trunk where the vista is wide and eat our cold victuals and contemplate these packed acres of swaying corn. Mr Digweed hardly moves his eyes but I know he's taking it all in, pronouncing on its quality by his silence. In the wilds where I was born, the prairie stretched as far as the horizon and the sky was big; but I've come to love this homely patchwork in yellows, greens and browns as much and more; and the hundreds of small farms, where even the largest of fields looks like somebody's back yard.

Herton lies away in the distance, an elevated spot surrounded by ash and sycamore woods: you can still see it from here. Now I've got some notions about that situation: history goes back a long ways in England and, as I am a man with a passing interest in antiquity, the site of an old castle intrigues me. Maybe I'll write a book on it now I'm gonna have some time. There's the old motte plain as day in the garden of Digweed's new house: nothing and no-one could come up the lane without you seeing them. I wouldn't be surprised if there was old ramparts, or the signs anyways, and a moat. I've had a look round for backfilled ditches and the like since I started reading about the old days hereabouts but I can't say I've had a lot of luck. I'm not talking about some huge castle with them high buttressed walls and drawbridges and damsels but more like a local fort, used the while by a Norman lord to control his land, and his villeins and slaves, keeping a force of mounted men and maybe his own sons to ride out over the holdings, collect dues and such else.

I haven't said much to Digweed on the subject, and when I did he reacted kinda predictable. There ain't a lot that makes him laugh aloud. But this did. 'Castle!' he shouted 'Well, well! In days of old when knights was bold …!' I grinned politely and told him that there would have been a water-filled ditch, an outer rampart with a kind of yard and a final defensive refuge on the motte. Nothing grand. 'Motte …?' he said '… that thing in the garden? Waddeecallit? A defensive mound? Tis tiny! But I s'pose this part of the country iddn all that important – just a lot of old farmers and shape'. Then he laughed all the harder.

Talking of sheep, I have put it to the old man that all his acres of fine wheat are surely that – fine. But out where I come from there's thousands upon thousands of acres of the stuff just waving in the breeze, year on year. Now, sooner or later, twelve maybe ten years down the road, that there wheat is going to start finding it's way across the ocean and when it does, the stuffing will be surely knocked out of English arable farming. That crop will be more plentiful and even though it's been shipped all the way across the Atlantic Ocean, it will be cheaper. 'So, if I was you William' I said 'I'd increase your flocks and expect sheep to be your main source of income in the future'.

Anyways, to begin at the end, we're sitting on this log just passing the time of day and drinking our small beer when Digweed, who hasn't spoke a lot, says on a sudden: 'Domestic arrangements working out alright, Arthur?' And I'm thinking this is the second time he's mentioned the ménage at the Home Farm in as many hours: I answer him (same as last time) that of course, surely they are. It's like he's probing, looking for something – almost like I've seen him look at Jane – he's waiting for me to drop a clue, it's like whatever's eating him he can't bring himself to say, only skirt about it. 'It's a big rambling house' I'm saying 'the three of us are quite comfortable, it's way too big now that you and Mrs Digweed and your family have moved next door. Is there something bothering you Mr Digweed? You seem very curious about my domestic arrangements'

I felt I could be direct, being as though I'm an old acquaintance. It's true, I've known old Digweed a long time, I know his instincts don't let him down. There ain't a lot he misses. He's acquired a bit more weight with age, he's a big rawboned man, when he was younger he always reminded me of some inquisitive sort of bird: he's got that narrow nose, some deal hooked, and that drawn-down mouth. Now that photographic portrait of his where he looks a bit crazy (he deliberately took on that expression, that people found so funny), defensive, dour, predatory … and that's the way he wants to be seen. You get the drift of what I'm saying? While he's sitting there on the log beside me – back straight, hands on knees – he looks like an old eagle just resting there, waiting for prey. Then he suddenly cranks his head round birdwise, one eye closed in a squint and the other fixed right at me like he's looking for dishonesty just to give itself away. And this single eye's penetrating and searching, probing the back of my mind. So I think the best thing is to look him straight back, and I'm right because he seems to accept it – as if he's made his judgement in a split second and I'm off the hook. Scared the living hell out of me.

'Oh well' he says then, getting on his feet with a grunt 'best get on' He leads the horses over. 'Us bedder be over Silton this afternoon, they'm drilling oats'.

So we ride over to Silton along the cart track, with Mr Digweed cursing the tough old brambles that snag him all the way, then we hack down through steep woods and take a look at the Devons at Broomworthy. By that time it's well on in the afternoon and the cloud's breaking up at last and the sun's coming through. Back round on the Long Lane we're almost walking the horses and enjoying the weather. Mr Digweed even goes so far as to comment on the primroses and the new leaf on the hazels and thorns. We talk awhile in a companionable way about desultory people we both know in the locality and all the time, even though we're nearly back, the old buzzard's still looking round, sidling his beast up to the gates and peering out over the fields, it's a full day's work to him, riding the crops, not a thing that's over in a morning. It's almost like he thinks this may be the last time he does it. By the time we clatter into the stable yard at High Herton, the long shadows of elms reach out across the ewes with their new lambs in the home enclosures.

When we dismount the young lad Georgie Boundy takes the horses. I can see Digweed's limping on his left side and he admits, with half a sorry grin, that there's bit of stiffness in his hip. His age is showing, I guess. Mine too. I'm not much younger than Digweed and I'm guessing it won't be too long before even he thinks to take a back seat and give his instructions to young John. I've more or less told Geoffrey that I want him to take over from me pretty soon, if Digweed agrees (I guess he might want to get a farm of his own settled on him and Jane). Then there's young Boundy, no more than seventeen, whose youth speaks volumes, spare and light and fresh-faced. We both stand and watch him stride sure-footed between the two horses, upright and slender in his waistcoat and short breeches, and when our glances leave him they touch in passing. We're thinking the same thoughts.

On the rebound of that passing glance, I broach the subject with Digweed here and now: he knows I've been grooming Geoffrey for years now, there was a kind of assumptive arrangement that he would succeed me. And I'm saying: 'I guess it might be time young Geoffrey took over from me, is that alright with you Bill?'

'I dunno why you'm workin at all John! You've got the means, you don't have to' Digweed says with his usual candour. 'Young Geoffrey can do the work, I know. Aye, then, let un start as soon as he will, long as you give un a bit more of your guidance until he settles in '

'I love this job, Bill, as you know but maybe I should get on with other things I've a mind to'

'Well, you'm talking about doin without, and I bin thinking on I, I suppose …'

Just then the subject of our discussion himself emerges from the house, says he's taking a letter over to Crocken before dark (sometimes he likes to do these things himself). When I beckon him over, Digweed tells him that he can assume my duties in a month, shakes his hand. And I know Geoffrey is delighted, he shakes my hand too, like the honest-dealing young man he is: his face has coloured up. Then Jane appears at a gentle trot, on that good-natured grey she's been riding these last few weeks, slows to a walk and waves. She must have been out on another of her mysterious jaunts. Geoffrey thanks us again and mounts up, trotting out to meet his wife. My son leans over from his saddle and kisses her welcome, he must also be telling her the news. I see her smile and rest her hand on his thigh as their beasts stand side by side head to tail. But Digweed is watching them with those eyes of his narrowed right down, and he's that absorbed I can scan his face without him knowing. And there it is – that hawkishness about him again, someone biding their time until their prey comes out into the open: I'd swear he's just waiting for his daughter to make some wrong move, in what direction I don't know. Then quite suddenly, he bids me good evening, and walks briskly away into the house.

But my mood won't be dampened. Jane dismounts with a hand on Boundy's shoulder and he takes the reins with a quick grin and she takes off her bonnet. We go in to the farmhouse together and I ask her was she pleased with Geoffrey's news, and she's very pleased. I took a leaf out of the old man's book and asked her straight how she's getting on with Mr Digweed these days and I swear she coloured up (although it could be she was still flushed from her ride). 'As well as ever' she says, with a prim little smile that don't mean anything and changes the subject to the temperament of horses, and the trouble she's having finding pupils for her school, the flag iris on the marshes … anything, really.

CHAPTER FIVE

Johanna

Early yesterday morning we followed a quiet winding river called by the locals Barley Water out of Marshburgh, then devious systems of narrow tracks of the kind I know at home: sunken banked ditches overhung with trees, where moted shafts of sunlight hover in the silence and springs chatter out of sight. A mulch of crisp leafage, beech–mast and ash keys muted the tramping of many feet, brambles snagged our clothes and the tails of the horses. There is to be a long road ahead of us, climbing ever higher. At first we were bearing eastward, then we followed another long combe northward, noisy with water, rising steady mile upon mile. De Bonville called out to the guides, asking the name (out of idle curiosity, presumably) of the quick shallow watercourse below us. They say it is known as the Sheep Brook. 'Ah, yes' our leader said mysteriously, as if such a name was only to be expected, as if being so called fitted exactly the order of his scheme. At times he is impenetrable.

On the following day, soon after breaking camp, we emerged onto high downland where the way is wide and the prospect open. The whole of the arm of the river which flows by the town is visible and all of the country it lies in. Before we left a few men mounted a cursory and half-hearted search for the man Martin and no trace of him was found. He was not popular, few questions were asked. It was assumed the tide had most likely carried him away. Roger de la Moule reassured us of that in his amiable way.

'Bringing him in in the middle of the night? Fighting with staves? His hands were bound you say? Well, most likely he'll have been taken out into the river on the ebb. He'll turn up in a creek somewhere I dare say, or be washed in on the strand, happens all the time ..... Bristol, is that where you're going? Ha! If I were any of you gentlemen, I would stay here, park up your waggons when they get here, pay me a nominal rent, you'll be much safer. Out there, anything could happen'

He had said it with real unease, his bluffness escaping him for a moment, as though 'out there' was black space. And I'm sure I'm not the only one to wonder why we have so outrun our waggons. Now that we're 'out here', the cold breeze of this deserted land runs its unwelcome fingers of ice across our faces, winter has arrived already, in September: back by All Soul's, I told Jeanne, though neither of us believed it. The way may well be bleak, little more than a beaten track, but it seems popular (judging by numerous hoof and foot prints, a body of men like our own has passed quite recently). The soil is grey, wet and heavily rutted, becoming ever wider as carts go further to the sides to avoid the quaggy centre.

By the view from where we sit, every way you look, the situation is clear. No-one says so, but we can very well see that the waggons are certainly lost. That shoulder of heather where we stopped and looked down at the town only four days ago lies well in the distance with the road looping down its flank like a length of discarded cord. The town itself is tucked away below it, out of sight (and, by now, almost out of mind). But every farm and village gives out a plume of dark smoke that drifts across the hills, merging like incense with the dull sky. Even those places we passed through such a short time ago, where we were eyed with such suspicion, burn. Those lands will now be wasted, by whom we do not know, only that it was not us the people should have feared, but others. There are men ahead and men behind, the whole world is fighting the whole world. For all we know, Marshburgh itself may be under siege already.

Were it not for Monsieur Jean de Ravelin, the gloom would be unrelieved – I love the man! I would not dare ride near him, but I catch myself sneaking looks: his burst of tightly curled fair hair, thick lips and mad eyes ... I see him with my eyes closed. Oh, this sounds terrible! What I mean is I admire the image of a greater man, that is all, not in any unnatural way – my name is not Canteloupe! I sometimes whisper 'de Ravelin' (I confess it) under my breath and it rolls off the tongue as easily as his words – begod, how he can talk! Fired by his extravagent offers of payment and visions of pillage and dissipation some half-dozen men (as well as the guides) were recruited in the town at his personal expense. He's up there now, at the head of the column, riding with the trusty scouts: *why two? Would not one have been enough?* They are pointing and he gazes along their signs and holds up his hand. Everyone halts. De Bonville has been in the rear for some while but now he rides up and joins de Ravelin. Quite distant, where the lonely trackway disappears, yellowish–grey smoke creeps across the horizon. De Bonville motions us forward without turning his head.

As we get closer, the source of the smoke is clearly a huddle of buildings set in trees straddling the road as it sweeps through the valley and up the other side. There is a stench of damp embers, and darker scents of overdone meat. The farmstead is in the last stages of destruction, a few charred timber posts are all that stand, all life is at a standstill, all is silent. As we draw nearer it seems that everything that moves here has been killed, even the dogs. There had been no quality of mercy shown. But it's an ill wind that blows nobody any good, gulls and carrion crows have been quietly busy. Those cadavers of human beings, seven in number which were found and laid out in a row for burial were nearly all missing their eyes. An opportunity for my lord de Bonville's priest to say *missa pro defunctis* and earn his keep.

Huddled together in a corner of the shell of the main house there was an old lady and two men of sundry ages. All were curled with their hands on their heads like run down game. There had been no struggle and the slaughter must have been an easy matter. All are partly burned and brutally cut, most of their clothes ripped away – I say *all* were curled with their hands on their heads, this is not quite so, the hairless dome of one of the men, partly stripped by crows, lay a few feet away. Outside, another man, crushed by a heavy cart against an oak, stood with his fists gripping the backboard, his teeth were bared as if he'd pushed himself to death. In the cart, one young woman, more or less naked, and two boys lie strangled with ropes.

We pick our way through the wreckage of what had clearly been a prosperous little farm: the people looked after themselves well enough, they had plenty of fodder and grain laid in the remains of it smouldered in a black heap where a barn had been, some of its uprights still glowed red in the heart.

As the burial detail start their digging, my lord de Bonville, myself and Jean Villon take five men and set out on foot with weapons drawn and helmets on, but a cursory tour of the outskirts of the farm reveals only desertion: a dismal prospect of trampled fields, in the corners stock surplus to the requirements of the looters slaughtered and left.

'So' I say (rather daringly, I suppose) in an undertone to de Bonville as we walked carefully forward (bearing his comments in Marshburgh in mind) 'this is what my father wanted you to be sure I saw?'

'Not precisely this, Ralphe' he said, his gaze never still, ranging all around, he walked like a man on eggs. 'But this might do. This is what men do when they're off the leash, when no-one's in charge. I've seen it often enough before'

'It's no great surprise, then' I say, trying to sound calm (and I *was* calm, rather underwhelmed and felt that I shouldn't be)

'Ralphe ... there is' continued de Bonville 'hatred ... blame' he seemed to wander a moment, then snap back, looking me straight in the eye. 'D'you know who most likely did this? The neighbours, almost certainly – some petty argument that simmered for years boiling over, an opportunity arises to settle it once and for all by the methods you see before you. Neighbour can slaughter neighbour because the state of anarchy allows them to without fear of retribution and the people who did this are probably still out there, they'll have got the taste and be moving on. And what shall we ourselves do without crops, animals or food? We'll find ourselves stealing someone else's because it's each for himself – smash and grab!'

'I think I get the gist of it, my lord, we too are plunderers. Is that not why we're here? There's never an excuse ...'

'Oh, Ralphe, you're an honest lad I think and it'll be a long time before you get even the slightest notion of "the gist"'

'I'm just recalling, my Lord, that part of the object of this expedition was to see what was out here to be got. You said so yourself'

'What will you be getting, Ralphe? No, don't answer that. When I wonder why I tolerate your rudeness, I think ...'

We have wandered into a fallow of three, three and a half acres, divided off from the pasture by a unlayered hedge of thorn, its berries gone, leaves starting to turn. Near the hedge is the old headland of long ryegrass and hoary nettles. One of the men is on his haunches apparently picking over a heap of clothing discarded in the ditch, then he seems to pick at the rags with greater curiosity ...

'You!' roars de Bonville 'I said no fucking looting!'

'But my lord!' returns the man, turning the heap as though it's alive, crossing himself 'a corpse ... un cadavre!' I see a pelt of yellow hair, a pale face with a dark bruise on the high bone of its cheek. She's plainly been lying there all night, the blond girl (thirteen, fourteen, I would venture) wet to the skin and barefoot. We send a man back for a beast and she drapes the saddle like a side of bacon.

By the time we return, seven corpses are covered and laid out in a long pit, the delvers sit tired and filthy, their shovels thrust in a mound of earth and stones. De Bonville's priest is about to begin his recitations over the grave. Seeing that there is an extra soul to be consigned, he waits in silence for it to be added but no one has the will to move, as if whoever does will make the death of this child real. In the end, myself and Villon wearily slide the girl off the saddle (I have her legs and I wrap her skirts around her calves so that she is godly and her flesh hidden). Though we are both tired, it is I who choose to stumble and almost fall at the edge of the trench: we have no choice but to let her go, lest the operation descends into compete fiasco. Thus, her *introit* to the next world is to roll into a cold pit of earth and flop boneless on her back. And she lies across three of the other bodies at the right angle to them. Jean Villon mutters his apologies to the sky. Something must be done, we both know it, and we go about righting her.

Villon closes her spread arms and starts to manoeuvre her by the armpits and I must reach again for her legs (awkwardly, from the other side of the pit). I am in a dream, groping for her feet, trying to avoid standing on any part of those she lies over. And as I touch her foot so help me God, it twitches! Then the whole body shudders, and heaves like a hooked fish. She lays her head to one side and coughs vomit. Villon leaps out of the pit, people are crying out and crossing themselves. The blond girl's eyes jerk open and look straight at me, and I cannot move for sheer terror. With a harsh, reedy sound her face buckles – as though the sight of me is too much – she throws up once more then lies still, flexing her fingers, clenching and unclenching her fists, gulping air as the humours return to her face. No one will go near her. I remain transfixed. I am aware of Villon on his knees and Guillame Canteloupe flat on the ground with his face in the soil. I don't know where the others are, I cannot raise my eyes from the girl who is now breathing quickly and working the stuff of her shift between finger and thumb.

Then my lord de Bonville himself is in the pit, treading unhandily over the spongy corpses. Passing an arm under the girl's neck and working it along under her back, he starts to lift her away from the corpse beneath her. At this point, as though she cannot bear to leave her soft bed, the blond girl opens her eyes and her mouth wide, and the purest of screams brings us all to our knees. Even the priest is dumb, kneebound, eyes to the skies.

But I think there was nothing miraculous. Look at it this way, her first experience on resurrection: a large travel-stained man picks her up and bears her away, why? To throw her down and spread her. So this is the same as the other life. And she knows better than to struggle, she is already familiar with the rough pain, the intrusion – she throws her head back like a dog and howls for lost content. Or so I think.

To his credit, de Bonville does not let her go. He holds her until she stops, meets her eye until she calms. 'She's been raped' he says to me 'she thinks we will do the same. Come on, come on! You two (he beckons) yes, you two!' They obey with reluctance. 'Take her and find somewhere dry, strip her, clean her and wrap her up in whatever you can find that's warm, bind her hand and foot and keep her guarded. You two only, no one else – she must sleep. Do nothing to frighten her and don't even think about taking advantage. Anyone, and I mean anyone, who even thinks about that I will kill them … personally.'

Later that evening, watching the moon gliding through reefs of broken cloud, an understanding of our situation comes to me *á propos* of absolutely nothing. I'm wondering if it really matters whether or not we get to Bristol. Perhaps the famous 'gist' is coming to me after all, perhaps all that Bonville says is true. Neither the Queen's party nor the King's party can claim me (though my Lord de Bonville must be of the King's, or else the Queen's, there is no fence he can safely sit upon). It is very simple: there are those who carry out murder, rape and destruction and those who avenge by murder, rape and destruction. Someone must have initiated the whole thing but now it moves along without them. All parties are interchangeable. There's no King and no Queen, so could it be that there's no God? The best thing is to keep one's mouth firmly shut and bear in mind that we now have Johanna. Our old friend the moon is not the only object of beauty to grace this decaying place.

How Perfect She Is

Now I swear this place – Daxworthy it's called – this bloody place is as godforsaken a hole in the fucking ground as you would ever find. It reeks of mildew and ash, there's animals lying about all over the place where they were chased and slaughtered by whatever madmen were here. De Bonville thinks it was the neighbours – ha! my lord de Bonville for whom I have the greatest respect says it was the *neighbours*! Most of us have the sense to want to move on, but we are held up by Bonville's insistence that the girl needs more rest before she is fit to travel. He holds her rather in awe (and young Mareschal is *spellbound* by her, totally captured) some are talking of 'an holy miracle', she who died and returned to life. For myself, there is only one miracle I would dearly like to see come about (and this needs to be addressed by The Almighty at his earliest convenience): a sudden and immoderate end to the shortage, nay the dearth, of strong drink.

I suffer! I suffer! BeGod how I suffer! Search as I will, there is not a single drop of anything fermented in this place. Not even remnants. Any looter worth his salt would have left some traces: broken jugs still smelling of ale, breached and discarded barrels, but there is not even a whiff of the smallest of small ales. So, our friends never found the stuff. And neither, as yet, have I. That there is none, I won't believe! The only person here who can help me is Saint Whatever-her-name-is, the Flaxen-Haired Precious One.

So this morning finds me, a Canteloupe in a desperate state of tremors and vapours, forced out into a brutal clarity of sunlight and made to visit the shelter where the girl lies. I must tell you that, in such a place as this, the rising of the sun is hardly a matter for celebration, for the light it throws on things – the dark is much better – and I've a throat like a cat's tongue and a head full of marbles.

Of course, she is still guarded at all times. I must make it clear to her keepers that I have come only to *see* her, to view the wonderful phenomenon. I will have to find a way to question her secretly. Signs, most likely. The universal sign of the pouring hand and the stretched throat, she will understand my need and point me toward it, ah no she can't, she is still bound, never mind she will have to point with her eyes. Do it for me young lady, for Christ's sake! So there are the two dullards seated like blocks either side of the girl's cot, staring at me, defying me to speak my business. She is lying on her back as she has been for days, that same position as when she was in the grave, when I made a bloody fool of myself, lying on the ground, washing my face in the earth. Even de Bonville himself tends her now and gives her water, he will not tolerate anyone else near her. But this a serious matter and I am a gentleman. Those two men say nothing, they don't have to. They have no intention of allowing me in any closer but as long as I don't move, they're not stopping me from looking. And now, despite the bruise on her temple swelling below the skin like a dark plum, she sleeps neatly, her head averted: she has almost invisible eyebrows, pale lips, in repose there's a tranquility about her that no one can deny. And I see there is a faint smile as though her mind is entertaining her as she sleeps. And that feeling is there again, damn it! .... that I must throw myself down and grovel. She could have been buried alive. *But see how perfect she is Canteloupe, you oaf!*

I will have to *exeunt* before my knees give way. Bugger it, I'll find the booze on my own. Then she opens her peculiar flinty eyes, you notice them straightaway, grey and tender (a strange mixture). She raises herself on her elbows and moves back in the cot, one of the wordless oafs takes off his coat and makes a rolled bolster for her back. She drops her head and sweeps her fingers through her hair (which is almost white) and when she looks up again the smile still hovers about her lips (which are almost invisible). I've seen nothing like it before, I am smitten. She examines ... no, *penetrates* ... me with her gaze and I feel that what is me, that I thought was only known to me, is being quickly read. Yes! She's opened me up like a book and she can read so fast. Her voice is unmusical, rather nasal, like a weak youth: 'there isn't any, messire, they took it all'.

And so it is I, William de Canteloupe, and two men whose names I don't know, who have the honour to be the first to hear the girl speak. If it were not so blasphemous, this could be the beginning of a biblical legend, or a parable. The information she gives – on the face of it the worst possible news – is not as staggering (as it were) as her very knowledge of my predicament before I have said even a word. I know I have a reputation as a toper but nothing of that could possibly have reached her here. And further, she follows on by saying: 'you have no problem'. And I realise she is right, the craving to which I have been used for so long has gone utterly, in its place is nothing and nothingness. *I feel absolutely nothing!* It comes first as a shock, then such a rush of childish joy that I feel I must bear the novelty away like a secret, once outside, I drop to my knees. There is a man on duty at the entrance to the shelter, he is pointedly ignoring me, as indeed he should, 'pissed again' is most likely his thought. Resting back on my heels, I tell him I will stay in the shelter as guard whilst he goes to my lord de Bonville and tells him that the young lady has found her voice.

So she tells me her name is Johanna. It is to me she describes her running flight, her escape as she thought it. And I find that I have all the time in the world to listen. She says she was with her father (*of the severed head? Does she know his head was cut from him, that the eyes of her family are crow-food?*) and his old parents, in the house and they begged her to save herself (we have no hope, they said). So she ran, twisting side to side from the flailing hands of the men. She says she knew them, they were near neighbours (alright, alright, my lord de Bonville was right). I watch her, lying on her back, still with bound hands, working her knees under the cover, showing me how she ran and ran. Then a sucker of thorn trips her and she falls winded, on the edge of the copse near where we found her. She gives up the chase then, and hands are all over her, an arm under her neck like the *seigneur* had handled her in the pit. She makes her eyes sleepy and says how she saw a face behind a curtain of mail, and he made her comfortable as he carried her, she could rest quiet against him. Believe it or not, she makes a snout of her face like a puppy (*I swear it is true!*); she mimes nuzzling a surcoat and smelling the must of earth and grass in its fabric. She clung to him, the man, and took the mail on his arm in her fist. But soon enough she was laid down by the hedge bottom where we found her. There were more men, voices she knew that sounded foreign: there was much laughter but no joke. She makes her head loll and her eyes stare blank (*at what? What was there to see in the ditch? Ragged nettles, little flags of wool plucked from sheep by the thorns*). And she says there was a cold breeze on her thighs, I can see her knees tenting the blanket as she raises and opens her legs. I am not afraid: this is how she does things. She says that hands held her knees apart and bent her legs back. I thought that if her hands were not tied she would have showed me that as well.

So Guy de Bonville is no fool then, after all. And she mimes the awful thing itself, her violation, I could see the intrusions were becoming less painful as she became accustomed to them, she shuts her eyes tight and grinds her teeth. She was left alone in the end, when they'd finished, and she says she slept, and later grazed some of the grass which her mouth could easily reach, for its bitterness.

I try to stop the flow of her memory, I tell her these are things I don't need to hear. She looks at me as if to say: 'you are a man, you need to hear them'. Of course, she is right, it is for my own benefit I wanted her to stop. I took the chance of touching her – the blockheads had let me move closer since she started talking – drawing a few pale strands of hair through my fingers. She carries on with her account in level tones: she is lying on the ground with the bad taste of grass in her mouth and rain starts to fall on her bare legs and tummy. Until dark she sustains herself by considering every detail of a common shoot of ivy in the hedge bottom, the star-like form of it and the configuration of its veins, and each blade of grass her eye can contemplate becomes not mundane but beautiful. Knowing what she will find when she returns home, the will to move has left her; and the rain is soaking through her clothing, the bruise on her head is tender, her insides are reamed and sore.

De Bonville asks me, after I have left her, if she has told me her name. I tell him Johanna. He says with a trace, I think, of envy that it seems only to be myself that she talks to. I tell him all that she's told me and I say that she tells it all so that you can clearly feel it and won't be quieted.

'Is she some kind of spirit would you say, then?' he asks suddenly.

'I wouldn't say so, my lord, no. She *has* spirit, inside her, there's a spirit about her – but I can't say she *is* a spirit. I was desperate for drink, that's why I went to her, I was certain she would know where they kept it – but she knew before I spoke what I wanted, and cured me'

'*Cured* you?'

'It is true. I no longer want to drink. I can face the world unadorned.'

'Can you begod? If only she could do that for everyone, how many problems would be removed at a stroke!'

'What happens, my lord, is this ... she can only help if what you want you cannot do without, and it makes you suffering ill. A man who enjoys a drink does not need a cure – obvious enough you might think, laughing in the alehouse or stumbling home in the dark. But think on it, and it is a deep saying. I'm sure she will speak to you soon and thank you for seeing to her care.'

I can feel Bonville looking very closely at me, as though he finds me a strange beast indeed. 'Well, Canteloupe, since you have gained the confidence of the young lady perhaps you can get her to describe the men who were here, every detail of them ...' he is strolling away from me now, slowly '...we're getting very short of food, by the way, and must move on in the morning.'

As everyone is so keen to be away from this desolate hole, the journey resumes with a good atmosphere. The men, of course, are happy to go where they're told and collect their money at the end of the day, but to some it is becoming increasingly aimless and, more importantly, profitless. The town of Bristol, nominally our destination, seems a long way off and of course the disappearance of our supply train doesn't help – much expense there, twenty draught horses, five heavy waggons, pack animals. But de Bonville seems unconcerned: either he is very rich or feels we can get along without our supplies.

The girl Johanna is mounted now, beside me on my left, preparing to ride (one of the few donkeys we have has been made available for her and its load is shared amongst the others). She is staring deadpan at the oblong of turned soil and its seven crosses of woven *noisette* to the right of us. Though I cannot spare her from the facts of life – and for all I know she might know more of them than I – nor can I resist shuffling forward to block her line of vision. As I hoped she is distracted, but not by myself but de Ravelin astride his strong grey at the front of the column, pointing at the sky and clowning like the madman he is, whilst the fine horse sidles and whinnies, even boxes the air in capriole. The girl suddenly giggles, then laughs aloud and a ripple like a breeze seems to flow over all the crowded heads before us. As if this is his cue, de Ravelin waves and shouts and the whole company starts to move.

Strangely, mounted on a pack animal, this girl has the dignity of a wealthy knight on an expensive courser; she walks the beast on, her strange white hair flowing over the rough sequanie she improvised from hessian. I say, or I was going to say, she rides like a trophy we have won – but we do not bear her, or display her. I think it is she that leads us, from the centre unseen, am I right?

The Siege At Gernsea

'You'll see, Ralphe' de Bonville had said to me 'how a dry period will turn Canteloupe into the sorest–headed of bears, he'll be at his most sarcastic and vicious'. But as far as I can tell, the opposite is true. He has become clear of eye and sure-minded, quite philosophical – and in the fight he has become untouchable! What skirmishes we've had on our way here have seen him fearless! He has for some reason taken to using a device of a bat, in black calfskin, on his helm and every time he charges in he comes out unscathed. Everyone knows that since he was forced into sobriety, something else is feeding his fire and it is her, the maid Johanna. That skinny girl with eyes like a cat has got into his heart. Though I know she is not quite perfect, for she has breathing fits where she doesn't sleep but wheezes and creaks half the night. Sometimes, during the day, her face is not radiant but drained, her eyes stare at nothing, her hair hangs lank and muddy, she breathes fearfully as if air is just more ill humours. But then the fits will pass, in a day or two, and she is the same as ever.

People are talking of Holy Wisdom, but there is no churchman here of enough rank to pronounce on her closeness to the Father. Some claim to love her, some sense the work of devils, some make a talisman of her. De Bonville's device is the wild goose (did I say?) wings spread as it lands on water, and his men are so liveried, his helmet so adorned; and she in her way has become a device for all of us, our party is recognised through her. When she does not have the choler in her chest, she is a proud maid, striking a pose and a steady glance – in fact, some see her as possessed by a madness that makes enemies back away, for fear of contagion, without a fight. I have no great liking for her, but I think she brings us Luck – those of us who fear the arrows of the enemy more than the fires of Hell saw that, when the Reaper came for her, she slipped away behind his back and that is enough for us.

Poor Jean Villon was carried from his horse by a bolt shot straight through his heart – there's no mail coat will save you from a lucky shot like that. I saw him leave his saddle with his arms spread and landed so, flat on his back like he was tied to a cross and dead as a stone! One of de Ravelin's trusty guides rode headlong into a low branch that ripped his shoulder crooked. And I was able to help him! I sat astride him and clamped him still as I saw my father do once at Herraton when a villein had an accident with his plough, then I yanked the arm back into its place. De Bonville, like de Ravelin and Canteloupe, has avoided injury thus far. I myself have bruising from a fall.

We've lost four of the peasant billmen, the Welsh bowmen are still present and correct, and we have one prisoner, a tediously cheerful Breton knight, our only saleable item. He rides with us, his wrists bound to his pommel, singing and telling old, fairly bad, jokes (though I will confess to the odd snigger). For instance of de Bonville's priest he asks: 'which man in the Holy Book was the most flexible?' and the priest, of course, chooses not to hear so the Breton answers his own question. 'Why Jésus Christ himself of course, who tied his arse to a tree and walked down to Jerusalem!' De Bonville laughed aloud, not at the joke which is as old as the hills but at the straight face of his humourless priest.

I say the knight rides with us but, to tell the truth, we have not ridden anywhere in a long time, and we are bogged down. It is now early November and I can't see us moving much before the Spring. We are at a castle my lord de Bonville knew of: he knew it was under blockade, and brought us here on the grounds that if you heard of a siege it was a good idea to join it. He says The King himself had caused the siege to be laid but left on a sudden (as apparently *Sa Majesté* is wont to do) for Trowbridge, taking nearly all his retinue and his flemish troops with him. 'Luckily for us', says de Bonville, 'the King is a good and cheerful soul but utterly scatterbrained: there's nothing wrong with being cheerful and good but being scatheaded means that few of his actions have plan or policy, a lot is left undone, there are pieces to pick up'.

Later I said to Bonville: 'my lord, I'm baffled. I am Ralphe Mareschal. I am present on this venture through my *vassalage* to you who are Guy de Bonville and you are present through your obligation to My Lord Of Gloucester and he, with the wind in its current direction, is the man of his half-sister the Empress'

'Quite so, Ralphe, your grasp of the pecking order is uncanny'. He was standing with arms folded, head to one side, one eye closed, the other twinkling.

'Now' I continue 'we are laying siege to a castle held by the Empress' man, whom we shall have to kill if an arrangement can't be come to. Technically I should be within the walls, not without. And so should you. Am I stupid?'

'No, no, Ralphe … you're not stupid, now are you? You are young. You're seeing things in black and white, like young men do. Try to see it this way: we have joined a siege initiated by our Sovereign Lord The King, therefore we are now representing – at least whilst we're here – *his* interests. At the present time in the history of this island, as everyone but you seems to have noticed, there are no bondings that could be called loyalties. You really do not have a problem, politically speaking: as long as you're with me, you are fulfilling your obligations and you can leave my own obligations to My Lord of Gloucester for me to deal with. This, Ralphe, is a War whosoever promotes it and I suggest you try to enjoy it and profit from it as much as you can.'

'But, my Lord, I am willing to be thought stupid …'

'Crap!' he barked 'you aren't listening to me! Ralphe … all you need to bear in mind is that we've tried and failed to negotiate with those inside and they *will not let us in*! So we'll have to fight our way in, we don't have time to go anywhere else and if we don't get into this so-called "castle" – which is no more than a fucking chicken shed! – if we don't kick in the door very soon, we'll be caught by the weather and even those of us lucky enough to survive will be in very very deep shit!'

This was the first and only political discussion I ever had with my lord de Bonville. I'd not seen this side of him at all often. I couldn't deny the accuracy of his summing-up of our situation (though I was put out to hear his comparison of Gernsea to a hen house, since it was rather similar to Herraton) but there was a weakness in his argument. Let's say he was pursued for vengeance and defeated, then his men (myself included) would be killed or ransomed as part of his goods – in that there was a problem. I had bear in mind that if, as my Lord de Bonville was continually pointing out, every man was looking out for himself, then I (as every a man as every other man) should be looking out for *my*self and take advantage of the situation. I was thinking, for the first time ever, that my *own* best interests were not *of necessity* the same as those of my Lord and Master whom I was supposedly born to serve.

To return to more pressing events: it must be a full month since we left the place called Daxworthy and the country about here has been quite thoroughly laid to waste and food is in very short supply. This place, despite its old timbers and ramshackle buildings, its air of desolation, is nevertheless fiercely guarded by a wizened, shrunken man called Roger Joliffe who seems willing to fight to the death and command the loyalty of several quite able fighters. Gernsea is a place of permanent drizzle at the end of the world, standing on raised ground where three roads meet and merge into one, then follow the sea coast north: the only 'view' we have from the spinneys of birch where we're camped are endless mudflats that stretch away into the hazy distance like pooled eel skin and merge into a steely sky. The only good news is that we were lucky enough to find a small acreage of untouched pasture where the few stray sheep we managed to round up on our way can graze under guard. The weather is damp and gloomy but perhaps not quite as bad as I'm saying, there have been odd warm and pleasant days: the grass is still green and growing but there'll be frost soon and after that forage will be impossible to find. So de Ravelin has volunteered to go off and obtain salt by whatever means he can so that we can start slaughtering.

Though no one looks forward to winter, we are (or most of us are) still alive and there is fresh water running through the woodland which is cover enough for us to move freely outside the range of their bowmen (who are very good, anyone who strays beyond a point we call the Three Beeches is liable to fall to a sniper's arrow). Some men are a couple of miles away felling ash and carpenters are working it to shape for the mantlet engines, which are our only chance of kicking in the door of this godforsaken fort. Oh yes, and Canteloupe is coaching me in the art of the late Jean Villon's lance. There must be worse ways of passing the time: at first I found it heavy but, now I'm used to it, I spend hours making passes and lunges at ivy figures stuffed with moss. He, Canteloupe, the new man, has made himself a shelter in the woods where he lives with the girl Johanna not in sin, as the rough humour of frustrated men would have it, but more as father and daughter, priestess and acolyte, call it what you will.

I am honoured to be sleeping in my lord de Bonville's tent! And he seems to have taken it upon himself to educate me, holding forth on all kinds of subjects at all hours of the day and night. Being a well-travelled man, he says that in

England we've been spoiled by peace and security for so long we think it is normal. On the continent, he says, situations like the one we find ourselves in are commonplace: there is constant feuding, castles spring up illegally all over the place, occupied by those whose allegiance is elastic. Many lords, he says, even the most honest of men, driven by being victims of plunder themselves, must plunder their neighbours in turn.

Of course, we are not the only men laying siege to the 'chicken shed' (by the way, the nickname has got around the men, they strut and pose just before the Three Beeches flapping their elbows and waving their arses at Joliffe's archers. I've heard a broody hen during the night, and the inevitable cock crow at first light: it's the Welshmen, who all seem very good at it). If some of the other forces here are mere remnants of the King's forces, his actual retinue must be huge: there are knights here covered in steel from head to foot with plate armour of a sort I've not seen before, and the engines they have beggar belief! We are put in our place indeed with our two mantlets. They have brought down granite from the moors at god knows what expense and employ masons to shape the stones into round shot for the onager, and there is a huge wheeled ram being made day and night by a team of carpenters. De Bonville has thrown in our lot with Oliver Pynchon, a large very rude man who drinks like a fish but has an apparently bottomless war chest: he is impressed by the luck of Canteloupe. Canteloupe and I have been given the task of negotiation with the enemy, Pynchon says that between us we are diplomacy itself, I talk well and Canteloupe scares them. I had never seen myself as an actor but I do quite enjoy our sessions – my job is reason and debate, Canteloupe's insult and threat.

It works thus: we walk out and plant our white flag in the open ground before the castle and the water. Jolliffe's men emerge from the portal with their own flag, and others begin to gather on the ramparts.

'What do you want today?' ask Jolliffe's men (as if they didn't know).

I say something like: 'we wish to talk with Alured' (this is the *nom de guerre* of Roger Jolliffe's main henchman, a ferocious bearded unfriendly man).

'He's busy' they say 'sharpening his wits'.

'Oh really' says Canteloupe 'there's a pity! Such a mighty effort for such a small return'

'Well' I continue 'I was only going to advise him, for the love of Jesus, to give up this place … does he not want a long life? It is so that the longer he stays in there, the closer comes his death, but of course this is nothing he hasn't heard before' I sigh with world–weariness 'such a godforsaken spot as this – I don't know what he finds to do with himself'

'None of your fucking business!' As expected, Alured himself surrounded by a large and noisy *entourage* has appeared on the gatehouse.

'Ah, Monsieur Alured, *bonjour*! Not so busy then that he cannot pass the time of day in polite conversation. The mark of a civilized man'

'Your friend is quiet today' says Alured, ignoring me. Canteloupe says nothing, stands with his arms akimbo, spits on the ground before him.

'He is weary of the siege' I say 'that's the truth.'

'Well why doesn't he fuck off home then and take that yellow–haired whore with him!' (This was the first time Johanna had been mentioned, I didn't know they knew of her).

'I think Monsieur Canteloupe' I continue 'would hate to go home and leave you alive. The fact is he could kill all of you single-handed, he just doesn't want to take all the credit for himself ... look monsieur (I spread my open hands to show they are empty) why die? why not live? God expects us to live our allotted span and not die for mere vanity! (I can sense Canteloupe struggling to keep a straight face, admittedly he couldn't in rehearsals} Surrender, my lord, please surrender, and we can all go home, we'll be with our families before the cold sets in. I'll be reasonable, Monsieur Jolliffe has one further week, after then we will be fully ready and you will all die. How can I, how could anyone, be fairer than that?'

'Well, Monsieur Whatever-your-bastard-name-is, I'm touched by your concern (as Alured began to speak his men set up a chorus of whistles and grunts, some wristed their groins, others were pissing down the stockade) perhaps you'd be so good as to tell that cowfucker Pynchon to ... '

Canteloupe interrupted 'the more your men piss on that old timber, monsieur, the quicker it will rot. You'd do well to listen to what my colleague has to say. He may be young but he knows what he's talking about. You've a week before we kick this fucking chicken shed (our own men are now strutting and cackling) to pieces and burn it to the ground and I'm looking forward to seeing you with your head up your arse, that's a tricky one to do for anyone especially fat bastards who don't bend – I'll do it the quick way and just cut it off and shove it up there!'

We usually walked away as Alured began to get into his stride. 'At least' he is saying   with a grin to cheers from his men 'my head and my arse are seperate which is more than can be said for your master Pynchon whose very anatomical peculiarity has forced him to spend his whole life talking shit!'

'Thankyou for your time monsieur, limited though it is'   I say, withdrawing and bowing. 'Do bear in mind what I say'

'Shit and fall back in it!' laughs Alured.

I bow low, turn and walk away. Canteloupe slaps his hand on his right arm and makes the sign of the stiff dick before he turns his back.

'And you!' Alured calls after him 'don't get her pregnant! What comes out will have a pig's tail and snappy teeth!'

I fear Canteloupe will crack, but no, he holds his temper, merely smirking and walking on, quite sure of himself.

Revenge

Oh yes! Now ... what a set-to yesterday! There was early fog, quite dense, and a flurry of arrows out of nowhere, then a body of mounted knights clattered across the water. They were just testing our strength – there's never any hand-to-hand, you know, they shy away from it (and who can blame them?) – an expensive little experiment I'd say. A couple of them ended up running for their lives back inside and there was horseflesh lying on the open ground near the water. Mareschal and Canteloupe, working as a pair these days, stood like a couple of idiots shouting after them, raising the two fingered salute as our archery thumped into the closing gates.   But they were forced to dive into the trees as the salvo was returned and I had fear of losing them.

Canteloupe has no excuse for such behaviour, Ralphe I suppose has his youth. His lance work really is coming along, a finely balanced young man. I saw him yesterday ream a foot soldier (and this from his mount!), toss him aside like a split sack, flick a mess of guts off the business end and ride on looking for more! But by God it's tedious, this place! My men are working with My Lord Pynchon, trying to force a breach in the outer wall below the motte, the timber looks old and flaky enough on the outside but each log has a solid heart which we must slowly break with axes. Constant cover is required, bowmen sit in the treetops; the enemy as they must drop big bastard rocks on us. You know with all the hardware we've accrued here, there's still nothing so effective as the dropped rock – there are men crippled already and one has died from a broken head.

But I've been thinking ... this seam of fine weather goes on and on as if someone up there likes us: the more the ground dries out, the closer we come to taking this bloody castle and going home. I say as much to Canteloupe catching out of the corner of my eye as I speak a blizzard of falling leaves spinning on the breeze ... I'm sitting with him in the place on the edge of the wood, out of the wind and out of sight where you can put your feet up and scan the country on the rear landward side of the castle ... a comfy spot, there's even a ledge of rock to sit on. I was there with Guillame Canteloupe. You know, I was wrong about him. Once a sot always a sot I said (even though he was worth more drunk than many of them sober). Anyway, the three of us were there, sitting like spare pricks at a wedding on the rocky bench: myself, Canteloupe and the girl (her breathing sickness has all but left her, she has now almost a bloom of health), she was pealing away with laughter at Canteloupe's account of that day's exchanges. Some of Jolliffe's erks – in the middle of the night – had pushed an old waggon into the wood, making a hell of a racket, got it well alight and tried to fire the trees but there's a squall like Noah's flood that douses it in minutes. Ha! So in the morning, of course, Alured does not emerge. 'Tell your master' said Mareschal to the erks standing very solemn and sheepish with the flag of parley 'that even God pisses on his efforts'.

But even as we laughed, the young 'witch' helpless with it pointing and laughing at the same time, out along the line of a hedge. I should be pleased to see men and weapons appearing ... reinforcements! But no, I don't think so, you could see a dark smudge moving over the fields, a rounded thing with legs like a phalanx of chukky-pigs from under a stone. By the time it reached the acres of fired stubble around us it had resolved itself into teams, waggons and men. A military cortège bechrist! But the girl had grown quiet and serious, resting her hand on Canteloupe's arm: the mounted men and foot are those who destroyed Daxworthy and murdered her family, she says. And why shouldn't they be?

There's a body of men, some mounted, of quite humble status apparently: a few peasant infantry and two knights at the head, no retinue to speak of ... in fact they *seem* to be sharing a squire, who carries the helms and shields of both (rather clumsily). The devices of owl and fox (rather crudely put together) are on their helms of the knights, just as the girl did describe to me, and I can see the crooked arm of a onager. I do try not to be judgemental, in case I myself am judged, so I can stop myself wondering for the moment where such an ill–assorted pair came across such an engine. Begod they're odd! One of them is a slab of beef with cropped hair and a layered chin, the other is quite different, narrow–faced with long dark hair tied back in a tail and draped over his shoulder. They are taking no trouble to swerve outward, clear of the archer's range and Canteloupe (bless him) is on his feet pointing at the castle, making the sign of the drawn bow, shooing them over to the left.

'Alright, young lady' I say 'I don't doubt that these are the men you say, they look ragged to be sure but they have a useful engine so we'll have them join the siege. You keep out of their way and out of sight for the moment, don't worry, they'll suffer later'.

The new arrivals were accepted into the pay of My Lord Pynchon without question. I let a couple of days pass before I went over, with an escort of men, to where trees had been cleared and their machine was being made ready and mounted: I couldn't help but admire it, standing on its chocked wheels like a dragon, a well-made piece of hardware indeed (from whom did they steal it, eh?) Now, the first priority of men such as these is their own comfort and their own protection. I wanted to give them the benefit of a little drama I'd prepared but they should be allowed to settle into their seats first. Canteloupe was with me and I told him to keep his distance and look out for trouble (something he should have no difficulty in doing) and bring the girl on my signal.

They were sitting side by side on a bench lashed up from coppiced hazel, waiting to be fed: the pot simmered, strung from a tripod over a red fire. There was something of the abandoned about them, a liquidity in their laughter, a nasal tone to their speech ... they would soon be dead men. They introduced themselves, John and John: the fatter one was John Swain and the slender hairy one John de Palmere and they say (rather surprisingly) they are the men of Roger de la Moule of Marshburgh. 'I am Guy de Bonville' I said 'I have met your Lord recently. A fair man. We stayed at Marshburgh Castle for three nights'

They invited me to share their meal, I declined politely enough. 'You travel on to Bristol?' asked Swain.

'Theoretically' I said. 'I will come to the point straight away, a point of law I think'. Here a quick glance flickered between them – this is a bonus of frankness, few people expect it – and when they looked back at me, as one squaring their shoulders, there was calculation in their eyes, de Palmere stroked the tail of hair that ran down across his shoulder. 'I believe I have come across the handiwork of you two gentlemen and your associates (as I spoke they did not blink but their gaze hardened), we passed through a stead called Daxworthy in a combe you come upon suddenly on the high downs two days out of Marshburgh. Do you know of it?'

'I've heard of it' said Swain, a lip tremor and a glimpse of tooth, thumbs locked into belt 'what of it?'

'I wanted to compliment you on the workmanlike way you dealt with the threat the people who lived there must have posed, and you followed the wise criminal's code and left nothing alive to tell the tale, but such untidiness! My men exerted themselves on your behalf to bury the dead. Could you not have spared the boys and the girl ... the dogs?'

'Dogs can't talk' said de Palmere with a sideways grin at Swain.

'I'm looking at two that are going to' and as I said this, de Palmere's grin snapped shut and he was reaching for his blade. Swain's eyes, secreted in slashed cushions of flesh, missed nothing: he stayed the arm of his companion without apparently taking his gaze from me. He had noticed Canteloupe – of whom he will almost certainly know already – slipping in a bolt.

'However' I continued 'you were quite thorough enough. We found the young lady (there was here a guffaw here from de Palmere, I was holding up a finger where Canteloupe could see it and crooking it slightly as we agreed) I noticed from her state that your party had taken it upon itself to introduce her, no doubt with great sensitivity, to the ways of carnal love ... and when you had all finished you left her to die'

'Talk, talk, talk. You are good at that my lord. Is he not a great talker?' When we had walked up to Swain and de Palmere, their people had not stopped what they were doing, seeing only a man coming to pay his respects to fellow warriors, nothing unusual. But now the silence was heavy: workmen banged, sawed and whistled away in the distance, a woodpecker knocked, and everyone near was watching and listening apparently to the hiss and crackle of fire and the quiet seething of game stew.

'She was a virgin!' I began quietly, but de Palmere cut me off, suddenly calm and confident, as if a threat had passed.

'Look!' he said 'we don't know what you're talking about. I know of Daxworthy, I've heard of the girl ... she was trouble and certainly no virgin (he looked about him for smirks, there was a murmur of laughter) what is she to you?'

'Crop blighter!' said Swain 'Witch! Bad all the way through!'

'Trouble, you say' I was trying to carry on with my planned speech, but I hadn't expected this, a man of my age should not be surprised. 'Unfortunately for you she is trouble, yes. You two gentleman have a problem. She belongs to me now, it is to me you will answer'.

As I become aware that Canteloupe is approaching with the girl, Swain and de Palmere are sitting very still. I would say the latter is in a dangerous state, a cold fury, but Swain doesn't take his eyes from me. He says: 'I know what is in your mind my lord, you think she's the daughter of a farmer, don't you? That that was her *family* out there ... ha! ... so what is it that goes on here, eh? A man like yourself, experienced, wealthy ... I'm asking myself, like my friend asked, what the fuck is she to you?'

'I care for her because she brings us luck and she has cheated Death'

De Palmere throws back his head and barks out a laugh and then ... 'the bitch is looking!' he cries. His teeth are bared and grinning, he's ready to suffer now.

'Sees right inside you, doesn't she?' I said 'there's nothing you can hide from her – she's right in there, right in your rotten heart – she'll chew you up and spit you out!' I didn't know where these words were coming from, I had not intended to speak in this way but I had no control.

But Swain was the most composed of any of us. He lowered his head and looked straight at me, not at the girl. 'My Lord de Bonville, our holdings are near Daxworthy, as you know we are the men of de la Moule, but we haven't been anywhere near home for quite a time. Like yourselves, we were forced to roam and get whatever was out there. We've been well north-east of here since the midsummer – I mean, did we approach here from Marshburgh way? Ask yourself ... did we?'

Well no, I had to admit they didn't. But I couldn't quite let it go. 'Where do men such as yourselves come by such a beast as this?' I indicated the crouching onager.

He raises his eyes briefly to heaven as though the whole thing is just too exasperating and he looks towards de Palmere but his friend was still staring at the girl. 'I don't know' continued Swain 'what you mean by "men such as ourselves" – poor men, ugly men, heathen men? – but we caught up with the engine marooned by the road surrounded by the corpses of its owners and, as you know, if you hear of a siege there's no harm in joining it. So we travelled along with the mechanics. You can ask my men or you can ask the engineers. Ask them where they met us and your proof is there ... we were nowhere near Daxworthy ...'

'But the girl says she knows you for the men who destroyed her home'. I admit that now I was faltering seriously, Canteloupe had moved up to my side:could these men be honest? There might be witnesses who could vouch for them. Everything must be done according to law.

'That bitch would, wouldn't she? And we need to be clear on the fact that Daxworthy is not and never was her "home" ... as my comrade here has told you, she's trouble. And he should know, the bitch put a blight on his wife and she died'

'So that's it! Revenge! What better motive than that ...?' I must make decisions and I must make very quickly, I have experience of the way men speak, I have learned to catch the meanings in their actions, what they do with their hands, how they look at you, direct or indirect. Now, these two were men like any other, odd–looking, lovers of comfort, idle of speech, droll of humour, but rather too easy to mock. Whilst I accept that I, in common with all other men, have prejudice of others, I like to keep it under control, for the sake of the law. I was thinking unbidden of the transformation of Canteloupe. As I have said, he is a man I trust and like, despite his rakish habits. But of late he has *not been himself.* The Canteloupe who stands beside me now is a new Canteloupe, an improved being, sober and strong, but something *is not there.* The old Canteloupe had it but the new Canteloupe does not. But still I'm not prepared to take the plunge of believing these two utterly. 'I think you are both lying ...'

'Then you are ill-informed, sir ... it is not I who am the liar. I would be much more careful in what you say!'

'Or what ....?' I said, bristling now, in no way will I have threats laid upon me by this fat bastard and his sallow familiar. I was aware of Canteloupe shifting his stance beside me. My doubts then disappeared at once. I saw Swain as the greater threat, I was keeping an eye on him, and I was aware of sounds all around, stealthy scratchings and scrapings, clicks and snaps, as both parties prepared for the scattering of blood.

Was she at Canteloupe's side where she should be? I could not look, I was concentrating on Swain. I had taken it for granted that there would be time to see the effect her approach would have on them, and it seemed clear that these two were less afraid of punishment than of the girl herself. You only had to follow de Palmere's gaze to see she was detaching herself from Canteloupe, a weapon of guaranteed destructive power. De Palmere's face was frozen and his teeth were still clenched as though under a spell ... yes by Jesus and Mary, a spell! I saw the movements of genuflection at Canteloupe's chest and the girl out of the corner of my eye was drifting like a fire ship out into no man's land. A figure was moving in close behind Swain and his partner, fetching an arrow from his quiver, but he was stopped in his tracks. I felt safe enough to look away and towards her. Her eyes glowed ashen and caustic, and she pushed a thin blade of sound into the air from her lips that grew until it penetrated every head She was pointing a finger at the archer who took the arrow he had selected and thrust it hard into his ear.

The fight that followed was simple and quick. Only Canteloupe and I were involved, he put a bolt in Swain's eye that killed him instantly and I felled de Palmere where he sat and he flopped to the ground like a landed fish. And that was that. Disappointing, really. Keep him alive, I said, we'll hang him. My Lord Pynchon will not be pleased at first, but he will have the engine and its crew: and none of the retinue such as it was of those two men fought, but laid down their arms.

And when later I am telling all this to an exhausted and cynical de Ravelin who has returned from his travels without a single grain of salt he says: 'high drama then, my lord – so it is true the girl can induce a man to kill himself by her voice alone? All very well, but we're nowhere near lifting the siege, are we? I go away, I come back after a fortnight and all has changed! Spirits have sunk, time drags, there's a bad atmosphere about the place, a row of graves. Frost has come, the grass has stopped growing. Even Canteloupe's moping about, he's looking again for his old comforter I suppose?'

'You mean the drink or the girl? He'll be lucky to find a drink here and the girl keeps herself to herself now and lives alone in her own shelter'.

'Ah! He has lost the miraculous, I was going to say Virgin, I'm sorry my Lord'

'So you should be, monsieur ... you think we should try to get back to Marshburgh don't you, for the winter?'

'I do. Look, we have yet to breach the rampart in any one place and let's face it there's a jinx, my Lord – too many stupid accidents. A man who fell asleep on guard losing his leg under the wheel of a waggon rolling on its own, brake disengaged. These are facts my Lord'.

'I know monsieur, I have heard these tales myself'

'... An artilleryman, very experienced, decapitated by the arm of that onager the first time it was fired in anger and poor young Mareschal sapped by the merest of arrow-nicks in his thigh, a plague of a wound which doesn't heal ... my lord Pynchon is certainly talking of winter elsewhere and if we don't move soon it'll be too late. And won't they be glad to see us at Marshburgh? The last time we saw it half the world seemed to be fighting over it!'

'Of course you're right my friend. You see it clear. Johanna, it's her. Ever since she's withdrawn our luck has run out. We must go. For Christ's sake look at the landscape of this place! Endless slopes of that rough wiregrass, the sea that's never anything but leaden grey and choppy, the roads that carry no traffic and stretch away to nothing, need I say more?'

'Not the most poetic of places, my lord. If you ask me we should kill that cove de Palmere, his life's worth nothing, or should I say not enough. The poor man lives in a nine foot pit, under weighted timber with his feet in water, I'd say he'll thank us for it! He certainly won't be worth a penny of de la Moule's money'.

'The men think he's bringing bad luck ... they'll blame anything, anyone but her ... but much as he'll be a weight round our neck, and keen as I am to see a rope round his own I must take our monsieur de Palmere back to Marshburgh where he can be hanged with the authority of his Lord and master. And I want de la Moule to confirm or deny certain things about the young lady Johanna'.

I go to tell her we have decided to leave. It was myself who had the new shelter built for her as she wanted, a rough tent of hazel branches thatched with grass where she spends her time alone, curled like a winter mouse. The moment she sees me she throws off her covers and pulls away her clothes in one movement and an arch of her back. Even with my head averted, I cannot avoid her nudity. 'Don't you look away' she says 'you've seen me naked before. Look messire, I must show you ...' And then she's working the dough of her white belly, very softly with her fingertips. She takes my hand and lays it there, places her hands over mine. 'There's a child in there' she says 'did you know? It's a boy child without a father and he's going to be called Guillame and he'll live in a place called Herraton. Do you know it?'

There are some things I will never understand.

CHAPTER SIX

Atmospheric Pressure

'You'll get used to the sway' says Mr Halloran the balloon aviator standing like a mast before a rocking horizon, a ruddy face smiling fiercely under its strapped hat. Geoffrey and I are hanging onto the ropes as though our lives depended on it.

'Mister Halloran! I was scared before we started, I didn't think I'd ever go up in this thing, and now I'm terrified! But I swear before God this is the greatest thing I've ever met with! We have no weight! Are we masters of the land and air or is it vicey-versy? Are you sure this bag of air will hold (and I'm looking upward at the dizzy height of silk, the wind is in my teeth) I mean it's big but is it strong? It's so thin'

'You ask a lot of questions Mister Trelease!' Mister Halloran tilts back his head and surveys the tight silk, he appears to be considering my statements. But Geoffrey has answers for me, he is peering down over the country but turns to speak around Halloran's back. 'It's not air, father, it's hydrogen gas, lighter than air, took a couple of days to fill'

'Don't tell your father that, he'll think we're going to blow up' says Mr Halloran cheerfully.

'*Gas!* A couple of *days!* Damn it, Geoffrey how much is in there?' I reckon they're both thinking the old fella's having another childhood and by Christ I won't argue with that! Okay it scares the living daylights out of me but I saw it yesterday rearing up over the trees on the Bonville Acres and I said to Geoffrey: 'what in God's name is that?' When he told me, I was spellbound. But I still didn't think it was there for me. At my age you think there's nothing new under the sun, but there is, believe me, and I'm glad to know it! The world's a lot simpler from up here'.

'Geoffrey, Geoffrey! Take a look down there, how it's all so clear. There's nobody, nothing human anyways, has ever seen the old motte from up here. You can see how Digweed's got them paths mown, like sunrays, how come I never noticed that before? It was called Herraton Bonnyville, I know that much'.

'Bonville, father, Herraton Bonville'. Geoffrey has his back to me again and he's shouting into the breeze out of the corner of his mouth.

'That's right, son, I'm getting all carried away here, but come on over here and take a look down at the motte through the trees. Now, you see that smudge on the ground that's the building that used to stand on it all them years ago, and there's the ditch round it, there's no amount of backfilling can hide it from up here! Fool that I was, I guessed its size all wrong. The bailey's a deal bigger than I thought, the whole of our house and garden you can see lies in a small corner of it. It's like someone tipped a bowl and all the loose stuff rolled out to one side'.

'You'll have to excuse Mr Trelease' Geoffrey is saying to Mr Halloran 'it's his birthday!'

I can see that Mr Halloran is amused in his rough way, he's seen it all before, once the terror's overcome and the customer starts to enjoy himself.

'Look at the whole place, Geoffrey, Digweed's Castle they call it. I can cover our small corner of the county with just a hand and it's pear-shaped! The track out to the fields goes all the way round, and the road up from Rafton skirts the bank with the hedge on it that was a rampart and there's Mr Hammond's men working on the tennis court, and we'll tell Mister Digweed all about it if they're slacking!'

'If they're slacking, father, Digweed'll already know'.

'True enough, son. There ain't a deal he misses'.

Oh yes, the old hawk's as sharp as ever, even if he is a bit stiff in the wing. He wished me luck but wasn't inclined to join us, he prefers the surface of the ground. He's not getting about so well now but he's not a lot older than me but, if you listen to him, sounds like he's done some hard graft in his time. And he walks with a stick now, for a good couple of years he said: 'beggared if I'll walk with a blessed stick, I'd lose it all the time' But that old stiffness in his hip got no better and now the arthritis has got him, like since he became a man of means and one of the leisured gentry he's kind of seized up. 'Balloon! (I can hear him say it) you won't catch me in a blessed balloon!' And he's accepting help these days in other ways: Jane always helped him with his bookwork now and then but now she spends time with him regular, dealing with business and correspondence. She's that keen she wouldn't come today on account of her being so busy with the Digweed correspondence.

'You see, Geoffrey, out in Canada we didn't rightly have anything you could call history and I'm not talking here about old time lords and ladies, jousts and romance, young men with blue eyes and flowing hair on prancing steeds'. Geoffrey's enjoying it, he's laughing away, my fine son.

'You are, father, you are talking so, you're a terribly sentimental man and its gotten worse with the years'.

'Alright, alright, what I mean is, it was a castle sure enough, the King would have given it to this fella called Bonville to administer. It'd be one of those way off the track forts the Normans had when they needed control over land right up to the edges of the country. Maybe it was built and kept up for a time as a far outpost but never really needed but can't you see them mounted knights, the King's retained men with their foot soldiers, riding out to gather the taxes?'

Now I've done with running Digweed's estate, I mean to get around to writing a short history ... I don't know, say 'The Life and Times of Herton' or some such thing (except that I don't know a lot about the life or the times of any place but I guess I know a little about history). Jane was keen when I told her, reckons there's no harm in it, so I asked her if she could help me out with the writing. It's like she's taken to writing these last few years, I don't think she knows I know, but she's been scribblin' away at something. Geoffrey reckons she keeps some sort of journal very private and locked away in her desk. Anyways, I'm going to have a shot at writing a history – even if only for my own pleasure and my grandchildren's. Ah now there's a thing ... grandchildren! Geoffrey and Jane've been wed five years and still there's no child.

Though he's right next to me I'm having to shout in Geoffrey's ear over the gusting wind: 'I'm getting to enjoy this ... a shame Jane couldn't come!'

'Not so much couldn't as wouldn't. She has her father's caution, she wouldn't trust her life to a mere basket under a bag of air!' shouts Geoffrey.

'The way I'm seeing it, Geoffrey, it's like as not the only chance we'll ever get to see the world as the eagle does – best take it'.

'I'm gad you see it that way, father' Now my son's got his hand on my shoulder, he's pointing a way out over the Coley marshes. 'Look' he says 'there's the old hut out on the marsh where Jane and me used to ride when we were courting … and all the barges out on the Banks!'

But I'm hardly listening to him, the wind has veered and is taking us back towards Herton and the fine grazing of Digweed's Devons and sheep, I can see the boundary drains of the marsh with tiny white swans, and the road twisting up toward the farm. I can see a buzzard coming in on the wing from that direction and it cruises in close, riding the breeze and watching. I'm thinking I'm equal to that bird, I've got a share in its element.

Sooner than I thought, we're passing rather low over the first trees of Marshall's Wood and our friend the buzzard sees what he's after and cuts under us quick, so quick I can hardly follow it and my focus is gone and the goddam basket's swaying like a bell. And out of the corner of my eye there it is, a strange growth of white in in a clearing of the green, but more like a species of beetle made of human flesh struggling and quivering on its back. There's two horses tethered and all. Goddam, I look away. But nevertheless, I have seen. Thank God Geoffrey's hasn't, I see the back of his head, his arm still pointing, his eyes still out over the marshes.

And that little scene has gone for ever – I'm thinking there's any number of beasts similar and that might not have been old Dido standing down there. But I won't get a second look, nor do I want one. I don't want to see her again, my daughter-in-law who does what she chooses but in the nicest possible way. You know, she must have …what? … a degree of self knowledge I'll never have. How she gets herself involved with them village children, gets their love and trust, even teaches them a few things. I'm glad my son is wed to her, it's as if I know he's safe. Oh surely I have my suspicions but I can't see no reason to tell him a thing – so what if it was Jane all bunched up somehow into that godforsaken knot?

I knew she wouldn't want to fly in this balloon thing, truth is I wanted Geoffrey on his own, relaxed, so's I could have a word with him. But I shan't get round to it now. Aren't there always things you want to say but years go by and you still never say them? It looks like Mister Halloran is taking us down: he's saying something about the wind veering again and shortage of time, he's pulling on thin ropes and letting the gas out, he must be heading down to Bonville Acres. So I've shot myself in the foot with this here birthday treat: I'd fondly imagined Geoffrey and I having a father-to-son kind of chat, up here alone in the blue yonder. What better chance is there going to be? But the whole thing's so overwhelming it takes away your worries as well as your breath.

In the end I guess I only really wanted to know that when I go and meet my maker I can be sure I'm leaving a good situation back here on earth. I ask Geoffrey, just as we're approaching terra firma at an alarming speed: 'things alright between you and Jane?'

'Of course', he says and looks at me a bit peculiar, 'things have always been alright between us – since we were kids – why d'you ask?' And then comes a terrific bump and a collapse of the mighty bag with a rush of wind and Mr Halloran shouting at the whole world: 'no naked flame!' I am on my knees staring at fleeing sheep, Geoffrey is laughing his head off and Mr Halloran is flinging an anchor at Digweed's turf.

And I can't answer that, Geoffrey, only with another question. But now I think I have the answer to that one too. The question was why Jane is so evidently and benignly satisfied … and I mean *satisfied* … when I know that my son can be nowhere near the whole cause of it?

There's two things happening here. One is that I know and love my daughter-in-law, there's always been something about her you can't argue with, can't describe, but it comes off her like steam (old Digweed sees it too, I've seen the way he looks at her). It's as though she nurtures a good seed just under the surface of her skin, and it flowers as a ruddy glow of warmth on her face, a frankness of the eye (I'm clumsy with words, just as well I would never attempt to say any of this to my son or any other living soul). My point is that this seed, these flowers, are richer than ever in their growth the more time goes on.

Which leads on to the Other Thing. I know I must try to stop thinking of my son as my little boy (she once called him beautiful) he's doing the job of running the estate and doing it well, he's a man. But what niggles me is that I well know that whatever it is that Jane is receiving there's an awful lot of it, and Geoffrey just doesn't have those kinds of quantities available.

But I can't deal with any of that now, in the chaos of the balloon's return to earth. After we have captured and weighted the huge bag and helped Mr Halloran coil the ropes, Geoffrey asks what we were talking about before we were so rudely interrupted and I can only say it's gone right out of my mind.

When we get home, Jane wants to hear all about the balloon flight. Being up there's made me tired so I leave it to Geoffrey. Nodding and laughing now and then, I watch Jane from the comfort of my carver and smoke a pipe. She's standing at the kitchen table facing us, letting the edge take her weight, resting her palms flat on the board. Every so often she casts her eyes down, or throws me a sidelong glance: there's that jaded ease about her again, that faint flush on her skin I talked of and I can see she's distracted, she's half-listening, she's really twitching her nose, trying to decipher a distant perfume, or dreaming with her eyes open. This is Jane Digweed, Mrs Jane Trelease, and was ever so ... has Geoffrey never noticed? For sure, she knows that I have. Perhaps it is she I should be talking to and not my son.

I had a chance the next day, when she suggested that we took our cold cuts out into her father's garden at midday. Geoffrey had to go off right after church and was likely to be out all day resolving a problem of several sick sheep on a distant farm. We sat over by the mound where a rustic bench and table were set up, near a roughly level piece of the yard where the tennis court was being built. Being the he Sabbath, the men weren't working. A memorable day, the weather was fine and warm, we walked out through one of the mown paths, swaying ryegrass a yard high either side of us and quickthorn bushes on the motte heavy with scent.

'I have finally succeeded' Jane said with a strange high laugh 'in getting father to restrain the gardener who apparently cannot last long without taking up the scythe'.

I thought there was some tension about her today. There sometimes was at this hour, after she had come out from the schoolroom and the children had gone home. But today there was no school and she didn't teach Sunday School. I often took this meal with her and, on weekdays when she took her long rides rather than helping Digweed in his office, she would ease down from the morning's activities, drink tea and chat but soon after, as the afternoon approached, distraction made her restless, and soon I would take myself off and leave her free to be off to the stables and old Dido. It was the rides, of course, that cured her restlessness. I've always been the sort of man who says nothing rather than something, I only knew the gist of what I was going to ask her, but I was determined.

'You're out riding this afternoon?' I said straightway after the tea and pleasantries.

'Oh yes. Most certainly.'

'I'd like to come with you, may I?'

She said nothing for a moment, but patted her hair, took the teapot and swirled it round, as if she was going to offer me another cup, sat for a moment idly turning over the sugar with a spoon and tapping it on the bowl. 'Well' she said eventually, with her eyes cast down, drawing on the teacloth with the spoon 'please Arthur do not be offended – we've known each other many years and you've never asked me this before. I suppose you wouldn't have when I was Jane Digweed. But really, it's something I always do alone. It was rare even that I went with Geoffrey. I am sorry, but I must go alone'

'Why is that? Where do you go?'

Then she moved her lip with something you couldn't really call a smile and gave a curious little shrug. 'I go wherever I want to go. A lot of places. This time of year I go over the fields a lot, in the woods when it's very hot. Autumn and Winter I prefer the marshes'

'Jane, dear' I began, leaning out over the cliff so far I was bound to fall 'how is it you always look so well?'

Now colour spread over her face and neck, she looked up for the first time, straight at me but I didn't flinch. I knew I had guessed right. She was stirring the sugar now with tremulous concentration. 'How do I? Why shouldn't I look well? We have a good life here, fresh air, good food.'

'Can I say what's on my mind, Jane? It won't hurt I promise'

She was smiling now, one of her dreamy smiles that drove her father and brothers to distraction. 'You best had, Arthur' she said 'you know you'll get an honest answer from me'

'I'll be straightforward then, when I say "well" I mean satisfied. There is something coming your way that comes neither from Geoffrey nor from fresh air and good victuals'. She sipped her tea steadily now in tiny amounts, as if to keep occupied, but her composure was regained, she looked across at me frankly over the rim of her cup. 'Don't worry' I said 'all I want, Jane, is to hear from your own lips that you and Geoffrey will always be man and wife "as long as you both shall live".

'Yes, Arthur, of course'. She sounded relieved. 'I have loved Geoffrey since I was able to love anyone. I love him with all my heart – all of it. But I cannot, as I think you have guessed, guarantee the "exclusion of all others" – except from my heart, that is'.

'I won't ask you to do that. I'm being selfish, Jane, I'm thinking of when the Lord comes to take me – you'll have to excuse my sentimental language – when He comes to take me I reckon I deserve to go with a clear conscience, happy that Geoffrey's well–being is assured'.

'As long as he is with me he will be happy. You know I will always make certain of that'

'I do know that, Jane'.

'And I will always be with him, just like I will always remember this conversation. Thankyou for trusting me, Arthur, and thankyou so much for loving me, that love will always be returned. Have you tried these saffron cakes? I admit I can't resist them'

Mr Digweed's Retirement

Mr Digweed, finally succumbing to pressure from his children, especially his two younger daughters, has allowed the construction of a tennis court in an area of the garden adjacent to the mound and near the boundary hedge. Most mornings now he makes his way up there and watches the men for a while, in his wake an arthritic and determined collie he has adopted from one of his shepherds.

It is his habit to lean for a while on his stick in the shade of a favoured sycamore and eventually when he can stand no longer he sits himself down on one of many rustic benches which his son John made in a fit of enthusiasm some ten years ago, before farming took away his leisure. As the old collie subsides to the grass with a grunt and dozes sighing at his feet, a young tabby cat, which has taken a liking to him, will often appear and settle on the old man's lap, rolling over, stretching and purring like a tuning fork under the fond caresses of his fingers. Though Mr Digweed well knows the men will not be comfortable with him sitting there, he doesn't care: he has not become so soft-hearted that he cannot take pleasure in witnessing every procedure in the laying out of the court. After all, he is paying.

He amuses himself by making calculations in his head of how much clay will be needed as compared to the amount which he sees going in to the shallow square of dead soil. He knows to a minute the time taken to extract and transport the shillet hardcore and grit, how far each man's wage is justified – but only out of interest of course, he would not *dream* of interfering. He cannot break the habits of a lifetime where he would know the market value of almost any given thing, the likely demand for it and what percentum of it would fall his way. Though in conversation, Mr Digweed restricts himself to polite comments on the weather and jovial gossip about mutual acquaintances, he knows within a few pennies how much Mr Hammond the contractor will take home with him after the job is finished and his costs have been met.

Though he did not expect to, Mr Digweed is enjoying his retirement. At first he lamented the stiffness in his joints to anyone who would listen, cursed his enforced domesticity; on the rare occasions when he went out he was confined to the roads in a driven carriage. No more could he ride the crops on his cob, alone or with Mr Trelease, and eat his lunch perched on some high hill. But slowly he has grown into these new ways and, having become accustomed to the luxury of doing absolutely nothing, finds it irresistible. Young John has taken over from him entirely: the old man hears his son's accounts of the various farms at mealtimes, he enquires after acquaintances, when asked he will give advice, otherwise he lets his son get on with it. He has even taken an interest in such topics as horticulture and local history. Occasionally, after he has spent a little time watching the tennis court take shape, he can be found 'having a word' with the gardener or stopping in to chat with Arthur Trelease, whose fancies on the past of Herton are promising to turn into a written account of some depth.

One morning, when the job was barely under way, and Mr Digweed was sitting on his bench in the sun pensively kneading the droning flank of the recumbent cat, Mr Hammond approached him, removing his hat.

'Morning Mr Digweed' he said.

'Morning John, lovely morning' said the old farmer. 'Do you like cats, John? I used to hate em, you know, but I don't mind this youngster, have you ever seen a living thing more contented, eh? I s'pose there's exceptions to everything!

I'm sorry, do sit yourself down, don't mind the old dog . You look like a man with a question'.

'I thank you, sir. I was just going to ask if some of the men could use that old bothy in the mound for keeping of their tools and what have you, just fer the time being'.

'Of course, of course. Mind you, tiddn all that pleasant in there I shouldn't think. Nobody's bin in there for yers. I'll have look tomorrow, just to see what's in there ... where's the key now? No matter, I'll find it'.

'I didn't mean to put you to any trouble, sir'

'That's alright, don't you worry John. I wouldn't mind taking a look in there'

And the following morning early, Mr Digweed extracted an oil–dropper from the chaos of the gardener's store, removed the old key from its hook on the wall and made his way over to the mound. It took him some time to free the lock and hinges before he was able to wrench open the ancient door and breathe again the earthy must of damp air and rotting timber. It had been some time since the light of the outside had entered the outhouse and fungi, quietly multiplying for years in the dark, was now crudely exposed, clinging like bleached flesh to the walls; and poor Mr Digweed coughed so much he was forced to hawk and spit, causing his old dog to wander off and pretend to amuse itself, looking back now and then with suspicion. The retired farmer, dabbing at his eyes with a handkerchief , struggling to regain his breath, is assailed by memories. Of course, he knew that his daughter's sketch books had vanished some years ago but it was with a smile of tolerance, almost mischief (which even now could surprise him) that he imagined the inappropriate and ribald comments the contractor's men would make if they came across them. Though he never saw his daughter's drawings again, he never forgot them either – occasionally they could drift unbidden across the landscape of his mind, or he glimpsed them in certain foreboding, stormy formations of cloud, even once he thought he saw the bargeman's formidable member resting on a hotbed in one of the garden frames. In fact, to be truthful, few days go by when he does not give some thought to his daughter's outrageous drawings. And what's more she got away with it! She! His daughter!

And Digweed cannot stop himself speculating, questions will occur to him. How it is that Jane is so happily wed to a man such as Geoffrey. Childhood friends, Geoffrey and Jane, quite inevitable, but man and wife! Man and wife! She and he so different like chalk and cheese you'd think, Jane so strapping and you know what, and Geoffrey like a rasher of bacon, not an ounce of fat on him nor an ounce of craft in him. *Come on, Digweed, you know very well why she wed Geoffrey ...*

Though retirement has allowed his mind to roam, Mr Digweed knows there are places he simply must not go. And the stranger's voice, right in his ear, unheard for years, tells him the same. There are still speculations which lead him – a man who has surely seen everything – along paths untrod through unknown lands, overwhelming odours, miles of bizarre vegetation, but he finds his way back quickly enough to the strait and narrow of agriculture and Profit and Loss because he knows how subtle growths and soft tendrils could drag him into places where he will be lost to the world for ever.

'I'm afraid tiddn in that clever a state, John. The hinges is that rusted in twas all I could do to get the door open and I'm beggared if I can shut it again'

'Well, Mr Digweed' says Mr Hammond 'I'm pretty well desperate to keep stuff under cover near the job – how would it be if I put new hinges on and did any other small repairs? Twould be worth it to me'.

'You'll do that fer the favour of using it?'

'I will'

'Then you're welcome' Mr Digweed and Mr Hammond are two men much of an age and they stay sitting. The sun is warm and the breeze pleasant. The old dog is lying on its side twitching its feet occasionally, chasing a dream rabbit across a dream pasture on a dream evening. 'You know' says the farmer eventually 'these days I'm content to get up each morning and survive till the end of the day, one time my head was full of the future, now tis full of the past – tis enough that th'almighty 's let me sit out yer through another spring of catkins, and they celandines, daffies and primroses'

Mr Hammond is staring ahead and vaguely amused by Mr Digweed's cogitations. He stretches out his legs, crosses his ankles and folds his arms.

'I won't let him cut the grass, you know, till all the flowers is gone' Mr Digweed carries on 'never used to think ort of flowers, can't eat em can ee?'

'How's the family?' asks Mr Hammond, apparently ignoring Mr Digweed's horticultural confessions. 'Well now, Jane's still running her little school and I'm beggared if the missus haven't joined er in the dairy ! Oh, Mrs Digweed's a prapper farmer's wife again now, enjoys a good laugh every morning while I'm out yer making a nuisance of meself'. Mr Hammond laughs politely and fills his pipe, settling in.

'I dunno' continues Mr Digweed 'I'm not so inclined as I was to be layin down the law about this and that. Looks like the twins will be marrying afore too long ... well, like I'd hoped I s'pose ... I'll be honest with ee, John, I've got on well in the world'

'That's true' says Mr Hammond solemnly.

'But you know I'm tired of it now and sometimes I couldn't give a tinker's cuss for any of it, I wanted my younger daughters to marry well and so they will, I can hardly complain. But what's the odds their husbands'll be pale and thin chaps who can't put anything in an honest to goodness way and don't have the strength of a fly between them and want to spend all their time playing tennis. To be honest with ee, I think I always misunderstood my Jane, a kinder young lady you could never come across ... well, there you are John!' Mr Digweed gets suddenly to his feet 'I've bin in there and sin it, tiddn so bad – you'll put new hinges on't for the favour of using it, I can't argue with that'

Then suddenly Digweed has gone. And Mr Hammond is left to smoke the pipe he has just lit alone. He is rather disappointed, having been prepared to settle and listen to Digweed's confidences, rare as they were. But then everyone knew Bill Digweed was like that ... a man who said a lot or nothing at all.

Some time after this, later in the summer, when the tennis court was almost done, Mr Digweed is resting from the heat of the sun beneath a large elm where a seat has been built round the girth. He is gazing down at the top of the old dog's head where it dozes, wedged between its white legs, now smudged with darker marks; and he recalls the animal in its heyday, lithe and fast, black and pure white, racing low round the flock, turning on a thought. And even now he sees its nose twitch as a breeze sweeps through, and sometimes an ear might lift at a sudden laugh or whistle from the few men left on the site, so a dog never sleeps.

Then there are sounds worthy of a raising of the head, an inclination of the ear, and Mr Digweed hears them too: sounds of delight, people shouting, someone holding forth that sounds a lot like Arthur Trelease. Mr Digweed sees a shadow grow on the grass before him and then the balloon, a boiled egg yards high with a tiny wicker cup strung beneath it, sails quietly into view over the canopy of leaves. And he catches odd phrases on the breeze: 'Digweed's Castle', 'pear-shaped!' He well knew his house was so called by some locals, he'd thought better of his former factotum ... but then he laughs so sharp and sudden that the dog wrenches his behind off the ground and stands staring. Castle be beggared! Arthur Trelease says that Lord Bonville – to whom Mr Digweed pays his rent each quarter – might once have 'held' a castle here. Now Mr Digweed well knows that his lordship, who owns all the land in this part of the county, lives miles away in Wiltshire and his house is by all accounts virtually a palace. He has certainly never been asked there. Now that's the sort of place you'd call a castle!

It being Arthur Trelease's birthday, Mr Digweed has already been over to the old house to wish his former factotum the best and taken a glass of rum with him. Rum! First thing in the morning! Mind you, it cheered him. A tradition, apparently, in the Trelease family. He'd heard rumours of this balloon flight and it was suggested light-heartedly that he should come along. Oh no one could deny this was a perfect day for it, but Digweed had watched the thing inflate, waxing huge above the Bonville Acres over the last couple of days: oh no, he could never be persuaded to perch in a glorified picnic hamper with no more between his feet and the surface of the earth than miles of thin air.

Now, he makes a bunch of knuckles over the head of his stick and hunches forward to follow the progress of the contraption. Despite the decline of his body and the inconvenient binding of his joints, Digweed's eyes and ears remain sharp. He sees an arm spread in a sweeping motion, hears a laugh of exuberance as the apparatus tacks out across the blue, toward Marshall's Wood, the Coley Strands and the sea. He can see Geoffrey standing still, gazing ahead, and his father gestures this way and that, Digweed smiles and fondly imagines the enthusiasm, the windy explanations, so typical of the man. And there's a buzzard he catches out of the corner of his eye, coasting above the balloon, maybe curious as to what this thing could be, barging through its element. But, of course, it's only scanning familiar territory, and soon enough sweeps earthward, curving round and under the illogical balloon, to score its kill from the heart of Marshall's Wood.

When the balloon has drifted far away and Digweed can no longer make out details he rests back on the bench for a moment, closes his eyes and nudges the old dog, who has lain down again, in the flank with the ferrule of his stick. 'Well then, old girl, it's time you and me went in for a bite' The old collie drags its rear end off the grass, shakes and stares. 'Neither of us have got long to go, what a pair we make, eh?' says Mr Digweed, moving off in no particular hurry toward the respectable bulk of Herton House.

Wild Garlic
12th March 1875: What I'm trying to do, gradually, is improve my writing style and I was looking through my desk the other day (to see if it had improved naturally through practice) and there it was plain as day, lying on the floor having slipped out from between the leaves of a very old notebook. 'Life on the Ocean Wave' by Jane Digweed. I wonder what father made of that one! Such a *tour de force* I still can't

bear to throw it away. There I'll be, years on, in my dotage (old Mrs Trelease who used to have the school) sitting quietly with this drawing and letting memory flesh it out. I will hear again the steady boom of breaking surf, the chattering of herring gulls, and recall sweet gormless Jago in all his glory levelling his first class member like a cannon across acres of flat sand – the cormorants ranged upon it (or 'shags' I should say) are fine evidence, if I may say it myself, of my own fertile wit (though it would appear that I shall always have to be happy with fertility only of wit). So what happened to George? It must be nine years since I last saw him. I hope the wastes of Canada to which Mr Digweed banished him are treating him well. ~~I fear sometimes that Geoffrey might~~ Come on Jane, use paragraphs!

I don't know how he could but sometimes I worry that Geoffrey might find my notebooks and see this picture and others – but if he did could he really in his heart of hearts dislike them?

Yes! Nine years since I've seen Jago. I can only hope that age has not withered him, any of him! (nor custom staled his infinite variety – I have acquired a very old Shakespeare which I can only just read, it is part of my endeavour to improve, but does he not skirt around his subject too much, is he not tedious?). To talk of age, that affliction has caught up with Mr Digweed quickly enough: but how it has mellowed him! I notice lately he's allowed a cat to befriend him! A cat! I've seen him fondling it on his lap, talking to it in that silly way people save for babies and pets. But he always revelled in his hatred of the creatures, booting the farm cats about and cursing their kittens and their greed (there was one old tabby he called 'Allguts' and shied windfall apples at it!). And that old dog trails about after him. He's gone from Lord High Hater Of Pets to Saint Francis Of Assisi, with animals and birds as his brothers and sisters! It will not be long before pigeons will perch on his shoulders and blackbirds eat out of his hand. But I must not be unkind and blame him for getting a bit soft in his old age. Best not to complain. He's seen us all through childhood and he never ever said a single word to me about my sketchbooks (though we both know what we both know). He's quite a remarkable man in his way. Mr Hammond (Trusty) and his men (some Carnal, some sub-Carnal, some Trusty) who are building the tennis court seem quite fond of him (but would they say if they weren't?) Matty (Super-Carnal) says: 'to be honest Mr Digweed's a bit off-putting, tis like having the boss breathing down your neck'. But even he will admit to liking my father for 'a nice enough old chap'. At least, says Matty, he don't tell you what he thinks ought to be done, they's the worst by a long way'.

15th March 1875: Matthew is four or five years younger than me and he already has one child and his wife is expecting another! He tells me that father's opened up the outhouse for the men, storage apparently, did it on his own. Perhaps he was afraid of what might still be in there, I must go

16th March 1875: That's it! 'I must go' That's all I wrote! Where must I go? I have completely forgotten. Geoffrey must think I'm desperate. I have to make sure he finishes off in me at least twice a week. Just in case the unexpected happens. I must have had absolutely nothing else to do, but this morning before I got up I found myself making all these calculations of the type I make in the dairy but instead of milk, I became involved (of all things!) in reckoning up the amount of male seed I have taken in over the last ten years. Can you believe it? I was so astonished at the results of my mental arithmetic that I had to confirm it on paper, I was here at the desk at the first crack of dawn scribbling away. So, according to my figures, working on the basis of a mean five dollops (or teaspoons) a week (that is twice with Geoffrey then three times, over a week, with other or others) then the resultant amount were it gathered together is roughly equal to almost three gallons (imagine three demijohns on a shelf full of the stuff!) But there's Still No Children! Definitely must be me, can't be Geoffrey. He's said nothing, my husband, bless him. My class at school, children, so simple. Motherhood. Having babies. Year after year. The world is full of children growing.

23rd March 1875: There are more examples of the mellowing of my esteemed father, mother has returned to the dairy! This morning there she was, as large as life, sleeves up, working! Never said anything, just appeared. We all have a good joke, and mother still has a sharp but tactful tongue, she is never hurtful or sarcastic, everyone likes her. She can rest from her role as Lady of the Manor (at least in the mornings) at which I must say she excels. I realise now that it's a long time since I've been very near her, we haven't had a lot to do with each other in recent years. But she brightens everything with her humour, I feel as if I haven't seen her since I was a child, when she 'made allowances', but now between us and Granny Hammond who's been here since the dawn of time we can make the young girls blush, although I have to be somewhat careful in case anything (so to speak) slips out. Suddenly, we're working and japing around at the expense of our men folk and I suspect it was ever so for all the women who have ever lived in this place at any time – perhaps even when it was a castle as Arthur says it was. Was I was too serious about the place, my knowledge half-learned?

10th April 1875: Mother and I had a laugh this morning about father's apparent conversion to the cause of cats. 'Ah yes' said mother 'My husband! That staunch enemy of anything feline, that keen drowner of kittens, that hurler of apples and swedes, even flinging a fork of dung at the most innocent of kittens and now what do we see but him, William Digweed of Herton House, clucking fondly over a black and white farmyard moggie!' Then she told me she'd be happy to live in the old house! None of us Digweeds will ever be 'refined', all we have is money. When the final accounts are read, we're no more or less than farmers. By the way, I have given up trying to improve my writing style, it doesn't need improving for what I have in mind. I shall leave it as it is. I hate paragraphs.

Later: Taking stock of my family:

<u>Father</u> bless him is wandering quietly through his dotage and has tired of airs and graces.

<u>Mother</u> still fit as a fiddle, sees a gap in Mr Digweed's armour, returns to being a farmer's wife.

<u>Myself</u> would rather lose the company of mile upon mile of county snobs than give up a quarter inch of my independence.

<u>The Boys</u> John is Mister Agriculture (a dedicated farmer, can talk of nothing else), Charlie is Mister Law (committed to his career, no time for anything else, largely absent in our capital city).

Which leaves the only harbingers of success, Betsy and Becca, or <u>Elizabeth and Rebecca</u> as I should say, their twin selves so recently emerged from the grooming of various educational institutions. I sound resentful, jealous even. This is not so, even though my sisters have grown pretty, and no less socially presentable (I'm coming to realise they are famous throughout the county, people will say: 'Oh yes, Mrs Trelease of course, the elder sister of the misses Digweed' as if I was some kind of forerunner, the first try that preceded the real success). They are still handsome and brown-eyed like me but have none of my bulk and colour; they have father's nose but without the pronounced hook, just a quite subtle angularity that I have heard called 'aquiline'. They do not walk but rather 'deport themselves', their skin is pale and smooth, their hands soft and tiny. Indeed they are perfect. It is acknowledged that they will go far. It is typical of them that even here in my private book, they get pages and everyone else a line or two. As I am becoming older (twenty–seven to be exact, an unthinkable age) I'm afraid my deportment has become somewhat adjusted from the ideal, at times I think I've developed a slight swagger, and my skin was always on the sanguine side. Oh, my sisters will go far. But there are roads down which they will never venture, to their own detriment. Their suitors, the tennis fiends (a new classification: Bandit) one is offish and weedy, the other has predatory teeth and cheekbones like beggar's knees ('the other', that's what Jago called it). Neither of them are 'sympathetic' and I know what I mean by this, no one else would. I am drawn to men by simple recognition, I know in a trice whether or not they'll give me pleasure, and neither of those two (not to say they won't eat their fill, given half a chance) is driven by hunger. But then my sisters, God bless them, would not entertain any idea of losing themselves. But I mean to. I shall 'lose myself' one of these days. I shall ride until I don't know where I am and live off nothing but sweet soft fruit and the thin air of paradise.

12th April 1875: Reading my last entry, written in the middle of the night, its tone would indicate that I don't like my sisters. This is not true. They were a true gift from God, my two lovely sisters: I cared for them when they were young as the eldest daughter must. I love them truly, as I must. It is just that I fear them not being happy in their lives.

3rd May 1875: Great white swathes of ramsons today in Marshall's Wood. I drew in potent draughts of it, walking the horse. Another summer coming, another life.

8th May 1875: Strange happenings today. I think I died and came back to life. I had seen Geoffrey and my father-in-law set off on their balloon excursion (wild horses would not drag me into that apparatus!) and I went off again to the dappled woods. A glorious blue morning! Matty goes into Rafton on Saturdays, and he's on his way back by mid-afternoon. We got started quietly enough. His breath was a little sharp with cider, he was fumbling and muttering, slow and methodical with his tongue. I was flat on my back, staring through the fresh green canopy of beech, so sleek and young and sappy, at an impossibly beautiful sky. I was in a delicious state of weakness, travelling nowhere, gawping at nothing. Matty was sometimes probing deep and stopping altogether right up inside (it was going nowhere for me, too slow, far too slow, a long moment of going nowhere). And then everything disappeared for a long time. There were dreams, inside me, of blind rhythm and I was in a place full of sky where nothing was surprising but anything could happen, where everything was mixed up with everything else. I was nowhere at all. I was just a pulse. My eyes saw nothing but they were open. I, Jane Trelease, was the dreamer, but I was any woman, with woman's insides and this woman for some reason was giving birth to a handspan's length of iron bar, pushing it out of her but it was too late and she felt it explode and melt.

I woke, ages later, naked as before, hot and greedy for air, everywhere was bathed in the scent of garlic, my legs were spread and thrusting like a swimmer's, my voice was appealing to the saviour by name from very far away and a dog was panting. A dog! My face bristled with points of fire, my head was skewed over, I was grinning fiercely at stems of bracken fern. My eyes focussed and stared crosswise at a mass of ramsons, ferns and campion, my breathing eased and I ran my tongue round the back of my front teeth over and over. So I came back to life, there were still teeth. And the dog? No dog but poor Matty. I gazed at him in wonder. Of course, I was here, still beneath him, he looked strangely hard and distant as if he didn't know me, I had left him on his own, he was still working, but I was weak and longed for rest, I tried to bring him back by searching his chest and his face with the tips of my fingers, his eyes flicked open suddenly and straightaway I slid my knuckles down under his belly, ~~found a horn that I forked with two fingers until it blew.~~ (This is too bad!) and trapped the snake with my two spread fingers until it kicked and stopped. How many times? I don't know. I was lost so utterly in the fragrance of garlic and perspiration and the smell of friction and seed, I turned away from Matty, exhausted, and fell asleep with his knees in the back of mine and his downy chest on the blades of my back. Then I must have reached true oblivion, beyond caring, deep in the woods, miles from anywhere, naked, and asleep! When I woke (again waking, from sleep?) my legs were wide again and he was leaning on one arm staring at me and exploring me with two fingers. Matty is a fine man, fair like Geoffrey but much hairier. The thatch on his chest is dense but very pale, braiding thick and honey-coloured as it runs down to his groin. I smile because I know it's all for me, the thing (I'm going to improve my vocabulary, for I have a plan) up-ended from a mane as copious as the hair on his head. There's a finer weave of down on his shoulder blades that I catch with my fingers as he rolls onto me and feeds it in, this tool handle, this flagpole. When the balloon floats into view, a perfect bulb of stretched silk strangely festooned with ropes, my eyes have already glazed over and a momentum is gathering that cannot be stopped. My God, yes, the balloon! And there was a hawk dropping out of the sky near us, and the small fearful cry of a young coney. I couldn't tell Matty, though my mouth was open, for he was oblivious. I was in a state of shock so calm that I heard my own breathing in the shell of Matty's ear, my tongue travelled round the backs of my teeth again and I wondered how long this can all last. The base of the 'basket' containing my husband and father-in-law drifted across my vision, tiny under the huge dome, Matty said something that sounded like 'where's the sun?'. I was utterly utterly helpless. I can't remember if I heard their voices, but I was sure Arthur had seen me, his face was there, at the edge of the basket, and his eyes. Meanwhile, the other Jane (I'll call her Jane Digweed), the one whose body stretches away below my neck, has gone crabwise for the man and he has half of her arse in each hand. They find, Jane Digweed and the man, that so docked together, if she pushes up and he bears down, they are a fine physical equation, a lesson in balance and she has only to make the most subtle of movements, as if her fanny is the mouth of a grazing fish, and she is made to succumb, to tolerate such a series of scandalously protracted waves of pleasure that the passage of the balloon, and Mrs Trelease, are forgotten entirely and Matty grunts an abrupt finale, fires his shot with such a lunge that our reciprocal geometry unravels in seconds. We collapsed, of course, in gales of laughter and there really was a balloon, for I saw it vanish over the trees out of the corner of my eye. When I told Matty he said ballocks. As I write, I still have tiny shards of him under my fingernails.

9th May 1875: Strange conversation with Arthur today. Of course he saw us, how could he not? I think we understand each other. How much of life is compromise, so that people can live together? Yesterday's account is more or less true. I think I could write something of some length about what I know, a book with paragraphs, but who on earth would publish such scandalous work? I cannot answer that question but I can answer another. Who on earth would read it? Everyone. Secretly.

In The Lock-Up

A series of quite vicious and blustery showers had seen the men rained off, so Matty Hammond and his father stood amongst the debris of the half-finished tennis court discussing technical matters. The world of green things was sluiced pleasantly clean, dried by a strong breeze, polished by bright sunlight, but the sky had not lost its metallic cast of grey and it was not especially warm, considering that the Hawthorns on the motte were in full flower. As they talked of time, profit and loss, etcetera the two men shivered.

'There'll be more yet' said John Hammond 'twill slow us up'

'We're not doin so bad, father' said Matty 'and there iddn that much else to go on to at present'

'But I've told Bill Digweed it'll be done afore the middle of June'

'Blame the weather, father, the weather' And the weather it was that forced them headlong into the outhouse where they stood in the doorway with folded arms as the latest bout of rain rattled like chains in the leaves and poured down the side of the motte in rivers. So heavy was the cloudburst that they retreated inside, tetchily moving a clutter of shovels, rakes, iron bars and wheelbarrows. Still the rain hissed in the tall grass outside and it was not long before it was running purposefully down the inner walls of the outhouse and pooling on the floor.

'Bugger me nothing much is gwain keep dry in yer' said the elder Mr Hammond, regretting the time and money spent in fitting new hinges. He was a man who hated enforced idleness, and stood with his hands in his pockets, casting his eyes about, desperate for interest. 'There ent much room in yer' he said 'I wonder what twas used fer?'

'I think it was the lock-up when this were a castle' said Matty.

'Nah! Tis too small!'

'Twas only a small castle!' said Matty 'or at least that's what Mister Trelease reckons anyway and he knows a bit about the place'

'Well, I shouldn't want to be locked up in yer for lung – they'd soon have my confession! Smelly damp old place. How long does ee reckon it's been yer then?'

'Seven or eight hunderd years, so he says'

'Bugger me! As lung as all that!' Mr Hammond cleared his throat 'I didn't know you'd bin talking to Arthur Trelease'

'More his daughter-in-law, really. Twas she that told me'

'Didn't know you'd bin talkin with Jane Trelease neither – but iddn er a lovely maid? Not at all stuck up like some of em, there was plenty of em in Rafton wouldn't have minded waking next to er each morning'

'Her sisters is better-looking' said Matty, hoping for a change of subject.

'Yes and no' Matty had never discussed women with his father before, he wanted the conversation to go elsewhere, but then '... the sisters is fine girls, but they'm like summin out of a book, you know what I mean, sort of untouchable. But Mrs Trelease, she's one of us, to be honest, Matt, er can still make the blood bang round my body and I ent never spoke a word to er in me life'

Matty, becoming increasingly alarmed at his father's candour, was saved from more of it by the sound of feet plashing nearby and the appearance of Arthur Trelease himself, running through the downpour with an oilskin thrown over his head, bearing down on them like a mad monk. Both men stood aside and let him rush in between them: 'Goddamit! Forgive me Lord .... got caught right out on Bonneville's, had to go out there to pick up this here oilskin that I left out there this afternoon.' Throwing the thing off his head, he shook it out of the doorway and hung it on a spade handle.

'Just the man' said Mr Hammond. 'Matty and me was just discussing this place, he reckons twas a lock-up. He says you know a bit about the history, sir'

'A lock–up!' Mr Trelease sneezed and shivered, and was immediately into his subject. 'Well now, you might be right, It had crossed my mind. Perfect for it no doubt, to be honest with you, Matthew, I've not much idea what it was, I'm surprised it's lasted this long. It's like no one can bring themselves to get rid of it, must have been here hundreds of years. Maybe it was where they put people who'd been so bad that they needed to be confined without windows, without nothing. Outside's the remains of them iron angle things like you'd slot a length of timber through to stop anybody getting out from inside. I think you may well be right!' .... *Now this young man as I see it, is sure to be the back of that writhing beast in the woods, his hair says it ...Jane would see him as 'beautiful'. He's like Geoffrey in some ways but he's all physical. I saw him there, his broad shoulders and back, a white hand on each scapula, the narrow waist and buttocks that were still. She, Jane, the upside-down why, was doing the moving. I saw a lot more than I want to remember. Damn it ... it won't go out of my head ... do I want it to?* 'There's one thing for sure, whoever was in here in winter wouldn't last long, with the floor like a goddam pond'

'Did you enjoy your flight last weekend, Mister Trelease?' Matthew had realised, during the week, from gossip, that there was a balloon as she had said and, of course, any passengers would have had a perfect view of all of him and parts of Mr Trelease's daughter-in-law. Too late, he wondered whether he should have opened his mouth at all.

...This is a decent lad I'm sure ...'Excellent, thankyou! A marvellous experience! I was only frightened a wee bit. No better way to see the world!' ... *But I can't get that construct out of my mind! ...A man and a woman in convex tension like a bridge that crosses a river in a single span, so perfect! Mr Brunel would appreciate it. Forgive me Mrs Trelease, I should be mortified I know but I'm past sixty and still learning ...*

Mr Hammond, who likes to be busy, is still casting his restless eye round the place. He has his pocket knife out and is poking the timbers suspiciously. 'Twill collapse forlung, this yer place. Should be shored up. If it goes, I reckon the whole side of the mound'll slip down with it. Needs bracing with strong elum. Should I raise it with Mister Digweed d'you think?'

Raise it? With Mr Digweed? 'I shouldn't think he'd want to spend money on it, couldn't you just fill it in?'

'Just as cheap to put in some new timbers I'd say, two men one day job done. Think how long it would take to fill it in, and look at the water running down in yer, twould wash the whole lot away and you'd be back where you started'

'To be honest with you Mr Hammond, the most likely outcome is that nothing at all will be done' Mr Trelease coughs and turns to the younger Mr Hammond. 'And how is your wife, Matthew, I believe she is carrying your second'

'Very fit, sir, three month to go, thankyou for asking'

'You're a lucky fellow' says Mr Trelease ... *and a hairy-backed one! I see it foaming out of the open neck of that shirt, the same hair! ...*

There is a flurry of small talk amongst the three men as the rain seems to ease, then it returns more vigorous than ever. Their chances of going their separate ways again diminish. Mr Hammond Senior continues with his desultory probing of the timbers, Matthew has picked up a spade and is turning the point in the wet ground without enthusiasm or interest. Mr Trelease stands in the entrance with an arm braced on each side of the door frame gazing wistfully out at the sheets of rain. A naturally contented man, he feels strangely disturbed, he finds himself envious of the lives of others, of the lives of the young. And not only is there the obvious and relentless passage of time, there is his own reasonableness. Ranging in his mind back over the generations of Treleases which have preceded him, he sees a succession of easy-going genial men, taking everything for granted. Had his wife not died out in Canada, they would surely have had more children, it's that word 'child' and that word 'children' ... simple words that belie the complex nature of what they describe ... *It must be her, Jane, it can't be Geoffrey. When we spoke at dinner time the other day I thought it was simply the one, but there must have been years of it. Poor Jane is barren. Poor me. I saw the flesh–knot unravel before I lost sight of it altogether and, you know the bad thing is I wish Geoffrey had been staring down, I wish he'd seen what I saw and I had not seen it! But he was looking the other way, as ever.*

'Mr Trelease! I think tis stopping. Home for a bite, I reckon'

'Of course, Mr Hammond. Very sorry. I think I drifted away there – I must be away. Thankyou Matthew' Mr Trelease takes his oilskin from the younger Hammond and the three men emerge from the outhouse into the sharp evening light. Water drips quietly from the leaves of sycamores and ash into the black earth.

'Best thing' said Mr Hammond Senior 'would be a good solid door on it and shut it right up'.

'Definitely' said Mr Trelease, watching the father and his son plodding back down the garden toward the house. *A well-built fellow for sure.*

'Of course!' said Mr Digweed with quite sudden emphasis when Mr Hammond's suggestion was put to him 'shut the blessed thing up fer good!'

CHAPTER SEVEN

Bandit Country

There was a round quickthorn tree, all on its own, standing on a slope, and a handful of starlings was flung from it, and the breeze seemed to throw them all about the white sky in leaping random shapes, and snatch them back as suddenly. A momentary distraction, watched by everyone, remarked on by no one. My Lord de Bonville has of course abandoned any hope of ever reaching Bristol, let alone further. We have ended up making our way back, tails between our legs, no excuses. We ride in single file across the same high downs we traversed a few months before; the weather is grey and windy. We are retreating back to Marshburgh, where we will sit out the worst of Winter, and it will cost My Lord a pretty penny. We, like the king himself, left the siege at Gernsea unfinished. Too many things went wrong there. Bristol was to have been our muster point, the base of my Lord of Gloucester, and we were expecting to be fighting northward again near the Wye River but my Lord de Bonville (I'm sure he is right, everyone more or less agrees) thinks there is no chance now of getting there in any useful formation. Several men are ill or wounded – my own left arm is useless, I must wear it strapped across my chest between two lengths of hazel!

We live on snared and slingshot rabbits and whatever of God's winged creatures can be removed from their element by the Welshmen who seem as good with the sling as with the bow. We spent six or seven quite pleasant nights (has it been the only highlight of our journey?) camped near the saltlands not far from Gernsea preparing to travel, when great numbers of geese who spent their days loafing and grazing around the marshy pools flew in each evening to forage in the old harvest fields and enough could be picked off by a salvo of arrows to feed almost everyone. And this each night! Which proves the goose is as brainless as they say.

'We'll gain more returning by way of Marshburgh' said my Lord de Bonville 'we'll see what luck can be had, whose cause we can join'. He looked unhappy until his face brightened and he said, thinking of the story of the King of Sweden 'I think our goose may well be cooked as far as Gernsea is concerned'. A weak enough attempt at a joke but amid the general disappointment and poverty of opportunity, amid the sheer fucking boredom of our situation it raised quite a laugh. It reminds me now of how fond I had grown of Alured's crude wit, how I actually missed the daily exchanges with him back at Gernsea, even though one of his mounted men broke my arm and would like to have killed me. But like everyone else, I had no choice but to leave, partly because I am nobbled and ... besides ... why differ from everyone else? I too must be committed to my own gain, above all other causes. As my Lord de Bonville rightly said, I can do no wrong by keeping my faith with him, is he not an honest man?

We are returning with a depleted party: a few less of the common men, Jean Villon dead and my Lord Pynchon, convinced he can break the siege, paid de Bonville and de Ravelin a sum of coin for certain of their men (though de Bonville would not part with his archers). The girl Johanna rides along on her donkey and speaks little. We still have two prisoners, the comical Breton knight and a morose de Palmere, who hates the girl to the point of obsession. He is convinced, though she denies it with her bearing, that she did his wife some harm. If he were not bound I'm sure he would kill her.

The nearer we draw to Marshburgh, the more restless she becomes. We shall approach it without revisiting the ruins of Daxworthy. De Ravelin, mad as ever, has give the town the name 'Broken Arrow' – I think I can see why, but of course de Bonville is baffled. The girl still rides close to Canteloupe, though she does not hold quite the same sway over him as she did. Is that how it should be said? Hold sway? Since he has become less thick with her, some of his old self (which I must say I preferred) has returned but he is still an abstainer as are we all, through necessity. La Johanna has acquired a cape (from where I can't say) which covers her entirely and she rides side saddle with her head bowed under a deep hood, like an abbess. I rarely come across her but I did this morning, hood thrown back she leant against a tree retching, I moved to help her and she looked at me, smiled and waved me away. Her eyes were large and empty, her skin paler than ever. She frightened me, I was glad I could not help and moved on quickly. As we finally approach the town on an afternoon of mizzle in early December, she will not enter the gates, choosing to lodge outside the walls.

I have a few privileges, since I still pass as a sort of factotum to my Lord de Bonville. I am able to warm my back before Roger de la Moule's hearth in his privy rooms whilst he and my lord sit facing each other rather gravely across an impressive oak board. It would appear that we have an unhappy, almost angry, de la Moule who cannot accept the death of his vassal Swain, and he is perturbed enough by his recent experiences, where land and holdings have been attacked, where he has had to part with vast sums of money in order to rid himself of the attentions of his neighbours. He protests that Swain and de Palmere were two of his most trusted. He mutters about the murder of gentlemen becoming commonplace. However, when de Bonville offers him assistance in his difficulties with his neighbours, this seems to cheer him, and my lord explains to him the circumstances of the demise of Swain and the capture of de Palmere.

'Daxworthy?' de la Moule runs his hand over his bare scalp several times, as though a rich growth of new hair has suddenly appeared 'there's no *girl* like you have described that lives there. There's the old ones, their daughter and her man, her brother and the two young boys. No one else. Oh yes, of course I know it has been ravaged, my men have told me. They say there was not a human trace there, just fresh graves – dug by your men no doubt – and dead animals in the fields. But this girl – blonde you say, thirteen or fourteen – lives nowhere that anyone knows'

'You know of her then, my Lord?' said de Bonville.

'Of course I know *of* her ... everyone here knows *of* her. And if these deeds were done at Daxworthy, you can be sure she carried them out'.

Though etiquette says I should keep my mouth shut, I hear myself shouting across the room from the hearth: 'she? but there was fire, everything was burned!' De Bonville looks sharply at me but makes no sign to quiet me. 'Was it *she* who pushed a heavy cart and crushed a grown man against a tree, did *she* throttle children and leave those people ... the old ones you call them ... slashed and cut, one with his head clean off? This girl Johanna did all that? Was that before or after she raped herself? '

'Enough now, Ralphe!' De Bonville bangs the board with his flat hand.

'Awful things you describe, young man, awful things ... and she is calling herself Johanna? Well, well. And pregnant I suppose, her permanent state, she is *always* up the duff and no one knows what happens to the brats. We must be glad she is outside the walls, but she will come in if she fancies and she thinks no one will see her. She must go from here! You must take her away – though if you make good your promise, de Bonville, she will help you persuade my neighbours to be more neighbourly, no doubt of that. Now, though you may not think so, de Palmere and Swain are good men, lazy perhaps … er, small failings only …. they fear God as they should. I have known them for many years, they hold land not all that far from Daxworthy, they were not responsible for the carnage at Daxworthy, take my word. Now then, what's all this the young man says about rape? On whose evidence was the girl you call Johanna raped?'

'Her own' said de Bonville.

'Worthless' said de la Moule, with a little sniff.

'And the evidence of my own eyes. She chose William Canteloupe to hear her story, he will tell you better than I ….'

'She has many stories, de Bonville. You tell it, we need not trouble monsieur Canteloupe'

'Very well. When she was found it was clear she had been violated by many men before being left to die, on her back, in a ditch, her skirts still thrown up, her legs still spread. There was much blood on her thighs and around her coynt. She seemed lifeless but after we had taken her back to Daxworthy and were committing her with the others, she came on a sudden back to life. She has a gift of sight and brings luck'

'One moment sir, hold your horses, too much all at once' Here de la Moule gave a little laugh. 'Very clever you know, that comrade of yours Jean de Ravelin … broken arrow, very clever .. I beg your pardon' At this point food and drink were brought into the room and set down, the conversation continued.

'There are many' de la Moule was saying 'Monsieur de Palmere amongst them, who would find your claim that she brings luck quite bitterly amusing. And you say that she came back to life. I am not surprised by that. She is surely a witch. Blood between her legs? How do you know it was her own blood? It could have been the blood of any one of the corpses you say you buried – it could have been beast's blood!'

I said then, out of turn: 'with respect my Lord, the beasts that lay in the fields had no mark on them, I think you are too suspicious!'

'Then how did they die – without a mark?'

'Ralphe, Ralphe' de Bonville looked sharply at me 'interrupt again and you must go. So how long have you known of this girl Sir Roger?'

'All my life'

'So you know her for a witch? Never ages, I suppose, if you've always known of her. Has she been with Devils?'

'Many say so. Men of authority, and others such as John de Palmere whose wife was taken away from him'

'Well, sir, I have seen her entirely naked and have seen her whole body and each part of it washed clean after she had regained life, and I admit there were no abusive signs around her female parts but neither were there any diabolical marks and so fine and light is her hair they would certainly have been seen. I cannot share your view of the young lady (here de la Moule gave another of his little sniffs) … however, to show appropriate goodwill I shall release de Palmere and pay whatever monies are due for his comrade. I can perhaps accept that those two men were not the perpetrators, but the girl identified them and she *was* terrified of them'

'Ha! you must believe me, sir, there is nothing she fears! But I am very pleased we have agreed an accommodation. Your help with my neighbours will be compensation enough for Monsieur Swain since his holding is one of those I was forced to relinquish'

'There is one thing I can confirm' said de Bonville 'whether or not she was raped, she is carrying a child'

Now Jeanne, so far away at Herraton, had faded from my mind a little. The girl who saw the stars as windows, or was it pinholes? She must be swelling now, a part of the way through her childbearing more than half

'Ha well! No good will come of that issue, rest assured' De la Moule sounded surprisingly bitter, though his face remained as bland as ever.

'Sir!' said de Bonville, suddenly brisk. 'We need a change of subject! Was my man Martin ever seen again?'

'Oh, no. Never. I'm afraid'

'There's one who won't miss him eh Ralphe?'

'We were expecting' continued de la Moule 'to find a cadaver on the shore by a bend of the river where such things often are left by the tide but there was no sign of him. Either he was swept out to sea or he still lives. If the ... er ... latter is the case, since he will be hanged if he appears here again, he may have joined up with any one of the groups of malefactors who seem of late to be breeding out there' He makes a sweeping gesture with his hands. *Out there.* He said it in the same way as he had before our departure months ago, in the same reptilian way.

'Well' said de Bonville 'we shall go *out there* very soon (at this point he winked at me across the room and I was forced to turn and admire a wall hanging depicting browsing deer and distant greyhounds) and perhaps we'll run into said Monsieur Martin, although for his sake I hope we don't. Tis a pity about young Ralphe's arm ... I say, Ralphe, you'll have to slap the horse's arse with your good hand and stand back whilst the villain swings!'

A week or so later, I was allowed to ride out with Canteloupe and a party of de la Moule's mounted men along the north bank of the river for reconnaissance. I had to give my word to de Bonville to stay away from trouble (on the grounds of impending fatherhood and disablement). It is decided apparently on the information of a whelkman, a trusty long in the pay of Roger de la Moule, to go inland. 'Into bandit country, Ralphe!' said a cheerful Canteloupe 'you stay to the rear now, or my Lord'll have my ballocks for breakfast!' and he canters away to the van. I would say his own breakfast was of the liquid variety. The whelkman says there is a camp of villains set into old quarry workings on the sheltered side of the wild bluff we descended when we first arrived here from Cleeve.

We follow a broad shallow stream inland as trees close in and the water narrows and turns to fresh. We gather on a stony strand where the river cuts into the meadows when it is high and as the horses drink, Canteloupe tells a long joke involving pins and chickens. There are acres of good meadow grazing between the water and the trees, in normal times cattle could stay out all through but these are not normal times. Everyone houses their animals now.

The way up toward the down and the old quarry is wider and more breathable than the acres of untouched woodland, single file beaten tracks and sheep trails. But there are several deep holes and gullies and de la Moule's men walk their beasts with caution. Soon we are in timber again around the quarry rim, creeping tidily on the qui vive through what appears to be silence but is in fact a riotous whispering of leaves, a crackling of dead twigs beneath the footfalls of stalkers, each liquid burst of the robin's song calls up a sliding blade. When a cough sounds loud, very close, an arrow goes to it straight away, and three flustered ewes bounce away through the brambles. No one laughs.

Then a log as long as a man swings in from nowhere to the front of the column, at great speed, lashed to a rope. One man is unhorsed and he takes another with him and the horses go down as well, if it were a game of keels a good strike would be cheered. There is a chaos of running men and horses cantering and kicking their heels, and everyone breaks away in all directions, as though thrown off the log as it pitches back and forth, striking trunks and spinning. Finally it comes to rest, hanging quietly, well lashed and balanced. 'Mother Of God' I hear Canteloupe curse 'what you might call crude but efficient, eh?'

The man hit first was stone dead before he hit the ground, the other stood like a dog on all fours gasping for breath but seemed otherwise uninjured. 'This is what it's like' two of de la Moule's old hands are humping the corpse onto its quieted horse 'they won't fight in the open, can't say as I blame em, they're clever bastards. See ...' He pointed upward and away where men in motley of green could be seen limbing like squirrels through the trees. As the winded soldier went off back to Marshburgh to administer the corpse, we stood two men down. And soon after, another went down writhing in pulses of blood as an arrow passed through his neck. So a charge had to made out of the woods to open ground before the level of casualties meant total retreat. What happened to me was that I lingered – there was difficulty with my rein gear, and complications with my slinged arm, I was absorbed in my own fumbling, cursing the cack-handed way I was forced to do the simplest things, and there was Canteloupe, helmetless, beckoning me but his arm swept right over his head and he disappeared. I was dragged from my horse and lying on my back, pain much worse than anything my arm could offer skewered into my side, into my very guts, and there was a mailed body slumped across me, which strangely comforted and warmed me until it was pulled off. Then I was in agony and slung over my saddle, I knew this was a decline which could only end in death.

Later, voices hum all around me and I'm shivering on a board, I turn my head and see piles of blood-soaked swaddling all over the floor; even after the bleeding is finally staunched, the sword that pierced me, it's spirit was still inside me like an auger of twisting fire. Only after a few hours (or days) did this pain subside to a monotonous agony. I could turn my head the other way and see the pious corpse of the man who had been the first to stop the log. But oddly enough, things were not all bad, oh no, the consequences of the disastrous foray into the old quarry were far from catastrophic, almost cheering. I was discussed and given two choices. One to stay at Marshburgh in relative comfort and hope to recover or, two, survive the journey back to Herraton where my wife would care for me.

I told de Bonville that though he was indeed fine-looking he was not my wife. I was desperate to see Jeanne, who I had known for years but hardly knew at all, who was carrying the child, she must care for me: or at least when my soul departed, she would be there to guide it to God. I was forced to take only shallow breaths, movement was out of the question. Yet it was agreed (such kindness!) that I should be tied in a chair – yes, *tied in a chair!* – and *carried* back to Herraton. De Bonville was determined that I should die at home or at least on the way home. It was possible that I might catch a last glimpse of Herraton before the Lord called me in. There was at least a chance of that. I was vaguely aware of whispered discussions from which de Ravelin and four of his men emerged as my escorts. De la Moule insisted that we take the girl Johanna.

'If that is indeed her name, which I doubt. My advice is to get shot of her as soon as you can'.

'It's a hard man who can abandon a carrying mother' I heard de Bonville say.

When it came to the girl, de la Moule was without pity. 'If it is born alive' he said 'leave the little bastard on the hillside and, if it isn't, then Glory be to God'

Oblivion

Autumn that year was long and unseasonably warm, the leaves seemed reluctant to leave their branches, even though the sun passed lower each day as the season wore on. St Michael's Eve (when Ralphe was due to come home though she knew he wouldn't) was a golden, rosy day which felt at last like the very end of summer. Madame Mareschal and Jeanne are working long into the afternoon with some of the younger girls, hoeing, raking and firming, setting out cabbage plants between the fruit trees for the spring. And Jeanne, as she shuffles along like an old dog on her hands and knees making holes with the stick, is distracted for the moment by visions of her absent husband. She sees him before her, leggy and sleek as a girl, fine-haired, blond. To her mother-in-law she says:

'But is he not simple as *simple*? One thing only on his mind'

Madame gives a little peal of laughter. 'Oh yes, that is Ralphe' she says 'and all other men'.

'I can look at him from outside, inside, upside down, as much as I like' says Jeanne 'and I swear there's nothing to him – I have plumbed the depths, and *rien d'autre*!'

'But my dear he is a young man'

She was really entertaining herself, of course she and Madame were talking at cross purposes. She was thinking how she loved Ralphe, how she had loved him years before her father let her know that an understanding had been reached with William Mareschal over her betrothal. It was not sex she was thinking of but Ralphe – *that* was the one thing on Ralphe's mind – Ralphe.

But then is Madame not right, the same could be said of all men whether or not you're talking about sex? There's a game they play (or played) to see how long they could go without speaking and she, Jeanne, always wins. It drives Ralphe to distraction. There was only *one* time when she ever lost the game: before they were married they would often make love in the dead of night on the rough ground outside the hall, and silence was essential. Jeanne drew in her lower lip with her teeth to keep her mouth shut and breathed heavily through her nose but on this occasion she couldn't keep her mouth shut. '*Oh ...*' she let slip twice '*oh, oh* just like that ... *oh, oh*' and he, Ralphe, stopped dead inside her and whispered in her ear 'did you say no?' and she said 'no'. So they laughed and laughed without a sound, gripping each other and shaking.

Oh the fool he is! So innocent! It is these little things she misses him for. And she finds she has no one else to talk to. And she misses him for his tenderness, despite what she says of him. 'It's like he's never seen a girl before' she said to her sister when she last saw her 'he's into everything like a little boy! He explores me, you know, with little ums and aahs – calls me little bird, and the very slightness of my bones excites him, he will run his finger along the curve of my foot and make these cooing sounds like a pigeon!' (Her sister, Maria, older but not yet married, lies on her back on the grass and squirms). 'But now' says Jeanne, suddenly 'he can do that with *any* whore he might come across in *any* place he finds himself! …. How much do I know him, Mary, how much, really? At least I was able to let him know for sure before he went off that he'll be a father soon – as if *that* or anything else can make him hurry back from my Lord de Bonville's war!'

'He'll be thinking of you, Jeanne, I'm sure'

'Thankyou for saying so, Mary, it's what sisters are for …. Oh dear, I'm so sorry … what an awful thing to say! It's well above a month now since he left … first crack of light in the sky he was up and ready, winter in the air, leaves looking a bit tired, just himself and a mule and a few bits of armour. And who knows if he'll be back this side of next Spring, the other side of Spring, or never. The begetter of this child inside me has just ridden off to I can't say where for I don't know how long. And he's completely on his own, travelling over wild country'.

'But you know he *has* to, Jeanne'

'And d'you know *where* he's to rendezvous with my Lord de Bonville? *Cleeve*! Of all the godforsaken places! If you ask me, my Lord de Bonville's becoming shady. What *is* he up to? Into what is he luring my innocent husband? What a fool I was, watching him disappear along the road to the high moor. I can see myself, hand faltering back to my side after his last wave, turning back to this ramshackle pretty little castle to face it alone'

'Oh you poor little thing …' croons Maria. 'Poor little baby' And they both laugh.

But she is not alone. There is her husband's mother. And what they find to do, Madame Mareschal and she, is work. All around Herraton they organise, superintend and labour. In such a place there's always something that needs doing somewhere, and they go about looking for it – and it works so well! Madame, a woman educated by priests, calls it Oblivion, which means forgetting. It's only at night that Jeanne has to acknowledge loneliness and call it so. They share the keys and the tallies, Jeanne has them one day, Madame Mareschal the next. They toil away from early in the morning until dusk, tilling their plots in the bailey themselves, tending the fowls and the fruit, and on days of rain they work on a huge *broderie* of Herraton for the wall, with the view of the sea.

Madame is determined, for they both know he will be gone a long time, to make sure Ralphe returns to order and efficiency. Not that he would recognise such a thing, jokes Madame, and nor would his father have done. They oversee the ploughing and the tending of the herd but since everyone knows it's not wise to upset a shepherd they leave the sheep to young Oswald. Madame is even talking of organising repairs to the fortifications, the old timbers on the outer rampart are far gone to rot, but there are few men who will do it. 'The world is something of a different place since Ralphe's grandfather built them fifty years ago' sighs Madame 'with forced labour you could get anything done. Guy de Bonville – or any other of old King Henry's men – will not be happy with the state of them'

Jeanne couldn't care less about the ramparts, and nor would Ralphe if he were here. Because the work is tedious, she becomes engrossed in the perfection of the holes she makes. Though the soil is naturally black and fine, it has been made rich with dung and straw, as she pushes in the whittled piece of thorn stick the sides remain entirely round. Out of obligation, she thinks she ought to have something to say to Madame about the ramparts, and she begins to rise from her knees and turn to her mother-in-law. The sun was lying close to the trees, low and intensely bright, straight into her eyes and, as she starts to speak, she raises her hand to shield them. 'I think' she says, wincing into the strong light, seeing only the shape of her mother-in-law in dark shadow 'I think ...' But she sinks back to her knees as though pierced and a pain like a sliver of wood burns into her. She still must avert her head from the sun, and she hears herself crying out far away, and something gives way inside her and gnaws its way to the outside, melting hot on her thigh. She finds herself back on all fours, staring in agony at the last hole she made, four inches deep, two inches in diameter, ready to receive its seedling. Perfect.

There never was a 'he' or a 'she'. She never saw *it* because Madame Mareschal dealt with *it* and said very little about *it* afterwards. The women told her she cried for Ralphe over and over. Madame said she was lucky to be alive at all and lucky that the poison didn't take her from them as well. 'Poison!' she cried 'Poison! Who would poison a little baby?' And Madame said 'no no my dear' that she had meant the poison and the bad blood that had got into her and driven the poor little soul to God, He must have wanted it that way, she said. Jeanne said: 'God *poisoned* me?' and Madame Mareschal told her to sleep in case the bad humours were still in her. And Jeanne would have asked God why He chose to fill her insides with griping bile but Madame's finger was between her lips and she was rubbing the sleeping powder on her teeth and when she slept there was Ralphe sitting in a chair outside in the world somewhere, he said Herraton many times but that was not all he said. She was so weak she could only envy him his easy chair.

It was a good sennight before she could bear the pain and sleep without the powder. Over and again, she saw Ralphe, but a different Ralphe, not so young. More like his father. There was a much older .... an old Ralphe in the woods sitting on a trunk beside her and he was speaking but his tongue was so long that it could and did reach down between her legs whilst his head was still next to hers. The tip of it wiggled its way into her and she cried and cried. Madame tended her well, always near, without her Jeanne would have died. When she came back, the first time she woke there was Madame cleaning the tears and sweat from her face with soft linen. Jeanne tells Madame that in her dream her late husband's tongue was over a yard long and before she can say how like a serpent it was, Madame is saying 'oh yes dear, I know what happened – it got so stretched over the years because all he used it for was licking the Bonville's arses'.

That was the first time in days that Jeanne laughed. And scarcely had the ring of laughter died away, almost as soon as she was up and about again, the man Jehan first appeared. He blew in with the breeze, travelling alone without baggage and sought what he called a 'position', begging Madame to employ him as our seneschal. Madame said she and Jeanne were coping well enough and we were not grand enough to have a seneschal. But he was a persistent man, saying he had done the job before on an estate up the country of a similar modest size; he mentioned *en passant* my lord de Bonville as though he was known to him. Whatever Madame said, she and her daughter-in-law were not coping *that* well and the services of a reliable steward would not go amiss. Apart from oblivion, there was another reason why Jeanne and Madame were working so hard: John Mareschal's old steward had died earlier in the year, before Ralphe left, and there was no-one to replace him. It was almost as though Jehan knew of this, though he could not possibly, only from Ralphe (when asked if he had come across Ralphe Mareschal, travelling with Guy de Bonville, he looked at the ground and seemed to speculate, then upward again and said with a level stare he feared he had not heard of such a young man).

So Jeanne and Madame Mareschal discussed the matter. The drive for oblivion was tiring them, there was no doubt of that. Madame was no longer young and Jeanne was still weak from the miscarriage, and a connection between long hours of work and that event could not be ruled out.

'But' said Madame 'he looks wild does he not? His hair! (which was dark and dry and bushy) And that hat! (which was battered and never left his head). And you can see he's been on the road a long while, Jeanne – he *looks* like a vagabond'.

'But *maman* anyone can fall on hard times, and he seems decent enough. If we pay him his wage, he will tidy himself up. You cannot expect a man down on his luck to dress like a king!'

'But don't you wonder Jeanne, why he is no longer steward on the estate he spoke of, which must be another de Bonville holding? I have questioned him on this and he told me he was tricked into making untrue declarations by a rival who had wanted his position and had been wrongly accused of falseness in his book-keeping. I will send someone in time to see if what he says is so, until then he could be useful to the men who will be working on the fortifications. We shall wait for Ralphe to come home, any decision should be his'.

The liking Jeanne took to Jehan at first seemed justified. He put real spirit into the work on the fortifications which until then had been patchy and half-hearted, the men were few and unwilling, but Jehan seemed to put spirit into them. It had been assumed he would be a labourer but before long he had taken charge, he had men out cutting timber at first light, he organised carts of stones to be rammed in behind the new stockades and the men seemed to work for him without stint.

At first, Jeanne was pleased to hear laughter and song on the air, the bustle of industry, she liked to go out and watch the work, for she was forced to rest as she recovered and spent long hours working indoors on the *broderie*. But gradually, she realised that the atmosphere was not as cheerful as it seemed. It sounded so, sure enough, but there was something unfriendly in the boisterousness, something *male*. And this was Jehan. The man she had seen as honest now had a confidence about him, she saw him now as crude and stocky, no charmer: and he had a way of looking at her that she wasn't happy about. Madame would laugh and click her tongue: 'all boys together, my dear, you know what they're like, Ralphe will know what to do with him when he comes back'. But Jeanne is thinking of the dream of Ralphe sitting in a chair, he couldn't move, he was helpless and she was helpless too, without him, without anyone.

It was not long before Jeanne developed an actual hatred of Jehan (if that was really his name). She found herself drawn, with a disgusted fascination, to watch him and 'his' men at their work. She saw him posing amongst them, making gestures with his arms and thrusting his hips to gales of wet laughter from the oafs. She came to think these antics were for her benefit, since he knew she was watching, but she could not catch him out, he was clever enough never to sneak looks in her direction. But he laughed with Madame and flattered her – Madame was clearly blind – and she such an experienced woman. When Madame says that Ralphe will know what to do with him, Jeanne assumes that what she means is he will know who 'Jehan' is for sure because he is fighting with Guy de Bonville. But it looks as though Madame intends to enjoy herself in the meantime.

As Jeanne works away quietly at the tapestry and early Autumn fades into the dank months of winter, she arrives at a solution, a way of satisfying an itch she has to humiliate Jehan. After a week of preparation, she walks in a leisurely way as she does on most days, over to the rampart for she knows he is standing on it with his back to her, making one of his imbecile gestures, tossing an invisible cock. She did not normally come this close and he, of course, had not seen her but some of the men had and were smirking. He was saying something like: 'what I wouldn't do to that if I got it up against a wall, what? Eh?'

One morning about a week before, Jeanne had stood down at the rampart early, before the men started work, and made calculations for a length of cord which she spun up from leftover yarn. Onto the end of this light cord she fixed a leather pocket into which she sewed a conker steeped in vinegar, especially selected for its weight. She had practiced with this makeshift weapon until she thought she had the precise speed and aim of its upward arc. So there she was, standing behind Jehan, who was so utterly absorbed in his storytelling and mime-fucking that he was unaware either of her or of the unease and amusement of his audience. He assumed, of course, they were laughing at his wit. But they could clearly see the young master's wife, in the flesh, working up the momentum of the sling by spinning it round and round, and *they* could see what was about to happen. They were agog. But not one of them alerted the storyteller to his fate.

'So young Denzil has her where he wants her' he is saying 'and he's got it in his hand stiff's a lance and is just about to ram it home when this fackin cat comes down out of the tree ...' And Jeanne has all the energy in the sling fully wound and is ready to hit the target with maximum force. Over weeks of observation, she knew just how the oaf stood: his legs were always half-akimbo, due partly to the themes of his stories and partly to the need to keep his balance on the rampart. '... A fackin cat, eh? Would you believe it? Come down right between them and dragged is claws over Denzil's cock' At that point the vitrified conker travelling at lethal speed makes a cleft in the centre of Jehan's scrotum with a sound like a closed fist and he falls like an ox. Jeanne walks away immediately, feeling a stunned silence at her back. Though she does not know it, she is not the only member of the Mareschal family in recent weeks to deal this former groom and aspiring steward's bollocks a crippling blow.

The First Homecoming

Even though the winter weather wasn't as bad as it could have been, it took all of a week to get to Mareschal's place at Herraton. The nights were clear and bitter cold, the days were sunny but never warm enough to steam off the damp and the frost. We carried poor Mareschal along beaten tracks and sunk lanes where rime lay unmelted all day and the ruts were hard as rock. Mareschal rode like a king in his specially made contraption with long handles and a canopy draped with waxen cloth. A carpenter had laboured the best part of two days to make it.

It's hard to tell what he's thinking, he speaks little. He weakens by the day, and the look in his eyes becomes more remote. The fair girl, still cowled like an abbess on her mule, assures us we will get him home before he dies. Apart from her, there is only myself and four men of Marshburgh whom I am paying. We can travel only as much in a day as the strain of carrying Mareschal's Throne can be borne by these strong, patient men. Ralphe is giving off an evil stench and the tight swaddling of his wound is foul. The girl tends him as she can, claims he is the father of her brat-to-be, which I don't believe for a moment. She knows both its name and the path of its future, she says. 'Monsieur de Ravelin, I see what is to come, I can't help it, it is a gift I have, I know all of this child's life from its birth to its death. I can tell you the story of Guillame Mareschal'

'No, no, no – spare me, spare us. Why should I want to know how a man will live? Yesterday, tomorrow, they're nothing to me. I don't give a bat's bollocks for any of it. If you know my death also, keep it to yourself, there's a good girl'

She laughed then, a pretty little peal like a stream flowing. 'We can be friends, monsieur, even though I know nothing of you, you are not even in my womb'

'Nor will I be, nor any extension of me'

She laughed again. What was it she extracted from Canteloupe? She never laughed when she spent so long in his company, and he became as grave as a bishop. Both are more cheerful now. And nor is *he* the father of her brat-to-be. The father is one of those who left her to die, the child was in her, seed sown, when we found her.

'You are not my type, young lady. Too thin and hungry-looking. I like some flesh, big girls with big brown eyes who move slowly and take their time'

'Cows by any other name'

'You're a sharp young lady. Tell me, since we're never likely to come across each other again, what were you doing out at Daxworthy?'

'Doing? Nothing. I don't live there, if that's what you're thinking. I don't live anywhere'

'But everyone knows of you'

'Everyone, yes. I am a local girl, I inhabit the Daxworthy area, I'm known in the town'

'You wouldn't go in there'

'No, de la Moule hates me. But I have friends outside the walls. I know you think I killed all the people at Daxworthy. I can kill, quite easily. But I did not kill them'.

'Why didn't you kill the men who raped you?'

'Because I required their seed'

'I have never come across a being like you' I heard myself sigh. 'You suffered at their hands, you were distressed, you were dead. And people think *I* am mad! You are what they call hereabouts pixilated'

'It's not true what they say, it's not catching. You can't *catch* madness, monsieur de Ravelin. You and I know that, we are both crazy. Let's keep it to ourselves'

'You're a very clever young lady, Johanna – is that really your name?'

'Yes and no'

'That's just the answer I expected. Forget it, we'll talk some more this evening'

After several days of travel we came to a wide silty bay and halted where two rivers joined and flowed into the sea to await the ferryman. The 'ferry' was a raft of alarmingly flimsy construction and the ferryman, hauling us across with great skill on a rope and pulley, was handsome and wordless. Then we trudged along the shore of the river which ran eastwards, wide and sandbanked like the one at Marshburgh and we crossed a large marsh on a causey of timber some three miles long. Acres of bleak dunes that Mareschal called The Warrennes were disposed to our right between us and the sea.

'I've made it' he managed to say 'I can see it now. There, up there is Herraton'. And I could see it, amongst trees at the top of a cleft at the rising end of a long valley. A road of sorts twisted up toward it. 'A fine position, Ralphe. They'll see us coming, your family, they can see us now I don't doubt'. I could just make out the shape of the keep on the motte above the trees, the fields had a peppering of sheep. It looked a pretty but a poor place.

The men, God Bless them, were at the end of their tether as we struggled up the road, which was a sunk track with neat ditch walls and trunks of beech and sweet chestnut coming right up to us atop them. There is no frost here and no breeze, a balmy place indeed but we are forced into single file and the girl has thrown back her cowl and started singing! An ungodly sound indeed but sweet (I cannot tell her age: sometimes she seems barely of an age to bleed and at others she has design in her eyes). The path is so narrow that the men are catching their knuckles on the ditching stone and swearing. They make no effort to quiet their profanity for her benefit and when I turn she sings a particularly high sweet note and smirks at the same time. The trees thin out as we come out into pasture and I can see the stockade, in rather bad repair I must say, de Bonville had said it was a peaceful place and indeed it is, at the outermost rim of the kingdom, in green pastures. A place which, if it were mine and I had a choice, I would never leave.

A pity then that we could not have arrived in better circumstances with better news. The moatwater is full of weed but the bridge over it looks newly built; further round the rampart, out of our sight as we approached, a small team of men seems to be replacing timber. Two working women were coming across the bailey to meet us: a reception committee I had not expected I must say – servants with soiled hands and coarse clothing. But as it turned out these worthy souls were Mareschal's wife, Jeanne – drawn-looking and very slight, not much older than our Madonna of the Mule – and Madame Mareschal, his mother.

'You have brought him all the way in this thing? Thankyou, oh thankyou! Oh God in Heaven he is dead!' She had drawn back the oiled cloth, and I who had spent nigh on seven days in his company had not really noticed how grotesque the poor fellow had come to look. There he was, lashed to his chair, a parody of domestic ease, head kept upright, tied to the chair back with a travel-stained strip of linen stuff. He looked as though he was resting after a devastating meal except that his arms were thin as a child's (the broken one still in its fetid sling of leather), his ankles were swollen like mottled plums, and his pallor was such his poor wife thinks he's dead. And even she, Jeanne Mareschal, could not help covering her nose and mouth at stench of the swaddling cloth round the wound in Ralphe's side. 'My God, my Holy God' she said softly 'what has happened here?'

'I'm so sorry. We did what we could'

'Who are you, monsieur?'

'I am Jean de Ravelin, vassal to Guy de Bonville. Poor Mareschal has a broken arm and a side wound as you see, acquired near a quarry by Marshburgh. The young lady with us has done what she can for him on the road. He is not dead but I'm afraid, as you can see, he is not good. A very brave man. It's not everyone who would be so carried back to his home'.

I could think of nothing else to say. Mareschal's wife looked at me as I spoke. I felt like an oaf.

'I'm sure you did your best' she said, quite graciously. 'Take your horse and your men and get rested, have something to eat. Is that the young lady you speak of?' The blonde girl had dismounted and was walking over toward us.

'She calls herself Johanna' I said.

'Calls herself? Is that not her name?'

'We don't know. We know nothing of her. She was the sole survivor of a massacre beyond Marshburgh. Roger de la Moule of Marshburgh seemed to think Johanna was an alias'

'We must get Ralphe indoors' said the older woman, his mother. 'Come, Jeanne. Help us here!' she called out to the gathering crowd and people came forward. Ralphe had not opened his eyes all through these conversations. Jeanne Mareschal had bent over her husband and was stroking his hair: 'we'll get you well, we'll get you well' she was saying.

The blond girl was still walking over meanwhile, the hood of her travelling cape was still thrown back and there was colour in her face (a thing I had never seen). No one stopped her and she, as was her way, spoke directly to Jeanne's bent back. 'You have lost a child, and I' she said, making a cradle with her hands beneath her swollen belly 'am gaining one'. I exchanged a glance with the elder Madame Mareschal, and shrugged as if to say: 'you see, this is the sort of thing she says, I don't know what she's talking about'. The older woman was shocked and speechless, but Jeanne's head turned slowly and she cast up her eyes which were red from tears. She looked ready to kill but the hate in her face quickly softened to curiosity. Once Johanna had such an effect on all of us, but it became lost in the lethargy that came over us in the closing stages of that fruitless siege. Now she had gone in an instant from looking sickly to almost healthy, she had colour as I said and her hair seemed to have a bloom about it, she was even smiling. 'Madame' I said 'she means no harm'. And I believed it.

As people helped to get Ralphe out of his chair and lay him to bed I noticed that one of the men who were working on the ramparts was not working at all but sitting. 'What's he doing here?' I asked.

'Jehan?' said Madame Mareschal 'he's helping us out at the moment, wants to be a steward. He just appeared one day. I've come not to trust him, and Jeanne hates him. I expect he's idling now. But he's an invalid, Jeanne made a sling and …'

'You're right not to trust him, Madame, Jehan is not his name. His name is Martin, he was a servant of my Lord de Bonville and his status now is fugitive rogue. The first thing your son did on meeting this man was to bring him to his knees for insolence and rightly so'

'Ralphe knows him?'

'Most certainly. The last I heard of him was that he escaped from your son and William Canteloupe who had him tied and were arresting him for attacking the former with a timber stave! We all thought him drowned at Marshburgh'

'Then he is here for revenge?'

'Quite possibly. But he won't have it'

So Martin was turned into a damp alcove cut into the side of the motte which doubled as lock-up and dead-house and the door barred. Once Ralphe was well, he would decide what to do with him. But unfortunately Ralphe never did get well and somehow, in the grief and confusion which followed his death, Martin was able yet again to simply melt away.

The Second Homecoming

On the last evening I was on the road back from Stoke Kevelle, the sky was so high and clear that I chose not to reach home, though I could easily have done so. Instead, I spent a sleepless night in a slack in the Warrennes, wrapped up tight I lay flat on my back on the cold sand, watching a thousand thousand stars tack round on their dark sea of nothing. And all night, conies and whatever other small creatures scurried, crept and snuffled about and the ocean droned in my ears and the breeze rattled the rough grass. My plan was to melt into the emptiness I saw above me, but in the end I just became bored, and my ears were cold. All night I slept with open eyes, which is not sleeping at all, and only in the early part of the morning, after the sun was up, did I sigh like a dog and sleep for hours.

It was the late afternoon before I drew near to my home, and a sweet light was falling on it – on it alone I swear. Have I died and been taken up into the Heavenly Host, am I seeing the Holy City? All around the sky looked bland and heavy, but shafts of sunlight shone on Herraton, I could clearly see the scaffold of Richard's new hall etched by the sun onto slaty cloud. I had assumed my mood would become heavier the closer I came to my home, but now I felt as weightless as a bird, I had no being at all. And I sneaked into the estate through my own woodland, like a thief, only squirrels knew of my arrival. I stumbled through my own door just after dusk, fell on my musty mattress and slept until almost first light.

Having spent most of the preceding day asleep, I was up and about quickly. I walked down through the woods in a foggy and grey dawn, limped about the fortress when only a few cottagers are stirring in their hovels and the animals are still quiet. Though walking in a dream and drained of all emotion, I could not escape pain: all my limbs were creaky and stiff and my foot, always worse in the early mornings, was particularly irksome. I thought of old Grillade with his own limp so like mine, of Angelica and the almost certainly by now late Guy de Bonville: how strange was that gathering in the dusty room at Stoke Kevelle. I still cannot quite grasp the importance of those few words Bonville gasped out. My father apparently not my father … my mother Johanna (that's what he said Johanna) … and bastardy. Johanna … Jeanne, they are similar names but no, there's no point in pretending, he meant my mother was someone unknown to me called Johanna and as for my father not being my father – there's no other interpretation to put on that! I have to accept that my history is unknown to me.

I have been wounded in battle twice only: a spear wound to the leg is simply that, a wound with blood and torn skin, the agony is unbearable but quite straightforward. This dull cramp of the whole spirit is far worse. So what am I to make of it, what am I to do? My non-father fatally wounded in an ambush, my non-mother raising the bastard child of some young girl and referring to him – that is me – as her son? I suddenly feel rather old and helpless, dragging my foot as though it's chained, a man without a history, just bones.

The shell of the new hall looms out of the fog, not a trace of the old home remains. Two dogs wander out from the skeleton of heavy timbers, shake and limber up, trying to catch my eye, but neither of them are mine. But then I see him! The real reason for this early morning expedition! Éclair sidles toward me from the other side of the motte – he knows me still! He stands and puts his paws on me, I almost pull off his ears. Éclair! What a dog, eh? What a dog! He dashes off and returns with a stick, drops it and waits. I throw the stick so hard I almost stumble and fall, there is soft laughter nearby, from where I cannot see. I'm not that interested. I walk on without looking back.

I was hoping the fog would keep me out of sight and let me have a good look round in solitude, haunt the place as I did not so long ago. But Herraton is small and being who I am, I cannot avoid having to stop and chat with various people. Old acquaintants and tenants. But since neither Richard de Bonville nor *maman* were here, there were no obligatory visits to make and the whole morning was frittered away in sentimental wanderings about my home, I can think of no other way to say it. Whatever comfort and security I have now I will keep but it seems it was never mine by right.

As I circled the motte I came to the old lock-up with its dry brittle and worm-eaten door. Its timbers had turned grey, mottled with orange spots and patches of moss. How long ago was it I'd bladed the eye of that oaf of a sergeant? More than thirty years I'd say. The lock still held though it was flaking with rust. A fillet of dry timber spun to the ground like an old bone as I worked the point of my hunting knife between two planks and twisted one of them away easily. I could not stop there, I destroyed the door systematically, stripping out the rest of the plankage with my bare hands and kicking in the frame. I took off the hauberk of fine chain I was wearing (which cost me several shillings in its day) and flung it into a corner of the empty chamber. I didn't know why but tears were filling my eyes and I was swearing viciously, kicking holes in the wall timbers with my good foot and spitting on the beaten earth.

When I was calmer, I saw Éclair standing in the doorway, his tail limp and wagging uncertainly, he was looking askance, ready to run, his stick forgotten at his feet. Dogs (God bless them), they know pain, fear and joy but they don't have 'moods'. They regulate our behaviour: if given the chance, they tell us when we've gone too far. 'Of course, Éclair, my apologies, we'll go about this in a more orderly way – I'm going to call you Ralphe now, after my non-father'. He barked concisely twice, picked up his stick and dropped it at my feet. 'Alright, young Ralphe' I said 'let's go up and see your old master, only you leave his sheep alone now …'

All day I walked about the acreage with Ralphe at my heels, logging each tree and field, taking stock. I came across Oswald on The Broomy Hill, standing like a dark shaft in a millstone of sheep, his two working bitches creeping and watching for breaks in the circle. He showed no surprise at seeing me. 'You'm getting on alright with thik dug then?' was all he said.

'I've called him Ralphe'

'Did you find out about un then, yer father?' He could see from my face that I had. 'Not what you wanted to hear I dare say'

'You knew and you never told me, Oswald'

'Not my place to tell *you* nothing'

'But we're friends, Oswald'

'Of a sort' he looked straight at me 'don't take it wrung now. Us've bin friends as much as us can but een the'end you'm the maister and I iddn. I could have told ee some things – leastways what I know – but tis bedder you should hear um from Lordy Bonville hisself. Did un tell ee ought about maidy Joanna?'

'Oswald, he hardly said anything. But that name was mentioned.'

'Tis er was your mother'

'So I gather'

'What they say about er is that er disappeared – well, I fer one reckon er's still about. I'll tell ee summat about thik maid, er was only yer a short time but my father died whilst er was. And my mother was worried because he hadn't been to church for years, she was worried that he might go down you-know-where and burn fer ever. I says to er that you couldn't expect a shepherd to be too strict on th'old churchgoing business cos his place was with his flock. That's what he'd taught me, see, you don't *never* leave your flock even if Old Nick eeself is standin to the door! So er says to me, half-laughing and half-crying as us stood by un een his winding-sheet "How d'you suppose the Good Lord's gwain know whether he's a shepherd or what un is?"

'Now this maidy Johanna was there nearby doin of summin or t'other, all that was said she'd heard and er went away and come back with a ball of sheep's fleece er'd plucked off a thorn bush and er bends over the coffin ever so tender and puts the wool between the poor old chap's fingers and er says, quite right: "there now, Saint Peter'll know him for a shepherd now and let him in because The Lord too is a shepherd who cares for his flock above all other things". And poor old mother was all come over and tearful with thanks, so if any bugger says that maid's evil – it iddn true!'

'Did they say it? That she was evil?'

'Oh aye. They said it. Said er was a witch who'd killed and destroyed, that er was one o they daemons who make swords slash and cut whilst held in no man's hand and make heavy things move on their own.'

'I thank you, Oswald, for telling me this story. You say she's still about, my mother?'

'I do think so. I think er's one of they beings that lives forever. I think I've seen her sometimes – a thin young maid with yellow hair. Now that I come to think o't, I've sin er all my life and er always looks the same'.

'Where do you see her, Oswald?'

'All over, nearly ever time when I'm up yer with the shape. I've seed er walkin, so have others'

'Earlier on you know, Oswald, I was in the old lock-up, flinging stuff around and cursing, I felt ready to fire the whole place, the new hall and everything and just walk away'

'You do what you must, sir, the place'll still be yer whatever you do. If I was you I would just walk away, never mind damaging ort. You've got the means, you could go and look for the maidy Joanne. I don't think er gets old like the rest of us, if er's yer mother twould be like you was only jest born. Yep, I reckon if you look for her you'll find her: are you sure you've never come across her afore?'

'Sure' I said, though at the back of my mind were certain things, like the sounds of leaves in the wind at night, the creeping of badgers in the woods, the thunder of Ponchard's hooves in the charge when he was in his prime.

I suppose my Lord de Bonville could yet have spun me a web of kindly lies, but he could not have invented a tale so bizarre or perhaps on second thoughts, he could. It could be all lies, perhaps he really did kill my father and he has made up this elaborate tale to amuse and excuse himself. What does Richard know of all this? Is he really the son of Guy de Bonville and my 'mother' (hereafter referred to as Lady de Bonville) – well, yes, I suppose he is. Five and forty years I have lived on this earth, and still I find the company of Oswald's rejected collie preferable to that of most human beings. Am I not, quite literally, a 'miserable old bastard'?

Apart from the men I have killed, who must have been perturbed, on the whole I have upset no one. Supposedly we are all men in the sight of God. But I *am* at fault for I bear grudges. Often a grudge does not survive contact or conversation with the grudgee, but I bear them for ever. I've never been ambitious, I look on Oswald as my closest friend. So what do I need to worry over? In the final reckoning at the gates, it may not matter who fucked who or who killed who or who took what from whom? Lady de Bonville and my half–brother (a fraction now open to question) have been told that Guy de Bonville, *chevalier, seigneur*, crusader and all the rest is at Death's Door and that they should hurry before he crosses the threshold. As intended, I missed them by taking a different route, we will have passed each other at a remove, and was it not always so?

After I left Oswald, Ralphe and I walked for miles. The fog lifted in the late morning and the weather was fine. I remembered the evening before and the light that seemed to be falling only on Herraton. And just as sweet a light falls on the rest of the world. I am what I am, a man under the sun and stars. The ground that supports me is the ground I will enter when I am dead and slowly become life again through the tracts of worms. Although he does not know it, I saved the life of Ralphe the dog, a life worth saving for he will keep me warm at night and give me company through the day all from the goodness of his heart. A simple creature like all of us are, simple creatures being and dying. I am sure my dog has a soul, I have seen it in his eyes, and I believe my horse has a mind and I suppose Lady de Bonville is a human being like any other whose hunger for my touch (even though I was not her son) was unfed and my father – oh God enough of all this! I will walk away (as Oswald counsels) and bear no grudges. I can seek God in starry skies, drift just above the grass without ever touching the ground – I'm looking for the girl, the *Madonna* Joanna, who will see me right.

CHAPTER EIGHT

Obscene Publications
10th February 1885: Nearly ten years has gone by since I last picked up this book. It has been, if the expression can be excused, festering in my drawers since 1876! It's true! I've had to give it a jolly good airing. Behind the hothouse stove in father's glasshouse there's a cavity where no one can find it, the gardeners (mostly Trusty, one or two Carnal) knew it was there but wouldn't have dreamt of touching it. I'm <u>so</u> glad now that I kept it up all those years ago: you can see, flipping through the pages, populated by motley people I might have forgotten. I will try and put some more in it now, even though the pages are spotted and mouldy, so that when I'm old it will be a comforter – the scandalous doings of Mrs Jane Trelease farmer's wife and 'fuckstress'! My vocabulary has changed in all directions, you will see, whoever you are.

An event sadly unrecorded by my pen was poor father passing away, in 1881. After he became a gentleman and felt he should no longer do practical work, I fear he very quickly declined, physically and mentally. In the end his hair thinned on top and went wild everywhere else, and he sat all day with his head slumped, repeating to himself 'I can manage' even though this was patently false. He kept mother up at all hours with his calling and his nightmares, but she is so patient, Mrs Digweed, so very patient. No one else could deal with him, not even myself I'm ashamed to say. Yes even I, used to dealing with awkward children, could not keep my temper, one day I threw

Later: threw what? Might have been a cactus in a pretty pot which I smashed on the wall. Poor Mr Digweed looked so <u>hurt</u> and <u>shocked</u> that I never again in the short time afterward that he lived as much as raised my voice in his presence.

So, what have I (dear Mrs Trelease, darling Jane) what have I been doing this past ten years? Ageing, for a start – I am nearly forty! I've been standing in a queue since birth, no particular queue, just a queue that's there and I've joined it, but this queue has been shuffling inexorably forward – and all along I've assumed that I'm no nearer whatever whatever is in store at the head of it but then, the person in front of me (Mr Digweed, of course) moves aside and it's <u>my turn</u>! Oh dear me! And the secretary or whatever he is rolls up the papers of my father and ties them with a neat little bow of red, hands it to his filing clerk and calls out 'next...!' without even looking up. And it's me! I'm next! I have been thinking of giving up the sexual act except within the sanctity of my marriage for some years but have not yet done so whilst there is still the faintest hope of a child.

I am digressing. Have I said that my vocabulary has spread out in all directions? Because I've let this journal lapse, that doesn't mean I've not been using the pen. I have. I have. In fact I have to get another three stories written before the end of May. My reading public will be panting for the latest works of William Jago and Ralph Marshall. My reading public? According to the wisdom of Mr Castle they are obviously men – married, of all ages, with good incomes who live in towns. I will quote him, the dear man: 'increasingly, Mrs Chetwynd now that we have railway trainsh and a poshtal system the goshpel can penetrate even the remotest cornersh of our realm where the utterly dubioush and I musht shay outrageous magazinesh for which I hope you will continue to produce your excellent shtories can be pashed around, and shecreted in sheldom-vishited byresh and barnsh or whatsoever they have out there'.

My task could not be simpler – to make the eyes and trousers of men bulge, their lips go dry and their hands wander to that which must be extricated and given the wrist. I must confess there are occasions when I myself, seduced by my own inventiveness, am compelled to lay aside my pen and seek relief in the same way (which I remember calling the Finger Thing but is really called Finger–Fucking). As far as Geoffrey is concerned, my consultations in London are with a savant called Doctor Alexander Dugdale, who keeps me abreast with the latest educational theory. Every six months I travel up there, enter a narrow thoroughfare near The Strand, Wychwell Street, where the disreputable but witty 'agent' who manages my literary output has his emporium at Number 47 amongst the rag and hand-me-down shops. In common with other such publishing establishments in the area, it has heavy oaken doors with hefty bolts and large men who stand on the other side of them with their arms folded and ask you your business through a tiny peep-hole. I could communicate only by letter but I rather enjoy my visits to Mr Norman Castle (neither Divine nor Trusty, unclassified but certainly not Carnal).

Despite his unprepossessing appearance, seedy premises and the blatant unlawfulness of his trade he strikes me as an honest man. He has never tried to find out my real name, nor has he ever shown the slightest shock or made the slightest criticism of my membership of the 'fairer sex'.

I have improved my vocabulary enormously, and in all directions (I must stop repeating myself) and Mr Castle greatly admires my writing and the money it makes for him. Though Geoffrey thought it totally unnecessary for the offspring of clodhoppers, I persuaded him (saying I was acting on the advice of Dr D) to part with the sum of fourteen shillings in order to provide a copy of Mr Roget's 'Thesaurus' and donate it to the school – of course I could well afford to buy it myself, but not officially. It has been a most valuable aid to composition – it took me all of three days to perfect my style, which requires a little wit and subtlety, but there is no need to burden oneself with such baggage as plot, story or character: the only requirements are that nothing should be allowed to obstruct the frequency of coupling (which should take place at every opportunity and in every situation) and that depth of character need go no further than the nadir of penetration of the (naturally enormous) male member into the syrupy chasm of the equivalent (naturally insatiable) female receptacle.

Mr Castle asks me some of the time for flowery effusions so that the more educated and sensitive of my readers will believe they are experiencing subliminal beauty rather than tossing themselves off in their studies, and at other times he will expect me to make myself familiar with all manner of low colloquialism. Some I have heard with my own ears through certain military connections, others I have conned from a book compiled in the last century by a Mr George Bell–Pritchard, a scholarly work full of all manner of expressions which Mr Castle obtained for me a few years ago. 'Here you are Mrs Chetwynd, and I advishe you to copy partsh of this, both for the purposhes of literature and … er … your own amushement'.

But is it not a tragedy, after half a lifetime of ramming, poking, pumping, quim-wedging, riding the cream-stick and general handy-dandy, that poor Mrs Trelease is not yet shot in the giblets?

3rd June 1885: Big tennis tournament today! The Herton Championship! A winner emerges triumphant at the end of the day after all the others have been 'knocked out'! Even the school is closed for the day and the children help with fetching balls and preparing drinks. The whole family is here: Becca and her husband (Mr and Mrs Charles Lebrecht), Liza and her husband (Mr and Mrs Alfred Dumble), John of course and Geoffrey and the more respectable tenants and tradesmen, such as dear Matty Hammond who is forever linked to balloons. Only Charlie is absent, due to court business.

The first ball was served at ten-thirty and there was a long break for luncheon in the shade of the sycamores, lolling about with our backs on the mound and laughing. And Geoffrey won (!) in a terribly gripping match against John Handford (Carnal) from Silston. He's become rather good – he's had a lot of practice, with Handford and the others. He was delighted! Beating Handford, who must be ten years younger than him, for the first time ever! I'm afraid time marches on, neither myself nor Geoffrey are quite the glossy young things we were, I am getting a bit on the heavy side I must say, though I was never as willowy as Geoffrey.

When the girls brought out the cold cuts and lemonade for luncheon and set them out, I was sitting on the side of the mound, where a sort of grass bench has been worn away and I was right behind Eddie Jones (Carnal once but run to fat) one of the tenants, and I saw him wink at Charlie Lebrecht (Trusty, I thought) and crook his finger. 'Interesting plot here for a Ralph Marshall tale, don't y'think? Tennis on a hot afternoon, wayward lob pursued by young sylph who's never had it into shrubbery, where lurks Ben the ploughboy in difficulties, trousers irreparably rent in a very convenient place and a hard-up you could hang your coat on!'

'Yes, yes indeed' replied my brother-in-law 'there's one just arrived you really should run your eyes over, parson's daughter on a train bouncing sternwise on a soldier's cock whilst his reverence dozes behind The Church Times. If I drop off says the dotard be sure to wake me up when you're almost there – oh father I think I shall she says. Damned if I know how they get away with it!

I'm always amazed that my works are so widely read and my wit so widely appreciated, simply everyone must be on Mr Castle's postal list! Is Geoffrey? My Lord, the possibility had never occurred to me, that I might be in my little office writing them and Geoffrey's next door in his study <u>reading them</u>! I was forced to feign a fit of coughing to disguise my mirth and those two turned their heads quite shocked as they didn't know I was so close. They would have been hoping that I hadn't heard their risky conversation, of course no lady could imagine in her wildest dreams that such scurrilous writing exists. I can't help wondering if the lovely Rebecca is aware of what her husband means when he says he is going to his study to 'attend to some business'.

18th January 1886: I've picked up a nasty head cold from one of the children and am forced to close the school and stay in bed. I can hardly hold a pen. My father-in-law has brought me up a plate of stew, dear man, but I don't think I can eat it. He says he has almost finished his history of Herton. It is a work of some length and detail I think. In the Middle Ages it was called Herraton, it's in the Domesday Book. It was held by the Bonvilles even then. He asked me to look up the name Marshall (as in Marshall's Wood) in Great Russell Street on one of my visits to London, and it does appear frequently though spelt Mar-e-schal.

Later: when I was dozing this afternoon, I half-dreamed about the marshes, and sketching. There was young Jane Digweed with firm skin and lustrous hair, virgo intacta, sketching the head of Jago, the first student at my newly-opened seminary (you see, I can't help it) who passed his practical examination with flying colours. Coarse as they come, but there was never a workman as skilled with the tool as he!

I was lying on my back in my frowsty sickbed with blocked nose, sore throat and streaming eyes yet I could hear piping curlews and chuckling gulls, clean river breakers shushing over gravel at ankle-depth, and smell that rich briny stench of the Coley Marshes. The same flavours clung to him – gormless Jago who couldn't believe his luck and myself squirming with curiosity. That oaf of a man will never be superseded. Dear John has brought me a hot toddy. Oh how I long for honest, dreamless, sleep.

10th May 1886: We were all here at Whitsuntide, the whole Digweed tribe. Mr Phillips brought out all his apparatus from Rafton and we posed en famille in the garden at the base of the mound where celandines and primroses are still massed – sometimes there seems such beauty in the world, more than it deserves – countless times I lay here when I was a child, on my side, curled up into the rise of the mound, staring at a single celandine. The complexity of such a simple thing is staggering, the perfect yellowness, the spray of pied green basal leaves, each one like a small heart. And this a single bloom out of thousands, is the world not like a machine? Each spring the whole mechanism gears up, clothes itself in yellow and white, for what reason those colours? God knows.

17th May 1886: Mr Phillips has printed the photograph and personally returned it to us. He is concerned that there is a strangeness about it. And indeed there is. The back row of the photograph is almost entirely composed of the male sex, them being taller of course, and on the right-hand end is Geoffrey, but next to him is a figure no one can account for. Some of the servants were in the picture: at the ends of rows or to one side, some sitting up on the slope above, and at first we thought she must be a new girl started as a domestic but none of the other staff know anything of her. She is sallow, thin and young, no more than fourteen, with a gaunt face and pale hair, invisible eyebrows, wide and conversant eyes. She looks vulnerable and inscrutable at once, it really is very peculiar. Everyone is agitated and no one has an explanation, not Geoffrey who stood right beside her, nor the rector (Divine?) who is very perturbed.

25th May 1886: It's the eyes – like they say, following you around. Slight though she is, she dominates the picture, even the taller men. Everyone thinks they're being watched. Visitors can't keep their eyes off it, even when talking, their gaze is drawn to it.

27th May 1886: Mother walked over to it today and turned it to the wall. She wants it burned but I said that it was still a family photograph. I have put it in my desk, in one of my old notebooks, along with my drawings.

3rd June 1886: Jago's back. George Jago! I saw him <u>riding</u> past, on a fine solid mare. He looks <u>very</u> well!

Jago Canadensis

And indeed he did. Jago looked comfortable enough as he leant on the rail of the *Mary Brownlow* as she cruised up the Avon below Clifton in early morning sun to the same port of Bristol that he had left, with his new box and a pocketful of change, twenty years before. He stands easy now, a solid man not quite young but certainly not old, his suit worn but well cared for, his hat brushed and clean: in fact the years have made him more handsome, his moustache is dark and thick with a faint peppering of grey. He must be the owner of a small firm of artisans, or a craftsman on his own account whose skills are rare enough for him to be paid well above the odds. Only his hands would tell the story of the work he has done, with their calluses and scars, dark marks here and there under the nails.

His employer Thomas Reardon was hard-bitten, tetchy, difficult and very religious with a thick scotch accent and a bald crown and such abundant facial hair that his long-suffering men would say his head was put on upside down. Jago, who hated the sight of him, nevertheless gained his trust by volunteering for stock fencing and other such work in remote places so often and with such enthusiasm that eventually he was given the tasks as a matter of course and left alone to do them. When he arrived in Rupert's Land he was given his year's pay in advance as promised and had spent hardly any of it. Opportunities for expenditure were few out on the lonely extremities of Reardon's land where it met the open prairie, therefore saving was not a problem. Of course, Jago well knew that his exile was due to the influence of Farmer Digweed, which made him the more determined to turn it to his advantage. The former bargee lead an exemplary life of abstinence and economy. His only luxury was the common one of tobacco and his sole entertainment – when he was not thinking wistfully of Rafton, Herton, old Bill Painter and young Jane Digweed – consisted of a portfolio of masturbatory fantasies so complex and utterly shameless that he rose from each indulgence shocked to the core and exhausted. His only social contacts, apart from the Reardons and those few of his work mates he came across, were Indians and the half-French Métis, whom he respected but did not trust. He would wave, of course, being a friendly soul, but he made sure one hand rested on the barrel of the carbine which followed him along whichever fence line he was working on. The Métis would sometimes glower, occasionally smile or else give him the stiff finger.

His stay in Rupert's Land lasted for much longer than he hoped. For the first two years he grafted away his days at the beck and call of Reardon, living in a rough lodge on the Assiniboine River, not far from Kirkboys with other men in his position. These men were all single, all Irish, and all of a certain age; they worked solely to provide the means for their monthly excursion. Jago went with them into Winnipeg at first, doing his share, drinking and banging away at the whores with the best of them, but strangely, he could not sustain it, he was laid low with a homesickness, a sensitive sentimentality he had not known himself capable of. Therefore Jago resolved to not just work, drink, fuck and die penniless in this desert place but gather what he could and return to England, even if it took decades.

He worked away at his solitary tasks, plotting his escape. After only three years he became free of Reardon the gangmaster, legally and financially. After that, as the rough and ready Rupert's Land became Manitoba and a province of Canada, and the Métis moved west into Saskatchewan, Jago worked as his own man and made a better living, even so it was fifteen years before he felt able to return to the mother country and buy into a business of his own. As he found himself cruising up an English river to an English port, his happiness was complete; Canada was vast and in places very beautiful, but along the Assiniboine snow lay for half the year, but Jago had turned even that to his advantage, in a single bleak winter he had taught himself to read and write and had been in correspondence over the last few months with the now elderly Bill Painter and had reached an agreement. He meant to acquire at least two more boats – Painter had told him of them, at Marshberry, moored and ready to work. So Jago had written further letters, secured these boats and arranged crews for them. He would return to the Coley Banks, but now he would be the master.

And so, a week after his return, having rented a property in Rafton, he walks a mare along the dyke and takes deep breaths of the tangy breeze – just for the sheer hell of it. There goes a man with all the time in the world, people would have said. During his years of solitude, he had picked up a habit of talking aloud to himself, as though passing the time of day with an acquaintance ... *seems to me th'old Coley's silted up a lot more, 'twon't be long and bigger boats won't be able to get down er. Still, my boats ain't big, they'm just big enough to make me a living. I shan't be overstretching meself, no fear of that. I can't believe how lucky I've bin, ridin along yer on a decent chestnut mare, taking me time, idly watchin men out there shovelling away at the banks earning me an honest shilling. I've done me bit, earned ever penny of the little bit I've got put away. I can look Jane – or Mrs Trelease I should say – in the eye. Can't say the same of th'old man ...I yer he's bin in his grave these five yers ...he weren't immortal then ...I remember her saying in that voice of hers, local mixed with a bit of posh – er didn't go to the high-class school her sisters went to, there's no local in their talking – 'marriage' er said to me, though twas none of my business ' is the duty of a girl. For her part is choosing the right man so that life can carry on, it shouldn't be taken <u>personally</u> if you see what I mean'*

Quite honestly I didn't see – I'd never heard an opinion like that, I would've thought twas summin you took <u>very</u> personally. But I don't like a lot of talk and I said so. 'This yer tongue' I said 'uv got bedder things to do than talk' and er was still tryin to speak as I pushed it into er mouth.

But I spose tis diffrent fer a woman. Tis alright fer a chap to be single, but a maid gets to be an old maid who's never ad it. So they says. There was places you could go in Rupert's Land, same as everywhere else, to scratch th'old itch with one of they Cree maids ...but most of the time I ad to scratch it meself. I think that's what kept me goin out there y'know. Pullin un off. A day didn't go by I can truthfully say when I didn't think about Jane Digweed – and what thoughts eh? I'd be doin summin ordinary like drivin in a nail or washin me trousers and there er'd be comin up behind me from somewhere back of me mind, real fuckish, and taking the shaft of un in er fist and I just had to give er a hand. Funny thing is I dread seein er but I spose tis bound to come about – <u>I</u> shan't know what to say or where to look but by Jesus didn't er ave an itch! A persistent one that needed vigorous scratchin, more vigorous than young Geoffrey Trelease could ever give – not that I'm saying er don't love him, I'm sure er do – but the best of both worlds suits her and the fact is you can't carry on like er unless you'm wed. I never gived her a babby and from what I hear no one else have neither – and it won't be from want of tryin ...

A few days after his arrival in Rafton, Jago had run into Matty Hammond on the quayside in *The Admiral Rodney*, and he listened with growing interest as Hammond told him of the tennis court up at Herton House.

'Now, as it appens I learned to play out in Canada' said Jago 'in the last few yers I was out there, it caught on big. Everybody who could afford it caught the bug. The winters was a bit grim – cold as a witch's tit – but the summers wasn't so bad. Once I was workin as me own boss I ended up gwain to some quite posh houses – they don't mind so much out there you bein a bit of the common sort and not havin sixpence to scratch yer arse with if you can play a game well – and I could! Not many could beat me once I'd learned and I learned quick.

'There was an old boy lived just outside Winnipeg who I was doin a bit for and he had a court, and one day the lad of the house were out there practising and he asked me if I wanted a go – I think he just wanted somebody to knock about with. So I takes hold of the racket and I was soon hitting the ball back to un and I told un I'd never played the game (or any other bliddy game come to that). He said I had a natural gift, so in the end I gets me own gear and I beats the best of um. And they took it well. Out there it ain't so much like it is over yer where you don't get nowhere if you've got a bit of the common about you and no money

'Tell ee what Matty I was over to Marshberry t'other day and I come across an interesting little book. Twas about the history of the hamlet of Herton and twas written by John Trelease! There was a lot of old waffle in it about lords and ladies and a drawing of how it would've looked in the old days with a wooden tower on top of the mound and a moat and a stockade and all that, and all the changes that have happened there in the last thousand yers, blah blah blah ...but d'you remember that maid us used to see about when us was kids? Pale and fair, thin as a rasher, all eyes and no eyebrows'

'A word in, George, if you please! Bugger me you can talk!'

'Sorry Matty tis all they years I spent on me own, soon as I see a human being unless tis a Cree or one o they bliddy Mettys I'm away'

'Course I remember the maid, nobody spoke to her and she spoke to nobody, you'd see er here and there, but nobody knowed where her lived, what about er anyhow?'

'Well now, in this yer book, there was summin about a legend of the girl-witch or some such thing. I knowed er from the way ee described her, like you say er was always about, all the time I've lived yer but you don't think nothing of it.'

'If twas a "legend" I've not heard of it' said Matty 'but come to think of it who was that bliddy maid? What was er name?'

'Buggered if I know'

'There's tournaments up there regular, to change the subject' said Matty

'Tournaments?'

'Tennis matches, up at Herton, you wanna get up there matey, there's one in a fortnight'

'Ain't they private then?'

'No, open invitation. They'm keen as mustard on the game. Mister Trelease specially'

'Well' said Jago 'I'm tempted, and I've got all me own gear for sure'

Oh my godfather's! Look at th'old hut! 'Twas always a ramshackle sort of a place but now 'tis more or less falled right down. If any of my men's out there they'll be able to see me, like I used to be able to see Miss Digweed, they'll think I'm keeping an eye on them – if I was honest I'd admit that I'm hoping she'll ride up yer and sit down beside me. I didn't think I'd want to but I would like to see her, I would but I can hardly go calling. We was never properly introduced! Then along comes tennis! A stroke of luck! Tis only a game after all.

Rude Awakening

'Geoffrey ... Geoffrey!' Ah, the voice of my wife singing softly to me from a sunlit glade miles away. 'Geof–FREY!'

'Oh my God! Alright, alright, alright!'

I've been sharing a hard wooden chair with a girl I've never met before, and she unwrapped a scarf that was wound round her whole body. I know what's happened, I've slept late again. Dammit! Only a half hour and I'm meant to be riding out with John. I'm always waking up in the middle of the night and not being able to sleep until I've sat downstairs awhile, I'll get a book out of my desk and have a read. Then I go back and have ridiculous dreams and then I oversleep ... *the girl was silky, young, quite flat-chested, neither willing nor unwilling. She was like that girl in the photograph, ah no Geoffrey she WAS the girl in the photograph! But she was dark. Was the hair on her head dark? So was it Jane? I hardly think so. Her thighs were suddenly and terribly astride me, something awkward that I had to prise open and search, it was hidden up inside there and I couldn't quite reach, behind the nave. I don't usually dream about girls ...* Anyways, there's no time now, got to rush. John's probably already pacing and picking about at the stables, looking for something to do whilst he waits for me: with any luck he'll get the boy to have my horse ready.

Then I'm hurrying quietly across the courtyard, pulling on my coat, and before I get to the stables I lean against the wall for a moment to let the fluster die down. My tongue still stings from hot gulped tea. Actually, I'm not strictly speaking late but my brother-in-law likes you to be early because he really is a very early sort of fellow. He's there, of course, talking to Boundy who's got my grey ready. Good man. John'll either wish me good afternoon or say he thought I'd got lost.

'Mr Trelease! Here you are. I thought you'd got lost!'
'I hope I'm not too late ... I think the clock's slow'
'It iddn the clock that's slow. Tis that missus of yours, keeping ee abed'. He's looking a bit askance at the ground, stroking his thick dark beard and then he laughs his laugh, a scoff that yelps and dies in an instant, takes you by surprise if you aren't used to it.

So we start off at a brisk trot, leaving Long Lane at the four cross way, and up over the downs: the weather's not cold or especially wet, just kind of dull. You know, John gets to look more and more like his father, not so tall and lean as old Digweed, but he's got the same hawky nose and small eyes, and he's like Jane with that ruddy sheen to his skin she still has. He was a skinny kid, but now he's so damn beefy and getting beefier: he's wearing his usual dark suit of clothes with a crisp white stock, on his head he's got a brand new grey bowler. He's balanced on his saddle like one of them big steam boilers, with a dome on top, a strong heavy fellow, fit as a fiddle, that no one would seek argument with. He'll leave me feeling weak as a woman. The last flash of this morning's dream passes before me oh goddam it! That girl's face right up against mine, her teeth, there was something about her teeth! It's a grin without cheer. Go away, go a–way!

'We'll drop down through Marshall's Wood' says John 'and up over Broadlands'

Broadlands. Right enough. He wants to take a look at the barley. There's nothing wrong with it. It was fine the last time I saw it, standing up nearly ready for cutting. 'We'll have to hope the rain holds off'.

'Oh' says John 'there'll be none of that wet stuff. It wouldn't dare'

That advice my father gave old Digweed still holds good. He went for sheep and dairy and sure enough the bottom's well on its way to dropping out of the wheat market. There's thousands of tons of it coming in from Canada and

America. There's men without work drifting away from the land. We turned a good part of our acreage over to pasture and there's thousands of sheep and hundreds of red cattle out there. John's as good a breeder as his father. There's a great shoal of ewes and half-grown lambs gathered on the slope as we come down from the top into Broadlands, marshalled by two expert dogs. As we ride down, they start to move in a tight drift across, down toward the old cow pasture at Seven Acres; them dogs is creeping low – the slightest sign of a sheep even *minded* to break away and quicker than hell would scorch a feather one of them dogs is right there.

'Don't you love watching them dogs working, John? I never tire of it'

'A good dug's like a good missus – worth more than money'

Now John Digweed is a bachelor. Far as I know he ain't interested in the fair sex at all. All he's interested in is farming – cows, crops, machines, drainage – he's got nothing else to do but be on time for everything. I'll bet he doesn't even have dreams. But that's the second remark he's made on the subject of married women this morning. I know him well enough and I know there's one woman in particular he must be talking about: my wife, his sister Jane. So what's he driving at? Let's hope it's nothing. I'm not in the mood for John Digweed's special form of straightforward obscurity, his nods and winks. I know he thinks I'm afraid to get my hands dirty.

As the morning drags on, he's got to stop and look at everything, talk to everyone. He hasn't found anything not to his liking yet. We're sitting watching the engines dragging a plough on a chain, and I'm still feeling peaky and washed-out, oily smoke's drifting over the field ... *she was silky as a baby, slender as a snake, the chair was one of the heavy wooden ones in the kitchen, she didn't want me at all but the dream demanded she offer herself up and I was obliged to search for whatever I'd lost up inside her. How in hell did it get there, whatever I'd lost? Makes no sense. Her soft hair's in my palm, and my fingers are searching reams of warm silk and I'm exhausted*

... It's them books, you know, them by William Jago. I ordered three of them a year ago now from the Post Office in Exeter (even Rafton's too close) and I *mean* to burn them but I haven't yet. On a sudden there's John Digweed, out of the blue, turning to me over his shoulder and shouting: 'Tennis! what d'you reckon to it?'

He well *knows* what I think of it! 'Great game! Of course, I love it, you know I do'.

'You've got to be just about the best player out of all of them that comes to Herton – there's not that many who can beat you'

I'd been thinking the same myself lately. 'I've improved in the last year, John' I said 'I can't deny it. But there's always someone better'

'Far as I know there is ... a chap used to live over in Rafton, been in Canada a few years, done all right fer himself and recently come back. From what I hear he's a tidy player and I reckon you and he ought to have a game, there's a few who'll stake money on't. His name's Jago, used to be a bargee now he's a barge-owner, bought the business off of Billy Painter'

'Canada?' What else could I say? 'Jago?' That name!

'What d'you reckon? Like to take him on?'

'Surely I would, John, surely. I'll take him on ... Mister Jago, you say?'

The more we carried on riding the acres, the more my mind cleared. We jawed and laughed with all and sundry, ate a cold lunch on a knoll near Silston where you could see Digweed's Castle away in the distance, and I was quietly thinking out a programme of practice. We walked over the sward where one of the herds would be turned out in a week or so, John was down on his haunches, setting a value on the grass, probing it with his fingers. 'Tis so good I could eat it meself ...' he was saying. And I too bent and grabbed a handful and inhaled that sharp green life-smell that comes off the juice of it.

'You wanna chew on some o that, Geoffrey, to give ee strength to take on the bargee. Does wonders fer the cows – they'll be frisky on it! Twill be a busier day than usual up at Herton, sure enough – serious money being wagered'll bring out the crowds. Us'll make an occasion out of it, beer and refreshments, the lot!'

'Jane'll be pleased for sure' I said 'she loves all that stuff'

The day was long and it was early evening before we rode back to Herton. During the afternoon, the sun had come out and even John had fallen quiet. 'I don't know if you've thought about it ever, John?' I ventured, for some reason.

'Thought about what Geoffrey? I should think the answer'll be no, whatever it is, I can't say I'm the thinkin sort'.

'Well, I was thinking, just riding along' I said truthfully, taking a bit of a plunge 'what is it that attracts people to each other? *Is* there anything you can put your finger on and say yes, that was it?'

'Oh dear, you're getting all serious now boy. Geoffrey, I dunno. You're askin the wrong feller, I'm married to the farm. There's wimmin about doing wimmin's work. I've no need of a wife'

'Jane and me – you know I always going to marry her, ever since we were children. I guess she's still teasing me about the way of talking I inherited from father ... I guess there's something about the *bearing* of someone – that's where it starts. Just something about the way someone walks, drinks a cup of tea, a certain way their hair falls, little habits like ...'

'Whoa, whoa! You're running away with me Geoffrey. What's brought all this on?'

'Oh, nothing. Best forget it' I lost my nerve and I think John was happy with that.

The issue is my married life. I don't know that I actually *like* the act (how could I have said that to John? Just as well I shut up when I did). My mind wanders for a start, I find myself thinking about something totally different; and Jane's eyes are always open, I can't meet them. She only closes them when she's helpless, and that's the only time I can look at her. But haven't we've always been happy, seriously so? I know she loves me even though she has agendas of her own. What I was trying to say to John (the wrong person at the wrong time, hopefully he's already forgotten) was that I don't know if I've ever been attracted to her *as a man* through instincts I've no control over. God knows we have a long history, as kids we were inseperable. Jane's always told me I'm beautiful – but a dog or a cloud or a building can be *that*!

The truth is I'm bored. Not with her, oh no never would I be bored with Jane. Who else could there be? But when it comes to what has become a twice-weekly ritual in our bed not only am I distracted but I'm convinced she's acting: for a while, after the honeymoon, she got to like it more. But she never *talks*, her eyes are open but she's not looking at me, she sighs and grits her teeth and I put the stuff inside – Jesus Christ I could put up with anything for the sake of young ones – what a home they'd have here! But poor Jane, you'll have to say it Geoffrey, poor Jane is barren.

'Are you happy, Geoffrey?'

I was hoping my brother-in-law would have forgotten my indiscretions already.

'Sure, John, I'm happy. Who wouldn't be?' I looked around me, at the sheep-studded downland, the fine evening.

'I'll think about what you said, Geoffrey. Is my sister happy?'

'You know Jane' I said, hopefully.

'I know Jane alright' he took off his bowler and slapped it against his thigh, smoothed his hair. 'If you iddn happy, Geoffrey, tiddn me you ought to be tellin … tis her'

'I never said I wasn't happy'

'I never said you said you wasn't'

'So' I said with a laugh 'nobody's said nothing at all'

John Digweed turned and looked straight at me. 'You think about yer tennis, Geoffrey, and bugger women'

He's right of course. Queer thing, this chap Jago sharing a surname with a certain author of scatological works. Jane is there, waiting, as we clatter into the stable yards. My lovely wife. As I thought, the prospect of the tennis tournament excites her, she is resting her palms on the lapels of my riding coat and offering her cheek. As the evening deepens, a chilly sea of stars assures me that if I wake in the dead hours and read, the fox will scream far away, the room will be a bath of cold moonlight, and I will search again those snail-like cavities in dreams of girls with bodies like boys.

The Final Set

You know what the first thing her says to me was? *Whilst you were out there did you do it much? Were there children?* I hadn't seed her fer nigh on twenty years and that's what her says to me. What a woman, eh? Can you credit it? 'Now and then' I answered her, a bit flummoxed I was, I must have sounded a bit snooty, it waddn what I'd been expectin. 'I wouldn't know whether there was children or no'.

'Ah' her says 'I know. In and out quick before everything freezes over'

I had to laugh in the end. 'Tiddn that cold out there, there is summer, y'know'

It was a while before I got to speak to her. I had plenty of time to wander around, first time I'd ever bin yer, in the grounds of th'actual house and twas a good do I must say! Everything laid on – lemonade stalls, beer tent, bookmakers, the town band from right over Marshberry, coloured flags hung out everywhere. There was a proper job umpire, funny little chap from up country. The weather was lovely. And I was treated like summin special, apparently twas expected to be a battle between me and young Mister Trelease and there waddn going to be a competition – because the game between meself and Geoffrey was the one everybody was yer for, there couldn't be no chance of either of us being being knocked out by small fry. Bugger me, I was thinkin, I iddn that good!

I was havin a glass of lemonade (they wouldn't let me pay fer nothing!)

and sittin on a bench in the morning sun watching the Digweeds, they was all gathered in front of a shelter with poles and a straw roof on the far side of the garden. Missus Jane Trelease was sittin on a bench lookin a bit peaky I thought, a bit thoughtful and moody. Her was wearing a plain pink dress trimmed with dark brown and a big hat full of folds like a walnut, there was a tabby cat on her lap and her was staring downward and to one side, looked as though her was studyin the Jack Russell one of her sisters was holding. Her husband was right behind her, lookin tall and serious, with his right hand on her shoulder and his left behind his back, sweeping back his jacket to show his weskit. He was lookin smart and fit to play, wearing his whites, pumps and cap. His racket was leaning against one of the posts of the shelter, ready for action. The two sisters was there with their husbands, and John Digweed stood there grim like a block of wood. I thought to meself I was in exalted company – twould probably be best if I could manage not to win.

I come across Missus Trelease whilst the warm–up games was going on. I was standing by the house lookin fer Matty Hammond who had me racket and me other gear and I was wondering whether to ask if I could go round the back with a ball or two and have a knock-up against one of the brick walls by the stable blocks. I says to her: 'morning to you Mrs Trelease' and I asked her if I could go round the stables and have a quiet knock-about. Her laughs out loud and grabs me arm straightaway. It's quicker this way her says and leads me off into the house! That was when her says to me: was there any children? I said I couldn't say cos mostly I never saw the ladies concerned again. You never married then? her says. Good Lord no, I says.

Now, I'd spent all those yers out in the middle of bliddy nowhere thinking a lot about her but, now I was face to face with her, her wasn't much like I remembered. Her asks me was I going to beat Geoffrey and I answers, sporting like, that the best man would win. Her smiles at me sort of lopsided then and I was thinkin her seemed a bit addled. Her was lookin very smart and well off, up close the dress was quality, and of course her was always above me, whatever I might think or feel about her – that was the truth, her was not fer the likes of me. In other ways her hadn't changed – out of the blue her says that her's more or less given it all up now and only does it with Geoffrey, I knew her was only sayin that because her was about to make an exception to the rule.

Us was standing just inside one of the back entrances to the house, and her reaches down – anybody could have seen! – and tests the length of un drew me trousers like her was down the market seein how fresh the carrots was. Her was lookin down, a bit vapourish, at what her was doin, and I was starin at the hat, the folds was all flower petals and there was thousands of um. Miss Digweed was calm and careless fifteen yer ago, and there was a sort of passion about Missus Trelease, but twas cold. 'Come on' her said, letting go of un and leadin me be the hand drew a long corridor to God knows where. 'I think you should have your knock-up in here' her said, looking drew a doorway into a washroom with sinks and long drainers and mangles.

'I know what you'm on upon' I said 'you'm tryin to sap me strength so that your husband'll win the game'

'How could you think such a thing?' her says 'just give me a lift, Mister Jago'

Her'd never called me that afore! I put me hands on her waist and lifted er onto one of the drainers. 'Lift me again, oaf!' her said, and when I did her lifted and spread the dress. Her wasn't wearing nothing underneath at all. Her sat there watching me pop me buttons, like her sat on the bench with the rest of um, lookin askance all sulky, all in pink with no drawers on. Her hooked her legs round me straightaway and I was obliged, perforce, to take the tiller and my God her was so buttery inside twas in up to the base straight away. Twas over quick as was bound to be, and I was minded to pull out whilst our luck still held and no one seen us – *but her wouldn't let me go!* Her kept her heels clamped to the backs of me legs and her was looking deadly serious. Her was starin at me and I was starin back at her, twas like her knew he'd stay up like a crowbar, her had un clamped tight and her was startin to slew round and round ever so gentle. Her give me a crooked little grin, took her hands off me shoulders, unpinned her hat and laid it down. 'What if somebody?' I started to say. 'Quiet now' her said, like her was talkin to an orse, running her hand down the side of me face. Er was merciless, nothing was going to stop her (that's what was different about her, desperation, want – er *wanted* me!)

There iddn nothing else a man can do if he's wedged inside a woman but carry on regardless. I got the bit between me teeth again and things got serious – at one time a pot fell on the floor with a terrible clatter and I was sure someone was going to dash in at any minute. But I spose they was all out watchin the games. And her wouldn't have cared if Mister Gladstone isself had walked in – her arms was crossed round the back of me neck and her chin was dug into me shoulder, and her was cussin and swearin like a navvy. I didn't know her knew such a way of speakin.

It took its time coming from afar off, and the closer it got the more up in th'air I felt. As the stuff shot into her, her let out a grunt through clenched teeth like her'd bin punched. I was terrified. When her let me go I was staggering and puffed out and her was leanin back on her elbows doe-eyed and red's a beetroot. I felt tired, really tired, I'm not as young as I was. There was a bucket of clean water under one of the sinks. 'We'd better cool off and compose ourselves' her said, lowering her voice suddenly, each word echoed in the empty room which was all stone and wood, pots and pans and crockery 'having arrived yet again at the end of the sentimental journey'.

'That's what tis is it?'

'In a manner of speaking ... I know a lot of colloquial expressions now'

'Them's *all* I know' I said, picking up her discarded hat and handing it to her. 'One-eyed bed snake. Know that one?'

'Of course. Fagin, isn't it?'

'Quite right'

We dabbed our faces, and her dipped her handkerchief in the pail and took it up between her parted legs. I shrugged off me braces and let me trousers down (the last thing I wanted was a damp patch on me whites) and sprinkled a bit of water over me cock and stood watching her push the long pin into her hat.

'How long are you going to stand like that?' her said, laughing.

'Lung as it takes un to dry off in th'air, no longer'

'Must be nearly time for your game' her said with a funny little grin. 'I should put it away, we must go, you go the way we came and I'll go out of the front'.

Soon as I was outside, I seed Matty Hammond out looking for me.

'Oh there you be' he said 'thought you'd gone home. Morning Mrs Trelease!'

She had appeared from the other side of the house, cool as you like, and I reckon my seed was still running down her thigh. 'Matthew! Good to see you, are you looking after this reprobate? Mister Jago's been practising his strokes around the back'.

'Has he now?' said Matty, smiling at Mrs Trelease and handing me the racket 'not too energetically I hope, there's such a thing as over–practising you know, George. Especially without a racket'.

'Are we on then, Mister Hammond?' I said quickly, spinnin me racket in me hand, tryin to look keen.

'Quarter of an hour, twelve o'clock sharp' he said.

Anyway, I was right. If Missus Trelease was more trying to sap my strength than just following her inclinations, that's exactly what her'd done. I sot down fer ten minutes in the shade of a tree, the quiet pause before the game – and I didn't want to get up again! And the minnit I steps out onto the court me legs is weak, me cock's sore and I'd lost a good part of me strength and disposition. The sun's beatin down, there's a noisy beery lot of buggers in the crowd, and Mister Trelease is standing up the other end looking cool as you like, slinging his racket from hand to hand and runnin on the spot! As we're knockin balls back and forth, I can see her sittin at the front and when I catch her eye I get a smirk: you naughty, naughty girl, I'm thinking, you won't get me with yer craft. After we've knocked about fer a few minutes, the umpire says: 'when you're ready, gentlemen'. The little umpire's even got a high chair – this is the properest game I've played I'm sure. You don't even have to pick up your own balls – there's two little girls doin it, Missus Trelease's nieces I should think. So we toss a coin fer first service, square up proper and 'Play…!'

Well now, Geoffrey Trelease wasn't nothing like as strong a striker of the ball as me. Even though I was on half rations he couldn't get my first few serves back over the net and, even when his stroke did get in the way of the ball, his arm just went stiff and the ball bounced off his racquet anyoldhow. I won the first set six games to love and I was thinking that Missus Trelease's ploy hadn't worked. Some of the crowd was with me, especially the noisy lot (gamblers I reckon), which was a bit off-puttin: them as was with Geoffrey Trelease was quiet.

But as we got into the second set, Geoffrey was starting to wear me down. He was fitter than he looked. He didn't have my strength but he was steady, and once he started to return my serves (he broke it in the second set), he was gettin the better of me in rallies. And the rallies was getting longer and longer, and he was getting craftier and cannier, dropping shots just over the net and lobbing into the corners so that I was running all over the shop. He won the second set and the third. So we was in for a long one, best of five.

There was a break after the third set fer half an hour. I drank a couple of glasses of lemonade and dipped me head in some cool water. I sat with Matty in the shade beside the court. 'Talk about anythin, Matty' I said to un 'just not tennis! I'll win or I won't win'

I seed Missus Trelease walking about with her husband, the two of um under her parasol, her arm in his, leaning her head on his shoulder. Right then, I'm thinking, I'll be showing you soon. I won the fourth set in short time – six games to three – and we went into the final one tired and determined. Both elements of the crowd was gettin noisy now that they would soon know which way their money was set to go. We was three games all and squaring up to each other like a couple of knights-in-armour, death before dishonour as I've heard em say. That's when I saw her, the maid, the thin blond girl, still looked the same as ever, sittin right next to Missus Trelease and talkin to her. Their heads was well together and their faces close. I was waitin fer Geoffrey to serve but when he did it just whizzed straight past me – I was trying to pay attention to the game and at the same time watch them two out of the corner of my eye. Can't be done, of course. The maid was doin the talking and Missus Trelease was listening close, they made an ill-matched pair, Jane so dark and buxom and the maid with her thin face, hair almost white, bony fingers drawing directions on the air.

So, I lost that game. He was four to three up in the final set. I shut it all out and concentrated, I fought back to leadin five games to four – I had Geoffrey on the run, he was still alert but his eyes looked beaten, he was a handsome chap but he'd lost his will. His mouth was down. I poured water over me head and towelled me face down when us changed ends for what, as far as I was concerned, would be the last game, I seed her over there looking at me. The maid was gone and a stranger sat beside her now. Her was looking straight at me with cow's eyes that made me feel weak and melty again. Now, I knew her was beggin something of me – but what was I meant to do? I'm thinkin I'm buggered if I'm going to let un win and anyway 'tis unsportin, and how could I do it without makin it obvious?

Me first serve of the last game was a cracker, left poor Geoffrey reeling then, as I'm bouncing the ball ready fer another I thinks of sand, acres of it, banks of it. Now that could put me off me stride but not altogether – if I still win, then so be it, I'll be the champion, I'll deserve it and the bookies'll take a drashin. So, as I'm sendin the ball back and forth, I starts working out how many tons of sand they would need for to build the wide new bridge they was talking of over the river at Marshberry. I was sure I'd get the contract – I hadn't bid for't yet but old Bill Painter reckoned he could swing it my way and I'd slipped him some notes to be sure o't.

So I does me office work, as always, in me head. The bridge was to be the best part of two hundred yard long, parapets two foot thick by four foot high, five spans – that'd be about forty yard each with four piers – and 'twas to be built with granite stone infilled with rubble and mortar. That means a bit over three hundred cubic yards! Let's say a third of that's infill, which leaves two hundred yards which is round about a hundred and thirty tons, a lot of sand, a lot of work and a bucketful of money. And that's how I managed to lose the game – sand!

But I still had enough of a grip for it not to notice and, though I slipped to six–five down, I still paid a bit more attention to't: three times I had the vantage and let it go back to deuce when we was on the last strokes of the last game. I let Geoffrey have it by serving a double fault on my last serve and I looked upset and muttered curses and all them beery lot who was backin me had gone quiet (bliddy fools should have put their money on the underdog) and Geoffrey's lot was clappin and shouting. I smiled broadly, strolled up to the net and shook Geoffrey's hand, clapped him on the shoulder. He was all hair and teeth, I've never seen a man so happy. I sneaked a look over at Missus Trelease and her was looking a bit quiet, looked like her was blushing, as well her might, she moved her lips: *thankyou*.

A few days after the tennis game, I had a letter from her:
My Dear Jago,

Thankyou so much. I have never seen Geoffrey so happy. He still talks of nothing else.

There is one last favour I would like to ask of you then I swear I will leave you alone. Could you possibly meet me in the garden of Herton House at a half past ten this coming Sunday evening? There is an old outhouse at the foot of the mound, could you meet me outside it? It will be quite alright, no one will see you. You need bring nothing but your assured good will and a full pouch of ammunition. This is positively the LAST TIME!
I do hope to see you there.

Yours in friendship
Jane Trelease
Herton Home Farm
27th July 1881

As her well knows, I'd do anything for her. A full pouch of ammunition! What a maid, what a turn of phrase! So when I gets there tis as black's a bag, cloudy and no moon: I can only just make out her face. Her skirts is rustling beside me in the dark as us walk round the mound and sit on one of the benches by the tennis court and her tells me about the maid who appeared in her photograph and I said that her'd always bin about. 'You know her?' her cries out and grabs me hand.

'No, I wouldn't say that. Nobody *knows* her. Have you read yer Father-in-law's book? There's summin about her in there. I couldn't say where her lived, but her was always about the village'

'Rafton, you mean?'

'Aye Rafton. It was like you saw her but her was always on the move, never seemed to stop and talk or go in the shop or ort like that. I dunno what er does and I wouldn't like to say whether her's on the side of the Christian or no'.

'Well, I'd never seen her before until the other day, one moment Mr Pargeter the auctioneer was beside me and the next moment he wasn't and there she was, as if Pargeter had *changed* into her. You must think I'm mad. Most peculiar big child's eyes, scanned you up and down, knew what you wanted before you knew yourself. Anyway, what she told me was, no chit–chat, introductions or anything else, just straight out with it, she said I must do it with you "your friend, Mister Jago" she said'

'Ha! Did you say you just had, twice'

'No, I did not! Really! ... And not with Geoffrey "your lawful husband" she said. The act must be performed at a certain time on the motte, as she called it, between half past ten and midnight on this day. And she sounded so sincere that you really had to do as she said. And I looked over at you then, you were just subjecting Geoffrey to one of those terrible services of yours, and when I looked back, there was Mr Pargeter again. I don't know what to make of it but I really must do as she says, my time is running out – you know what I mean don't you? So I'm afraid I've got to ask you to fuck me one last time'

'I ent never heard a proper woman say that word'

'What? Not even in the wastes of Canada where there's no vicar?'

'Come on then, Missus Trelease, let's get on with it'. I takes her hand and leads her back round the mound to the outhouse. But she breaks away and flattens herself against the door and raises her arms like I'm pointing a rifle at her (I could tell twas a new door for it smelt strongly of resin, and the planks was firm).

Her draws me up against her and I lifts her clothes out the way whilst she works on me fly buttons.

'This is called a knee-trembler' her says, fumbling it out and running the flat of her hand over it.

'I know' I says 'I thought we was s'posed to do it on the mound'

'So we shall' her says, raising her legs and guiding it home 'but I don't want it to be all over in a minute, this will be my only chance and I want to enjoy it'

What did her mean by 'only chance'? Buggered if I know.

When us gets up on the mound, 'tis even darker because of all the trees, and the wind was getting up. There was continual swishin from the leaves of th'oaks and sycamores. When her was naked her was jest a white shape of a female thing with a dark mane on her head and a brush stroke between her legs. Her knelt down and sat atop me for a minnit or two, kneadin me chest and groomin the fine hair with her fingers. Her reaches behind her and I say he's ready, don't worry. Her lifts herself up and downward, holds him upright like a stick of rhubarb and hunkers slowly down on him until he's firmly wedged in. That's summin her's never done afore. Actually, 'twas almost painful. 'Lean forward' I says and her laughs softly (that's another thing her's never done) but she does so, rests her palms back on me chest and works away, her'd never really taken the lead afore.

'You'm milkin me like a bliddy animal' I said.

'I'm sorry' her said.

I s'pose this was summin the thin maid must have said to her to do. I'm not all that happy but I know what it means to her. I've never had to put up with it like twas just a job of work afore. I was thinking how do I know tis really Jane Digweed kneelin up there – it looked sort of like her, far as I could tell, but it *wasn't* her. Not really.

Suddenly her flops down on all fours, driving backwards onto me, palms on the grass beside my shoulders and her bubbies hanging straight in me face. Like a drowning man who finds a piece of flotsam, I've got hold of one in each hand and I'm hanging on for dear life and I'm wishing it would all be over. Funny, but I was cut off from her, smothered by soft milky flesh and I didn't know what was there crouched over me but whatever it waddn gwain give up until the goods was provided. At some time Jane was makin a huffing sound like a train and at the same time I heard that little chuckly laugh, so it waddn her doin it. You know when you'm not going to be able to come, there's circumstances when you can't – I put my hand on her arm and squeezed gently, her understood and reached back down and put a finger each side of him at the base and worked them up and down … and I was off thinkin about sand again! I was thinkin whether or not twould pay me to get another boat, and another three or four men to work it. It come up on me then, the approach of a sting, and I pushed un right in and that's where the stuff went, buckets of it – that's what her wanted and that's what her got – where did it all come from, eh?

I could breathe freely again once her got off me, leg-over like her was dismounting an orse, her body was a smudge of white on the dark, and the wind was still rushing in the trees, a few spots of rain was in the air. I was cold. Her seemed happy lyin on her back, as far as I could tell her legs was crossed. I reached over and rested a hand on her breast. 'I'm stopping it running away' her said 'thankyou so much, George'. And that were that. Her said that her'd not bother me again, that this was 'positively the last time' but I wouldn't have minded if her had bothered me again – er could have bothered me til Judgement Day as much as her liked. I always regretted it, but I never seed her again.

CHAPTER NINE

Pete Florence

Grammar Schools, institutions which now barely exist, were common when I was at school. In the prehistoric past, if you passed the eleven plus and got a couple of 'O' levels you were saved from window cleaning, clod hopping, painting and decorating, drilling holes in roads and all that other menial stuff carried out by morons. You wouldn't have to shovel shit, you could wear tidy clothes and a collar and tie. And I was thinking (whilst digging a pond if you want to know) what a cheat I was: I've taken the money society provided for my education and deliberately failed to become (say) a local government officer, a pharmacist, a librarian, general practitioner or area manager. Indeed, my salary rises, if it rises at all, not by increments but by luck and guesswork. I followed my nose into a manual job, and I keep my brains to myself ... self, self, selfish! ... but I get to drive a digger, and design gardens.

I do what I like. I won't be told a thing. Am I grateful to the taxpayer? ... am I bollocks. I'm paid sums of money by many different people (hopefully in notes but, if there is absolutely no alternative, I must bow to the inevitable and be a taxpayer myself!) Impecunity is often my lot, physical and mental debilitation, for I'm a devoted hands-on designer and builder of gardens and *I* find my work, *I* execute it and *I* get paid for it. Independence is a beautiful thing – and speaking of beautiful things, that day I was digging the pond was no different to any other day, for as I sat on the machine drinking tea I recalled the job at Herton Home Farm, and Joanne. Yet again. Jo.

I'm going back a couple of years now. In my trade, as in most, there are slack times. The weather, Christmas, summer holidays, you know ... sometimes the dead months of winter are fine, sometimes they're not ... January, February, and a good part of March are survivable to differing degrees, but to get through them you need a lot of coal in your tender. Often enough you're in the stagnant waters of a certain well-known creek, lacking the necessary paddle. What was that phrase, one of many used by the Americans in the Gulf War, sporting their suits of sand and leaves? Not collateral damage – though that was a good one – but *nightmare scenario*. For me, this is where a dread of predators and starvation sets in, when Autumn becomes November and nothing new's come in – is the carcass of the old year picked *quite* clean?

On January the fourth 1999, as a filmgoer might button his coat in the cinema foyer, still spiritually inhabiting that land where Americans (invariably) of both sexes (eerily fit, dermatologically correct, dentally immaculate) deceive and shout each other down before choreographed gun violence finishes them off ... this filmgoer turns up his collar, blinks tiredly out into the drizzle that sweeps across the headlights of departing cars like smoke ... oh I'm sorry, I'm talking again, thinking I'm clever. OK, all that really happened was I stuck my head out of my foxhole after the Christmas break and mentally sniffed the air. I had told Julie nothing of the impending demise of Pete Florence Plc, she had already gone to work, I had pottered for an hour or so, eaten a couple of boiled eggs, made a flask of tea. New year, New job I was thinking. Outside, in the world, the air was thin and the morning frosty. As I walked through my overgrown brittle grass I was passing the key to my white 1900 cc diesel van through the flame of my Zippo. The lock gave with a few twists and the door seals cracked and sighed.

As I waited for the heater to thin out the windscreen ice and wished the spider that lived strung between the roof and the dashboard good morning, I rolled a cigarette and pushed one of the unboxed tapes that littered the passenger footwell into the stereo. It turned out to be *Highway 61 Revisited*, first side, first track viz. *Like a Rolling Stone*. Very fitting, the perfect accompaniment for someone sweeping out into the world with nowhere to actually go and nothing to actually do. Music well over thirty years old, a listener ten years older again. Standing on the brink as I was, with the little band of creditors approaching across the downs headed, as ever, by the taxman in his wingèd helmet, ready to push me over. What I needed, of course, was an honest-to-goodness, time-consuming, highly profitable garden reconstruction. Now!

You know I'm going to get one don't you? Why else would I be droning on? What is a landscape contractor without a landscape, as much use as … a cardboard spade? I can amuse myself with fanciful language, parody my situation, bore myself endlessly: I'm awfully well-spoken (can't you tell?) and educated, and I know it. I'm a proper Thesaurus of Words and Phrases in human form am I not?

So I was driving about, through hard winter sunshine, over puddles of road ice, touring the DIY sheds in Marshbury, cheerfully burning diesel I couldn't afford, buying things I sort of needed. A little collection of small items accrued on the passenger seat – shakeproof washers (assorted), cork insoles, rubber grommets (assorted), jubilee clips (assorted), a set of adjustable funnels, a cheap hand-operated paper shredder. I took a couple of broken tools to Mr Bennett, welder and general fixer, of Rafton. The following day I spent at the lock-up I rented in that town servicing the machines; sharpening blades and tines, tightening nuts, changing oil.

Whatever little bits of work there were, I was leaving Finbar to deal with them; let's keep him just busy enough so that his eye skims over the horticultural job adverts out of curiosity rather than need. In spite of his pikey earring, baseball cap and prehistoric Ford Fiesta, I wouldn't like to lose Finbar. He's been with me four years now – he's keen, borderline competent, rather witty. I've grown quite fond of the silly bastard.

But of course, the sun didn't set on the horticultural empire of Pete Florence, at least not this year.

For it came to pass that I was parked near the Coley, one of my favourite spots, where the dunes end and the mudflats begin, near the end of the dyke where small boats are pulled up above the tideline round a group of ramshackle huts. I was drinking tea and eating a pasty; it must have been a Thursday, for I was perusing the deaths and sits vac in the *Marshbury Advertiser*, and seeing what dreadful crimes had been committed and if anyone I knew had committed them. There was the bizarre account of a man who, 'after years of abuse and provocation', had killed his neighbour's cat and pegged it to said neighbour's washing line. I stared through the window at the sandbanks – to what part of the animal was the peg attached, and whatever could have 'provoked' such a thing?

But even this dark vision of an innocent animal sacrificed was easier to digest than my 'pasty'. I'd vaguely noticed a certain gamy *je ne sais quoi* about the taste of it. Holding it at eye level, I peered at the pinkish emulsion within – was there really such a meat as this? Of such colour, such texture? I really could force no more of it down and I tossed the remains into the back where it was caught and devoured by the unscrupulous dog.

Placing my head on the rest and closing my eyes, for some reason I fell to feeling sorry for Finbar. I *could* lay him off now, I'd only have to drive out to Gernsea where he was spreading wood peelings in a windswept garden above the sea and get it over with, take the fork out of his hands and do it myself. But nah! Gernsea's miles away, I'd best let him get on for another few days. Hope against hope. I sat and watched the tide race up the Coley, covering the banks of sand, filling the deep channel, behind the windscreen the sun was too warm but I just couldn't be bothered to get out. I let young Bobby out and he ran on the sands, flinging himself down and rolling on his back, pedalling his legs like a fool. And I remembered that I hadn't switched on the mobile all morning, and when I rummaged through the door pocket and found it there it was, a voice message. Possibly to be remembered as the last time she spoke to me; Julie, my wife, in from work, passing on a name and a number.

And lo, it was the sort of job (big space, lots of machinery, creative licence) that comes round only every couple of years. A tasty meal that perks up the dull diet of suburban back gardens which, like it or not, one has to nibble on to subsist. As I walked the site (it wasn't far way, up at Herton, I saw it the same afternoon) the sun was low and bright, the sky clear, and the more I saw the better I felt; I expect an addict would call it a rush. I knew the place vaguely, I'd seen it from a distance whilst out with the dog. A silage clamp of black plastic battened down with tyres, a cluster of roofs and stone outbuildings halfway up the hill, set into the end of a wooded cleave surrounded by a patchwork of fields grazed with sheep. Nearby a large, bland, house with a tongue-shaped acre or so of overgrown garden behind it, what looked like a mound rising at the far end, covered in trees. Though I'd lived here all my life, I'd never really been near the place, you wouldn't, unless you had business to.

The new owners of Herton Home Farm were Michael and Virginia Darwin, down from the environs of London, looking for a slower pace of life that only equity could provide. Like many others of their income range and provenance, they had netted an old mixed farm that the family had been forced to let go, with a residue of land, had the builders working on the inside for months and now it was to be my turn. (Builders, *ergo* beneath rutted, compacted and rubble-strewn ground lie concrete blocks, wire, string and plastic sheeting).

I was early. A middle-aged lady with dark bobbed hair and lipstick had stuck her head out of an upstairs window and shouted 'ten minutes, Mr Florence ... you are he?'

'I am ...' I said and spent twenty minutes ambling round the old farmyard. Empty cattle housing and milking parlours of concrete and corrugated asbestos stood alongside ancient outbuildings with thick stone walls and recessed doors of tarred, scratched and pock–marked timber, carved here and there with clear sets of initials going back into the last century: J D 1853, G T 1855. There was one massive old barn where the doors were half off their hinges and I was able to squeeze through a gap between them; inside, the familiar detritus of agriculture decayed quietly in the dust-moted sunlight that streamed through a high opening in the gable. Rusting lengths of wiggly tin strewn or stacked, hundreds of used fencing stakes in a neat pile, rolls of silage wrap and barbed wire, an ancient and tyreless tractor with a metal seat like a melba spoon in which sat a black cat which leapt away, and ran through another doorway that came out onto a yard of rippled concrete with weed-infested joints where hay-frames and the skeletons of old gates, greened and sagging, were stacked against the wall. Eventually, I made a cigarette, sat on a stone roller in a small cobbled yard, and waited.

'We're going to use that ...!' The lady with the dark hair had appeared suddenly. She was a short, energetic woman wearing a waxed gilet and green wellingtons, she now had a red alice band in her hair, and greenish shadow on her eyelids. Rising from the roller, throwing away the cigarette and shaking her offered hand, I asked what it was she was going to use.

'I'm sorry, the roller ... it needs to be stuck upright in the ground'.

'Absolutely. Put it in gravel surrounded by low to medium ornamental grasses, you can't go wrong' I said.

'This way' she said 'I'll show you what you're up against'

As we strolled off into the depths of the garden, we skirted the edges of a massive area of strange mounds of ivy, old teasel and thistle heads, thickets of desiccated bramble six feet high which sloped gently to a curving stagnant stream.

'Is that a *moat*?'

'We think so ...'

'So that mound has to be a motte ...'

'And we're walking through the bailey ...' she said with a smile. 'I hope you won't find it too daunting ...'

'I don't mind being daunted' I said truthfully, staring at two large and utterly decrepit chicken houses which stood near an inexplicable corner of ditch walling. The hedges hadn't been laid for decades. Daunting? I loved it.

'The mound wasn't part of this land, but we've bought it and a little bit that surrounds it from the old boys at Herton House. They seemed quite glad to be rid of it.'

'What's that flat area near the mound?'

'We think it was a tennis court. D'you think you can do it, Mr Florence? Give us an estimate for turning this wilderness into something we can live with?'

'Oh yes' I said 'certainly I can'.

She left me then to walk the site on my own. The plot started off narrow and widened out quite a way, shaped more like a pear than a tongue; skirting, at the far end, right the way round the mound, which was not as high as it looked from the road. The old tennis court was long-neglected, hidden by the scrappy remains of last summer's dandelion, dock and plantain. Because the boundaries kept veering off at odd tangents, measuring was a long process; I drank a lot of Virginia's coffee, took a few photographs of the place sitting in its surroundings.

'I do things the old-fashioned way, I'm afraid, I don't have a computer'

'Michael has several computers' said Virginia.

When I'd drawn up the skeleton of the first scaled plan, there was a little over an acre to play about with; to the farmer a postage stamp but to the gardener a large blank canvas.

The lawned areas and planting were not a problem, a few curved pen strokes dealt with them, but we discussed the mound at some length. Despite being at the far end of the garden, it's domination was inevitable, there was no other option but to lead all else to it. Four metres high, twenty metres across on the top which was well overgrown with ash and sycamore. Levelling it was out of the question. Most likely it was a scheduled monument. It was the sort of thing you didn't touch. So I said I would have to see what I could come up with. 'By the way' I added 'you'll see the whole thing's pear-shaped – let's hope that's not how it goes'

Virginia was happy enough to laugh at this, and I knew we would get on. And what of Michael, oft referred to but never seen out of doors? The only glimpses I ever caught of him were through a window, of a thin concentrated face at a keyboard, under an anglepoise.

In a week, I was back with a finished drawing and an estimate that would bankrupt a small African state. 'How about' I said as Virginia, Michael (out at last) and I stood in the windy sunlight each holding a part of the plan, trying to keep it from blowing off the picnic table they'd set up in a small area they'd cleared themselves.

'How about?' said Virginia.

'How about cutting four alcoves into the mound, four large notches retained with dry stone about half the height of it, with a flagstone seat in each one – I've seen plenty of good slate about. And there could be a flight of steps – I've drawn them in, see, there – next to one of them so that you can get to the top. Then you can sit up there and face any point of the compass you like (for the view was extensive in all directions, the best aspect west to the Warrens and the sea where soundless traffic swept down through the valley of trees). Then the trees can be thinned out and underplanted with bulbs and perennials, and you've got shade without being too dark. That door in the face of the mound, do you know what's behind it?' They didn't.

Their house, Herton Home Farm, was an antiquated rambling Devon longhouse of a fairly common type but Herton House, a hundred yards away, was planted on the landscape like a monolithic slab. I mean, it *looked* empty. I thought it *was* empty. Its walls were bland and bombproof of old cement render covered in spots of yellow lichen, like any one of the military remnants that littered The Warrens, still there after fifty years, except that it was far older than that. Its high curtainless casements with flaking paintwork stared straight at you but revealed nothing. The main door had a pillared portico and was heavy enough to stop a tank, but the oddest feature of Herton House by far was appended to its north side, possibly for the accommodation of awkward or insane members of the family, a windowless tower with crenallations, its only visible access a tiny postern door.

'That house' I said before I left 'is very odd'

'Oh *isn't* it!' said Virginia 'a great drab hulk! It's Grade II listed you know, must be that funny castle thing stuck on the end'

'I've never seen a place so bland, did you say there were two people living there?'

'Yes, Mr Digweed's a retired farmer and Mr Trelease I don't know about, just the two of them rattling about in there. They make a living buying up and restoring 'antique' furniture'.

'Digweed?' I said, rather predictably 'with a name like that we could do with him in here!'

A Small Collection of Relics

Of course, they went for it, Michael and Virginia, praise be to God.

'There's one thing it would be fair to warn you of' said Viginia before I left after our second meeting 'there is a local man, Sergeant Cawsand, I've more or less promised him – he's a bit of an archaeologist – that he can dig around a bit when the site's stripped. I hope you won't mind'. There was a little chuntering on my part about the job being held up, I wasn't keen. 'Of course' said Virginia, sustaining the dream 'if it holds you up, we don't mind paying. You know, sort of compensation.'

I rang Finbar the same evening. 'Finbar, it's me. We can stop scratching and pissing about, Herton's on'.

'Yes!' he cried, I could feel him punch the air down the phone line. 'It's a long job yeah?'

'It's a long job'

We were there for three months. Lock, stock and barrow. And archaeologists.

Once we were on site and doing necessary brushcutting, felling and burning before the serious work could begin, one of the first things Virginia said was 'We'd really like that awful hedge grubbed out and replaced by something we can manage.'

'But Virginia' I said 'that hedge is worth a thousand of almost anything else I can think of. It's Box, utterly priceless; a boundary hedge more than a century old, we could hoick it out with a digger in half an hour, but we really musn't'.

So pruning was agreed to be the answer. Finbar and I made a start on bringing it to heel.

'You should see it over there, Pete' said Finbar, backing down the ladder 'you won't believe it'.

Where I was expecting neglect and dereliction, the Digweed/Trelease side of the hedge appeared to be neatly trimmed, and the Digweed/Trelease garden consisted of a well thought out grid system of vegetable and fruit plots divided with mown baulks, and a small apple orchard where the trees had obviously been knowledgeably pruned since they were planted.

I descended the ladder like Moses and lo, I made utterance: 'many people have wonderful apple trees but they don't know what to do with them, year after year they let them go and the fruit decays on the lawn'

'Right' said Finbar 'so these two don't buy their fruit and veg down Tesco's'.

By the first week of February, I'd got a local contractor in with a wheel digger and we started stripping the site. He destroyed the poultry houses in half an hour and dropped them on the fire (the fires at Herton were many and tall, satisfying conflagrations that warmed the winter days). Three quite illegal and very deep holes were dug in different areas into which went the wriggly tin, more than one tractor carcass and anything else that Michael and Virginia wanted to get rid of. On top of all that went the scraped off vegetation, the bramble roots, the thick mats of rough grassland and on top of that fresh topsoil pushed flat by the machine's fore loader. And whilst the machine worked, Finbar and I were up on the mound, thinning out and pruning trees. Not only did the weather smile upon us, day after day of high cloud and sunlight, but coffee with quality biscuits from Marks & Spencer in Marshbury appeared regularly.

'What I reckon' said Finbar, as he and I and Barry Hammond the digger driver sat on top of the mound smoking and drinking coffee 'is that what our arses are parked on here is a motte'.

'Us used to come up yer when us was kids' said Barry 'Rat's Castle us used to call un. Ee wuz a moody fucker, old man Digweed who lives over there, sometimes ee'd chase us off, othertimes ee'd ignore us. Ee's family farmed all this land for hundreds of yers and ee's like the last of um and that George Trelease, he's related to un. When us used to come up yer, the mound was in that garden, now 'tis in this one'

'The boundaries have been redrawn? Now, that's interesting. What's a motte then, Finbar?' I asked though I already knew.

'It's a defensive mound, right, but as a rule it's a bit higher than this one. And there's a moated area round it called a bailey, there's the moat over there'.

'It's paying off then, Finbar, all these history programmes you watch on satellite TV' I said 'It's an old castle, right?' I was getting to my feet, and so were the others. I've never quite got used to being 'in charge'. If I had sat all day, would they also?

'Onward I suppose. Right, Barry, we'll start carving slices out of this motte, like it's a Christmas pud. Take out four wedges about four feet across – no, six feet cos I've got to make walls each side. There's canes to mark the centres, cut the backs flat and push them in'.

Barry looked askance. An agricultural man, he was bemused by this sort of pettifogging earthmoving. 'Let's ope the fuckin thing don't cave in' he said.

'There's always a chance of that. I reckon it must be hollow behind that door. You start on the other three and we'll try and have that door out by hand'

Barry swung up into his cab and starting up the machine, sliding the feet into the turf and swinging the backhoe round with a hiss; the knife to cut the cake. Finbar and I broke the lock on the door and started to work it open with crowbars. It was built of the same timber, black with preservative, as many of the other doors on the farm buildings but much heavier and hadn't been moved for a long time. The hinges were fused with rust, we were getting nowhere.

I walked round to Barry. 'We cant shift it, you'll have to rip the bastard out!'

Barry plucked away the door and its frame, scooped it up and dumped it to one side, and we were left looking at what amounted to a closet without a roof, a sentry box shored up on three sides with timber so old and brittle that a baby with one arm could easily tear it down. The joints were bursting with fine tree roots and fungus, the floor was beaten earth, and there was absolutely nothing in there.

Each of the alcoves sliced from the mound was to be floored with the excellent slate flags that I'd seen scattered about all over the place. I set Finbar to digging out the floor of the old outhouse so we could put down a base for the flags and went off on a tour with Barry, picking them up in his front bucket. There were some in the barn I'd looked in on my first visit, some supporting a rusted out and empty oil drum, and many stacked against a wall in the old cobbled yard.

When I got back, Finbar had made small progress because the ground was well compacted and took some digging. There was a clay pipe of the kind Victorian workmen always have stuck in their spade beards and the inevitable fragments of willow pattern crockery. As I was digging round the edges the fork kept snagging and I was cursing and muttering about plastic and stuff but Finbar rightly pointed out that when the door was made and put there, plastic hadn't been invented. 'Then it's got to be fucking binder twine, that was invented for sure, the farmer's friend, the devil invented that'.

Finbar got down on his knees, and scrabbled with his fingers. A shape emerged like a cat's ear.

'It's a dead moggie' I said.

'No it ain't' said Finbar, excited 'It's oilskin! It's an oilskin bag! Get a spade under it and prise it up!'

'Yes, boss' I said dryly, taking the spade and working it under the shapeless package.

'It must be old' said Finbar 'just cloth waterproofed with oil'

'I know what oilskin is, Finbar'

With a gentle touch I didn't know he had, Finbar placed the oilskin bag on a piece of old ply and carried it over to the picnic table and barbecue near the house. Its drawstring had perished long ago, age and damp had made the pelt of cloth very fragile; he held it open with a barbecue skewer that was lying on the table whilst one by one he extracted the jumble of objects inside it. A collection of tiny coloured pebbles, a piece of metal about to go to dust but which still resembled a thin blade.

'That's a *spur*!' I said as Finbar extracted a round of starred metal. 'How old is *that* for God's sake?'

'Pete, pass us over them barbecue tongs, the rest of it's too far in and I don't want to put my hand in there'

'Yes sir, straight away sir'

'Right' said Finbar 'here we go. One piece of ... oh, what?... finely knitted metal, like chain mail'

'This is all very medieval, Finbar ... when's that Captain Scarlett or whatever his name is coming? Not bloody yet, let's hope. There's work to do. You can bet he'll be very interested in this fucking old bag. We don't have to mention this'

'Can it be chain mail ...?' Finbar was chuntering away, peering into the bag. With his skewer and tongs he looked like a surgeon performing a *post mortem* on one of those leather-skinned cadavers out of ancient bogs in Denmark. 'You'd think that'd perish wouldn't you? ... OK, two locks of hair, one dark, one fair *and* there's something else, right inside'.

He produced then a shard of slate with lettering on it, childish writing which must have taken great patience, meticulous care and a very fine brush: **These relicts gathered and buried here by Jane Digweed & Geoffrey Trelease, Year of Our Lord 1853.**

Really. That's exactly what it said. It sounds so corny, as if I've made it up. 'The names' I said to Finbar 'same as the two old boys next door. This is their little private and secret collection. Some of this stuff 's much older than eighteen fifty-three. If these two kids gathered this stuff around here how much more is there?'

'We ought to get them archaeologists round here now!' Finbar was excited.

'No. I don't think they should know about this. Let Major Catastrophe or whatever his name is dig up what he likes but we should put this little lot back in the bag and give it to Mr Digweed and Mr Trelease, it rightly belongs to them. And I want to get some more work done before we get held up. For a start, I want Barry to get the alcoves done so that we can work on them while the arkos are farting about'.

'But y'know it might be important stuff' poor Finbar seemed genuinely aggrieved, he took off his cap and peered again into the bag, as though he could spirit out more artefacts to make his case.

'Finbar, all those people do is dig up old bodies that should be left alone to rest and poke them about, digitally enhance them, find out exactly what the poor old sods died of. I hate it!'

'I never knew you was religious Pete'

'I'm not. For fuck's sake just put the stuff back and give it to me'

I needed this collection of small relics as my passport into the world of Messrs Digweed and Trelease. I wanted to get into that house, talk to those people. I'm not sure why.

The Antiquarian Imperative

The archaeologists were good and bad news. There was Tony Cawsand and, later on, his daughter.

Tony was a friendly man, garrulous. He'd been in the army for most of his life. When we met he shook my hand, called me Pete straight away. 'We must try not to get in each other's way. I hope we can work around each other. Ginny told me you weren't happy. Ah! you've cut slices out of the motte, god knows why but it gives me a chance to have a look at the profiles.'

It was hard not to like him. He had a way of making you comfortable. Despite my chuntering earlier about bloody arkos holding me up I heard myself saying 'not a problem, we'll organise it so we don't clash, we'll share the digger, and if I can't work because you're in my way I'll just have to find something else to do, like nothing. Compensation's been discussed'

'It has. I'm glad we'll get along, Pete. You seem like a man with an education, so what are you doing digging holes?' I shrugged and turned away. 'Sorry' he said immediately 'none of my business. Don't mind me'.

When he arrived he set himself up in the old yard, parked his winnebago (as he called it) on the concrete and put up a couple of trestles in the old milking parlour to lay out his finds. 'Morning Pete!' He was wearing jeans and what must have been his old army jacket with a knitted hat pulled down over his ears. 'All set up?' I asked.

'Getting there. I'm having a brew would you like some?'

'Give me a quarter of an hour' I said

We sat on a trestle and drank coffee. 'Where's your mate today?'

'Finbar? He's on another job down in Rafton. Couple of days'

'This is so exciting for me' he said 'getting myself a dig! Bit of luck, meeting the Darwins. Ran into them at the Local History Society AGM at the Red Lion down in Marshbury. Said they'd just moved here and wanted to know about the area. They sort of buttonholed me, bought me a drink; being "Chairman of the Committee" I have to show an interest if there's potential for new members. You'll find me very straightforward, Pete'.

'I've noticed. You'll find *me* the opposite'.

He laughed. 'Michael – tall and quiet, easy to ignore, with the kind of smile that's not a smile, a bored man keen to escape (which made two of us). Virginia – not bad looking for her age, hair suspiciously dark, a bit on the scatty side but marbles all present and correct. But my god I thought these people are boring, I was casting about for an excuse to get away, until they said *where* they'd moved into. Herton Home Farm! I'd seen it up for sale in the *Advertiser* – 'delightful seventeenth century longhouse, full of character, in need of some modernisation, idyllic rural situation, undulating picturesque countryside' and all the rest of that Estate Agent crap – then **SOLD** went up across the corner. I was for taking the drastic step, paying a visit, introducing myself, get a foot in the door, but like so much else I never got round to it. When it was still part of old Digweed's empire – have you met him yet? – the awkward old bastard wouldn't let me anywhere near it.

'I was that keen I tried to go over his head to Lord Bonville himself, but even His Holiness wasn't willing to contradict Digweed, chuntered on about did I know how long he'd been there, how many generations, respect his wishes and all that bollocks. I said all I wanted to do was a dig, archaeology, scientific research, you never know I said it could put Herton on the map. "But Sarnt Cawsand" he said down his nose "it already is *on the map*" and he might just as well have added *you stupid little man*. Fucking Guards Officer ... farthead.

'I'd seen it, my name on posters: *Tony Cawsand talks about his excavations at Herraton Bonville. Marshbury Museum. 7.30*. But no. That was that, I'd have to give up on it. Let a rich medieval site sit there laughing at me. Then God sent me Mike and Ginny Darwin'

'I'll drink to that!' I said. I told him that getting this job had saved my bacon.

'Talking of bacon' he said 'I don't know what Michael does, haven't asked, but it must bring home lorry loads, whole sides of the stuff if they could afford what Bonville was asking for the place, not much change out of half a million! D'you know what he does?'

'Nope. Involves a lot of sitting and tapping keys'

'Quite frankly I think he's a bit of a prick. Ginny's alright though, somebody's mother, I got on with her straightaway. Anyway, once I'd allowed them to buy me a pint I had no trouble broaching the subject of the possible archaeological significance of Herraton Castle. The old name drew them in. "Really? Herraton? Is it in the Domesday Book?" ... Of course, I said, and they were full of questions. Hooked good and proper ... are you local, Pete?

'Yes'

'You don't sound it. *They're* from Surrey, of course. Is there anyone left in Surrey? Leatherhead, or that neck of the woods. And there's another stroke of luck. I was in the Army twenty–two years, five of them just down the road at Pirbright. "Good heavens!" she said "we could have passed each other in Waitrose and never known it!" Great sense of fun, Ginny, likes a good laugh, and I was in! Before you got here I waded out there, through the grass and nettles, snagged my joggers on the bramble clumps, struggled up to the top of the motte, sat on the bench and sighed. Don't you love it, Tony, I said to myself. Field work!

'Anyway, I mustn't hold you up. I'm a bit of a talker. You'll have to excuse me. I must get moving anyway, only here to off load a few things. Got to take my daughter into Marshbury. She wants a laptop for the catalogue, bless her, and there's the dentist, root canal work, very expensive'.

Yes, Tony was 'a bit of a talker'. He was a user of time. I tended to avoid him when I had anything to do that had to be finished. But he was likeable enough, I didn't mind passing the time of day with him when it suited me. One day, when I was discussing something with Virginia, he came over and said 'thank god you're not a builder!'

'No I'm not a builder, Tony, strictly garden design and construction. Why, what if I was?'

'I'm afraid you'd set me off on a pet subject'

I laughed. 'But I have, haven't I? You're going off on it anyway'

'OK... builders, right ... unreliable but cheery. Totally incapable of bearing silence, only able to converse on topics related to television, sport or copulation. And they must "sing" at every opportunity – in the seventies it was Englebert Humperdinck ... po–lease release me, let me GO! ... Abba or Tom Jones ... my my MY Deelilah! why why WHY Deelilah! ... Christ knows what it is these days. And when the live music dries up it gets worse, along comes Radio Drivel, loud as you like all day (Virginia was laughing her socks off by now) dreadful mediocre stuff and between tracks what passes for philosophy in DJ speak, cretinous humour, the sad opinions of 'listeners' – people who start every sentence with *I'm sorry* as though what they're about to say might sound boneheaded, might have made even Adolf Hitler blush but nevertheless is the way things REALLY ARE, out there on the streets. And the motorway tailbacks, inter–celebrity relationships, meticulous analysis of every aspect of football'.

'You're not fond of builders then Tony?'

'Or popular radio' said Virginia. 'Well, Tony, Mr Florence is very nice and he's definitely not a builder and he's Radio Four Man personified'.

After she'd gone, Cawsand turned to me. 'You're well in there, mate, no mistake'.

So where was Tony's mythical daughter? Virginia told me something of her. Her name was Joanne, she helped him out with his records. Even she had not yet met her. I was drinking her coffee, chomping on a wedge of Victoria sponge, standing in one of the half-finished alcoves. 'Where's Tony today?' I asked. Virginia said he had to see to something to do with Joanne. 'What happened to his wife?'

'There's a bit of a story there' said Virginia 'he's never been married. You know he's an ex-soldier? ... well, he came across Joanne, if that's the right way of putting it, in a trashed village in Bosnia. Poor girl had no one. Somebody, Serbs I suppose, came to the place whilst she was off on an errand ... when she got back the house was burning, her parents were shot, her brothers, the sow and her piglets, the dogs ... her grandfather'd been strung up on the barn, more or less crucified. When she saw what had happened she threw herself against the wall, tried to break her own neck, and knocked herself out. Soon after the British turned up and took her off in the back of the APC'

'He told you all this? Sounds awful. He brought her back, adopted her?'

'So it would seem. You'll almost certainly meet her, during Easter, when she's off school'

As well as the 'winnebago', Tony had a car and each day he drove off home with the two helpers he had, back to Rafton, where he apparently lived. One afternoon he came over to me. 'Pete' he said 'it's my birthday today'

'Oh, really' I said 'many happy returns'

'The big Five-O. You and I get on alright' he said 'I don't know many people and those I do know bore me a bit. I wondered if you'd like to come out for a few beers tonight down in Rafton. Will the missus let you out?' He laughed uneasily.

I was interested. And it was true we did get on. So I ended up drinking the evening away with him in various hostelries in Rafton. I lived about three miles outside the village and was walking home. He insisted on coming some of the way with me. I gravitated to my favourite spot by the Coley. The night was cold and clear, the moon gibbous, the beach ashen. We accounted for most of a bottle of port between us, staring out over the steely water through a gap in the dunes.

'I'll tell you about her' he said 'Joanne. Wonderful girl. One afternoon, moving on from the malodorous basement of the engineering works in Sasoko ... (it was hard to say how drunk he was, his speech was steady, only occasionally slurred) ... about which I shall *never* say a *single* word so don't ask! I was up top on the Warrior with Captain Worrall, used to call him Woolly Worrall. We stood there as ever in silence, not knowing what was going to be round the corner, on our grand sightseeing tour of the chamber of horrors, clearing up after these ... pigs I was going to say, but pigs are intelligent friendly animals. So I won't insult them by comparing them with the Serb Irregulars.

'What we *all* thought *all* the time was I AM PISSED RIGHT OFF WITH THIS FUCKING PLACE but there was no point in saying it. Men with all the gear – better than anyone else has got out there – who can't fire a *shot*! Look but don't touch, don't do anything about anything. Then Worrall's getting something over the radio and he's talking to Daz down below – 'do a left Daz ... left, got it?' We're suddenly off to Dovici Most – which even if it hadn't just been visited by Sammy the Serb would be an A1 fucking dump!

'We came past a couple of wriggly tin barns and round into the narrow street. The Warriors were big fish in a small pond, the exhaust banged against the walls of the houses and shot back and forth, a storm of noise with no one to hear it. You knew everyone was going to be dead. Even now I can't think straight. Have you got a cigarette, Pete? I've run out. Thanks ... you see it in Ulster, neighbour killing neighbour, or not objecting if their neighbours are killed by a third party. But this was worse. The bitter smoky fog we'd got used to swirling and drifting, heat, the reek of burning, the *sound* of burning – cars on their sides, on their backs, like dead chukky-pigs, everywhere that quiet rumble, that confident sound fire makes as it eats, the little pops, bangs and gurgles, as it digests everything. The rain started pissing down the moment we left the vehicle. I said I'm not coming here again next year, I'm sticking with Lanzarote ... ha!

'There'd been no *firefight* – that's what Worrall was getting on the radio. They said firefight and they said Dovici Most. There wasn't a *trace* of anything military there! They drive about in cars and lorries flying their flag, with hand guns and rifles, but some of them were getting more serious stuff from Milosevic. There'd been mortars there ... plenty of fire in Dovici Most, but no fighting. Nobody was about like I said. Or nobody alive at any rate. There was no firefight, sir, just a massacre.

'We moved on foot down the street. There was a house, nothing we hadn't seen before. Maybe I'd just had enough. This one was going to change my life. I only had a year left to do, I was already doing the courses for civilian life, I don't really know what made me wangle a tour in Bosnia for myself. I must be some kind of pervert! Anyway, the house was an empty shell of hot fire, flames shooting out the windows, there's a tree with brown leaves, washing on the line drying more quickly than the woman who hung it out could have hoped. A dress, a pair of child's socks, tee shirts. And round to the side two women dressed in jumble, and boys in cheap sports trousers and thin dark jackets, and an Alsatian puppy roaming round them, snouting hopelessly under dead arms. All done on behalf of those two or three with houses still in one piece and a cross on the wall who supposedly qualify as human beings and needn't be herded out and shot.

'*Over here Sarn't Cawsand!* It was Worrall over by a tupenny-hapenny lean-to and inside it was a girl with her back straight, legs splayed flat, head slumped as though she'd been thrown against the wall. "Broken neck" said Worrall. Her hair was very light, like it was bleached. "A child, sergeant, just a child" and he lifted her chin. I was going to tell the idiot not to move her head. "I hate these fucking people" he was saying. She was so pale, her eyebrows so light you could hardly see them, her face was mottled with vibrant shadow and fire was flickering all around us. Then her eyes opened. And we, neither of us religious men, dropped to our knees. It was like she'd come *back to life*! I'm fucking sure she was dead. But I'm sorry. I don't talk to many people. That's why I talk so much'

'It's alright, Tony'.

Strangely, *I* ended up walking with *him* to his door that night. I marched back and forth, covered quite a few miles. Halfway to my house, back to his, then back again to mine. Just as well it was Friday. He lived in Lion Row, a quiet cul-de-sac too narrow for cars, near the quay, lined with tiny cottages. 'You know' he said as he was turning and fishing in his pockets for his keys 'I don't know her *real* name to this day, it's like that with her' he winced and jerked his thumb over his shoulder at the moon, riding high at the end of the road, sliced neatly in two by a flagpole.

'Like what Tony, the moon?'

'Yes, the moon, the moon. Made of the same stuff as earth, lovely to look upon, but utterly deserted and cold as a witch's tit!'

'G'night Tony' He sounded so desperate I felt sorry for him. His shoulders had slumped and I put my hand on his coat and squeezed. 'I'll have to leave you to it' As I walked away he seemed to be scraping his key around the lock for ages before he found a connection.

One morning a lunar, mythical, Joanne appeared glowing in the passenger seat of Tony's car. Her looks were unusual rather than attractive. Though light-skinned, slender, within an ace of skin and bone, she walked with her pelvis as though for an audience. The clothes she wore always fitted tightly and she strode purposefully with her whole body. That first time I saw her, she wore dark blue jeans and a bottle green roll neck sweater, a black laptop bag slung over one shoulder. I was with Finbar, we'd been to the milking parlour to give Cawsand a hand moving his filing cabinets. She dispensed a quick nod and a single-use smile. From what Tony had said of her life I hadn't expected this pared-down confidence, this economy – as if she had *chosen* the absolute minimum of flesh she had on her bones because it was no more than she needed.

I kid you not. She was tall, she *walked tall* like a painted image or a wax figure come to life, she was beyond blond, hair bleached white, parted simply and shoulder long; her skin was so pale and stretched that her eyes seemed to be struggling out of their sockets. And that's what I was drawn to. Her eyes. Blue-grey, cold and immodest, infantile and highly intelligent at once. I shrugged as if the weather had suddenly changed, even then fingers were searching me, the long nail of one ran up my spine making me squirm. I looked round. She didn't. By Christ I fancied her. Things *could* change. It wasn't all over.

Sometimes she would march over to where Tony and the others were picking and scraping, gather the bagged bits and pieces and take them round to the milking parlour and the tables.

'How old d'you reckon she is? said Finbar one morning 'she looks like she couldn't lift a feather but I reckon she's hard as nails' I'd watched him watching her. I think he was afraid of her. Nor did her prescence necessarily have a good effect on Cawsand's mood. One afternoon he came out of the winnebago rather suddenly, cradling his coffee, and slammed the door. He came over to where Finbar and I were working.

'So, Tony' I said with a smile 'how's it going?'

He ignored my question, put down his coffee and got his cigarettes out. 'You know' he said 'she's a great girl, I wouldn't be without her for the world but there were *hundreds* of refugees, civilian wounded and traumatised in Bosnia. I told you how I found her didn't I?'

'You did'

'She didn't seem to have a home – nor did many. She was a bit of a lost soul – so were many. She doesn't have a name, she doesn't have a memory, at least not one she wants to part with, there were no official records of her. The family name was Alibegovic and there was meant to be a daughter called Jelena (who matched Jo's description, but not entirely) who disappeared presumed killed'

'How old is she then?' said Finbar.

'When she was found, more than five years ago, she was fourteen. The authorities accepted that she must be the unaccounted-for daughter but I decided to call her Joanne. For a new life. Good God! It sounds like I'm talking about a dog I picked up at the RSPCA ... ha! But she had no objection, didn't care *what* she was called – Jelena Alibegovic, Joanne Cawsand, Felicity Crump, Mila Drascova, so what? She hasn't changed you know, I mean she *looks* the same as ever, so fourteen, nineteen ... whatever'

'Who d'you reckon she is then?' asked Finbar with his usual tact.

Tony Cawsand took the question in his stride, it was what he was driving at after all. 'I don't know, my friend, I don't know' he shrugged and sighed, said over his shoulder as he walked away: 'why don't you guys come over later on and see what we've got from the medieval levels? There's some interesting stuff'.

'He's a funny old sod' said Finbar quietly. 'You've got to know him, how does a sergeant in the army end up an archaeologist?'

'You know, Finbar, believe it or not I've never asked him'

Starshine

Of course, there were still those items which the ex-sergeant had no chance of finding because for a fortnight, true to my intentions, I had kept the little oilskin bag of relics in a cavity under the passenger seat of the van, in a padded jiffy parcel. One late afternoon, when the weather was wet, I let Finbar go off early and wandered up the lane and turned into the driveway of Herton House. Obviously this driveway had once been a broad sweep of raked gravel but now it was reduced to a pair of gritty tracks with a central strip of grass and nettles. Under dark clouds, through a heavy, dripping silence I approached what must be the remnants of a civilisation lost for years behind a screen of rampant hydrangea, rhododendron and holly. I heard only the bite of my own footsteps and the sound of water slipping between tiers of glossy leaves and sliding quietly into the black earth.

The house sat bland and solid, each window shut tight. Never had I come across a building so stripped of anything that could have given it charm, never was there a front door more closed, more assured of its own bulk. It hadn't been opened in years and had no intention of being opened now, I was toying with comparisons to the House on the Hill, Castle Dracula, sharp white Transylvanian teeth until I saw the homely sign on one of the door panels, hand written, laminated, with a right–pointing arrow: **Will callers please go to the back entrance and ring the bell.** As I walked toward the corner of the house, I passed the little postern door and, instinctively, I walked faster the quicker to round the rough walls of the windowless castellated annexe behind which for all I knew, mad Aunt Agapanthus burbled away her endless days or a depraved Balkan baron exhausted by bouts of nocturnal feeding rested in his sarcophagus.

But that's me, flippant as ever, clever clever, and so wrong about so many things. I assumed the paving in the rear courtyard, when I got there, was weed-choked and neglected – of course it should be. But in fact the joints of the slate flags had been carefully planted with phlox, thrift and camomile. The back entrance, another heavy black door, lay across this old courtyard. On one side of the quadrangle were old stable blocks which I assumed were full of furniture: a prehistoric Land Rover and a newer Luton van stood parked alongside them. Quite ornate cloister-like walkways took up the other two angles, with japanned and finialed lamps bolted every few yards, strangely urban ornamentation in such a place as Herton. As I turned toward the door I noticed a gate between two of the outbuildings and caught a glimpse of the meticulous grid of veg plots I'd seen from the top of the box hedge.

The bell-pull slid out on grease and shot back with a soft thud. A butler's bell sprung on the end of some Heath Robinson system of wires, was presumably tinkling in some remote part of the house. A long time passed and all was still quiet, I was about to walk away and leave it for another day when the door was abruptly opened by a tall, sparely built elderly man with filmy brown eyes and a hook nose, smoking a hand-rolled cigarette. He eyed me with cynical suspicion, as if waiting for a sales pitch, the appearance of a clipboard or a sample case. He looked over my shoulder to see if I was alone, scanned me quickly from head to foot. I was wasting his time. 'Yes ... what?'

'Ah ... right. I'm sorry to trouble you, I don't know if you're Mr Digweed or Mr Trelease. My name's Pete Florence and I'm working on the garden next door. I've found something you might be interested in' I had been standing with the jiffy bag behind my back, I now produced it 'it might even belong to you'

'That it?' He looked at it sideways, like a bird. 'What is it?'

'A collection of relics, found it in the old outhouse in the side of the motte. "A collection of relics" that's what was written on the slate, it's old. A hundred and fifty odd years'

Suddenly he must have decided to trust me for he stepped aside and I was allowed over the threshold, into Herton House, vaguely aware that this might be a privilege few were granted. If there was to be any kind of friendship, this must be its beginning.

The kitchen was large and lived in, with a bouquet of Marmite and new bread, a chess game was set up on the refectory table. The chairs were old and worn smooth. 'I'm Arthur Digweed' he filled the kettle and placed it on the Rayburn 'd'you play chess?'

'Well, let's say I know *how* to play chess but I'm no good at it, you won't get much of a game out of me I'm afraid'.

'Pity. I'll make a cup of tea in a minnit. Let's see what you've got then'.

I spread the contents of the oilskin bag on the kitchen table. Arthur Digweed stared for a moment, pushed the items round with his finger, picked up one of the tiny pebbles.

'The little piece of slate' I said 'turn it over'.

By now, another man had appeared in the room, much the same age as Digweed but stockier, with a half–grown beard. 'George come over yer, see what this chap've found in the ground ... where exactly did ee find it?'

'Under the floor of the old shed in the side of the motte'

'The lock–up, you'm talking of' said the other man who I assumed was George Trelease. His voice was soft and friendly, despite appearances. 'Well bugger me. Pass me glasses Arthur willee. What's this? "Jane Digweed and Geoffrey Trelease – eighteen fifty-three!"'

'I thought I'd better give this to you gentlemen, my asisstant was all for giving it to the arkos'

'Quite right too' said Arthur Digweed. 'Very thoughtful of you. This is private stuff, nobody else's business. Mind you, Cawsand's alright. George knows un bedder than I do. He's alright innee George that Tony Cawsand?'

'That's an old dagger that is' said George Trelease 'have to look after that twill be brittle as hell. Cawsand? He iddn a bad sort of bloke, ex-army y'know, he's bin trying to get into the garden fer yers to scratch about but Arthur wouldn't let un. He must've got round they new people. He's bin yer to see us once or twice because my great-grandfather wrote a book on the history of Herton and I knows a bit about it meself'

'He's got a maid with un now, you sin her?' said Arthur Digweed, swirling hot water in the teapot 'says her's his daughter but her iddn'.

'He adopted her' I said 'sort of rescued her. Her whole family were killed in Yugoslavia'

'Tis a sad state of affairs out there' said George. 'What is it they'm callin it? Ethnic cleansing? Tis just bliddy murder, pure and simple ... anyway Jane Digweed and Geoffrey Trelease, that's my granny and granfer that is! Bugger me, eh? Thanks ever so much fer not lettin the sergeant get hold of this; they'm always diggin people up and pokin about, they archaeologists, tryin to find out what they died uv and such. Tis really none of their bliddy business!'

'We know a lot about our family' said Arthur 'they're interconnected see. Years ago, George's people used to live in the old farmhouse and two of the upstairs rooms was knocked into one ... oh, must be forty yer ago now, nineteen fifty six? I say knocked into one, but these rooms was one big one before and they'd been stud partitioned with lath and plaster. When they was knocking down the partition, out fell this package. From the wall cavity'.

'There's surprise packages turning up here all the time if you ask me'

'Oh aye! And I've just thought! There's a photo in with that package, from 1886, you know it George. Tis a family photo, and that maid that's with Sergeant Cawsand looks just like a maid that's in that photo'

She crossed my mind just then, Joanne, I can think of no other way to put it. The image of her, eyes wide open, staring straight at me, clear and cold, *crossed my mind* like a ghost image, a poor TV signal. 'Just like her?' I said.

'The dead spit' said Arthur Digweed. 'You married?'

I made an affirmative sound. I didn't want to bring Julie into this room, even the notion of her, there was no possibility of her involvement. She went nowhere with me, did nothing with me. I haven't mentioned her, have I? This is why. She wants no part of my life.

'Children?' Arthur Digweed seemed intent on family enquiries. I was equally intent on avoiding them. I turned to George Trelease, who was holding a lock of blond hair up to the light. 'All our family's fair' he said 'just like all the Digweeds is dark'

'What was in your package then Mr Trelease? Just family photos?'

'My Gud no!' he said 'if twas only photos it wouldn't have been hid in the wall. There was good reason to hide it I can tell ee. There was notebooks and a couple of drawings and this one photo. I'll show you the photo, since you've bin good enough to save this stuff from they wadeecallum?' he snickered 'arkos?'

He left the room and Arthur Digweed, whistling softly, busied himself with the teapot. I sat back and rested, and I realised tension was going out of me, just resting was something I hardly ever experienced. The dentist's chair, where I'm powerless to change whatever's being done to me, is one of the few places I totally relax and resign myself totally to another being, albeit the dentist. George Trelease was back quickly with a green card document wallet which he opened it and flicked through. 'Yer' he said 'this is it, the whole lot of um, Digweeds and Treleases, there's Jane Trelease and there's Geoffrey and there's the maid on the end of the back row, next to un. The only woman in a row of men. Er's tall'

I'd seen her immediately, I didn't need to be shown. This was not just a blond female who bore a resemblance to Joanne, it *was* Joanne. 'Jesus Christ, that's her!' I felt female fingers groping for me again, like when I first saw her, when the merest flit of a smile like low sunlight winking off broken ice acknowledged me, and she carried on striding away without looking back away down the path and I stood in the aftermath of her, agog, inhaling her sex like a dog. And there she was in the photograph, even across more than a century of time and the medium of a camera my stare still rebounded back at me off the polished glass of her eyes.

'Funny–looking maid. Tis true though, what they say about the eyes in pictures following you about. The rest of um looks normal enough but she's a ... I'm right aren't I? She looks like that maid of Cawsand's'

'Oh yes, Mr Trelease, you're quite right'

Arthur Digweed had poured tea and filled a plate of biscuits – Digestive, Custard Creams, Thin Arrowroot, Nice – he too was a remnant of times past. 'I was glad to see you berryin all that bliddy rubbish' he said with a wink to George Trelease 'tis illegal y'know. And I'll tell you summin else that might be. I've read they notebooks, and there's parts of um where my eyes was out on stalks! If I was old Jane I would have got rid of them.'

'Oh, come on Arthur, they iddn that bad! Tis only through they that I know how my father was conceived *and* I know why he was called George *and* I know my grandfer Geoffrey weren't his father, so my grandfer Geoffrey iddn my grandfer at all!'

'Complicated old business, eh?' Arthur Digweed offered the biscuits with a smirk 'from what *I* can gather, Jane Digweed, Jane Trelease as she became, wanted children desperate, just loved kiddies. You know there's a building looks a bit like a house-cum-church just across from the Home Farm? ... well, she ran a school for the local kiddies in that buildin, more or less paid for it out of her own pocket. But however much she tried (and, believe me, no-one could have tried harder) she couldn't get pregnant. Now, these things here were little things her and Geoffrey gathered when they were exploring, they grew up together, they were childhood sweethearts. Can you see it in your mind's eye, when they were kiddies and the world was unknown? There was no-one she was closer to than Geoffrey Trelease and yet she couldn't conceive, couldn't have his children. No. Tis a bad world. George's granfer was a chap called George Jago, worked on the barges down near Rafton. Tis all there in they notebooks. There's even a drawin of un – but I shan't hangin it on the wall I can tell ee!'

There were other occasions when I drank tea *chez* Digweed but I never roamed further into the house than that warm kitchen, I was never asked. They were friendly enough, at least toward me, but there was a reservedness about them which I neither would nor could penetrate. They tolerated me as long as I listened to what they said and was not too curious myself. One day, for instance, I asked why there was a bit of a castle stuck on the end of the house. The reply was that William Digweed had a lot of money and no sense of humour and that was that. But I knew that if I waited long enough, if I was a good boy, one day I would be allowed to read the notebooks.

I don't think the two things are related, but it was not long after my first encounter with Messrs Digweed and Trelease I began to descend the slippery slope, and was reverting rapidly to daydreaming. After work or at weekends as long as I had the energy I would walk in the dark, in deserted places, so that I could imagine myself out of the present and into a past less populated: so that I could feel bodiless. I already had nobody in the other sense – Julie had said nothing to me for weeks, the house was unkempt, the cupboards smelled of fungus, the bath had a tidemark, the garden was sad and battered, and only the dog was still happy. There's not much point in going into it, neither of us cared about the other, I must take my share of the blame and that's it, over and done with. I knew I must find a life; and, until I could invent a new one, an old one refurbished would just have to do.

I had the freedom of a young man made empty by the experience of an older one – I was nothing and I was nowhere. Near the end of the month, when the job at Herton was getting on for half done, the weather settled down cold and clear; and I took to walking with Bobby the dog along the shore down by the Coley, for the brackish mystery of the air and the star-laden sky. Maybe I dreamed of meeting some other soul down there, on the empty coast. I must have conveniently forgotten that I was past forty, and that there were no 'other souls', and if there were they were all busy or spoken for, and that the friendship of an animal was all I could expect.

Although the sky at night is utterly predictable, I never knew in advance what would be there; my knowledge of astronomy was patchy and unscientific, and I took things as they came. On this particular night the Moon was veiled and disappointing, hovering dim in the East to South-East – but in the West, over the sea, four planets were stacked up one above the other! Mercury, Jupiter and Venus seemed to drift together obliquely like a procession of flares fired out over the water; and Saturn was there too, at the same angle but high and solitary. As I threw limbs of driftwood for the running shadow of Bobby or sat watching the tide race quietly in, the three bright planets descended slowly in echelon toward the sea. Of course I was brooding, thinking that work was still slow in coming in, after Herton there would be still be nothing left to do – my wife had put up the closed sign, my life was a product which had been discontinued, and time was moving fast. I was hypnotised by self-pity. Out beyond the dunes the sea droned, the rising Coley whispered on the gravelly shore and there was a screaming sound in the distance that I couldn't identify. Then a voice that I could.

I should have been utterly shocked but all I felt was a shiver of lust, then tranquillity, and confidence.

'Time' she said out of the darkness 'moves neither fast nor slow'.

She appeared as if I had willed it. Someone, after all, was looking after me. But I hadn't seen her on the shore where she would have stood out against the river; she must have come out of the dunes on one of the tracks from Rafton. I didn't turn my head, but I sensed her sit quietly down on the sand and cross her legs. I reached out and rested a hand on her knee. There was only the light of stars but I could make out her bright hair, and the shrouded bloom of her pale face hovering above a sheath of dark clothing.

'It's good to see you' I said 'and don't think I'm surprised. I hoped for it. I *wanted* you to be here. And you know my thoughts, I'm not surprised at that either'

'So, Mister Thoroughly Unsurprised, what do you do out here on your own?' She spoke with only a slight accent, which I assumed was Balkan.

'I think. So, how can I help you, Joanne?'

'Cho! My name to you is Cho'

'Tony says he doesn't know your real name. It upsets him.'

'Tony is a kind man. I like Choanne, it suits me OK'

I started to roll a cigarette and I struck my lighter to make sure I had the sticky side of the paper. 'Tell me about Time then, Jo' I said. She wasn't looking at me. Her knees were drawn up and she was resting her chin on her arms, staring straight out across the river to the other bank. 'Not now Mister Florence, not now, there's nothing to tell about it anyway. Time is just Time. That's all I meant. It doesn't move fast or slow, it just moves' She was easy, talking to me like this, in the middle of nowhere, in the middle of the night. The world belonged just to us.

She was picking up fistfuls of sand and letting it run through her fingers. 'I can't believe I'm sitting here talking to you' I said. The flax of her hair flowed from her head, spilled over her knees and thighs. I wanted to hold it, that hair, and study it strand by strand. 'Bandit country over there' I said, instead 't'other side of the Coley where they eat their own young'. And she laughed, a brief, polite little snort, then her hand was on my shoulder and she was on her feet.

'Bugger Time!' she said 'I will throw wood for your dog. What is his name called?'

'He's called Bobby'.

'Ha! Well! I will call him Smokey. It's what he's like, you can hardly see him, a little cloud of smoke on the sand' Then she was running with Bobby, calling him Smokey, confirming this by plying him with the kind of short, chunky driftwood he loved. They seemed made for each other. He'd *be* Smokey, if *she* said so. She ran all over the beach with him and down to the edge of the river; when she came back both girl and dog were breathless. Bobby chose to lie next to her, flat out, panting on the cool sand, reeking of the sticking mud that lay near the river.

'Not only have you tried to re-name my dog just like that' I said, laughing 'but you've worn the poor animal out!' She was still breathing heavily and lying flat on her back. 'Is *your* tongue hanging out? I can't quite see' I reached over toward the blur of her face and found her cheek, I felt the heat of her breath on my wrist; then she covered the back of my hand with hers and steered it to her mouth, she trailed the hard tip of her tongue rather slowly across my palm. Erection was instantaneous.

With the certain attraction of bodies – gravity, magnetism – my head was approaching hers through the dark. 'My tongue?' she said 'hanging out? Oh yes'. And it slid fearlessly into my mouth. Joanne's tongue.

Her free hand was moving in my hair, her little finger was probing my ear and though lust was now unstoppable, there was some sweet delay. Drawing off her boots for instance, a pleasant distraction, the leather so soft and lined with fleece, like peeling away the skin of a fruit. As she was springing the button of her jeans and working the zip, I made her wait whilst I massaged the skin of her calf (for they were *flared*, her jeans, fashion had come full circle over the difference between our ages). I took off my coat, shirt and sweatshirt, crying out in the cold air; she was struggling out of her own coat and spreading it beside her, moving over onto it, making an arch and twisting out of her jeans. I was on my knees between her spread legs, lowering my trousers; my cock had shrunk to the size of a peanut and I threw my overcoat back on before I froze to death. 'Jesus Christ it's cold!' I said, wrapping myself and my coat round her. She crossed her ankles on my lower back and we stayed locked together, naked in a sandwich of woolly coats, exchanging heat, charging up slowly.

She was a kisser, Joanne, a snogger. I would say like a teenager but of course she *was* a teenager. So we kissed at great length, even when I was hard again she seemed in no hurry; I spent an age working two crossed fingers inside her with my thumb resting in her soft nap of hair. I was sure I was dreaming. But when I took my fingers out, she reached down straight away and guided me in. Inevitably, after such a preamble, the act itself was of baboon-like brevity; and I was lying face down with sand in my nostrils, tracing her lips with tacky fingers and she was licking them clean. 'I don't believe it' I said.

By eleven o'clock we were walking back toward Rafton on the long dyke, in no particular hurry. Saturn, the last of the four falling planets, was disappearing below the dunes, and Bobby/Smokey was trotting tidily, watching our flanks. 'They say it's an anaesthetic' she said.

'What, sex? Who says?'

'*They* say. OK? It's right for you, Mister Florence. You are not a relaxed man'

'Well, I certainly feel as though I'm not really here, I don't *believe* I'm here … I've no weight. I might as well be on that planet. I think we need to do it again.'

'Not now, Pete. And you would *not* like it on Saturn'

'You called me Pete'

'A slip of the tongue'

'You know? That's Saturn?'

'Of course I know it's Saturn. And the others in descending order were Venus, Jupiter and Mercury. Saturn's very big, all clouds, spins fast like candy floss'

'But it's very beautiful' I took her hand.

'It would float, if there was a sea that big. There was a woman who lived at Herraton once, who thought as a girl that the sky was a black cloth full of holes held up to a strong light'

'Oh yes, lived at Herton? Recently?'

'Ages ago. She was called Jeanne Mareschal'

'That name rings a bell, Tony's mentioned it, Domesday Book and all that. But did you say you *knew* her?'

'I did yes, I did know her. I was much younger then. I gave my child to her. They called him Gwilliam or something'

'You gave her your child. You had a *child*?'

'Quite so. Girls do. I was attacked by a group of men in the hills somewhere over there' She pointed back the other way, in the general direction of Marshbury. 'They all fucked me and left me in a ditch, by a hedge'

I was shocked not so much by the event but by her calm description of it. 'So how old were you then? I mean how old *are* you? I'm not even sure what we did just now was legal'

'The same'

'The same?'

'The same age as I am now'

'So this happened, like, the other day?'

'No, I told you Mister Florence didn't I? Ages ago!'

'*When*?'

'Eleven Thirty Five'

'Not the *time of day*, Joanne! When was it these men raped you?'

'E-le-ven Thir-ty FIVE!'

I laughed.

She stopped and opened her mouth and closed her eyes as if she was about to scream. 'I'm sorry Jo' I said 'not the right time to laugh' We'd reached the metalled road at the end of the dyke; Rafton lay one way, my house the other. There was a house on the other side of the road with an outdoor light on a garage.

'OK' she said 'You're a lucky man. I'm going home now, I will be seeing you in the morning. You can behave as though nothing has happened please'

'Go careful, Jo. Sleep tight'. I could see she was looking straight at me, and I felt suddenly drained, as though more than seed had been extracted from me. She was reading me, scanning information from me.

'Yes?' she was saying. 'Yes? You behave as though nothing has happened. I will help you then. OK?'

'Yes, Jo. You help me' I put my hand on her shoulder. 'Goodnight kiss ...?' But she turned quickly and strode away with her arms folded, like she walked around the site at Herton. She would soon be back in the little house tucked away near the quay. I stood and watched her departing back, she never turned, and she never looked around. The knowledge that I would never be likely to understand a word she said left me feeling good, oddly enough. I was smiling to myself ... 'you can behave as though nothing has happened' ... her language may be clumsy and quaint, I thought, but the way she communicated was beyond speech. She could use her tongue, indeed she could. Words were wasted on it.

CHAPTER TEN

The Mobile Home

Pete Florence, what can I say on him? He's not a bad bloke, not exactly unkind. Like he lets me go early sometimes and he'll still pay the full day. But he don't have all that much in the way of consideration? Like my name's Finbar Grounds, right, and one of the first things he ever said to me was ... don't take this wrong he said, but an anagram of your name would be dung for brains. And this was, like, more or less as soon as we met – he must've been thinking about it whilst we was talking. And I was so pissed off I spent loads of time trying to work out some clever anagram for him but the best I could come up with was petrol fence and perfect lone. The first was just silly but the second's got, like, something to it? Like he's a sort of a lone type and he thinks he's perfect.

He gets on well with that archaeologist. Two of a kind maybe. If me life depended on it I'd have to say I think he's an arsehole, Cawsand I mean, not Pete. He wears this like Crocodile Dundee hat and one of them green things with no sleeves and lots of pockets and stuff. Army type and full of himself. The two or three lads who work for him call him their Great Leader. I'm buggered if I'd want to do what they do, you know, crawling about all day on all fours in all sorts of weather picking and scraping with trowels and stuff for shit money. Every so often one of them'll pry some like absolutely minute shapeless thing out of the dirt and call for head arko and he'll poke it around in the palm of his hand, and peer at it through a glass until he can say it's like a button or bit of pottery or a petrified sheep's bollock. Barry Hammond hates him. He's off his JCB now and Cawsand's got him perched on this poxy little thing like a toy and the instructions he gives him are like so precise and fiddly? Makes me laugh, old Barry winking over at me and sticking his tongue out the corner of his mouth and shutting one eye like he's *really* concentrating.

And who takes all the bagged–up little bits of history and stuff away to the old cowsheds? The lovely Joanne. The blonde babe from Bosnia. Thin as a fucking rake. And she ain't really his daughter. One day last week me and Pete was having a bit of a crack about her and Cawsand, like he was having it away with her sort of thing (only Pete called it a 'sexual liaison') – I said it must be like fucking a skeleton and he said: 'Imagine the motor home rattling on its wheels to the grinding of bones in the dead of night'. That's how he talks, like funny but you're not quite sure. Only this week he's been different, he don't say anything about her, in fact he don't say much about anything.

Jo? She's got these, like, *really* thin lips without any colour, no eyebrows that you'd notice, no hips to speak of and no tits. She ain't my cup of tea at all, know what I mean? The lads doing the digging and scraping are OK, students apparently. Know what? I reckon old Pete fancies her, when she's about he's like, edgy? You can't just say to him what's going on because he'll cold-shoulder you ... none of your business, keep yer trunk out ... that's what he's like. But he never speaks to her apart from civilities, and she don't say a lot but she looks, right, and I mean *looks*. She makes my skin crawl, actually. It's like she knows you inside out? She makes me feel like I'm worth a few pence less than a dog turd. I don't know if that's how she treats the Head Arko, but he's such an ignorant sod he probably don't notice.

While they're here, we're not busy. We're poncing about doing little bits of handwork, and we have to follow on behind them. One morning early, we're raking over a rough corner ready for seed and the Head Arko's turbo diesel draws up, Jo's in there with him as usual. 'Morning, Mister Florence!' he shouts over to Pete 'Joanne's got a plan of the motte and bailey worked out, thought you might like to see it. I'll just bang the kettle on. Come in when you're ready. One sugar and milk for the both of you, right?'

And this is a great honour for me! Like whod've guessed that the lowly Finbar Grounds would've been asked into the great man's mobile home. Pete raked over another couple of yards just in case anybody thought we didn't have anything better to do and I finished filling the barrow with stones and crap and went off for a slash while he went on in. The motor home looked sort of big from the outside but inside it was tiny, you had to watch where you put yer elbows and stuff. The Croc's there washing up mugs at the sink, like doing domestic stuff, the great man himself. And Pete's there sitting down at this table that's not much bigger that a Frisbee y'know, and Jo's on the other side of it and she's looking straight at him and he's looking straight at her. And it was like there was stuff passing between them, like they was locked together and while I'm like taking all this in I somehow catch my toe on the step and I end up halfway through the door on all fours like a fucking dog angling for a biscuit. Embarrassing or what?

'Do mind the step' says Cawsand, turning from the sink.

'Drunk already' says Pete.

And Jo, right, just giggles like a little girl, that's probably the only time I'll ever hear her laugh. No one says you OK Finbar or nothing like that. I just have to get up and say 'whatever' and flex me knees and try and stay like dignified? Anyway I've put paid to whatever kind of vibes was going down between her and Mister Florence. He's *got* to be fucking her on the quiet. I know he's not all that happy with his missus. So anyway Jo gets busy suddenly and, like, takes off her coat and plugs in her laptop. I'm still standin in the doorway watching and yeah she's dead thin like I said but I've gotta admit she's neat, nothing outa place. The rattle of bones goes through me mind, like when we was having a laugh the other week.

She boots up the laptop anyway and stares at the screen with them bug eyes. Pete's rolling a fag. 'OK' she says in that icy way of hers, O as in Orange, 'OK ... here we are'.

Pete and me close in from different directions so we're standing either side of her. A rose between two thorns I could say but it's more like ... what? Like I'm really confused. Her hair's parted neatly and I can see the white skin. I haven't seen hair like it. She's wearing a tight black top like she usually does and if I look down her back I can see the outline of her bra. You wonder why she wears one. Her fingers are like really bony and white and dead fast on the keyboard. Up it comes on the screen, her plan of the old castle. I have to lean forward so that my hand's on the back of her chair, I'm that close to her I can feel heat coming off her face and I can smell her hair.

'As it would have been from about 1080 until about 1150, you will see how all the known fahm buildings, including Herton House, is inside the old bailey, you see the outer bailey is around 45 metres by 45 metres and the motte is about 22 metres square'

'And she's done this in ten days!' said Cawsand, still with his back to us pouring boiled water into the cups. 'How does she do it eh? It's almost like she was there and walked around the place. Software that cost an arm and a leg, bit of imagination and a lot of skill. That's my girl!'

I was looking at a shape like a fried egg with the mound as the yolk but over in one corner was the flat area with sloping sides, what's called in the trade the bailey. And the plate it was on was the moat. When she put it into 3D you could see the bailey had, like, wooden stakes and stuff driven in all round it. It was well drawn. It was like the Croc said, like you were really there, and she was guiding us through it with the mouse. 'We'd like to do some digging on top of the motte, if you don't mind …' Now, Pete's been bitching away ever since they got here about them holding us up but all he did was gave a shrug like it's all the same to him, whatever, and I felt Jo's shoulder against my thigh suddenly and I realise that Pete's shrug has given her a nudge – so he's been standing there resting his own thigh right up against her. I knew he was banging her.

'There's evidence of a fair amount of building up on the motte' Cawsand's saying as he's spooning in sugar and stirring. Pete's got his hand on Jo's shoulder but she shrugs it off. 'Very interesting…' Cawsand's rambling on '… either it was one of those places the Normans knocked up soon after the conquest to subdue the natives and fairly quickly decommissioned, say after less than a century, or else it was built during the Anarchy for the duration, We think it was built in the late Eleventh Century and that the mound was reduced by the mid Twelfth'

I'm not getting involved in this. Don't know what he's going on about.

'Anarchy?' Pete's saying. Cawsand turns and brings the cups of coffee over. Jo leans back from the computer and stretches her arms, me and Pete moves away. 'What anarchy's that? My grasp of medieval history is weak I'm afraid'

'*The* Anarchy, with capital letters' The sergeant sits with us. 'Rape, loot and pillage, plunder, murder, and torture. The worst kind of yobbo on the loose with carte blanche. Nothing like it before or since, at least in this country'.

That's well gross. I've seen films with people being burned alive and tied to cartwheels and stuff.

'From around Eleven thirty-five up to the mid-fifties' says Joanne 'and the earlier buildings are from soon after the Conquest, from the ten-eighties up until the mid twelfth century. Might have been on the site of a Saxon farmstead…'

I'd taken my coffee and moved over to the doorway. I was watching her as she spoke; she was, like, shifting in her seat and sort of playing about with the buttons of her mouse, caressing them with two fingers? And she was looking straight at *me*, I don't know why. Those eyes of hers, like fucking marbles. Oh yeah, I saw the way she and Pete were looking at each other and this was well different. They were sort of talking to each other but she wasn't giving me anything, just scanning me quickly as she spoke. It was like having yer clothes peeled away, like having something removed and not just yer appendix but like something useful?

'If nobody minds' I said 'I'm going outside to drink this'. I mean that's well rude but I couldn't help it. She was pushing me away as good as like she'd put her palm on me chest and shoved me.

'You OK Finbar?' said Pete.

No I'm fucking not I thought. 'Yeah, I'm OK. It's nothing personal'.

'I'll be there in a minute' Pete said. He looked a bit worried. Like I said he ain't a bad sort of bloke. But he wasn't going to leave until he was ready. Fair enough. I sat on one of the camp chairs where the Croc's team, who were now appearing for work, ate their lunch in good weather. I was glad to be outside. Considering it was only the first few days of March the weather wasn't bad; the bits of the garden we hadn't touched were full of daffs and the sun was warm. In a few minutes, and he must have knocked back his coffee like it was tequila, Cawsand strides past with a set of lines and an armful of short stakes, on his way up to the top of the motte where he started ordering his lads around and pegging out.

Then Pete came out. 'What's up Finbar?'

I had to lie me head off didn't I? I couldn't say I was exhausted. I couldn't say she's like a magnet. 'Yeah' I said 'I'm all right. I just came over a bit funny in there, like dizzy y'know. Just give me five, I'll be there in a minute. And I just want to have another look at that plan and stuff, I've got an idea'. But Pete didn't say 'Bollocks, Finbar! You don't have ideas!' He just said 'OK see you in a minute. You can tell me your idea'. And once you felt a bit sorry for him he weren't scary at all.

So when I went back in she was in there alone, still sitting at the table, looking at me over her coffee cup, with her thin white face and her dead grey eyes. I walked over to the sink and put my cup down on the drainer. It felt like I was walking through, like really *thick* air?

'You were sniffing my hair' she said 'lemons, it smells of. My shampoo is lemony. You have a problem Mister Grounds'

'What is it you want, Joanne?'

'Your boss also wished to know what I want. Well, I don't want anything. He got what he wanted well enough. Now, you have a problem as I have said – don't look at the floor! – your girlfriend'

'Hayley? You don't know Hayley! So what's going on here?'

'She works at the Bonville Arms, all right, and you are very jealous of the men, the customers. Jealousy is your problem, Finbar. Now what if your Hayley had seen you studying the plan of the motte and smelling my hair and thinking about my tits, such as they are. Why shouldn't she be jealous? You don't think of her much do you? She doesn't cross your mind from one hour to the next, but you can still manage a bit of jealousy. And you think I've arranged for you to come back in here so that we can be alone, so that now or later you can fuck me. And you would too wouldn't you?'

I was totally gobsmacked, there wasn't nothing I could say. Like she was *so* right I couldn't argue with her. I've lived with Hayley for, like, ages and have I mentioned her? Well, no.

'Your girl Hayley loves you, you won't dare upset her will you?'

'Ah, no'

'And now you're thinking what about Mr Florence? Mr Florence's wife does not love him and he does not love her. That is his problem and his solution is different, it involves sex. So, the Bonville Arms, I knew a Lord de Bonville'

You *know* Lord Bonville?'

'I *knew* a Lord *de* Bonville, I said, long time ago'

'In Bosnia, you knew a Lord Bonville? You are a very strange lady' I said and for some reason held out my hand.

'Don't even think about it' she said.

There wasn't anywhere I could have hid. She saw it all. Put me right in my place. No more skeleton jokes and stuff, I spose. So when I came out of the Croc's mobile home I felt like Zig from the planet Zog stepping out of his space ship onto unknown terrain and like my head had been through, what, a cheese grater?

Hardly A Love Nest

In the end, Sergeant Cawsand and his merry band were there not two weeks but two weeks and two days. Cawsand took away a little collection of odds and ends but I think it was mostly the ordinary detritus of human settlement, nothing entire or exciting. Mundane items people create, use and throw to one side. The collection of things Finbar and I came across were more interesting but Tony, Michael, Virginia, still know nothing of them. I expect Joanne knows, since she knows everything.

Events conspired to leave me at Herton alone for a week. Me, working to a price with nothing much to go on to afterwards. You're right, I did sod all. It was a good week in most ways. Some fine spring weather, the thorn hedges starting to break, celandines. This was shortly after Julie actually went, deprived me of her physical presence (the movie they said would never be made!) and I was left alone with Bobby and a house soon to be on the market. I was devastated ... well, a bit devastated ... okay, not very devastated. Actually I walked in a dream of inane ecstasy, smiling at strangers. Ruin at last! Michael and Virginia went off to New Zealand for three weeks and poor young Finbar, due to an excess of shovelling (for which I blame Tony Cawsand, since much had to be done by hand during his régime) had put his back out and I made him go home and rest it, it'll take a week to clear up I said and offered to lend him my stick.

So I was suddenly and utterly alone in all the aspects of my life. Only the dog was with me. And Joanne. She is why I took to making gentle small talk with the newsagent from whom I bought my tobacco, stroking other people's dogs, and smiling at children. A sweet time of leisure and a certain emptiness of mind. I was on site at Herton every day but I tended to work in the mornings and potter in the afternoons, waiting for the return of Finbar.

Though I've lived here all my life, I was surprised at the number of places I'd never been, like the wood called Marshall's Wood which I must have seen so many times and never entered. If you went over the fields from Herton and came back toward it through Marshall's Wood you saw the castle quite suddenly, on a spur of high land, unmistakably military. From this direction the motte was high and clear against the sky rather than hidden behind the farm buildings, and I discovered a small network of lanes that seemed either to end with a gateway at the edge of the wood or else turn back on themselves. Most of them were sunk well below the wood floor, banked and retained with thousands of finger-wide flakes of shillet rock. Part of it was spruce plantation, some of it natural growth of birch and sweet chestnut, there were outcrops of rock and small pools beside the track, broken sunlight and mossy stumps, springs that trickled like tears down glossy green faces of rock. You couldn't help thinking of the past; George Trelease had said it, we too would soon be the past.

Yes, I was alone verging on lonely, and I even missed Finbar. He was a good lad with a sense of humour like my own, an habitual asker of questions that he felt I must as an older man be able to answer – like when did Mao Tse Tung come to power in China, how long was the battle of Stalingrad, what was the capital of North Korea. (In the end, Virginia had to be asked to look that one up. 'Pyong Yang!'

came from her like a war cry out of the window of her husband's office 'so says the Internet!') Just before Finbar's stance degenerated into a permanent stoop he had taken to making subtle (for him) remarks about Jo, little comments like 'no more jokes about shagging skeletons, then Pete'. It was when he was singing 'dem bones, dem bones, dem dry bones' that I caught him right in the mouth with a flung banana skin.

To dislike Finbar is impossible. He told me that Jo reckoned she knew Lord Bonville and I said that was quite likely. There was nothing she didn't know. He was afraid of her, I'm certain of it. 'What do we know about her Pete?' he said 'if she's from Yugoslavia how come she knows Bonville? *And* she knew Hayley worked in the pub. She's hardly out of school for Christ's sake' I told him carelessly that I didn't care where she came from or where she was going, that all that mattered was she was here now.

'She makes me feel good, Finbar, simple as that. You're younger than I am, a lot of things make *you* feel good, and it's all sensation, am I right? (a snort of laughter) Oh, you can laugh but I haven't had much in the way of sensation for a long time and she is pure sensation, believe me'

I myself had 'stolen' Julie from another man, a friend; and I knew the imperatives of attraction, I knew that there were impulses you should simply follow, life being short.

There were only two places where I met Jo. One was Marshall's Wood, the other was a derelict farmstead up on the downs. I knew it, I had passed it several times on the road between Marshbury and the sea coast, and it was hardly a love nest. I had known it since I was a child, from an early age I studied the local ordnance survey map and it was called Dagworthy. I don't remember it as anything but derelict, a rare survival, the land around it farmed by others but the house and buildings let go and left, not even bought up by incomers. 'A bleak spot' I said when she insisted on going up there.

Bleak indeed. The house had no windows intact and smelled of musty neglect; most of the plaster lay on the floorboards, prised long ago from the walls by damp and rain, the few pieces of mortar that were left clung to the stonework like ancient continents. The dairy sheds were roofless and the old cow stalls green and brittle; the cobbles of the yard were slippery with moss and weed. Amongst the other outbuildings, open to the wind and strewn with litter, only one barn was more or less intact. We managed a few home comforts: blankets, what straw we could gather together, a wind-up lamp, a bottle of wine. Bobby/Smokey either curled up near us or else roamed round and about, looking in from time to time.

It was assumed by both of us that there was never any question of our relationship becoming public knowledge. She insisted we should not be seen together. I would pick her up on the outskirts of Rafton and we would drive through Marshbury and up on the downs in the dark. Always in the dark. Tony Cawsand knew nothing of it; she must have made some excuse to him for her absences but I, afraid of breaking the spell, never asked.

'We don't have to be in this godforsaken place, Jo, we can go to my house'

'Your wife' she said

'My wife's gone' I said, sighing with relief and annoyance.

'She will be back'

On one evening during my Week of Peace, we went up there, in the dark, and had sex without delay, removing only necessary items of clothing. Later, naked but for socks, we lay a long time face to face under a mound of blankets and coats, talking softly. I could have told this to anyone, friends if I had them, even Finbar, that there are moments of great privacy between two people – there *still* are! – but then he probably doesn't know that such moments of post-coital intimacy cannot necessarily be taken for granted. He isn't old enough to know how the colour of love can fade from red through pink to grey.

I became aware that Jo was telling me that it was away near here where she was raped. In the dark, in the middle of nowhere, I could listen forever to the soft passivity of her voice. I believed her and I didn't. Belief was not that important, my hands idled all over her skin as she spoke, up and down her flank, the cage of her ribs, over the hard buttons of her spine; and all the time she was reciting horrible events, apart from slight changes in the pressure of her fingertips on my shoulder blades, she never moved.

She talked of ivy and the smell of earth, the bitter grass she chewed; of being carried first by one man, then another. Though both were men they were utterly different: where one was taking her in some haste to be laid out for sex, the other was bearing her away quite gently (for he thought she was dead) to be draped over a horse. This latter man was Lord de Bonville. Nothing was easier with Jo than to be happily marooned on this island of the unknown where all belief was suspended. I had not forgotten the night on the beach by the Warrens, the four falling planets, and the bitter cold. Oh yes, she was every bit as cold and unreachable as Cawsand had said. But then I didn't want to *reach* her. I was lost in her body, the use of it she gave me and between times I was happy to listen to her, to whatever she was saying in that cool and quirky accent.

It was hard to reach someone who spoke of being tumbled into a grave, of being officially dead. She must have died many times. You could only stop wondering and listen. It's here she said, the grave, I could show Tony the archaeologist where he should dig; he would find them, the headless man, the old lady, the mother and her children, the father crushed against a tree by a cart.

'I don't need to know all this Jo' I whispered in the dark

'I know what you need to know' she said. 'Man after man fuck fuck fuck and they told me to shut my eyes but I wouldn't – I could have dealt with them, nobody tells me what to do, you Mister Florence must never try it. I made them feel watched so that they went about the business without any violence, rather gently, discussing their actions quietly, politely waiting their turn, like gentlemen (her body was quivering against me and I thought she was crying but she was laughing!). I told myself it was not so bad. I know what you think. Have you understood what I am? Many have hated me, many men. Those men left me for dead, in the rain, staring at stinging nettles. You, Mister Florence, do not love me and have been good enough not to spoil things. You want a body. You want sex. Well, have it Mister Florence, while you can'

'Thankyou, Miss Ex. I will. Before I'm completely past it, if that's what you mean. You are completely heartless, I've never come across anyone like it'.

'Miss Ex is not my name'
'That's OK. I don't want to know the real one'
'I shan't be telling you'
'Finbar's back'

'What about it?'

'You did it'

'No. He did it. Shovellink. You need this week alone'

'I do need it. Are you watching over me, and looking after me? Will you be *there* for me?' I laughed.

'You are a stupid man, Mister Florence' she said 'at the weekend I will see you in the Wood, I will be there for you then'

'Saturday afternoon, Miss Ex. I'm spending the morning with Messrs Digweed & Trelease, I'll be having another look at your photograph'

'Ah yes, I was not in that photograph, not truly. I never stood there, next to her husband'.

Cold Madonna

I had become an occasional but habitual visitor to Herton House, so much so that I was privileged enough to drive straight into the back courtyard and park next to the engine of George and Arthur's import and export enterprise, the Luton van. Wearing weekend clothes, similar to my working clothes but newer, I sat for a moment before I got out of the van. Terracotta and stone planting troughs were loaded with dwarf daffodils, spring squill and bright azaleas around the edges of the courtyard and either side of the door. As a gardener I couldn't fault the two old boys on their taste. It was a fresh, green yellow and blue sort of morning and when I got out of the van I limbered up, rocking on the balls of my feet, flexing the joints of my fingers – for I was on a promise.

If I cared to look in on Saturday morning, George had assured me that he would show me all of his granny's journals and drawings. And true to his word, he dumped them all on the kitchen table. 'There you go then' he said 'Arthur's gone into Marshbury and I'm gwain out to the garden. Have fun and help yourself to whatever you can find. There's milk in the fridge, kettle's simmerin. Don't let un boil dry'

Well, there was not that much to sum up the life of Mrs Jane Trelease, a modest little stack of nine manuscript books, tied parcel fashion with raffia. She was a sporadic diarist, not the sort to make meticulous entries each morning and evening; she wrote only when she had something to say or when she felt like it. There were gaps of months, even years. As I read it became clear that she received far more entries than she made, for his grandmother's abiding interest was copulation. I realised why old George's eyes must have stood out on stalks, double take after double take. Her diaries were no *Lark Rise To Candleford,* there was no nostalgia, no quotable insights into nineteenth century rural life, no game old characters. Though she made the occasional attempt to get off the subject (teaching, her family, this and that), she couldn't keep off sex for longer than a paragraph.

After an hour or so, by the time I had rescued the kettle from boiling dry and called George in for a cup of tea, I was well into the1870's. The sun had climbed higher and it truly was a lovely morning, I had found George moving a hoe with practised ease through the dark loam between immaculate rows of young peas, a careful man doing a meticulous job. 'Much obliged' he said, taking his tea, 'waddyreckon then?'

'Interesting' I said, rather lamely. 'Its still there, you know, or some form of it, the old hut down by the Coley'

'Tiddn the same one' said George 'can't be'

I knew it so well, the banks of sucking mud, the old hulks. It hasn't changed, a new generation of hulks lie there now, and the new hut that replaced the old has become the old one in its turn. As Joanne said, Time is utterly predictable, moving neither fast or slow. I'd sat inside that knackered old shed many times years ago, it was the kind of den where you'd mess about with the other boys from school, ogling magazines that someone found in a train compartment or someone else found in a litter bin, and smoking illicit fags. I felt I knew Jane Digweed straightaway, she too was led there by a secret sexual imperative, the satisfaction of her intense curiosity. She moved on from the Finger Thing (as she called it) and without a qualm let the sand and gravel merchant's assistant George Jago fuck her rigid.

I didn't get to the first diary for a while for I didn't read them in order but when I picked it up a drawing and a photograph fell out. The drawing made me laugh out loud. 'Life on the Ocean Wave' Jane Digweed 1863: rolling surf and a naked man, scaled up, rearing out of the waves pointing a massive erection along the beach. Waves were breaking over the reef of his cock, and the cormorants, my God what a laugh, ranked all along it like butler's coats on a washing line! Could this be the very penis, the conduit of the sperm of the very bargee that generated George's father?

A pity that she who could draw with such wit and skill and who could have written the most transcendent filth was reduced (though willingly) to writing stagy and tacky pornography under male pseudonyms. But how I would love to read her work, despite what I've said. Who might have a collection of mid nineteenth century written pornography? Surely someone. I must ask Finbar, he who surfs the net, no problem he'll say, straight to it – www.cornyoldporn.co.uk – the complete works of Ralph Marshall and William Jago in ten languages and a choice of fonts. If, as is generally assumed these nineteenth century men were so buttoned-up, they would surely need pornography to *be* that buttoned-up. They couldn't be dignified all the time. In private they could copulate with whomever their imagination could call forth. Jane knew her market. Ever since printing was invented, ever since the first man (or woman) could draw there must have been pornography.

The photograph was the same one that I saw before, the solid Victorian household gathered in ranks before the solid Victorian edifice. So which of the figures was Jane?

George pointed out a dark-haired woman wearing a hat with many folds and curls turning her face away and down from the camera. The man behind her was tall, fair-haired and lithe, resting his hand on her shoulder. I thought she looked disappointed, unhappy. It was not at all how I'd imagined her. 'The chap behind her is Geoffrey Trelease, her husband, who I thought for yers was my granfer. And on the other side of her right on the end there's the blond maid who nobody knew, no one seen her before or since. Tis in one of they journal books. Nobody liked the picture, everybody but Jane wanted to get rid of it'

'You know that's Cawsand's daughter, George, it doesn't just look like her, it *is* her'

'I can't say nothing about that'

'It's her, George. On the back of this photo – 1869. How can that be?'

'Buggered if I know. Weird-looking scrawny maid er is though'

He was looking at me askance and smirking. I felt myself blush – me, a man in his forties! As I looked down at the photograph, I was smirking myself.

'She's not as scrawny as she looks' I said 'nor as young'

'Just as bliddy well, or you'd have the police round for sure. Statue Tree Rape they call it'

'Bugger off George' I said laughing. George was like Finbar, impossible to dislike.

I studied the photograph after George went back to his garden peas, more to distract me from my own embarrassment than anything else. No one was supposed to know about me and Jo so how did that wily old sod find out? The Digweeds were a big family. Father, Mother, two sons, Jane and her twin sisters – all the young children at the front, the servants to the sides, even the gardeners with calico aprons and boots. What went through my mind as I scanned the gathered household and its servants? Only her of course, the real flesh and blood Jo. I found myself whispering parts of that poem of Keats, so well known as to be a cliché, *La Belle Dame sans Merci*. When I first read it, I naïvely thought that narcotic addiction produced visionary people, those prepared to risk everything to feed their imagination, rather than car audio thieves and shoplifters. But still the poem, to me, was all about the thraldom of the addict to his drug. When she's finished teasing you with her beauty and letting you so sweetly forget your pain, this silken, pliant, sighing belle dame kicks you out of bed onto the cold floor and leaves you hungry. Needless to say, the taming of this heartless bitch is just out of your grasp; a little more of the drug might help but in the meantime it's moved a little further away. Your addiction arises from her, she never quite does what you really need her to do.

At first I thought Mrs Trelease looked unhappy, turning askance, but perhaps she's just thinking about something else, looking out of the photograph into her own world. She's what they called handsome then with very dark hair and dark eyes, robustly built. No, she's not unhappy, she's turning away with a subtle smile. She'll be thinking about sex. She was more generous and good-hearted than Joanne (or whatever she called herself then) who was neither 'comely' nor well-furnished, builders on scaffolds wouldn't give her a second look and if they did they'd regret it: she was sexless, ruthless and peaky, more like a catwalk model than a belle dame.

And was she addictive? I mean Joanne. I had wanted to think about Jane Trelease, her warm features and her demure sideways look but instead … could you be *addicted* to Joanne? She was aloof and bland sure enough, perfect for those who tended to dependency. My God, what am I talking about? She's cold, without emotion … but I can't get her out of my mind? Madonna, cold Madonna. I said it aloud, George was whistling in the distance as he hoed. Cold Madonna. It means nothing. Read on …

30th August 1889: My son's laugh is an explosion of delight, I know I will have no trouble with him. He dashed all around the mound at top speed today, laughing his little head off. He's a gem, my reward for waiting. 'George Trelease, son of Geoffrey and Jane' scratched in the old book in the vestry, there for all time, but only half true I'm afraid. I even love to fret about him, creeping into his room and listening for his breathing, I can rest my fingers on the soft down on his cheek and feel the touch of his breath – he sleeps so deep and he plays so rough! What a crowd there was out in the garden today with all G's cousins! My Georgie talks <u>all</u> the time and <u>shouts</u> – young William was chasing him up and down the mound with spread arms and roaring like a dragon – 'not so rough Billy!' Becca was calling. Not so rough. My sisters have been prolific, despite their unattractive qualities, their husbands do not lack lead in their pencils.

Years ago I had those categories, what were they? Divine, Trusty and Carnal. There must be another now – Deadblock. Poor Geoffrey has no idea that four years ago, up on that mound in the middle of the night, I extracted the seed for our son from Jago. Why do I keep saying 'poor' Geoffrey – he's never been a happier man – so delighted to be a father at last. John, too, has a small brood of Digweeds, Charlie has yet to produce issue but then he isn't married and marriage, as I can attest, is the only way to produce recognisable children. Outrageous fact: though King Henry the First had twenty-one children only one (called Matilda) was official and that started off something called The Anarchy.

10th September 1889: My brother's boys are absolute Digweed males, idle and not keen to learn, I mean idle in the mind for they are keen enough to work. George is a handsome dreamy child, lively when roused, dark and curly and ruddy like an Egyptian.

10th January 1895: So who was that sapless girl whose name I never knew? She had an accent, don't know what – foreign. Strange, bland face without colour. Her hair, her skin, even her eyes were *drained* of colour. I had to take her advice, though, I just had to. If I hadn't, no Georgie. Even though I never spoke a word to her she knew what I wanted – I've forgotten a lot of what she whispered in my ear on the day of that tennis match when Jago and I rattled the cooking pots. I haven't seen Jago since. I think he was upset, rightly so I suppose. I treated him like a seed drill and sent him on his way as soon as I was sure I'd captured the stuff as the girl said. All fours it was, she said, but face to face and work it hard, stay locked like a dog – she was very crude actually for such a slight young thing, quite exciting – oh, I really mustn't think about it!

There was something in my father-in-law's history of Herton that throws light on who she was, I'm sure.

3rd April 1897: Have I taken others into account, as I should? My father? Jago? My sisters? My husband? Have I been a cold fish to all of them? Most likely yes, I have. To be ultimately fair to myself, I have always put Geoffrey first. I have given my life to him, no matter what ways I've given myself to others – I haven't given them any of my self, only temporary use of my body. My whole self has always belonged to Geoffrey. Arthur understood that, dear man. Geoffrey has always had my heart – so there, I haven't always been bad.

6th May 1897: I am retiring. Fifty-two years old. Long enough I'm sure. William Jago wrote his last scurrilous tale a few years ago and now it is time for Ralph Marshall to screw the cap on his pen for the last time. In the past few years I've gone back to sketching, I deal with Mr Norman Castle's son now, providing illustrations for his ridiculous stories. Faces of women in degrees of absorption, lopsided grins and protruding tongues (the readers like 'sweet pain', 'sweet moan', 'little whimpers of pleasure'). I had to produce a drawing this evening for the morning's post, George and Geoffrey were out riding and I was able to quickly execute an armchair fuck, the invisible man's hands under each knee and half his shaft upside on to us, so that the rib of the keel sits snug in the notch at the top of the vulva. The girl's face is pleasantly shocked as if she had walked into the room naked as usual and slid down with a sigh into her favourite chair without realising that it was so fortuitously occupied by a naked man who forthwith impales her with what must be a stocky branch of walnut and with the fruit still on it! I must give her the tiniest flare of the nostrils and show the very edges of her teeth where they grip the lower lip and leave her hands, plain and unadorned maiden's hands, resting tidily on her thighs. How awfully slight and fair she is, this girl, and so exposed. Her eyes stare straight at us, but I've allowed her a small round hat like a soldier's, and the invisible man has kept his boots on. I couldn't help laughing – I know they'll like it. But why do I carry on? I don't have need of the money.

Later: Mr Thomas the younger (still Carnal) has delivered a whole set of new and grown-up clothes for George, who is to go travelling with his cousins. He took my drawing to the post in Rafton – I doubt that my drawings are within the law, but they're not harmful – to amuse myself I tried to think of a name to recommend for this behatted Jezebel – Amarantha? Harriet? Charlotte? What name goes best with such a bony frame, such bleached hair? What about, ha! ha! ... what about La Belle Dame Sans Merci! No, young Mr Castle would never permit it! He'll say she's a housemaid and call her Susan, or Jane, or Mary Anne. Oh, those poets I read in far off times to show mother that I was improving myself, I hated all of them except John Keats.

23rd December 1912: Oh my dear soul, I'm a real old biddy now. I must burn the contents of my desk. George must not find my collection – what ever would he think? Trouble is, my fingers are not as nimble as they were, and my legs are stiff. All those years ago I burned my early sketchbooks in the dream of the apple orchard, in the absence of the gardener who provided the flames – oh, what was his name? I hear myself laughing. I will ask the carpenters (one Carnal, one Deadblock) to put them in the wall they're making – or else I might have to burn them here, in the grate. Doddery old soul like me could easily start a fire.

Marshall's Wood

Because I'd left the van parked at Herton and walked over to Marshall's Wood I entered it at an unfamiliar angle, down a green lane I didn't know, through a pungent two-dog farm called Thorney. I climbed a dilapidated stile in the corner of a large sloping field and sat for a moment on the step before dawdling on down the sunken lane I found myself in. I didn't know it – I thought I knew every track and footpath in the area, but I hadn't ever been along this one. It was just wide enough for two sheep and the banks were retained with very old ditch walls which had collapsed in places, but I could hear and then see the stream quite a way below, so I knew more or less where I should go.

The day had not lived up to its bright start and as a breeze began to build branches were sawing and creaking, dark cloud crept across the sky above the canopy of spruce, a few spots of the wet stuff were falling. I got my bearings when I joined a track I knew and Joanne was where I thought she'd be – keeping out of the cold in an old quarry working, a mossy cove full of leaf litter and birch saplings, halfway down the slope. She was sitting with her legs drawn up, arms straight down and her back against a slab of rock. Her face was tilted up into the light rain and her eyes were closed.

I picked up a small cone and lobbed it, bouncing it off the rock behind her so that it dropped onto her shoulder and rolled to the ground. She stuck out her tongue without opening her eyes. 'I know it's you Mister Florence' she said with a sigh 'throwing silly little cones about'

'But it might not have been. It might be someone not half so benevolent or handsome, an axe murderer, or the old man of the woods who eats children'

'You really think you are *benevolent*? *Handsome*? Get real, Florence!

Anyway you don't have an axe, and where is my friend Smokey? You can't walk any place without a dog'

'I might not have an axe with me right here and now, but I do possess an axe and Bobby thankyou for your enquiry is having a day at home, he looked a bit peaky this morning and didn't show much enthusiasm for going out, it's not like him. I left him saying goodbye with his eyes, snout between his front feet, like a good dog.'

'Alright Mister Florence' she laughed softly. 'I'm here, and I wouldn't be here for just anyone'

'I know I'm very lucky' I sat down beside her and shackled her kneecap in spread fingers. Her hand spread on mine and squeezed, as if a stray blossom had drifted from a tree and come to rest on an old raised root, her impossibly graceful white fingers worked between the tanned scaliness of my own. I thought of reptiles. 'Well' I said 'It's getting harder'

'Fight it, Mister Florence. Keep it in your trousers. I shan't want that today'

I laughed. 'You don't mean that, Jo'

'I mean it Mister Florence'

'Anyway, I wasn't going to say what you thought I was going to say, you shouldn't interrupt. What I was going to say was it's getting harder to understand that old photograph, the Digweed family group 1869, the full team with reserves and coaches and groundsmen. I was looking at it this very morning. You know, it's the one you're not in. When George pointed out his grandmother Jane I was disappointed; she was looking away from the camera, a bit pensive and sullen, it's not how I'd imagined her. She even looked sallow, I pictured her big and dusky. Her husband was tall and fair and a bit hard-faced but you Miss Ex, you were radiant, stellar, like one of those portraits of young noblewomen, the niece of the Prince of somewhere Italian, thirteen or fourteen, you look so good with your hair drawn back and down, one of those little flowery hats perched on top'

'Ah Mister Florence, how your tongue runs away with you. You could be three times my age, three times, but even so you don't have to go to all this trouble to get a fuck'

'You really say the most romantic things Jo. How is it a pretty young thing like you gets hard and cynical?'

'Ha! I am not like that Mister Florence, not so hard and cynical as you say, and I'm not so young, I've told you. I can tell you Jane was never sallow, but she did sometimes look unhappy when her guard was down – though she wasn't, ever. She was a *distracted* lady, all the time on the look out you know'

'Joanne, I'm not listening to you I'm sorry. What I'm thinking is what an actress you are, how there's not a serious bone in your body. What *is* all this "Mister Florence" stuff? I can't believe you're real.'

'That's my hand there, on yours. That's a real hand. But you're right not to think that I'm real. Your wife will come back'

'God forbid! Let's not mention "the wife", please. What were we on about? I'll keep my mouth shut, I won't question you. "On the lookout", that's what you said of Jane Trelease, she was a woman not averse to a bit of the old rock and roll'

'She liked to fuck. You would love her if she was alive now wouldn't you?'

'With ninety per cent of my heart. Jo, you're always saying fuck'

'So what Mister Florence, you're always changing the subject – to me'

'To be honest Jo I'm shocked by women who swear, I want to shrink away. I come from a long line of dissenting tradesmen, shipwrights from Devonport and shopkeepers from …'

'Dissenting? What is that? Something English?'

'Oh, Methodist. Weslyan.'

'Uptight Bible types? Well if they want to call it Rock and Roll, it's all right'

'They wouldn't even call it that. Copulation was never discussed'

'But now Mister Florence, time has gone by and they're not watching over you – so now you can call it fucking if you want'

'Oh whatever, Joanne, whatever' She was kneading my knuckles with her palm. 'So how can you say, sweet Celandine, that you're not in this photograph? If you're not, then someone identical to you is. It's alright, I believe you about the medieval stuff, I really think you were there, and you knew Jane Trelease'

'I don't care if you believe me or not – your belief or disbelief does not change what is true'. She looked down and laughed to herself. 'I spoke once to Mrs Trelease to give her guidance'

'Guidance?'

'On how to get pregnant, actually. It's something I'm very good at'.

'Really! Was it on style, this advice'

'Angle of penetration, location and partner, that's all'

'The boatman'

'Certainly. And I stood next to Mr Geoffrey Trelease. I'll tell you something, Tony, Mr Cawsand, has accused me loudly of being offish'

'Offish? Has he?'

'*You are unreachable* he says – he means cold, he also means frigid – but this Geoffrey Trelease was in …'

'A class of his own?' I offered.

'Yes. His own department. I could not *at*tract or *dis*tract him. A tall man, good-looking, blond and graceful, but only interested in other men'

'Well …' I extricated my hand and started to make a cigarette '… that might explain a few things. I read her diaries too – at last! I've been angling for months to get a look at them'.

'Congratulations! You're finding a way to keep your hands occupied. Jane Trelease's husband was homosexual'

'An uphill gardener'

'Whatever clever way you want to put it. So, were they satisfactory then, these diaries?' Joanne closed her eyes again and sighed.

'Very interesting' I was smoking now and I laid my free hand on the inside of her thigh, I moved it upward slowly but she clamped it in her fist.

'No Mister Florence, I told you I won't do it today, it is not necessary. I don't always want to. I am not like Jane Trelease'.

'Not necessary?'

'Anyway it's raining and it is cold. Why are we still here getting wet?'

I laughed. 'Alright, we must move. There's a cave we can just squeeze into'.

'I know it' she said 'you haven't given up hope then, to get in there we would have to lie together as one'

I laughed again. 'Lie together as one! Oh, yes'

'There is nothing else on your mind ever than your prick?'

'It's you Joanne, you, when I'm with you I think of little else, you don't know how hard it is having such a thing to live with'

'I know how hard it is, Mister Florence, thankyou. Quite so for a man of your age'

'Now you're winding me up. We can just go up to Dagworthy, it's a bit more hospitable up there. Or I could walk back to Herton and pick up the van – take you back in to Rafton'

'OK, in a moment' We stood up and she smoothed her coat and stamped her feet. 'Let's keep under the trees, by the way, Tony has spoken to me on the subject of you.'

'Sounds ominous' I said coolly enough to the back of her dark coat and her fall of light hair, but I was being ignored, I felt adolescent. 'Is there a problem?' I remembered how Cawsand had declaimed at the moon that night (not very long ago) outside his house – *cold as a witch's tit!* 'How are you with him? Is there anything between you?'

'He is not a happy man about this, but there is no jealousy. He is a proper man, not like you' She turned and smiled.

'How do they find out, these people? George Trelease knows as well'

She was not listening to me. 'Tony is a kind man, even though I don't need his kindness. Kindness makes him feel better. I think he will have followed me'

'Today? Followed you? What? You never told me he followed you!'

'Only sometimes'

'You mean he's here somewhere?'

'Very likely, yes'

I had a clear picture of Tony Cawsand with his face smeared in dark cream, an olive beanie, automatic sidearm shoved in his belt. I wanted to laugh but couldn't. 'D'you take absolutely *every*thing in your stride Jo? Is there nothing that shocks you?' So we worked our way down the steep slope between poles of spruce, and I was watching all the time for a dark green shadow stalking us. We came down to the edge of the stream, slithering undignified down a bank of ivy onto the beaten track that wound along beside it in a daylight of loud water and scattered primroses toward the road. I took Joanne by the shoulders. 'We won't come to anything serious Jo, I know that, but I so need you, human company …'

'You are serious today Mister Florence for a change. People have said to me that I'm not human … (I was only half-listening to this girl I didn't know, still scanning the woods above us for Cawsand) … don't worry, you won't run into him' She rested her palms on my chest and pushed gently. 'Off you go now to get your van, Pete'.

She never called me Pete, always Mister Florence or nothing. 'You're staying here?' I said.

'Of course. I'll wait for you at the gate at the end of this track. I'll sit here for a while, the rain is stopping. Maybe we will go on up to the farm. Get on with you, off you go. I will deal with Tony.'

You couldn't argue with Joanne. I did what I was told and walked back up to Herton.

The rain had more or less stopped as I got in the van and I was just about to start it when George Trelease appeared, strolling across the yard, flapping the water from his large red and white umbrella. He waved casually and walked on.

I got out again. 'George!'

'Hello!'

'George, how did you know about me and Joanne?'

'The sergeant told me'

'When?'

'Er ... Monday. I seed un in Rafton'

'Was he upset?'

'Didn't seem so, no. I wouldn't say he was happy about it, but ee waddn upset. Resigned to it, I'd say. Tiddn nothing of my business'

'Of course not, I'm sorry'

'Only thing I will say is er's a young maid but er's not as young as er looks'

'I know that, George. I'll see you during the week, have a good weekend'

On the road from Herton down towards Rafton, you must take a right turn where it levels out and that takes you into the lane that runs past the gateway where Jo should be waiting, at the edge of Marshall's Wood. Not far from this turning, a herd of Friesian cattle crosses the lane twice a day at this time of year; as I rounded the bend the farmer had strung his length of twine between the two metal gates and was seeing his cattle across. Cows seldom hurry and the herd was on the large side, a hundred or a hundred and twenty.

So I switched off the engine, rolled a cigarette and sat. I could see the wood not so far away, on the other side of the valley, spindly larch and thick green spruce ranked up the slope just so, like soldiers. And above the stumbling of the cattle I heard the long single note of a scream come out of the trees – no fear or pain in it – just a sound with a purpose, a sound that at this distance could drill into your ear, close up I'm sure your head would be prised apart.

There was a message in the scream that I absorbed without understanding. One or two of the beasts had turned to look, lowered their heads and raised their eyes, then lumbered gently forward again. I found myself admiring their build, their glossy good health, their steadiness. I envied them that for I had been pinned to my seat by the scream – I would have done anything to avoid thinking about it. I'd even heard it before, way in the distance, that clear night on the Warrens when she appeared out of nowhere – the same functional scream, fired like a defensive weapon. Joanne could deal with anything and that was the sound of her dealing with the Sergeant. That was why she was so keen to get rid of me, sending me back to Herton for the van. When the last cow blundered across and the farmer tossed his length of twine into the hedge, I gave him a smile that he did not return and drove reluctantly on toward the wood. Whatever had happened would still be there. There was nothing I could do.

Joanne was waiting by the gate as we'd arranged, sitting on the top bar. There was no sign of Cawsand. She didn't move as I came over, just parted her legs and I put a hand on each thigh.

'So the scream' I said, working my hands upward. 'What was that all about?'

'About nothing, Mr Florence. About pitch and decibels'

'Anything in close range of that would be finished I reckon. Tony was following us wasn't he? You said he might'

'He was'

'And where might he be now?'

She jerked her thumb over her shoulder, and gazed at me with those huge blank eyes. I reached up and ran my fingers down her face.

'So what was it with you and Mr Cawsand?'

She took my wrists and moved my hands away, rested them again on her thighs, 'Leave them there' she said 'that's OK'. I was looking straight back into her eyes until she started to speak again, then I watched my thumbs moving back and forth on the cloth of her jeans as she spoke. 'I told you Mister Florence there was nothing *with* me and Tony. You think I'm a cold-hearted bitch don't you? There was a priest, Guy de Bonville's priest, called me a Basilisk to my face, but his men were sure I was a Miracle' she laughed 'sent to help them in their stupid war until things went bad, then it was all my fault. And you hate me don't you? Cold Madonna, that's what you think, or some bullshit like that'

I was no longer surprised at the gift she had, that she knew my thoughts. I looked up then and met her eyes again.

'You, Mister Florence, are not afraid of me, you believe what I say because to you nothing is real. Everything is a joke. How d'you know I'm not just a liar, a big liar, that all I say is not just crap? You are mentally idle Mister Florence, clever enough to entertain yourself but not so clever that others are entertained by you. I have helped people in my time but who have you helped?'

'I'm not going to flinch, Joanne' I said even though I was reeling from this attack. 'Why lay into me like this? I can assure you I'm quite harmless'

'That I know. We'll go and see Tony if you want' she said 'it's OK he's not dead'.

I'd have to take her at her word that he was alive, because he certainly didn't look it. He was lying on his back on the path by the stream; there was a pair of binoculars in the hedge where he'd thrown them to leave his hands free, and they were still covering his ears.

'He's paralysed and he's not conscious'

'Otherwise he's fine' I said.

'Leave him to wake up' she said briskly 'you and I must go on to the farm'.

'But it's going to rain again, he'll get ill. If you couldn't kill him, the damp and cold will'

'He'll be OK. Leave him. I didn't say I couldn't have killed him. If you want to know, there was nothing at all between us, I must think you are talking of sex, I've said he was a kind man over and over and he was but he was a lonely man like you. He was like you in many ways, he couldn't understand similar things'

'Are you sure he's not dead? You're talking about him in the past tense'.

'Come, Mister Florence, get in your white van and take us to the farm. I will tell you about Mister Cawsand on the way …'

So why is it I call him Mister Florence? Maybe it's his age, he's like a teacher you call Mister because he's older, and because he has no relationship to you. The main struggle with him is to help him relax, to stop him looking over his shoulder as though someone's at his back all the time. You know, he told me the only time he ever relaxes is in the dentist's chair – what kind of man is this who looks forward to the tooth-puller? He says he has to do nothing at all, just lie there and his life is totally in the hands of someone else. Florence is a sad man. And that plank Finbar standing behind me in the caravan sniffing my hair like a dog and thinking about my tits until I flattened him (is that how it's said?) with the girl Hayley – I, the cat, scratched the mongrel's nose. Of course I could have encouraged him, he couldn't have stopped himself, he would risk life without his girl for a five-minute fuck with this babe from Bosnia. They all will.

Now Mister Florence knows how to make a fuck last. I mean the second one, the one for me, after he's got the first one, his, out of the way. Though Finbar will tell me he's not friendly at all – a moody man, often sarcastic. He drives very steady with his thumbs on the wheel. He's wearing that green fleece and jeans again – denim can't suit him, he's too old for it. Sometimes he looks old and dull with his thin long face and those scary squared off sideburns, I guess he's always had them – he's never stood there before the bathroom mirror and felt like changing his face in a fell swoop and shaving the bloody things off. His thumbs, blunted and squat with etched lines, but he knows what to do with those thumbs. 'You treat me like something precious, Mister Florence. You are afraid I will be damaged' I said to him once, since then he has taken to working me inside like he's moulding a pot. 'Tell me when it hurts' he says.

Here we come up the long steady hill, soon we'll see the place I was born. I can't believe how well I know this road – long before this tarmac thing for the benefit of cars it was a stony track worn in the muddy ground by feet and horses, herds and flocks. Pete (I'll call him Pete to myself) is a steady driver, you feel safe with him even though only I am really safe because I cannot die ...

'Alright Mister Florence ... Tony Cawsand. Since there must always be men, I had Tony down as the kinder sort, I had to put myself in his way because I saw how the war affected him. He needed a reward'

'You, Miss Ex? A reward?'

'That's right. I put myself in his way because he needed a daughter or someone, a son or whatever. He was a poor sad soldier. The British are more like police than soldiers'

'Come along now sir, pull the tank over, this attitude's not getting us anywhere'

'You take the piss if you want Mister Florence. Those men out here ... right here, see ... eight hundred years ago were proper soldiers, little men with nothing in their heads, made into big men because someone, a thief who had fallen out with another thief, gave them the means of killing and left them to it. They thought I expect that what they did to me was worse than death but they gave me the voice you heard' *He has stopped the van now in the courtyard of Daxworthy amongst the nettles and damp dust.* 'Tony Cawsand is far too nice a man to be a proper soldier but now Mister Florence he's become what they call here a "stalker"'

'Are you sure you haven't had sex with him?'

'I think I would know if I had. I don't do it with quite everybody, he's never touched me. But all the same he's all over me: he leaves me to myself all the time, he never makes me do anything, but all the time you can feel him thinking about you, even when there's walls between you or miles of distance you can feel him *thinking*. He would harm *you* if he could, if I let him. Of course he knows, I haven't told him, you haven't told him, but he knows'

'Everyone knows as far as I can see, even old George bloody Trelease'.

'So when he came along the path swinging his binoculars on a string I had to fell him. Anyway, as I was saying, there are always men. Each time I break the surface in this world only things and objects have changed; the people, the characters, are just the same. And I'm always giving birth, each time I descend here there is the male seed, and the way it is absorbed is pleasant, it is the simplest thing to acquire, men are all slaves to their pricks. Even now I have a child in me, a teacher's child, a real teacher not like you who acts like one'

'A child? One of your teachers?'

I must upset Mister Florence now, so that he doesn't miss me when I go. Soon. 'Yes, one of my teachers, a teacher of mathematics older even than you, almost retired. I was astride him without underwear at three forty-five on a Monday afternoon. And he came in fat jets in less than twenty seconds, grinning all over his face, didn't even take his trousers off, and I told him he should have taken them off, for now there were stains he might not be able to explain to his wife and he said he had not spoken to her for eighteen months and "mere stains" were none of her business. We laughed together as he pulled the hood back over his cock and I put my knickers back on. "Thankyou Joanne" he said "I really didn't think things like this were likely to happen to me". "No problem" I said, and I knew as I spoke that one of his sperm was on its way, the Chosen One with the pointy snout and a strong tail; and those still hanging around from the day before donated by you and a boy called Vince Somebody would be swept aside'

'Vince Somebody?'

'Vince, I don't know his other name, his phone rang and he had to find his coveralls'

'Where were you?'

'On the deck in the back of his van with painting brushes and rollers, there was a spirity sweet smell that clung to my skin for ages, even after a shower. "Yeah, this is Vince" he said when he found his phone. That's how I know his name. Whenever I come to this place I get pregnant, it's the only reason I'm here. Guillame Mareschal's fathers were all rapists, in those days I couldn't tell which from which. And there was poor little Maria who lived only fifteen months who knew only 1831 and some of 1832: her father was a sailor called Bill Ridd whose wife was big trouble and threw fishheads at him, swung at his head with an oar or threw the cat and its new-born litter out of the window, Bill drank all the time when he was on dry land and had five children all girls. I met them all, lovely girls, but they never met Maria'

'You're making up every word of this, Jo. You've made up everything. I must be dreaming. Everything you've told me is'

'Like a dream, Mister Florence'

'All that medieval stuff, Jane Trelease'

'I told you I was not in that photograph. Now Mister Florence I will get out of your van and walk away. I'm afraid you will only ever see me again in fantasies, or I should say recollections of reality. In that way I will stay with you always, you will only have to close your eyes and I will be there in whatever way you care to remember. Can you remember every time? You will now. Tony will recover but his memory will be impaired, especially where you and I are concerned. That is good'

So she simply walked away across a wide tussocky field, across the yard of the old farm and out through a steel gate canted off its hinges. I watched her go, for I couldn't move. As she strolled on and away her clothes seemed to replace themselves, the old ones dissolving into new, like some trick of photography. A tight, brief skirt had replaced the jeans, and the woollen coat she wore was gone, instead her arms were bare and her hair lay down her back on some kind of sleeveless blouse. She didn't look back but once she looked sideways, and I swear she was wearing an alice band. I sat and stared, gripping the steering wheel as though if I let it go I would shoot off into space. She was all legs like a schoolgirl, I would miss those legs terribly, she had the most beautiful smooth white legs. And there was a scent like molten rubber, a smell of friction and sticky oil, the skirt she wore was peeled back above the navel and someone's hands pushed her knees flat on the grass. It must have been sometime in the middle nineteen-sixties, I was young, certainly a virgin; there was a man kneeling, but it wasn't me, I must have been watching. She was as young as I, but sweet and hard as nails. This wasn't the first time that hesitation had let someone else take away an opportunity that was rightly mine. As they say, he who hesitates is lost. I stared hopelessly across the field, almost inclined to laugh but not quite. The thighs of the man (I never knew his name) were braced like a frog's, and her pale ankles were crossed on the small of his back, what pretty feet she had. Goodbye Choanne. Not a fantasy of course, but a recollection of reality.